# All Our Games

Erika Mitterer

# All our Games

CAMDEN HOUSE

*All Our Games* is the authorized translation from the German of the work *Alle unsere Spiele*, published by Josef Knecht-Carolusdruckerei, Frankfurt am Main.

*All Our Games* is published simultaneously as volume 39 in *Studies in German Literature, Linguistics, and Culture* edited by James Hardin and Gunther Holst.

Set in Palatino type and printed on acid-free paper.
© Copyright 1988 by

CAMDEN HOUSE, INC.
Drawer 2025
Columbia, South Carolina 29202 USA

Library of Congress Catalog Card Number: 88–70101

*First Edition*

ISBN:0–938100–61–0

Printed by Thomson-Shore, Inc.
Dexter, Michigan

### Translator's Preface

I have long hoped to introduce to the English speaking public the work of the dean of Austrian women writers, Erika Mitterer, and am pleased to do so now in this translation of her most recent novel.

*All Our Games* is the first book—of some thirty I have translated from the German for various publishers—that I have done "on spec" as they say. I did so because the artistry of the novel persuaded me, and because it tells in fiction, but with absolute veracity, the story of Vienna during that terrible period between 1938 and 1945, after Austria was engulfed by Nazi Germany. The oh, so attractive Vienna of the tourists does not appear in this book. Instead we experience the lives of a truly Viennese family: the daughter, Helga Wegschneider, in love with an SS man, both mesmerized by Hitler's "mission," and their increasing despair as they realize that they have embraced an evil cause. We are presented with her father, mother, and two brothers, who sense the madness in the Führer's goals, and are gradually drawn into the resistance movement. Courage, disillusionment, and horror are given their due.

Germans and Austrians speak the same language, but with a difference. Each has its own amusing dialects, but it has been my experience that Austrian German, when purely spoken, is the more felicitous language, less convoluted, less ponderous, not as complicated philosophically as German in its native form, or let us say simply: Austrian German is more accessible and therefore easier to translate into so much sparser English. This is certainly so in the case of Erika Mitterer's style.

Here we are dealing with a famous writer of poetry as well as prose, and inevitably a certain lyricism is present in in her writing, giving it a poetic quality that never seems to detract from the stark realism of her subject but tends rather to intensify it. This was more difficult to capture and a real challenge for the translator.

This, I felt, was the book with which to introduce, in English, an Austrian writer who has received the highest honors for literary achievement in her own country. I hope therefore that *All Our Games* may be an auspicious start.

Catherine Hutter
Hamden, Ct.

Yesterday, my child, as we lit the votive light for your grandparents because it is the custom in our country to think of the dead once a year, you asked me, "What sort of a person was your father? You never talk about him." You didn't look at me as you asked the question, and I answered evasively, "But Uri speaks about him often, doesn't she?" True, you said, she talked about his childhood, and you intimated that you were getting a little tired of being told constantly how much you resembled him. "I would like to know what he was like as your father, not the way your grandmother remembers him as her child."

I found this an astonishing distinction for a fifteen-year-old boy to make. You added, as if you had to substantiate your wish, "After all, Uri is very old. She gets things mixed up."

"But she is wise," I said, embarrassed by the unaccustomed word, even though it was apt.

I began to wonder how I could describe my father to you, because it was not easy. All I could think of were superficial things. I told you that he spoke softly, was always self-controlled, and demanded of us children that we be polite and well-mannered under every circumstance. "None of that would mean anything to me!" you exclaimed, and I had to laugh. In the meantime we had reached the crowded center path of the cemetery, and I gave myself up to the rare, relaxed mood of this folk festival of mourning. Apparently I am still susceptible to popular influences.

I regret that Mother, in accordance with her shy and basically lonely nature, couldn't have had a grave on the slopes of one of the romantic old cemeteries on the outskirts of villages that have become incorporated long ago, in Grinzing or Nussdorf or Ober-Sankt Veit, but naturally she had to be buried beside Father, under the wide stone slab in this metropolis of the dead, crisscrossed by right angled lanes, in the Central Cemetery, across which the biting winds of the Hungarian steppes blow almost constantly.

I thought I could discern for the first time a certain opposition in you toward this customary visit to the cemetery. Why this gesture once every year? Who profits by it? Who thinks of All Souls anymore, anyway? No one. At best one is mourning something that can't be brought back, and the living, touched by a breath of decay, draw closer. Isn't it hypocrisy to participate?

You didn't say any of this, my silent son. Your ironically twisted lips and the thin, sharp frown between your brows betrayed your thoughts. Oh, everything would be much simpler if you would talk more!

To dispel your ill humor, I decided to buy you a frankfurter at one of the stands, because there wasn't going to be any chance for lunch. We were in a hurry to catch our train. When you picked up the subject again on our way home, I was surprised. Was I hoping you had forgotten it? "Was he tall?" you asked. "Was he blond?"

"He was a little taller than I," I replied, and then, "No. I don't think he was really blond. I'd say his hair was light brown. But I only remember him as gray." And you said, "So he wasn't as blond as my father," in a tone of finality. Or had you expected that I was going to talk to you about your father at last?

In the night, as I lay awake, it seemed like that to me. You hadn't asked any more questions when I had shaken my head and agreed, "No. Not as blond as that." And it became clear to me that one day I would have to speak honestly with you about it. In the morning, though, I knew I would never be able to bring myself to do so. If Uri were a few years younger, I would ask her to do it for me, but she is really ancient now. You may be right in that she gets things "mixed up," although I've never noticed it. She only leaves a lot of things out when she talks, things she doesn't feel are important.

Since I want you to know everything, in spite of the fact that I don't feel equal to telling it, I shall write it down for you, at the risk of it taking a long time. When I was a young girl, I used to enjoy keeping a diary. What I thought and felt became clearer as I wrote, and I always did feel a need for clarity. This may have been what frightened off some of my schoolmates so that they turned to less exacting colleagues for friendship. The wholeheartedness and exclusiveness of my friendships, the mercilessness of my contempt when I was disappointed — that was what I was like at an age when one most needs someone to pour out one's heart to, I mean as a girl (boys are different) at twelve, thirteen, fourteen, all alone. That was why I kept a diary and wrote in it regularly, pages and pages. This stopped gradually when I made friends with those who thought and felt as I did, when I had to prove myself among them, and finally when I was given tasks and duties to perform.

As I write, I can't help feeling constantly that none of this could possibly interest you. Where to start? Every moment in my life is arbitrary. So let me begin with the day I met Horst Ulbig on my way home from school. However, for you to understand the events that then turned out to be so important to me, I must first describe the situation as it was at the time. It was spring 1940, the first war spring, two years therefore after Austria had ceased to exist. Called the Ostmark now, it had become a province in the German Reich, and Vienna one of its many large cities.

My father, a senior civil servant in the administration, had belonged to a student fraternity in his youth, the aim of which had been to create a situation in which national boundaries would conform as nearly as possible to folk borders. So in spite of being a devout Catholic and loyal civil servant, he greeted the dissolution of his fatherland into the Greater German Reich with reservations — one might almost say with satisfaction tempered by anxiety. Because after all, the Greater Fatherland, which he had longed to be a part of all his life, had by then been under National Socialist leadership for five years, ruled by men whose foreign policy aims seemed worth striving for, but whose methods were, to say the least, questionable. His modest joy over being "brought home to the German Reich" therefore did not tempt my father to join the party, on the contrary — he hoped that the influence of so many "fellow countrymen" who felt as he did would gradually moderate their disreputable methods. Austrians — no, *Ostmärker*, as we were called — were after all men with a "gentle" power, which in the course of events would prevail of its own accord. Unrealistic dreamers like these could be found in our government offices, could be heard lecturing at our universities and preaching from our pulpits, empowered by their superiors who thought they were as wise as Solomon when actually they were as timid as churchmice.

But enough of this. Hindsight is so easy. I do have to tell you though, that in spite of the fact that my parents never mentioned these inner conflicts in my presence, I was somehow aware of them. It is nearly always impossible to hide one's perplexities from one's children. I was almost sixteen, a grown-up girl, and when those in authority tried to curb my independence too much, I reminded myself and others that Grandmother — your great grandmother Uri — was already married at my age! But in all ethical decisions, only a clear cut yes or no carried weight with me. I definitely sensed my parents' reservations when faced with historic developments, but I thought they were just too old to adjust to a new world order. That was what we were taught in school and especially in the youth organization of which I was an enthusiastic member.

What bothered me more was that my brothers didn't seem to share my enthusiasm. But I was accustomed to their superior attitude by not taking them seriously either. Not Albert, who stuck to his room where he brooded, who didn't enjoy any kind of sport; and not Walter, who was lazy and insolent, and whose major ambition seemed to be to swindle his way up into the next grade with a minimum of knowledge, who read nothing but detective stories, went to Wild West pictures, and secretly visited dance halls in the suburbs. I half-despised, half-envied him, but never betrayed him. He should have realized this, and to this day I grieve that he didn't.

So I was never contradicted at home when I quoted the slogan: *"Am deutschen Wesen wird die Welt genesen!"* — "The German spirit will heal the world!" But neither did I hear an echo.

I felt very much alone until the day on which I want to start this account of my memories, the day I saw Horst again, just when I was beginning to feel a little unsure of myself, because my father considered it his duty to bring to my attention the dubiousness of some slogans, for instance: *Recht ist was dem Volke nützt!* — What is good for the people is right! Also the un-Christian behavior and inhumanity of the persecution of the Jews. But then he would console himself and me by referring to the power takeover of the National Socialists as comparable, in its revolutionary thrust, to the regeneration of France in 1789, when so much innocent blood had been shed. The discrimination against even the expelling of a small minority could perhaps be considered a lesser, possibly even an unavoidable evil. Thus he tried to ease his own conscience by first demanding criticism from me, then invalidating it!

I found out by chance that although drastic punishment was meted out for such offenses, my mother had given one of our food cards to a doctor who had looked after us children, a Jewess whose license to practice had been withdrawn immediately. I admired my mother for what she had done, but felt it had been wrong. However, I didn't say anything about it since no one asked for my opinion. At the time nobody I knew considered an extermination of the Jews possible. You will find this incomprehensible when you have read Hitler's book, *Mein Kampf,* the Bible of the movement.

But back to that day in spring and the schoolgirl on her way home, who was still thinking of the praise given her by her Greek professor: "You summarized this chapter about the sacrifice of Iphigenia very well, Wegscheider, although your interpretation is slightly unorthodox," and who now began to think how she could get her parents' consent to taking an evening course in first aid. They were against it because it meant coming home after dark. In those days the streets were dark, all lights were forbidden as an air-raid precaution. But Albert would soon leave for the front — I envied him for it, and I knew Walter did too — and I, a big, strong girl, had to be home every day at six like a child!

"Helga! What are you so angry about? Don't you know me anymore? I recognized you at once!"

The young man who was addressing me with every indication of pleasure was a tall, blond SS man. He was blocking my way and I stared at him, baffled. He did look familiar, but I didn't recognize him right away, and I mumbled, "Horst?" before I was quite sure it was he.

"Well, at last!" He laughed and shook my hand vigorously. "How is Albert? Has he left for the front yet?"

I told him that Albert was expecting to be called up any day. "Is that so?" Horst sounded thoughtful. We had quite naturally started to walk on side by side. "Albert in uniform. Somehow hard to imagine."

"But one could feel the same way about you," I told him, and he looked serious at once. "That's why I didn't recognize you."

"I'm trying to change." His tone was curt. "I'm glad to see that I'm evidently succeeding."

"Don't you play anymore?" I asked, because I had the feeling he was waiting for me to ask just that, and the alacrity with which he responded seemed to prove me right. "No. Of course not! There's no time for that now. But what was Albert doing ... I mean, before he was drafted? ... Law? ... Really? I always thought he'd be a philosopher one day."

"And why did we never hear from you?" I asked.

He explained that he had moved to Graz with his father. "There were times when I wanted to write, but I was afraid some of you might have thought it odd."

"I don't know what the boys think odd," I said.

Now we were standing in front of our house, and I wondered if I should ask him to come in, when just then Walter came toward us from the opposite direction. He raised his eyebrows ironically when he saw who was with me, recognized Horst, greeted him and without further ado took him into the house. His pleasure at meeting Horst surprised me because he had often made fun of Albert's musical "genius." It was a long time before I realized that it wasn't the encounter with Horst that Walter had found so opportune, but the appearance of an impressive SS man in our apartment. Walter had always known how to size up a situation and recognize its advantages at a glance, even as a child.

Our parents were reserved but friendly. Only Albert was taciturn, almost rude. Today I think that perhaps he had been fonder of young Horst than we had realized and was shocked by the change in him.

But now I must tell you at last who Horst really was. I have thought this over for quite some time, and the midday meal we had that day seems to me the best beginning for my story. However, I keep having to add things before we can finally sit down at the dining room table and Katie brings in the soup. Katie was our maid. She left us soon after that to work in a munitions factory where she could earn more money. She, who knew Horst least of all, apparently saw no change in him except for the fact that they had "sheared" him, as she put it, and laughed.

Three years before, Albert had been Horst's tutor for several months. His father was conductor at the Vienna Volksoper, after various engagements in German cities. Horst's school years had therefore been disrupted frequently, and his marks indicated that he might not be able to achieve every scholar's goal and graduate. The school principal recommended Albert — not a brilliant but a reliable student — to tutor Horst, and that was how it came about that he was in our home almost daily. In spite of his intelligence he wasn't really interested in what he was supposed to gain here in the way of intellectual ammunition because he felt predestined to become a musician. He wanted to be a violinist even if he never got farther in life than playing second violin in a spa orchestra! But that was just what his father wanted to avoid. He insisted on Horst's finishing school first. Horst worked hard, and Albert's standing in school also benefited by his pupil's progress.

Horst protested against this enforced bourgeois life by his behavior. He let his hair fall wildly over his forehead, he wore colorful sweaters and snapped out of his sloppy posture only when he noticed my mother's amused glance. He had no mother. We presumed she was dead, but he told me later that after a brief marriage, she had run away with another man. His father never mentioned her. When asked why he had never married again, Horst had said with a strange smile, "I would never have let him!" At the time I thought he was joking, but I never forgot that smile. All that though came years later. How difficult it is to tell things chronologically!

We sat around the table, Katie made her remark about Horst's short hair, I found that it suited him, also his slightly hooked nose which had grown larger, giving his profile a certain bird-of-prey ambience. But what had changed him most was his new, stiff, almost ramrod posture and the jerkiness of his movements, as if everything were a bit of an effort. My mother seemed to be thinking along the same lines because suddenly, as was a way she had, she interrupted the general conversation by asking, "But why did you of all people join the SS, Horst?"

Walter tried desperately to catch her eye as he shook his head almost imperceptibly. Horst answered slowly, "What do you mean, Mrs. Wegscheider? I simply volunteered, and since I met all the necessary qualifications ... my great-grandfather owned property in Friesland ..."

"How interesting!" said my mother. "You never mentioned it. How long will you be staying in Vienna?"

Horst didn't know. Probably a few weeks.

When he left, Walter asked him cordially to come again, and Mother was friendly, implying that she too would be pleased if he did. For her he was the boy who had no mother and had gone in and out of her home almost daily, and who didn't seem too happy in his own skin. The uniform meant nothing to her.

"*Servus!*" I said, as we shook hands, and he asked softly, looking me in the eye, "Shall I really come again?"

I reddened. With pleasure or embarrassment? Because didn't his question betray the fact that he had noticed my father's and Albert's reserve? Or was it out of a defiance aimed at my family, who were forcing me to affirm a cordiality Horst might well misunderstand? Even then I was fully aware of how vain young men were. But I overcame my shyness and said almost eagerly, "But of course! Come! We're so well-suited to each other."

As soon as I'd said it, I was startled, but he replied seriously and softly and pressed my hand as he said it, "That makes me *very* happy." Then he let go my hand, straightened up, clicked his heels, said "Heil Hitler!" and left hastily.

Perhaps that was the moment I fell in love with him, although I preferred not to recognize my feelings for a long time. Anyway, I thought of him a great deal. Wasn't it strange that he had said "*du*" to me so naturally? After all, in the meantime both of us had grown up, and before that we hadn't known each other very well. I decided that I should have said "*Sie*" to him and thus corrected him tactfully. But this only occurred to me hours later.

Oh dear! I see that I ran through lunch too fast. So much took place during this meal that I was aware of only subconsciously. Why do so many things only come clear to us after the fact?

Language ... and this only came clear to me years later when I tried to do translations ... is much wiser than the individuals who use it. "Come clear" means that a certain unclear, dim or veiled perception was present the moment it happened; we recognize only later the meaning of what we have seen. But what didn't mean anything to us at the time, we weren't aware of! To be aware ... the entire procedure is contained in this word with which the truth creeps up on us. But why does the truth creep up on us instead of walking straight up to us surely and courageously as would be appropriate to its proud nature? Or so we think in our innocence. I'll tell you why: When the truth is naked and ugly, it creeps up on us cowering in the dark depths of our inner selves. It doesn't want to be noticed because nobody would like it.

I have already said that I noticed how cordially Walter greeted Horst and said good bye to him. But did I really interpret Albert's reserve at the time as a sign that he didn't like the change in Horst because he had been fond of the eighteen-year-old boy who had been so different? ... Stop! At the time I was still keeping a diary, and I think I wrote about this first visit of Horst's. I'll go and see. Tomorrow morning. All my old papers are in a trunk in the attic. Now I must use the quiet evening hours to recall things as honestly as I can.

(I just went to your room to cover you up. You still kick all your clothes off like a little boy. When I rearrange them you sometimes open your eyes, their lids heavy with sleep, and purse your lips in the whisper of a kiss. And often, even when you were still a child, I stood besides you and prayed: Protect him, dear God. I can't. Take this kiss, dear God. I don't deserve it.)

*As honestly as I can.* That's what I just wrote. But will what I write be suitable for your eyes? Certainly not! And why not? Because I am your mother. Because there seems to be an intolerable perversity in forcing you to see me as a young girl. And *as honestly as I can* means erasing the many years that lie between today and the day before yesterday, means plunging into the continuous presence of the agony I have tried so hard to forget. Although, when I complained so bitterly in the beginning that I couldn't, *could not* forget, Uri said sternly, "You're not supposed to forget! He who forgets has lived in vain."

I don't want to descend into the past, into the fire of the ever-present. I don't want to, but I must. In order to press out of the mildewed grapes in the cellar of my consciousness the pure wine that I owe you ...

Was it the fact that I was terribly sleepy yesterday that made me paint such a banal and pathetic picture? Are the ingredients that I detest, that would make it an unpalatable poison — self-glorification and self-pity — already seeping into that ostensibly pure wine? But there is plenty of time for correction. First of all, to stay with the metaphor — the grapes have to be pressed. The refining process comes later. Otherwise it will happen to me as it did to Orpheus: when he turned around, Eurydice slipped back into the underworld.

Eurydice and Iphigenia ... when I was young I loved them like sisters. I was not an honor student because I studied especially hard — on the contrary — I was one of those few children who are as moved by the appeal of mythology as they are excited by the crystalline comparisons of natural science. What you so often find dull, I found absorbing. I lack a feeling for the chronology of events; everything that happened before I was born belongs to the past, with no perspective: Alexander no farther removed than Bismarck, Saint Joan no farther away than Madame Curie. This may be a very feminine, perhaps exclusively feminine approach to hero worship. My Greek professor was certainly perplexed and disturbed that morning by my temperamental attack on Agamemnon, who in a dual cowardice not only wanted to obey the monstrous demand of the goddess and slaughter his daughter, but also tried to parry his wife's protest by a clear-cut lie.

As we sat at the table with our taciturn friend, I was thinking about my Greek professor's objection: Iphigenia herself had demanded that her father obey the goddess. She of all people, in the purity of her serene emotions, had given the loftier command precedence over the mere obligation to family. For the moment I had been disarmed without being able to agree.

Conversation during the meal was fairly labored, so I talked about my Iphigenia argument. My brothers didn't seem interested, but Horst watched me and listened attentively. "What point are you trying to make?" asked my father. "This old myth really says nothing but that one must make the greatest personal sacrifice for the universal good."

"But Father," I cried, "that's not true! Naturally the sons have to go to war, that's obvious, because you can't win a battle without men. But ... would you drown me in the Danube so that there would be a wind to sail your ships?"

Everybody laughed. "Fortunately I don't have any ships," said my father, still smiling, and Walter added, "And anyway, on the Danube you don't need a wind!"

I declared, annoyed now, that at the last moment the goddess had wanted to spare Agamemnon this senseless war, because of what concern was his brother's debauched wife to him? If only he had had the sense and humaneness to deserve it!

My father raised the same objection as my professor had: the fact that Iphigenia was perfectly willing to be sacrificed was decisive.

"No!" I insisted, and looked straight at my father in order to avoid Horst's eyes. He was blushing and I had no idea why. "She felt that her father had made up his mind already and simply didn't know how he was going to break it to her. She wanted to help him. Adults never have the courage to say clearly yes or no."

Mother interposed gently that the older one became, the more likely one was to see both sides of everything — at times also the bad side of a good thing. Now Horst stood by me. "But we'll never make any progress, Mrs. Wegscheider, if we keep walking on the same spot. Why not a false single misstep rather than endless hesitation and deliberation?" And I felt he was on my side.

I tried to start all over again but Mother interrupted me. "These old stories are so grim," she said. "The only past in which I would have liked to live is the Biedermeier period. A very unheroic time, granted, but do women have to be heroic? Is that what you're thinking, Horst?"

At last he looked away from me: perhaps that was what Mother had wanted. "Certainly not, Mrs. Wegscheider," he replied politely.

"You are an artist," she went on, ignoring his involuntary negative gesture. "The other day I found a delightful little miniature in an antique shop. I must show it to you."

We had just finished eating. Father pushed back his chair and mumbled, "You'll have to excuse me," but Walter stopped him with the request: might he bring a few friends home with him on Wednesday? Would Father mind? "After dinner, of course," he added hastily when he saw Mother's doubtful expression. Wednesday was their bridge evening at the house of friends and Walter promised that everyone would go home by eleven. "I won't be home either," I said quickly. "That's the night I start my first-aid class." Nobody demurred, and I was delighted with my diplomacy. Now, if the subject came up again later, I had no intention of letting them stop me.

"Who is coming?" my father asked.

"Well, to begin with, Clemens Schindler, the one who's with the scouts," said Walter. He had met up with him again a little while ago.

Mother was immediately interested. "Isn't he the one who wanted to be a priest?"

"Yes. And he *is* a priest now and isn't in touch with anybody anymore. That's why I'm arranging this evening." Suddenly Walter turned to Horst and said, "Why don't you come? I think you'd find it interesting." But Horst had to be in barracks.

Strange that the conversation about Iphigenia comes back to me only now. Not that I had forgotten it, but I hadn't intended to go into such detail about it, or where will it end? I can't write a whole book! Only the important things ... only the facts. But what is fact? Nothing we can grasp unless we see it as in a mirror, detached from our personal experience. (Because facts hurt too much. You can't describe a toothache, only endure it.) Perhaps our conversation was such a reflection. As I look back now, it seems so.

I have found the diary and I must tell you that I was startled when I read it. For a while I was tempted to use only one or two paragraphs, but now I'm going to copy it all, even the passages that are definitely embarrassing. Especially those passages!

Met Horst Ulbig on the way home from school, former pupil of Albert's. Hardly recognized him. Looks wonderful in his black SS uniform. Took him home with me. Mother asked in all innocence: "Why did you of all people join the SS?" Horst wasn't offended, at least I don't think he was. I'm afraid Mother is altogether against it. No wonder, if all one reads is Stifter, Ebner-Eschenbach, Hofmannsthal, all the detached romanticists. On Mother's Day I am going to give her Hölderlin, also a romanticist but a prophet as well. I can understand Mother, but Father's attitude is puzzling. On March 13th, when the Führer came to Vienna, he wept with enthusiasm, and now? Only because the new masters in the ministry don't please him? How can one be so small? Is there a government anywhere with which one can agree one hundred percent? During the last years, whenever we, Albert and I, complained about the church and the political sermons, Father set us right: the church is a human institution and as such also prone to error. Then he would have a long discussion with the boys about how this could be reconciled with the infallibility of the Pope. I didn't pay much attention. In my opinion such dogma doesn't fit into our times any more than the nuns in their dusty black habits and their faces — no foreheads — framed in white — in other words not at all! All these things are relics from other eras. Like the whales!

So the church with its incredible demands and almost two thousand years of experience may make mistakes, but National Socialism, which is only seven years old, may not? And my father professes to be a Catholic! "Church politics have nothing to do with my faith!" But he doesn't want to join the Party because of its "false methods." Dear Father, those false methods have nothing to do with *my* faith.

I should be studying physics, but first I must write what — no, not startled me today but astonished me profoundly. I know that Papa loves me best. Mama says all fathers favor their daughters. We spoke about Agamemnon and Iphigenia, and I asked, "But imagine if I was Iphigenia. Would you sacrifice me so that your ships could sail?" and he wriggled out of it! "I don't have any ships ..." some sort of joke like that. Everybody laughed and I felt like a fool. At the time I was annoyed, but as I think back, I'm quite pleased. Perhaps my father is a heroic man after all.

If he is, he'll find his way to us, and when Father's for it, Mother soon will be too. Out of her need for harmony. That's why women are so often poor fighters, because of their intense need for harmony.

And Albert? He is a brooder. He can never make up his mind about anything. Besides, he's a born loner. Never joined a youth group. Walter was at least a scout for a while. I thought the army would be good for Albert, but can't see any sign of it yet.

Walter? He's not to be taken seriously and may be against it as a matter of principle. First he was against Dollfuss and Starhemberg. I think he's just as much against Hitler now. Why doesn't he say so? Is he afraid perhaps I might report him? But anyway, he's not really interested in anything but football and dancing. He's still so young. A sixteen-year-old girl is much older than a boy of seventeen. We have to be patient with him.

Why am I so anxious that every member of my family be "converted"?

Funny that Horst said *"du"* to me right away. Impertinent, actually. Maybe he'll pick me up at school one day. How I'd love to see their faces!

"Satisfactory" on my physics exam. Too bad! Because when you're no longer "excellent" they say right away: of course! Nothing on her mind but the *Bund deutscher Mädchen* and her first-aid course. As if they weren't more important! Besides, they aren't even to blame; it's all your fault, my beloved diary! So ... strict measures have to be taken. From now on only important events told as briefly as possible. And feelings. Because feelings are events too, or, to put it another way: without feelings there would be no events!

Next event: my sixteenth birthday. I've asked for a fat novel: *Nation With No Living Space*[1] by Hans Grimm. Very expensive. And silk stockings. Will I get them? At my age one is allegedly too young for everything: for silk stockings, for *Faust II*, for Colette — and for love!

I got them! Two pairs! And the Grimm. Mama said, "I looked at it briefly. I like it. I'll read it too." Bravo, Mama! Meanwhile I've read the novel by Colette that Marietta loaned me — in secret, of course. Horrible! I'm almost ashamed that I read it through to the end, but I was curious. Nothing but sexuality, real French decadence. I told Marietta just how I felt about it. *I* see love quite differently. "Probably because you don't know anything about it!" she said. Really nasty! "Certainly not as much as you," I said scathingly, and she turned quite pale, she was so furious. It was like the garden scene in *Maria Stuart*. By the way — a magnificent production! But I can't seem to keep up with events. Only the most important thing before I stop: Horst came to fetch me! *Not* at school, thank God, but at the corner of Mariahilferstrasse. With red roses! With sixteen red roses! I was so flabbergasted, I don't think I thanked him adequately. All I could do was ask him over and over again, "How did you know the date?" "I know a lot more than you realize," he said, and unfortunately I blushed. Stupid of me! Because after all, what could he possibly know?

But isn't it beautiful to get your first red roses on your sixteenth birthday? Dear Diary, isn't it beautiful?

---

[1] *Volk ohne Raum*, 1926.

How lucky that he wasn't waiting for me at school. The look Walter gave me was quite enough. Papa and Mama were surprisingly tactful.

The first red roses were also the last, my son, that I was ever to receive. I know — we have plenty of them. Uri had all the beds turned and everything replanted at a time when our neighbors were still growing nothing but cabbages and potatoes. And you take it as a matter of course that we have roses in our garden and in the house in summer, like the lilacs in April, the peonies in May, the asters and dahlias in autumn. But I was a city child, and red roses were no ordinary flowers. They were a symbol. And I thought now the "red roses" period of my life had begun and was so proud of it, yet at the same time filled with a faint rejection and fear, as if I were acquiescing to something final by accepting them. And that's just what I was doing ...

"I could never love a girl who didn't have the same world outlook as I did!" Horst admitted to me soon afterwards. "I can understand that very well," I replied, without looking at him. In our case any further explanations were unnecessary: his uniform was his world outlook. Once, though, I came up to him and Walter just as Horst was saying, "You mustn't think I find *everything* that's happening right. But we young people aren't here to stand to one side and criticize. We have to go along with things and try to change what we feel is wrong."

"Quite right," said Walter. Lately he'd been strangely inclined to agree with other people's opinions. But then he asked, "What do you consider wrong, for instance?"

"The Odin cult and all that hullabaloo," Horst replied. "I don't believe in going back over a millennium and a half! These visionaries overlook the fact that Wagner also wrote *Parsifal*, and that the Meistersinger were Christians!"

"So you're a Christian too?"

"Naturally! What else could I be?"

"Then join us on Wednesday, do!" Walter repeated his invitation. "A few of my friends will be there, and a young priest, and we're going to read the Bible together."

Horst declined. To begin with, he wasn't free, and besides — he was a Protestant. "That wouldn't bother us," said Walter, and Horst was smiling as he said that if they were going to read the Bible, they were half-Protestants anyway!

At last I could get in a word and declared loudly that I simply couldn't believe it. It was just a pretext. "Since when are you interested in ... in things like that?" I asked Walter.

"A pretext for what?" Walter's tone was sharp, and when I couldn't think of an answer because the word had slipped out thoughtlessly, he told me to come and see for myself. I was welcome anytime. He knew very well that I was doing something else on Wednesday.

Horst paid no attention to our little spat; he was used to the rough tone between us from earlier days. He assured Walter that if he could free himself, he would like to come, and Walter stressed again that the others would be glad to see "an enlivening of the discussion." I noted this because it wasn't at all the way Walter usually spoke. It was probably the language of the young priest. Horst said later, "I like your brother. He's made of the right stuff. You can depend on him when I'm gone."

"But I can't even talk to him!" I protested. "He doesn't take me seriously, and I don't take him seriously, ever!"

"Talking isn't so important, not if one is cut of the same cloth."

"But it's so wonderful that you and I *can* talk to each other," I protested gently, and Horst pressed my hand and said, "I'm going to write to you. Will you write too?"

"Yes," I said. "Of course! Certainly!"

That was all we promised each other at the time. It sufficed, although we didn't see each other again for a whole year.

Perhaps if we had seen each other regularly during those decisive years, we might not have become so inseparable. If Horst had been present, or at least where I could reach him, my development — I mean now the development of my critical side, which only begins to unfold during these early years, and the fact that I would have grown accustomed to his dazzling appearance, might have gradually put some distance between us. I could have asked him how he felt about certain news that seeped through to me —"horror propaganda" was the official term. If he had brushed them off lightly as malicious inventions, or declared that the Führer certainly knew nothing about them and would set things right in due course, my opposition would have been aroused. Naturally one couldn't write about things like that, so I had to find out on my own the answers Horst might have given otherwise.

Our sparse correspondence — although we wrote with increasing frequency — expressed little more than repeated assurances that we would not forget each other. At first in such trivial phrases as "I miss you. There's no one I can really talk to." Or, from him, "Think of me sometimes. I need it." But in time these communications expanded, without either of us realizing it, to repeated promises to be faithful to each other. In both cases the promise was always *given*, never asked for.

Even during the first year Horst went so far once as to write that it would be wicked of him to try to tie me down beyond death, because if "the deadly bullet" were to kill him, it would be my duty as an attractive young girl to give the Fatherland many healthy children. That was the first time a letter of his depressed and infuriated me. I tore it up and didn't refer to it in any way, which Horst probably took as silent assent. Objectively he was right, of course, but in our relationship I felt there shouldn't be this kind of objectivity. I didn't want to count on my friend's death as a possibility! After all, the poor mother of a very sick child wouldn't dress his brothers or sisters in his clothes as long as he was still breathing. I can remember thinking of this analogy at the time, and I tried to excuse Horst by telling myself that a man's thinking was basically unsentimental.

Now, however, when I recall this poor cliché-ridden letter which was perhaps intended to hide the desperate fear of death, and how it angered me, I think I was so bitterly unhappy for a quite different reason: before Horst had even proposed to me, before I had even had a chance to express my willingness to bear his children, he was disposing of me after his death! I became increasingly indignant over the fact that everything took place between us so wordlessly, as a matter of course, so that he didn't have to make the slightest effort to win me.

*Had* he really won me? Weren't the two of us actually imagining it all? Wouldn't it have been my parents' duty to offer a little opposition? Sometimes my protest went so far that I began to look at Walter's friends critically. Couldn't one of them perhaps interest me? But none of them could compare with my Siegfried in his black uniform! Except for Schindler, they were even a little shorter than I, a circumstance that at the time seemed to make anything but comradely feelings out of the question. Just the same, I was annoyed that, with one exception, they treated me like a schoolgirl.

The other day I brought down from the attic the little package of my letters, which Horst left in his father's apartment on his first leave, together with my diary, but I have only now been able to bring myself to read them! And there I see: *They treat me like an immature child. Look who's talking!*

As I read these lines yesterday, they gave me food for thought. Is it a distortion of perspective when it seems to me today that at the time I *was* the ignorant child the boys saw in me? Is this only one of the corrections with which we involuntarily change the expression on our faces in front of a mirror? Am I exaggerating my naiveté in these entries to have an alibi?

Oh no, my son! I truly believe that in spite of good report cards and serious feelings, I was a little fool! Or, if I want to be really fair to myself, besides good marks and all seriousness, I was a vain little creature who was furious that she made no impression on schoolboys like Walter's friends, yet was loved by an SS man! Didn't they sense at all how experienced I was already? Horst and I had kissed long and passionately when we had said good bye, even if neither of us ever mentioned it.

In the beginning I waited for Horst to mention it. Did he think I could forget it, or did he want to forget it? Was he ashamed of the intensity of his feelings? I was much too reticent to remind him of it, too reticent and too proud. And in the end my disappointment over the dispassionate tone of his letters changed abruptly to smoldering rage over the unreasonable demand to give the state healthy children after the death of my beloved! Was this stifling rage that threatened to choke me a first ominous rebellion against a fate that trampled on everything gentle and promising ... that was to be like a letter on which the words had been smeared by rain or sweat, with only a few legible ones left that had no connection? *Hunger. Shame. Stupidity. Desolation. Scorn. Vileness.*

Much later I received mutilated letters like that from Horst. I wasn't desperate because I couldn't read most of them. Whoever could still write was still alive! Whoever was still alive could come back! After Stalingrad, that was a comforting thought.

As a matter of fact, I am trying now for the first time to decipher the mutilated piece of paper that has the text of my life written on it, on which only a few words are left that are not illegible or garbled. In order to tell *you* the most important things, I must first know everything myself. Exactly what I have been struggling not to do all these years. Whether it was Uri asking me to do it in her indirect, gentle way, or the stern priest, demanding in the confessional: just *that* was what I now had to take upon myself. Let everything become present once more, live through it all again and suddenly I remember what he said to the girl who was crying uncontrollably: "You feel like a sacrificial lamb, and *that* is your true sin, which God can't forgive until you recognize and repent!" And I ran home and screamed at Uri, "Why did you send me to church? What does an unworldly priest know about the life of a woman? *You* don't go to church or believe in anything!"

"But *you* believe," she answered quietly.

I see I am losing the thread. Later I'll tell you a lot about Uri, but right now we are still in the year 1940 and I was writing about Walter's friends who treated me like an ignorant child.

Surely, even in more peaceful times, every person at least once in his life cries out over a revelation: "So that's the way it is!" And feels horribly deceived. But if he would be perfectly honest he would have to conclude, simply by the fact that he recognized all the connections in a flash, that they must have been known to him all along; it's just that he didn't want to face them. We prefer to accept the impossible as fact, even go so far as to look upon our indolence as humility — why should we know anything better than the next man? — before we try to get to the bottom of a thing, if the basis of our self-satisfaction may be taken from us in doing so.

How can I describe what I was able to observe at home during the war years without you shaking your head and saying, "But you should have known!" No, my child. One can't know what one doesn't want to believe.

So Walter assembled a small Bible group regularly in our apartment — Walter, who even as a child had protested against having to fulfill his religious obligations! *He*, reading the Bible, he of all people, who had nothing but detective stories on his bedside table or under his pillow. But I told myself that this had had to be the good influence of Clemens Schindler whom Walter had been fond of when he had been a scout, because Clemens had been willing to accept more responsibility than any of the other leaders and had given the boys who were entrusted to him as much freedom as possible; and the younger boys had accepted the fact that someone who excelled in sports was also a brilliant scholar. And it certainly was to their advantage that the adults trusted him just as much as the boys did. Was he trying to convert them now? He had my blessing. I went to my first-aid class. I wanted to be able to *do* something if bombs ever fell on the city. Should I take a nursing course after my graduation and go to the front? Perhaps I would recognize Horst among the badly but not fatally wounded. Unfortunately the war would probably not last that long ...

I snapped out of my waking dreams. Had I said "unfortunately"?

Naturally I was referring only to the beautiful image of a nurse dressed all in white, laying a cool compress on the feverish brow of a wounded soldier ... A cynical slogan reached even my ears a few years later: *Children, enjoy the war! The peace will be dreadful!* I wouldn't have been so indignant about it if I hadn't sensed the core of truth in it: all of us, yes, we enjoyed the war.

I can see you pause with a puzzled smile as you read that last sentence. Haven't you heard us talk about nothing but the horror of those days? Didn't we spice the lunch you took to school with the admonition to be thankful because during the war children hadn't had as much butter all day as you had on your sandwich? When you didn't want to get out of your warm bed in the morning, didn't I tell you how during the last war years school had started at seven so that children could be home before the daily bombing attacks at noon? And you heard about boys who had been called up for flak duty long before their final exams and had never returned, or had come back as cripples. Your dark eyes looked at me seriously, you listened to me respectfully and didn't dare to protest, yet I knew what you were thinking: how wonderful it would be to be called up for flak duty before the next Latin test! How much more interesting it would be to spend a night in the cellar now and again than to always have to turn out the light at nine! And that there was really little difference between coming back from flak duty a cripple or maimed after a Sunday outing in the car.

Since you never said any of there things, probably because you didn't want to hurt our feelings, Uri's and mine — after all, we're only women — we were never able to refute them. But now I have written and shall let it stand: we enjoyed the war! Not all of us, certainly not all of us, but many of us. Let us take a look at the people about whom I have written so far. First –my father. He was happy over coming home to the Reich. He was soon disappointed,however, when it became evident that as an *Ostmärker* and non-party member he was practically a second-rate citizen, and as a practicing Catholic even suspected of clerical leanings which came fairly close to treason. Perhaps these circumstances made it easier for him to choose actual treason in the end. The war preserved him from quite a few unpleasantnesses because many of the more important civil servants joined up, and dozens whose absolute loyalty to the ousted regime was assumed had either been arrested as early as 1938 or dismissed. But an administration can't function without a main body of experts. As long as the war lasted, my father could feel secure in his position. And his position was more than a job to him, Gottfried. I don't know if you young people can understand that, because evidently it is the amount of money earned that determines one's social status today, whereas a civil servant like my father actually felt himself to be a representative of that order which the Apostle Paul said comes from God!

If the possibility of working for the government hadn't opened up for my father, I think he would have become a judge or a prosecutor, never a defense lawyer who also has to take on doubtful cases. I have already explained to you why he was so happy about the Anschluss. The gradual demotion he experienced as the years went by was certainly shattering, but what weighed even more heavily upon him was the knowledge that it had to be wrong to support a government that occasionally, when it seemed opportune, deferred to the authority of Almighty God, but constantly and blatantly acted in contradiction to it.

And my mother? I turn the pages back and am astonished that I wrote so little about her. Actually I mention her only in passing. I told you about two apparently contradictory traits: it was a matter of complete indifference to her what uniform a hungry young guest, whom she had known since he was a boy, was wearing, yet it had been she who had expressed our astonishment: How do you happen to be wearing this uniform?

That's what she was like. She rarely criticized, yet nothing escaped her, and when there was something she didn't understand, she asked. (Until she was no longer able to ask.) To see her as she really was you must forget the sad picture that your two visits to the old people's home have certainly impressed upon you. I am so happy that you can watch Uri aging, that you can see old age can be dignified, peaceful, and a gradual detachment from the trivial business of daily life. Because I think Uri's forgetfulness rests mainly on her disinclination to take unimportant things into consideration. Naturally this includes things that are important to the material progression of life, such as everything concerned with money, quarrels with her neighbors — and your difficulties in school and prowess in sports, am I right? So why does she ask me about them, you'll want to know. Out of politeness, my boy. She doesn't want to shame us by letting us notice how unimportant our troubles are. Perhaps she is thinking: oh dear ... if it means so much to Helga that Gottfried doesn't get left back ... so she asks you if you passed your physics exam, and you are irritated and say, "It was a chemistry exam!" And she smiles and says, "Oh, I see. Isn't it all the same thing?"

Perhaps you would like to know what *is* important to Uri. Then watch her once; watch the way she examines the fruit in the apple pantry every week, with her eyes behind their thick glasses and with her gentle wrinkled hands, but with her nose too, because she leans over the frames and her nostrils flare as if she could tell the kind of apple and how ripe it is by its smell as well as by its color and shape. Or watch her in winter, filling the shells of nuts with margarine and hanging them on the branches in front of her window for the titmice, her favorite guests. And there are other things you could watch that mean a lot to your great-grandmother. Today you pay no attention to them, you may even make fun of them a little, but some day, when you are older and recall them, you may think of them with pleasure.

But I wanted to write at last about my mother. Everybody said she was beautiful. Sometimes Father asked us to admire her beauty but that embarrassed us; in a way it seemed almost improper. I should say it embarrassed *me*, because I don't know how my brothers felt about it. Psychologists declare that all little boys love their mothers in the same way they later love their girl friends and wives ...

I keep forgetting for *whom* I am writing these memories, but that doesn't matter. Perhaps I have to forget it or I shall make no headway. Later I'll make a summary ... Can it possibly interest the boy what his grandmother looked like in middle age? She was dainty, she wore size-five shoes and had blue-black hair, probably the heritage of the South Tirolean branch of her family; her round, golden-brown eyes too. *I* have big feet, small light eyes, and when I was fifteen I was already a handspan taller then she. She complained about it sometimes, found me "unfeminine", stern, reserved, and "Shockingly honest." She didn't approve of telling people straight to their faces what they didn't want to know, and she tried to stop me from doing it. "Talk is silver, silence is golden!" she said often. "Do a thing but don't neglect the other!" was one of her favorite sayings. As you can imagine, I didn't have much use for either.

She was totally without pretensions of any kind, and it never occurred to her, as it does to so many women, that since she had been brought up in a well-to-do household she was entitled to lifelong comforts. She declared that there were no boring people, and she denied the existence of menial work. When there was something dirty to do one put on rubber gloves, and in the presence of taciturn or pedantic, long-winded people she would pick up one of her beloved flower embroidery pieces, which she designed herself. "You have no idea what interesting thoughts such a 'boring' person can express if one just gives him the time," she told us cheerfully, and we had to admire rather than feel sorry for her. And she liked that.

Walter had flattered her unquestioningly as a child; still, I think she favored Albert. She could sense his silent, deep devotion, and of the three of us he needed her most. But her blitheness, which made it possible for her to see the good side of everything, had developed in him a tortuous indecisiveness: if *all* his fellow students were nice boys, *whom* should he chose as a friend? The first one to come along? The boy who sat besides him? Or the boy who attached himself to him and wanted to be his friend? "All of them!" Mother would have told him in her carefree fashion, but "none of them" was Albert's decision. He was just as talented in humanistic subjects as in the sciences, so — what should he study? "Be an engineer or a chemist!" said Mother. "They have the best chance." "Is that all I'm supposed to consider?" asked Albert. Couldn't one be effective as a humanist in the defense of a lost cause just *because* it didn't fit in with the spirit of the times? "Wonderful!" exclaimed Mother. "So defend a lost cause. Just as long as you're happy!"

"Oh, Mother! We aren't here to be happy!"

"So what are we supposed to be?" Mother asked, her tone a little sharp.

She was sitting in the window seat, her flower embroidery in her hands. Now she put it down, took off her glasses and looked across the table where we two slowpokes were still eating. That was when I got into the argument. I always tried to keep quite when my parents were talking seriously to my older brothers, but I never did stick it out for very long. This time I was on Albert's side. "We are supposed to sacrifice ourselves!" I cried excitedly.

Mother sighed impatiently and put on her glasses again. She didn't like exaggerated outbursts. Albert stared at me as if noticing for the first time that I was a human being. "Yes ... maybe," he said hesitantly, "Helga is quite right."

Mother went on with her embroidery. "And a humanist has more opportunity for that than a technologist?" she asked, a note of irony in her voice. "Could be," Albert replied, pushed back his chair and left the room.

"Sons used to learn the same things as their fathers," Mother said sadly, "For boys like Albert everything was so much simpler in those days ..."

Well, things became "simple" for Albert too. The war came and nobody asked him any more what he wanted to do. He had to be a soldier. I wondered if he brooded over what he would do later. I don't think so. He probably thought: time enough for that when it came.

And the time came ...

My mother hated the war, but she hated it like a natural catastrophe that overwhelmed mankind. Nobody could have wanted such a disaster or caused it; nobody could stop it. Because there had always been wars, just as there had always been plagues and floods and catastrophic fires. When there was talk of the "envy of the other nations" — rarely enough in our house — or of England's "hypocrisy," of France's "lust for revenge," or the duplicity of the Czechs, and finally of the Jews, which incorporated all the bad traits of every nation on earth within themselves, and who were using the power of their immense wealth to further the encirclement and destruction of Germany ... when Mother had to listen to talk like that she remained silent. Silence is golden ... But I had the unpleasant feeling that she didn't believe a word of it! In her opinion people were by nature good and became bad only when they were desperate. She trusted everyone. Father had to insist energetically that the door to our apartment be locked. Cupboards were locked only before Christmas. Even when there were workmen in the apartment, everything remained open and accessible. I don't know if there was ever anything missing; if there was, Mother wouldn't have mentioned it.

We children considered her naive and romantic, in our disapproving affection. We were still quite young when we began to believe ourselves wiser than she in some respects. If I declare today that she too was content during the war, as a matter of fact just because of the war, then the only way I can explain it is by her capacity to see the best side of everything. When rations got scarcer, she declared we were all eating too much anyway. Or: Now the foolish dictatorship of fashion had ended and everybody can wear what they have and what suits them. "What suits me?" I cried bitterly when I had to wear my shabby loden coat in winter too because the points on our ration cards were always needed for more pressing items. And the boys teased her. "Mother has always loved antiques!"

She admitted that she didn't feel at ease with brand-new things. Something perfectly beautiful was beautiful right from the start, but only kings could afford treasures like that. Ordinary people like us should be grateful when our inexpensive little ornaments were given a certain dignity by the patina of age. I can remember so well how troubled I was, almost hurt, when I realized that Mother didn't really like our apartment, which I found so elegant and homey, that she liked only a few things in it, things any child would find superfluous — the Meissen bowl in the glass cupboard, or the little Persian rug, its muted blue, light gray and red gleaming in front of her sewing table by the window.

I have already mentioned that Katie left us during the first war summer; after that an older woman came to clean twice a week. Mother, who had spent practically no time in the kitchen, cooked, and usually managed it so that we didn't leave the table hungry. Father felt sorry for her, but she was grateful for the chore of filling our hungry stomachs. What was really necessary was always the most fun, she declared, and none of us was so tactless as to ask her how necessary her embroidery was.

Once Father teased her — I think it was on her birthday, and they had saved a bottle of "army" champagne for the occasion. I can't remember whether Albert had brought it or whether Father had somehow wangled it. All I know is that during the war champagne was the thing to drink on festive occasions, whereas before the war only cheap wine had been served. After my father had praised the food exhaustively, he reminded

Mother that as a bride she had assured him, "But I'm never going to cook! You know that. I simply can't stand the sight of raw meat!"

"I still can't stand the sight of it," Mother said cheerfully. "Unfortunately I don't often get the chance!"

All of us laughed, and the boys declared indignantly that *they* would never have married a girl who had said anything like that. Mother turned to Father and said gaily, "If the poor fellows are going to size up a woman by what she *says*, then it serves them right, doesn't it?" "But what else should we go by?" asked Albert, who always gave the grown-ups the cue they were waiting for; this time, though, Walter was quicker. "By their legs, of course!" he said, and got a gentle slap from Father, and all of us laughed again.

I laughed too, naturally, but I sat there among them the whole time like a stranger and thought of Horst. He and I — we *meant* what we said and wrote to each other. We were the kind of people who, once we'd said *a* quite consequently said *b*. The war had been necessary, so the war was good. What Napoleon had tried to do, Hitler would achieve: the uniting of Europe under its most mature nation. There were already signs that even in countries inimical to us, the best people were forming National Socialist cells. They didn't want the Jews in their midst anymore, even though they were a scarcely noticeable minority in those countries and didn't pose a threat, as they did to us.

We realized that the Führer was blamed worldwide for nothing so much as for the persecution of the Jews. Why, he asked, and we echoed him, didn't the world accept joyously those whom he was expelling? If the Jews were really so capable and decent, why hadn't such sparsely settled countries as Canada or Australia opened their gates wide long before the war, instead of making Jewish immigration more difficult all the time? Now and then you could already read in a speech or newspaper article that dreadful phrase, "the final solution" to the Jewish question — not, however, with its later connotation. We saw something vague in it, such as the settling of the Jews in some climatically unfavorable region in Poland, or the establishment of a Jewish state in Madagascar after the war. It wouldn't be easy for them, but who could say it was easy for Germany to live in a world of enemies? The Jews would have to make great sacrifices before settling down in peace, but didn't we too have to sacrifice much innocent blood because the rich people among the Western powers refused to grant us the *Lebensraum* which our diligent population simply had to have to thrive?

I see, my child, that I have almost succeeded in writing an editorial of those days, so that you can understand how things were presented to us. But, you will ask, were there many people who believed it? Oh yes! Because at all times there are people who will believe anything they read in the paper, and in those days this was made easier because every paper said the same thing. There were plenty of people who knew the Jews only by sight. Others had done business with them. There might have been

one Jewish merchant who had saddled them with bad goods, or a Jewish
cattleman who had cheated them, or a Jewish doctor who had been unable to save the life of an incurably ill relative. There was a joke: Every
German knows *one* decent Jew.

There were two Jewish girls in my class. One of them was baptized
and took religious instruction with us. She was smart, witty and lazy, and
we liked her because she let us copy her work, made fun of our teachers,
and had no ambition whatsoever. There were no rumors about her racial
origin until she was suddenly gone and we were told that her family had
moved to Switzerland. We were sorry but felt it was best for her.

The second Jewish girl was shy and not very talented. She went on
coming to school until March 10, 1938. Then we were told that her family
had moved to another district. If you are going to ask me what became of
her — I don't know. After all, we had never seen each other outside
school. Nobody ever mentioned the Jewish girls, and their places were
soon filled by two girls who had moved to the Ostmark from the Reich.

I knew Frau Dr. Feldstein very well. She was the one to whom Mother
had given one of our food cards. She had been our doctor and had taken
care of us when we were children. We respected her and never dared to
protest any of her sometimes quite unpleasant orders. Very often she
made us fast, prescribed "apple days" and "juice days," practiced all the
simple therapeutic methods long before they were fashionable, and rarely
prescribed strong medication. She was dead set against rich desserts,
white bread, candy and ice cream. You can imagine that we were not very
fond of her. But when she walked into the room and we could feel the
sharp gaze of her big dark eyes and the grasp of her cool hand around
our damp hot little fingers, then all fear and restlessness were gone; all
we had to do was obey her and we would soon be well again. I must
admit that once Walter managed to feign appendix pains for a whole
week when he had good reason for not wanting to go to school. But very
different authorities were later fooled by his talent for dissembling.

Frau Dr. Feldstein never received money from my parents. She was a
public health doctor. Once, when Albert had pneumonia, she had to
make two night calls. My father, with some embarrassment, offered her
the standard fee, but she refused it almost rudely. She had only done her
duty, and for that the public health insurance would pay her. She started
visiting her patients early in the morning and her office hours lasted until
late in the evening. She was also an excellent cellist. I don't know how
Mother got that bit of information out of her, but because Mother was so
absent minded and seemed to be not in the least curious, she often found
out more about people than others would have. They went to concerts together a few times: mother got the tickets. Unlike the rest of the family,
she was very musical. Every now and then she was invited to Sunday
evening chamber-music concerts in the villa of a wealthy family in
Pötzleinsdorf when Frau Dr. Feldstein was playing the cello. On the following day Mother would report animatedly and with gentle humor on

everything that had been offered besides the music. "First rate" and sumptuous! But the music had been "first rate" too. And when Frau Dr. Feldstein played, that was when she got her "real face!" Father, who didn't think very much of intellectual women, asked skeptically, "So what did she look like then?" Mother smiled and said, "Like a woman."

But Frau Dr. Feldstein had less and less opportunity for such private pleasures, and by the time Hitler marched into Austria, Mother hadn't heard from her in months. She tried to reach her by phone but couldn't get a connection. Father said that surely she had emigrated long ago, such a clever woman. But Mother finally managed to find out that Frau Dr. Feldstein was working at the Rothschild Hospital and was also living there. My father found this very sensible. Nothing could happen to her there. After which the subject wasn't brought up again, at least not in my presence.

Now, since Katie had left us, Mother sometimes sent me to do the shopping, and I noticed that she only gave me four ration cards. Finally, tired of making excuses, she admitted that Frau Dr. Feldstein had the fifth one. "Do you still see her?" I asked, startled. My mother gave an evasive answer.

I was afraid the thing might leak out — the ration cards given to Jews were marked differently — and if that happened, Mother would be arrested and I ... quite possibly they would expel me from the *Bund deutscher Mädchen*, would throw me out, disgraced. So I dared to protest. "But Mother! That's forbidden! Just imagine if everybody ..." but she didn't let me finish. "I know," she said, "but we're not doing anybody any harm, at worst, ourselves." And she went on, her voice urgent, "Without this woman your brother might not be alive." That we couldn't call our lives our own any longer, that we were part of a national community and our lives belonged to the Führer, this she quite evidently couldn't grasp.

I spoke to Horst about it, naturally without mentioning what was actually going on, and he advised me to be patient. Older people needed time to adjust to changed circumstances. He was going through the same thing with his father. "At every historic turning point, people are divided into those who see into the future and recognize new goals and those who cling to the frail ideals of the past. Sometimes I find it difficult to overcome some deeply rooted prejudices." I just read this in one of his letters that lies before me. Couldn't "Thou shalt not kill" also be considered a deeply rooted prejudice?

I have told you all this in such detail so as to make a short scene, which I must write about now, more comprehensible. Perhaps also to put off telling it a little longer? It was very short. A few minutes and it was all over. For years I wanted to forget it and managed to forget it, then a dream brought it back to me. Since then I haven't been able to put it out of my mind. And when things go badly for me, I see it clearly, and tell myself: Serves you right! And when you vex me and my first impulse is to turn away angrily, I say to myself: he is *my* son. I have no right to be angry with him.

For some time now I had been the leader of a group of eleven and twelve-year-old girls. On Sundays we hiked, I had to call them up for inspection, or we went collecting for various causes. I took my leadership very seriously. The children sensed my enthusiasm and liked me, in spite of the fact that I was strict.

One Sunday morning at the end of October — it was still dark — I had assembled my little troop and we were singing as we marched through the fog. I had to stay back for a moment — I think one of the girls had torn a strap — and I was annoyed when the others didn't march on in step as I had ordered but instead stopped to watch something. "What's going on there?" I asked brusquely.

The little girl standing besides me said, "I think they're loading Jews. The SA like to do that on Sunday morning."

A pertinent answer with no special inflection. And she was right. "Forward march!" I commanded as soon as we had caught up with the others. I cast a quick shy glance at the big truck filled with people. A lot of things are necessary, I thought, which one does not like to see. In the same way I had always avoided the pig-slaughtering festivals in the country. Some children, though, are mysteriously drawn to such things. Walter, by the way, was such a child.

My girls didn't march on snappily as I had taught them. My command couldn't compete with the jokes of the driver, a smart SA man, even though one could hardly understand him. He spoke the dialect of a faraway province. Two other SA men were supervising the transport. They were standing nearby indolently, smoking. "Whoops!" one of them cried as the last person, an old man, fell back a second time in his efforts to clamber up. "Take it easy, gramp! We're not gonna leave without you!"

A few of the girls giggled. But I was staring at the woman who leaned forward now, both arms outstretched to help the old man. She looked like Frau Dr. Feldstein. Frau Dr. Feldstein would look like that twenty years from now ...

I couldn't see the woman's features clearly in the glaring light of a lamp post that was obscured by the fog every now and then, but the woman evidently sensed the astonishment with which I was staring at her because, when the old man finally got his footing among the dark, mute people crowded in the truck, she turned around and looked down at me. I could feel a stab of horror shoot through my heart because she smiled suddenly, a gentle little smile of recognition in which grief and pleasure seemed combined. But now there was added another emotion when she saw my brown jacket and the insignia, and with a sweeping glance took in the troop I was leading. She despises me, I thought. Yet it wasn't contempt that erased her smile and darkened her tired eyes in their deep hollows. How arrogant she is! I thought. But she was always arrogant! I hate her! My face was burning with shame. *I could sense that she felt sorry for me.*

One of the SA men must have noticed that something was going on. He spat out his cigarette and stamped on it with his boot. He gave his comrades a sign, they raised the tailgate and the driver started the motor. The SA man gave me a sharp look, then mustered his prisoners as if he wanted to find out which one of them I knew. But now Frau Dr. Feldstein was gazing just as apathetically into the fog as all the rest. It isn't she at all, I decided. I'd just imagined it. The woman is an absolute stranger. The SA man was staring at me again. Now he stretched out his arm and yelled, "How about it girls, let's hear it! Heil Hitler! Death to Judah!" And my girls, who never waited for a sign from me when they were supposed to give the German greeting, turned their pale, embarrassed faces to me. "Heil Hitler!" I cried.

Was I hoarse or were there tears in my throat? It wasn't she at all, I told myself, and at the same time: Why does she despise me? I can't help it! Let her hate me! I hate her too! Why do they let themselves be loaded into a truck like cattle? Why don't they prefer to die first?

My hand knew what it had to do, my arm, my voice. "Death to Judah!" I cried. It sounded bright as a fanfare. All my girls joined in and we marched in step, without looking back. We heard the motor roar like a wild beast escaping its cage, but we didn't see the truck again. It drove off in the other direction. The children began to sing, "Today Germany hears us, tomorrow the whole world!"

Now there was no way back for me. I had reached the point of no return. And I realized only then that until this moment I had been vacillating. But now everything was settled. Finally. "Today Germany knows it, tomorrow the whole world!" And at this very moment I also felt that I had made the wrong decision. But it was irrevocable. Horst, I thought, Horst is on our side too. I would have liked to cry, but that was impossible – I wasn't alone. So we sang. We sang all the songs we knew and woke the Sunday sleepers out of their morning slumber.

One can never be so utterly alone later in life, alone like a motherless child, as one can be at sixteen. Why don't adults talk to us about the things that decide our lives? Why did no one speak frankly to me? That's what I asked myself over and over again, asked Uri and the stern priest in the confessional in the years of my rage. How can it be possible that loving parents, who in times of need won't eat a piece of bread without sharing it with their children, how can it be possible *that they keep the truth to themselves?* And at the time I found a frightful and cruel explanation that I still consider valid, only thank God I have changed my position in the meantime and see it in a very different light today, namely the recognition that *the victim must be ignorant.* The less he knows, the more innocent he is, the more precious he is to the gods!

As alone as a motherless child, I just said. But I had a gentle, loving mother who wished everyone well. So why didn't she help me? She helped her sons and probably felt that I had to be spared from dangerous secrets. But that is how one "spares" the animal to be sacrificed! Gives it the best grass to graze on, preserves it from all hard labor so that its pelt may be glossy and beautiful, its motions free and fearless, its stance erect and noble when the time to slaughter it has come!

Never, my son, never will I spare you in such a fashion.

I have a frightful night behind me. There is supposed to be something called partial blindness. One believes one is seeing things normally but a part of the retina is receiving no light.

As I was trying to get to sleep I thought as usual of all the things that had to be attended to on the following day: an hour in the afternoon had to be reserved to help you with your mathematics, and I wanted to spend the evening writing again. I stretched out contentedly and closed my eyes and saw a sentence, the last sentence I wrote yesterday: *Never will I spare you in such a fashion.* And realized: that's all I've done until now. Nothing else! Just like my parents whom I have reproached so bitterly, I have kept the truth to myself because I was afraid it would be too much for you. As if a young person were not capable of bearing any knowledge as long as he doesn't feel one is hiding something worse. Gottfried, at last I dare to confront you, and me … yes, me too, with the whole truth.

Why didn't my mother talk to me? I asked myself over and over again. Because surely she knew me well enough to realize that denouncing my family to the secret police was impossible for the kind of person I was. Even if they thought they couldn't convince me, they must have known I wasn't capable of such baseness. But when I told this to the priest I have already mentioned, who at first was very patient with me, he demanded that I cease being arrogant: at a certain time and in certain situations everyone was capable of any vileness. Because all of us had crucified Christ. He had a way of expressing himself that always moved my wholly personal matters so far away, I could suddenly see them in proportion, and that gave them a pathos which made the most banal ones seem important and significant. I would have liked to protest, but then I had to think of my raised arm and "Death to Judah!" and had to concede that he was right. Yet I don't believe I would have betrayed my parents. After all — I loved them.

You pass through two strange experiences as you grow older. One is that the same thing seems to be happening to you all the time. And my Theme with Variations apparently is to be brought down to earth with a bang. The fortissimo came in the spring of 1945. To let it sound again, to strengthen your ears and heart so that you can bear it, is the purpose of my writing.

Even as a child I wasn't brought down to earth as gently as others, for instance, the moment when I realized that there was no Christ Child bringing us presents on Christmas Eve, that our parents had made fools of us with all this business of secrecy and locked rooms. That was how Walter enlightened me rudely one day, perhaps because he was so proud of what he'd just found out. But why? Why? I asked in my despair, and became even sadder when Father tried to get out of it by saying that, in a higher sense, the fairy tale was true because after all, the gifts came from the good Lord, and in our joy over the birth of His son, we wanted to make each other happy ...

But I felt deceived. They had wanted to make me happy with a lie and warm themselves at my happiness! And suddenly it seemed to me — and this was the worst part — that I hadn't really believed in the Christ Child either, and had only played along with them to please them and myself.

So that was the first time I was brought down to earth with a bang, and it was always like that, had to be for someone who had her head in the clouds, because the clouds don't hold you up.

In the black stillness of the night everything seems possible to the rebellious spirit, everything seems simple. A girl who has been miserable for a long time because she doesn't know if the boy she longs for loves her, decides, with tears of relief, to ask him. Because what is worse than uncertainty? And hard hit as I was by my most recent rude descent to earth last night, I wanted to rush straight into your room, wake you up, tell you ... tell you what? That you have no father? That the man in the picture you look at so often and so thoughtfully is not your father? That you will never know your paternal origin because I don't know it either. I wanted to beg you to forgive me for having brought you up with a lie because I considered the truth too horrifying for a child. But of course I decided to wait until morning. And when morning came I woke you as I always do, with the same injunction to hurry. You swallowed your breakfast standing because yesterday you forgot to inflate the tires on your bicycle and had to attend to it now. I didn't say, "Today you stay home. I have to talk to you." I said, "Then hurry!" and from the bay window watched you ride off into the mild winter morning. No snow yet. Again I felt: It is impossible. I must at least prepare him. Is what I am writing becoming so detailed because I want to drag out this preparation as long as possible?

But I have come to a decision. I shall prepare you in another way. We will visit a children's village together, one of those homes which a wise and charitable man founded in order to make happy people out of orphans, rejected children, and children of criminals, by giving them what they needed most — love and security. Then we will talk about the fact that it doesn't really matter what a child's origins are, but how he grows up.

Yes. That's a good idea. That way we will get to the subject quite impersonally.

I wonder how often my mother watched me going off to school, perhaps deciding too to bring up the subject some day in general terms: the theme of the wickedness of rule by force and the possibility of resistance.

But she never did. She had a husband and two sons, and my innocence was the best protection they had. She certainly also thought: "and mine." Or — and this thorn will remain forever in my side — did she love me less than she did the others?

But I ... why have I remained silent until now? I have only you.

Yes. That is why I am afraid with all the power of fear in me — for you. And this is the second thing I experience only now: all mothers are dreadful cowards.

When I got home that evening from our outing, Mother ran a bath for me right away because she could see how chilled I was after the long ride home in my wet clothes. When I was in bed, the brought me a plate of hot soup and sat down besides me while I ate. She was so gentle and loving, and I felt as secure as a little child. For a moment I thought how good it would be to tell her everything and then ask: It couldn't have been Frau Dr. Feldstein, could it? But I didn't dare. I was sure Mother knew nothing about such transports, and feared her horror and having to justify such measures to her. Never in all the years would I have been as incapable of doing so as I was at that moment. So I asked her to make me a cup of linden tea to ward off a possible cold, and while I was sipping it I said, "If I was still a child, would you read to me now?"

"Would you like me to?" Mother sounded surprised.

I avoided a direct answer. "You read me the fairy tale of the Singing, Soaring Lark a hundred times but I can't remember exactly what happens in it."

"I think," said Mother, "that is one of those stories in which the father promises the devil to give him the first thing that comes to meet him when he gets home. He is thinking of his dog or cat, but then it turns out to be his favorite daughter ..."

"Yes, I know. But was the girl saved?"

"Now *that* I don't remember either," Mother said, took my plate and straightened my covers. "And now sleep well. You have a mathematics test tomorrow, so you must be rested." She turned out the light and I fell asleep. I was an obedient child.

But I dreamt that my father came home from a journey and rang the bell wildly, which he did whenever he had a surprise for us. I raced with the boys to the door — we were all children at the time — and got there first. I flung open the door and wanted to throw my arms around him but he pushed me away and cried, "*You?* Why are *you* opening the door?" And I was startled and thought: He knows that I cried "Death to Judah!" That's why he doesn't want me to kiss him! Because it would be a Judas kiss! The specific logic of the dream made this absolutely clear to me. I began to cry, and my tears woke me partially. I floated up into that more transparent sleep in which the light of consciousness begins to shine. Why am I crying? I asked myself. It's all wrong. He pushed me away because he had promised to give the first thing he met to the devil, and he didn't want it to be me. But of course that's all in vain ...

You can't imagine how infinitely soothing it was to be damned and not be responsible for it! I fell asleep again and didn't wake up until I heard Mother calling, "Helga! Wake up! Hurry! You have a mathematics test your first period!"

All terror was gone, submerged; all I could feel was the prickly tension that went with any written test. Mathematics was the only subject in which it was difficult for me to get good marks. But this time I managed to solve all the problems easily, and I went home feeling relieved.

Mother had baked a meat loaf. There was more oatmeal in it than meat, but it tasted good and Father was surprised. "A Sunday dinner in the middle of the week?"

"Yes," said Mother, looking down at her plate. "Our meat rations seem to go farther again."

"Good," said Father.

Didn't he wonder why they suddenly went farther? I was evidently the only one who knew. And now I also knew that I had not been mistaken when I had recognized the woman in the truck who had aged so much. But that already seemed far away. It belonged to the past, immutably, and was therefore meaningless. "Would you like some more?" Mother asked, and I said, "Please."

It is mysterious — what events we remember and which ones we forget. When two people meet and recall past hours experienced together, they soon discover to their amazement, or with distrust, or, if they are very close, with horror, that one of them remembers things the other has forgotten completely.

After writing these last pages yesterday, I realized that I needed help. Would Uri be the one to provide it? All I could do was try to find out, I decided, and went to her room. She was sitting by the window, looking out with her red-rimmed eyes dimmed by the cataracts that come with very old age. Without turning around she said, "What is it, my child?"

This is one of my blessings: as long as she lives, I may remain a child, I, who when still young had to become the legal guardian of my own mother. So I confessed my plan to write down my past for you. She said nothing. "Do you think that's wrong?" I asked. "Am I a coward because this way I don't have to talk about it?"

"No. Why?" she said. "If you can bring it off."

"But that's just it!" I cried. "I started with so much courage. It seemed the right thing to do and high time that it was done. High time! Because Gottfried isn't a child any more. He has the right to know where he comes from."

She corrected me thoughtfully. "You mean where he *doesn't* come from, don't you?" and I blushed like a child whose teacher has to point out the correct answer. "Yes," I said. "Only now I suddenly discover how

many trivial things I remember, whereas the really important, the decisive things I know about only through other people or because I read
them some time or other in the paper." And it was then that Uri said
something strange. "One only remembers the things one doesn't want to
forget when they are happening."

I was astounded! I don't have to tell you that Uri is anything but what
today comes under the heading of "psychological." "You mean we make
up our minds what we want to remember right away, at the time it happens?"

"Certainly," she said firmly. After a short pause she told me that her
earliest memory was of a nightmare she had had before she was three
years old. At the time, on awakening just as she was about to be destroyed, she thought: I must remember this. This lion that was chasing me
doesn't exist. My flight through all those passages, the doors I banged
shut which he was able to push open with his mighty head, his hot breath
on the nape of my neck ... none of it was real. I dreamt it all. Here I am,
lying in my bed, still shivering, all wet with tears and sweat, but nothing
has happened to me. I've got to remember this, and when the lion comes
again I shall not be afraid. I shall tell him, "There is no you. I know I am
only dreaming you."

She was silent. You won't want to believe, Gottfried, that she spoke at
such length, with no interruption. But I wasn't satisfied. I asked, "And ...
and did you really say that to him?"

She smiled and turned around to face me ... until now she hadn't
looked away from the swaying branches in front of the window ... and
she said, "But he never came back! A lion you don't believe in ... what
sort of a figure would he cut?"

Do you remember, Gottfried, how you asked me a few years ago,
"Does Uri believe in *anything*?" And I put you right vehemently. "Of
course she believes. How can you think she doesn't?"

"But what does she believe in?" you asked. "She doesn't believe in
hell, she doesn't believe in the devil ..."

I didn't let you finish. It would have been terrible to hear you say,
"And she doesn't believe in the good Lord either!" It would have been
very difficult to deny that she didn't believe in the "good Lord" either, so
I answered quickly, cutting your question in half, "Gottfried, she believes
*in the truth*. And God is the truth. Think about it."

I recalled this conversation when she told me about the lion who
never came back because she had decided not to be afraid of him. But it
didn't help me in my perplexity. "You know, Uri," I said, trying to make
my difficulties clearer. "I want the boy to have the right outlook on everything. And actually I know so little about my father, even about my
brothers. After all, how well do we understand our older brothers? Later I
was told about the sacrifices they made, their bravery, their loyalty to
their friends, but I noticed hardly any of this. I saw through many of

Walter's petty deceits and despised them. As far as I was concerned he was lazy, a flirt, a star of the suburban nightclubs until he was called up. And after that I never saw him again."

"You saw him once," said Uri.

"Yes!" I cried. "Once more! But that was the time all of you told me it wasn't he!" And Uri admitted softly, "I know. We had to do that. But how could you believe us rather than your own eyes?"

I said nothing, but still, after almost two decades, I was hot with rage. Uri, however, understood me; that was why she asked gently, "Is it your intention to settle the rights and wrongs of *others*? Nobody can expect you to do that, child. Not even your son. Write what you experienced. That will suffice."

"Thank you, Uri," I said, and felt ashamed, and went to my room to destroy what I had written — all those reminiscences of the singing, soaring lark and the girl whom her father wanted to sacrifice on the altar of a goddess to protect his warships ... but then I thought that some of the facts could be left in after all, so I read the whole thing through for the first time and discovered a quite different picture of the young girl than I had seen before I had begun to describe her. It had become like me in an unusual and surprising way. And because I find it startling, I'll let it stand and continue as best I can.

Albert wasn't sent to the front; instead he was stationed in barracks in Mecklenburg and had to wait. My parents were of course happy to know he was safe, but he seemed to take this transitional period exceptionally hard. He wrote the strangest letters. Mother read them aloud to us when everyone's work was done and none of us had to go out again, or wanted to. They were always addressed to Mother even if they started off with "My dear parents," or "Dear Family."

It is possible that I remember these first letters so well because they were preceded by a ceremony of sorts. The dishes had to be removed, the table cleared, the ceiling light turned out; Father and Walter put the papers away, and only then would Mother start to read, and I wondered why her voice always trembled a little at the beginning. And there wasn't really anything very exciting in the letters. Once I can remember Albert complaining that there was nothing to do, and I, who didn't know whether I was coming or going with tests, courses, evening chores, inspections and collecting for the Winter Relief Fund, cried out thoughtlessly, "Lucky Albert!" Mother looked at me reproachfully, and as she read on I was already regretting my thoughtlessness. It was like a sort of purgatory, Albert wrote, because there was no point in taking up one's personal life again. That was why one shouldn't send him any books or at best something light that he could throw away after reading. His only consolation was that even in this teeming desert one was still granted the privilege of making "human contacts." This would interest Walter especially ...

I wanted to exchange an amused glance of understanding, with Walter, because we both had often made fun of Albert's turgid way of expressing himself. Walter, however, was paying no attention to me but was listening closely to what Mother was reading. This little observation was a piece in the puzzle that I was to recognize in its entirety only much later.

Albert also sent Walter the message that he should work hard and prepare for his exams. "And what about me?" I cried, feeling hurt. "In your case it goes without saying that you'll get through them very well," Father said to pacify me, and stroked my hair. "You're our good girl."

I can't reconstruct the situation today. Was he already involved with what the boys were up to? I think Walter let him in on it only when he had to, perhaps after the visit of the Gestapo; but it is quite possible that they had asked him, just as they had asked me, to participate in the Bible meetings, in which case he would have found out what was going on quite naturally. I never asked. Today I wonder why. But it doesn't really matter ...

In my case, however, they always made a point of telling who had been at the meetings: a few friends from a former Wandervogel group, but also, introduced by Clemens Schindler, a young man from a proletarian background, whose name was Pepi. He was a mechanic. He differed from Walter's old friends only in the proper way he dressed, the pedantic way he spoke and in his rather ceremonious politeness. He was small and stocky, and his intelligent eyes behind their thick glasses were sharp. Beside Walter he gave the impression of being "intellectual," and if this designation isn't supposed to cover only knowledge acquired in school but also the urge to ask fundamental questions, then he was intellectual too.

Once, turning back hastily because I had forgotten a notebook, I bumped into Pepi in the hall, laughed, cried "Sorry!" and ran off, but not before I had noticed that he had blushed, and I wondered why. The idea that this little mechanic could fall in love with me like any student — or SS man — didn't occur to me. When on another occasion I was made aware of this, I was again rudely brought down to earth and realized at the same time how little a true, humane sense of equality was mine by nature. And the prejudices of which we are not aware hurt the other person most deeply.

I made up my mind to find out some time what really took place at these Bible meetings. All I had to do was eavesdrop. But before I got around to it, I met Clemens Schindler on the stairs, and he stopped me. It was such a pity that I never had time on Wednesdays, he said. "I'm sorry too," I told him, "but I don't think I'd fit in anyway."

"Why not?" he asked, looking at me seriously. "How can you know ahead of time?"

It made me feel uncomfortable. I would lose out in every dispute. After all, as a priest, he was experienced in convincing people, whereas all I knew was how to discuss things with twelve-year-olds. Coward that I was, I pretended that he hadn't understood me. "What would I be doing in there with you as the only girl?" I asked. "I know that the Bible doesn't have a very high opinion of women."

"That's a bold statement! Do you happen to know the Book of Ruth? ... Well, there you are! Don't reject something you know so little about ahead of time. And you wouldn't have to remain the only girl. We need to grow!" Whereupon I was rude.

"Don't you ever reject things you don't know much about?"

He was silent for a moment. Evidently he was giving what I had said some thought. But I was in a hurry. As you know, I am overly punctual. That is an inborn trait which you lose only when nothing means anything more to you. When for a while I no longer considered time important, I ceased to see the whole world and my place in it as important. But that was much later. Right then I looked at my watch and said brusquely, "I don't share your faith!" He looked so startled that I added vaguely, "Still, I wish you success," and was about to run off, but he took my hand and said urgently, "Success? At what?"

I replied breezily, "At your efforts to convert us," and freed myself.

I found out later that this conversation convinced Clemens Schindler that I knew everything that their little group was working for, that I even approved of it but didn't want to become involved. I had told him categorically that it wasn't right for a girl. Such misunderstandings are possible when one doesn't show one's true colors. And I was prevented from doing that, not only because I was afraid of his cogent arguments but also because I wanted to spare him. Let him be happy in his illusions as long as he left me in peace.

But now I must tell you when I lost the faith in which I was brought up.

As a child I went to church rarely and never to mass. My father's deep-rooted Catholicism lacked the southern naiveté, also often found among us, that believes you can impregnate a child with piety by force of habit. To have a little child at his side when he prayed, curiously taking note of every move he made and trying to imitate him, would have bothered him just because he believed in what he was doing. And so I was seven years old before I attended high mass at my mother's side after explicit instruction in the catechism and classes in religion. The tears ran down my face, and I wanted to help the Savior. I wanted to stop Him from sacrificing himself for me because I felt I wasn't worthy of it and never would be. "No, no!" I sobbed as the priest lifted the chalice, and I realized how miserably futile my wishes were when he raised it to his lips and drank. My whole body trembling, I buried my face in my mother's lap. I did not want Jesus to die for me. I didn't want *Him* to atone for my sins. I wanted to do that myself. It wasn't fair of him to make it impossible for me to sin by this rite, to attach such an inhuman, such a divine weight, that would one day drag me down into the depths of hell, to everything wrong I would do from now on. Because I had to, wanted to continue to do wrong.

Mother whispered soothing words to me: it would be over soon. In just a few minutes we'd be out in the sunshine again ... Yes, yes. But nothing could undo the fact that my sins would become the cross of Jesus.

I am sure you will say that a seven-year-old child couldn't possibly think along such lines. I swear ... no, please, try to recall the experiences of your earliest childhood. Which ones? I don't know. The umbilical cord was cut long ago. Since then you live and feel in a different world from mine. But whatever your fears or joys were, can you deny that it is possible for a child to be aware of *everything* ahead of time, just as it sees with its eyes and hears with its ears? Only the interpretation — *that* comes later. And I wonder if it is always entirely right ...

On the way home, as I slowly calmed down, I noticed that Mother had been joined by one of our neighbors, and gradually I began to follow what they were saying. Yes, I had had chicken pox not long ago, my mother explained. "But she's been back in school now for a week ... Yes, you're quite right: children remain overly sensitive after an infection. After Walter had the measles he suddenly threw his plate of spinach against the wall, can you imagine?"

What a glorious hot feeling my defiant rebellion in church had been compared with the icy void that gripped me now as I began to get the gist of what the women were saying: a horrible disenchantment! Walter throws his plate of spinach against the wall, I burst into tears at mass; the one comes from the measles, the other is a result of chicken pox ... That's the way adults see the world! After all, they must know.

Gottfried, I think from that day on I tried to find my way without God. And for many years I managed very well. I *did* go to communion and was confirmed, just as I submitted to other conventions such as writing to Grandmother on her nameday or dressing better, and putting on fresh underwear on Sunday. I accepted religious rites as honorable symbols like Mother, Grandmother, and most of my elders, but Father? He was so sad anyway ... a good thing he still had his toy balloon. I was not going to puncture it.

My short, misleading conversation with Clemens prevented me from eavesdropping on the Wednesday night meeting. One is ashamed to steal what has been offered freely. And to know what they were up to wasn't really very important to me. The only thing that mattered that year was my dream, the dream I called Horst. It had a core of good, hard realism: our comradeship in arms in the fight for a new world. We wanted to be its conquerors like shining knights; we didn't want to be like the mercenaries who had jumped on the bandwagon (and we saw painfully how numerous they were in the Party) who snapped up everything that could be useful to them. If they remained incorrigible, our intention was to throw them out at the right moment. What was the right moment? The moment when we didn't need them any more. When the fight against the enemy outside was over, we hoped the big purge of the Party would begin.

But Horst and I were more than comrades because our union was exclusive. "I have only you!" we wrote to each other, and I was sure these were words only a lover writes to his beloved. That someone drowning might also cry these words aloud to his rescuer — how could I possibly have known that at the time?

"I can't talk to anyone but you. Sometimes I get the feeling that older people don't seem capable anymore of taking things seriously; the many disappointments have made them indifferent or cynical." That was the sort of thing I wrote to Horst, and he replied, "I love you because you are totally lacking in frivolity. I promise to die rather than to become cynical. When I can't believe anymore, then I shan't want to live either."

Didn't these words startle me at the time? I can't remember. I might even have been proud of them. Most women are deceived by men who don't keep their word; my man betrayed me by keeping his.

Sometimes I wondered secretly why my parents didn't interfere with our relationship in any way; they never even asked about it. I received mail more frequently from Horst than they did from Albert! Nobody seemed surprised. How is he? they asked sympathetically. I was allowed to bake something every week — a cake or cookies — and include them in my army packages, and I knitted a lot: socks, mittens, ear muffs. I believe I experienced a great deal of the joy of a solicitous wife and mother ahead of time when I sat up evenings with an aching back, knitting. Sometimes I dreamed of how I would knit a soft, baby-blue woolen jacket for my first son, later, in that promised time of peace which no one could really imagine. Then I would feel a vague longing which was soon gone. There are girls who long passionately for a child at sixteen, even earlier, who can't pass a baby carriage in the park without thinking, "I like that one," or, "Mine will be prettier." But I was awkward and embarrassed in the presence of little children. As far as I was concerned there was so much to do, to learn, to change the world; I wanted to be a part of it and not waste my best strength washing and cooking, baking and sewing. What did Mother get out of us anyway? I thought heretically, when, with all the means of propaganda, having a lot of children was praised as a woman's true joy. If I did happen to think of soft baby wool on my needles as I sat knitting coarse socks for a man, then it was a highly unrealistic dream, just as fluttering snowflakes can make us think longingly of petals falling on a past or future day in spring. One knows there are such things, but one doesn't believe they will ever happen. I wanted to have a child someday, but right now I wanted Horst and our life together.

Did I really want Horst? Did I want love? Or did I only want to go on dreaming a dream that gave me time, that spared me, that cast a protective cloak over me, like the Madonna's, to ward off all desires, even my own?

My schoolmates would have found me romantic and sentimental, but all they knew was that I had a "friend," an SS man who was at the front. This they respected. For most of these very young creatures love was a purely biological factor, miscegenation was a sin against the nation which, as in the case of thoroughbreds, could not be expunged. Fortunately there was no opportunity for it. Everything else was a private affair and primarily a question of personal hygiene. Every girl had to find out for herself what kept her healthy and efficient; that was all the "morality" expected of us. To invest too much emotion in sexual experiences was considered reactionary. The slogan: The German woman doesn't smoke! could be seen in many public places; nor was she to be amused by dancing like Negroes, but there were no orders about the more intimate aspects of her life, at least not yet.

I'm afraid I know much better today what I wanted to feel at the time than what I actually felt. I am sure I always tried to recognize the outside world and the people around me as they really were ever since I was able to think — that is — ever since I began to made comparisons. As a child, when I heard for the first time the saying love is blind, I rejected it vehemently. Because to love someone always meant to me, whether I liked it or not, to place the one I loved in a sharper light than any of the others, to recognize him more clearly. That is why to people like me love means to love *nevertheless*. But perhaps everyone is like me ... or no one. I didn't love Horst because he was a hero but because he, a talented, passionate musician, preferred to be a hero rather than an artist. I felt that he had wished to realize something difficult and contrary to his true nature. That he had to oppose his father, who had been dissatisfied with his son's decision, must already have been hard for him. Basically he tended toward compromise and needed the approval of those closest to him. Because his father had refused it, he had attached himself to me when he had seen that his uniform not only surprised me, but that above all it pleased me! I think he noticed it before I did. Two children left alone ... what could be more natural than for them to walk hand in hand? Or is all this too far fetched? Was it simply a case of two young people deciding to go steady as thousands of others were doing? That we were "meant for each other," as the saying goes?

It was my intention to tell only the facts, and to tell them chronologically, in a way that would make comprehensible the necessity of all the seeming coincidences that shape our fate. There are few words that contradict their original meaning in their everyday usage as much as the word coincidence. Because surely coincidence means an event that takes place without any intention or influence on our part, something predestined, a dispensation that happens to us. But we use the word for anything that hasn't been planned, a trifling "irregularity," proof of the incoherence of our world. Coincidences in this sense, however, could happen only in the chaos before creation. But are we godless people perhaps actually living in the chaos before creation?

If one steps back a little, one can see the weave of the fabric which before seemed to consist only of tangled, colored threads. The basically simple facts of my life — and your birth — require so many more circumstantial explanations than I had expected, or I would never have started to write. For quite some time now I have been writing for myself more than for you. This stepping back from the fabric is what takes place when I write, and to stop now would mean that I close my eyes deliberately the moment I begin to recognize something ... something, to be sure, that I don't like at all.

How far I have strayed from my intention to tell you simply, clearly and concisely, and in all honesty, what happened before you were born! Is it possible that the efforts to be honest impair clarity? For instance, there is the indubitable fact: that was the year I loved Horst above everything else. That was why I had no idea what was going on at home. Now I ask myself: was I constantly afraid for him? Was I indifferent to everything taking place around me, with only the one thought on my mind that he should come back, that he should soon be with me again? No. I wasn't really afraid for him; I rarely thought of our future together. Nor did I try to picture what he was experiencing in France. Whenever a shiver passed through me: Does Horst have to kill now? *Can* he kill? I hastily consoled myself with the foolish platitude: one can always do what one has to do. Nor did I ask myself whether he would remain the same, so far away, and not only spatially, or whether unimaginable experiences wouldn't perhaps alienate him from himself and with that also from me? Today I know: I didn't really love him. I loved the dream of a great love, the wonderful, soft protective cloak that prevented me from feeling the coldness of the times and the estrangement from my family, who had silently crossed to the other side and were gently, gently drawing up the bridge, doubtlessly in the reassuring delusion that they would somehow manage to rescue me at the last moment ...

Before I fell asleep, usually dead tired, I would let the sweet legend of our love story run through my mind like a film; and so that it might be a little richer, last a little longer, and not pass quite so quickly, with only the few words of consent, the warm, parched way he looked at my lips when I spoke, the trusting way we walked hand in hand in the empty residential streets, the roses, and the bitter sweet farewell, with the one and only kiss which had been like a seal on all unspoken protestations ... in order that the fairy tale might last a little longer, I would begin with how we two shy children had first met, an event I had to make up because I had absolutely no memory of our first meeting.

With these visions I spun a web of unlimited possibilities around myself, all of them equally attractive: dying together heroically for the Fatherland; living in poverty and peril as pioneers in some newly conquered territory, or a life of travel with a famous young violinist for whom I made the strange big cities of the world seem like home by my presence, my motherly anxiety, my understanding of his inner self. Actually I didn't believe any of it. Or does it seem like that to me today because nothing ever came of it?

Gottfried, young love is so dangerous because its dreams grow wildly, like tropical vines, around the delicate stem of life. Soon I began to feel a cold breath of disappointment when one of Horst's ineffectual little letters came, and I can remember thinking once, startled: Do I still love him? But I *wanted* to love him! Where there was no determination to love, there could be no faithfulness. Faithfulness is nothing but the determination to make love last.

I must have written something like this to Horst, because his excited answer lies in front of me. He had never doubted my faithfulness! He would consider any such doubt a desecration of our friendship (he wrote friendship!) ... But he too promised to do his very best to remain faithful to me in every way.

The moment I read this I knew he wasn't succeeding; that in the vulgar sense, which I had hardly ever thought of, he had been untrue to me.

At first I was indignant. It didn't hurt me, it hurt my pride. Even more than the fact itself, which seemed to me nothing but a lack of self-control, not really a deception or anything like that, I was indignant that he had let me guess it through such faint hearted assurances. He shouldn't have revealed himself to me. How happy I had been, believing in his strength.

I never mentioned this promise again, and I soon calmed down. Since I wasn't his wife yet, I had no right to be angry with him. But the ideas that today's young girls have about the necessities of a man's sex life are just as strange as the complete ignorance of earlier generations. Now they know all — well, almost all — about everything, but it doesn't do them much good as long as they've had no experience. For a long time I thought that people embraced and kissed out of exuberance, but did everything else when they wanted a child, and I tended to imagine it as something unpleasant and certainly extremely embarrassing, an understandable mistake after the absolutely incontestable sex education we had been given in our natural history class.

At sixteen I had a vague idea that this wasn't quite the way things worked because I had heard enough about illegitimate and unwanted children, and at the time motion pictures were already presenting exciting visual instruction, even if not in as graphic detail as is common today. So in the end I felt that Horst's unfaithfulness was mainly my fault, and I decided to marry him just as soon as possible. Surely he would get leave one day. Then, I thought, both of us would be immune against temptation — he from the charms of French women and I ... well now, against what was I supposed to be immune? Perhaps against the inclination to doubt some of the new directives and to measure right and wrong according to the age-old Commandments?

In the meantime, however, the period of the great victories had begun. Every announcement aroused a triumphant, wholly personal happiness in me, a beacon light confirming that our way was the right way — behind our Führer, who could see farther and plan more audaciously than all of us.

My parents and everyone I knew were happy about the good news too. My father, however, occasionally had some strange things to say about what was going on; for instance, that the French perhaps realized now that it wasn't so easy to oppose Hitler's artillery and bombs as they had so recklessly urged our last chancellor to do. And my unpredictable mother said, "Victory or defeat — the main thing is that the war be over soon!"

And that's what all of us believed. Walter declared, "It looks as if they won't be needing me anymore," and Father and Mother said, "Thank God!" And I thought haughtily, "What's he good for anyway, the lazy wretch?" But things didn't move as fast as all of us had expected. Because England didn't give up, not even after Dunkirk.

Once I came home earlier than usual and heard a vehement argument between my parents and Walter, who wanted to volunteer. Mother was saying, "But I have only you!" *And what about me*, I thought in a sudden wave of jealousy. Do only the boys count? Father insisted that Walter finish school first; later he'd never have the willpower to go back to it. "I can stay in the army," Walter said casually, with a strange look at me, and my father cried angrily, "That's no profession!" And when I interposed sharply, "How can you say that?" he defended what he had said, a little embarrassed, with the explanation that in normal times a soldier's life consisted of little but waiting. "I want my sons (again, my sons!) to have a fulfilled life, not to spend their days preparing for an event that everybody must hope will never come!"

Furious over such considerations, right in the middle of a war, I cried, "But there is no such thing as normal times!" and my mother said bitterly, "And there are no more normal people!"

"There you are!" Walter was smiling, and I thought: he's won. To my astonishment though he went on going to school and hating it ... until autumn.

Until autumn. In between there was summer. What a difference there was between the summers of our school years and those that came later! To me the former seem like islands of tranquility embedded in the current of events. During summer vacation one didn't grow older and the world stayed the same ... perhaps because we went almost every year to where the world changed most slowly: to the Alpine peasants.

My father was still a student when he had first discovered the farm, high above the Pitztal, and he had felt so happy there under the care of the young farmer's wife, that instead of staying a night, he had stayed a whole week and gone back again and again — alone at first, then with my mother at the end of their honeymoon, later with us children as soon as whoever happened to be the littlest one at the time was over the worst. Thus the farm became a second home for us, and we definitely gave the Gschwandtner-mother the authority of a second mother, and discovered to our astonishment how different mothers could be. The peasant woman had three children ... I almost wrote *besides us*. They were considerably older than we were and already took the place of hired hand and maid. Besides, she always had one or two foster children, shadowy little creatures who were experiencing friendliness and were given a feeling of security for the first time in their lives with her, and weren't allowed to leave until they could count on being treated well elsewhere as good workers.

For us there was always a large room in which I slept with my parents, and a bare little one for the boys. During the first years the two women cooked together at the big brick stove; later Frau Gschwandtner took care of our meals. The two mothers appreciated each other just because they were so different. We learned early that intelligence was not dependent on school learning and that decency had nothing to do with city manners. When our Gschwandtner-mother said once, "Helga'd make a good mountain peasant," I felt proud, and when I think of it, I believe I never did receive a greater compliment. Walter asked, "What about me? I'd like to be a peasant." But she just looked at him with a twinkle in her eye. "You'd do real good as a hunter, or better yet — a poacher, eh?" She was smiling, but then she became serious. "Be thankful you can learn, boy ... be truly thankful."

Oh dear God, of what concern could Frau Gschwandtner possibly be to you, my son? She is dead and her farm burnt to the ground. Why do I bring up this lost paradise anyway? Because it was part of my childhood, a timeless island in the whirlwind passing of the years? Probably because of something this peasant woman said in that summer of 1940, the summer of many victories, and so that you should know who spoke those words that sounded to me like an alarum. But I? All I did was turn over on my other side ...

We had just arrived and unpacked and were sitting on the bench outside the house in the last mild rays of the sun. Mother said sadly that we had hoped to the last minute that all of us could come, that Albert would be with us, because since the end of May one had kept hoping that the war would be over by now. "But God cain't let that happen!" the peasant woman cried passionately. "We'd be sheer despert an' have to stop believin' in Him if He let *them* win the war too!" "But ..." Mother's voice was weak. Father laid his hand over hers. There was no but, there was no answer to it — the Gschwandtner-mother's only son was at the front too ... I looked at Walter. He began to clean our shoes as if he hadn't heard. So it was up to me to say something. But I couldn't utter any of the stock phrases that usually came to me so easily. "Come and eat," said the peasant woman. "I've made fritters. Let that be, Walter. Melcher will clean them later."

The moment to show my colors had passed. I ate my fritters and felt guilty. We didn't have anything as rich and good at home anymore ...

I can remember very little else about this summer except that it fulfilled one great wish: a real climb up one of the three-thousand-meter Alps. Father had climbed the Wildspitze two years before with the boys, but they hadn't been able to take me along because I was ill at the time. Now one of the native guides asked if anyone wanted to join his party. He was taking a German couple up and could easily take four on his rope. My parents at once said Walter and I could go.

The weather was glorious — clear and cool. The couple from North Germany were great talkers, but while climbing they discovered, to their amusement, that you got winded. The last Alpine roses were still bright among the rocks; hawk and buzzard circled overhead, and later we saw the Alpine jackdaw flying below us. The glacier rose gently, our companions caught their breath again and started to talk, practically without cease, with jokes and banality, with sarcasm and a condescending amiability toward us *Ostmärker* that was more offensive than open criticism. They never stopped drawing comparisons between our country and its inhabitants and their homeland. Although they were right in many respects and were generous in their recognition of the beauty of the landscape and the robust native quality of the population, I understood my father's antipathy toward his new colleagues for the first time, and felt sorry for him. These people, in their naiveté, behaved like the conquerors of a backward province that had to be cautiously civilized.

Mountain guides are usually taciturn. Ours, who at the Gschwandtner farm had chatted reflectively, his small glass of Enzian in his hand, didn't say a word for hours. Walter, though, kept leading the couple on, much to my annoyance. Above all he seemed interested in their profession. Both were employed in a factory that had been converted to armaments. He listened to what they had to say with apparent respect, an amiable savage, I thought angrily, ready to be tamed. If he was putting on an act, he was doing much too good a job of it. I had no idea that he was just starting to work out a little routine for himself. When the man finally declared, "Where *we* come from the people are efficient, diligent, and extremely consistent; you *Ostmärker* are better at the art of living. You're altogether more at home with the arts, ha-ha, together with wine, women and song." I said quickly, before Walter could perhaps agree with him, "Do you really believe that this art of living could have made Adolf Hitler Reichschancellor and commander-in-chief?"

"No, no!" His wife tried anxiously to shut her husband up. "I'm afraid you've just put your foot in it, hubby!"

"Well, I guess when an *Ostmärker* is a go-getter, he goes a hundred and fifty percent!" The man laughed and added, "But the exception makes the rule!" And wasn't there edelweiss here anywhere?

At last our guide spoke. You could find edelweiss wherever there were no tourists, but not on the ice, naturally! We should please move a little faster, the snow would soon be too soft, and he looked at me as he said it — at me! Of the four of us! Walter said nothing and looked annoyed. I had vexed all of them. Again, I was all alone.

"A good thing that you're German but not like them!" I wrote to Horst in my next letter. "Or I would start insulting the Heinies too, which is beginning to be the fashion in Vienna." A fashion that has lasted a long time, Gottfried, right up to the present day.

Strange, how people won't admit when they've made a mistake. They've paid for it dearly. Is it more honorable to be cheated? This is a tactic I find wretched in an individual, much less in the case of a nation. That was something I couldn't understand about my father. It is incomprehensible that a man of his integrity should not have recognized how contemptible this attitude was.

But I am way ahead of myself. We have not yet reached the year 1945. Not for a long time ...

Why is the present so obscure, the person closest to one sometimes so far away? While you were walking besides me yesterday, Gottfried, so obviously bored and feeling superior ... I couldn't understand it. And then your question, which perhaps should have made me happy or reassured me, but which only succeeded in startling me. Was that the result of my clever idea to visit the children's village?

Of course we saw a lot of things, but very few children. And that a fifteen-year-old boy doesn't find the homey practicality of such little houses interesting — that I can understand. Since a different house is exhibited every week for the guests who are donors, or who, it is hoped, will become donors, the house mother has to be present to show people around, this besides her daily housework. Naturally she keeps the children out of sight as much as possible if only to spare them obtrusive questioning. So all we saw was a baby sleeping peacefully in its crib, and a twelve-year-old boy in the kitchen, drying what was left of the lunch dishes. When I said, "I guess you have an exceptionally good boy there," the young woman smiled and shook her head. "Jest like yours." You looked embarrassed and grinned. But then, among bathtubs and showers and washbasins at various heights, I did screw up my courage to ask an important question besides all my admiration for so much functional effort. "Did you ever have a child with such bad tendencies that it couldn't adjust to a new community like this, that it could even have had a bad influence on the others?"

"Takes a while for them to get the hang of it," the house mother replied. "Took our Peter almost a year. He saw his father go for his mother with an axe when he was jest a kid; after that he was in eight foster homes. Not much chance to find out that everybody's trying to do their best for him. Not till little Hansl came to us … the one that cried so much … that's when it suddenly worked for Peter."

But I persisted. "And that a child has to be sent away again — that never happens?" I asked. Only when the child was sick, she replied, physically or mentally, and needed medical attention. The way the simple woman said it sounded as if she had learned it by rote, perhaps because she was speaking High German now. Still I wasn't satisfied, because why had I brought you here? I wanted to be told explicitly, in front of you, what I so much wanted to believe. (Because what we so much want to believe, we probably *don't* believe.)

"You mean to say that there is no such thing as a basically bad child, only those who have been hurt by their environment?"

She looked at me, her big round eyes wide with astonishment. "But that ain't right!" she cried, paused for a moment, gave the matter some thought and went on hesitantly, "We're all bad, ain't we? Because of original sin? None of us stay the way nature made us."

"Yes, of course," I said, ashamed, and added unintentionally, "Excuse me."

Meanwhile she had led us into the boy' dormitory. "I must admit, it ain't always as neat as this," she said.

"I should hope not," you replied cheekily, and secretly I had to agree with you. It looked like a barracks — the beds neatly made, nothing lying around. I wondered if the junk children love was tucked away in some closet. It was all bright enough but lifeless.

We thanked her, I put some money in the collection box at the entrance and wondered how so many glass windowpanes could survive the residency of eight boys. While we were walking to the bus — you were delighted with the first snow of the year — I said casually, "Isn't it wonderful, the things that are suddenly possible when one determined person has a good idea? But the most remarkable part of it is that there are so many women who can love obstinate, recalcitrant children as if they were their own. And that in this way the children can forget all the dreadful things that lie behind them, and the past doesn't have any power over them anymore." Oh dear God, how I did beat about the bush!

You stopped me. "But who can know that?" you said. "They're not going to talk about it."

I was already beginning to lose the ground under my feet. "Well, anyway," I said, "They all grow up to be decent people. Experience has taught us that. They learn something useful …"

"Yes. And they don't become a public burden. So the money's well spent."

"Gottfried!" I cried. "What's the matter with you? I wasn't thinking of the money at all but of ... but of the splendid proof ..."

You looked at me silently, "Proof of what?"

I pulled myself together. "Proof that it doesn't make any difference what a person's origins are as long as he grows up in an atmosphere of love and trust."

"Sure," you said, and looked as if you were thinking of the ski trips that lay ahead. But then you quoted calmly, "*Pater semper incertus.*" I was dumbfounded. You went on calmly, "That's why I can't understand why people have anything against artificial insemination, since it doesn't make any difference who the father is."

"But I didn't say that!" I cried. Why? I had you just where I wanted you and tried to drag you away from it. "I don't think we have the right to decide over life and death, not at all." I said helplessly.

Just then the bus came and we got in. A young girl offered me her seat. I already had some gray hairs. You remained standing in front of me, then you learned forward, smiling, and said softly, "It's a good thing for me that you think the way you do."

"What do you mean?" I asked, but you had already gone a few steps farther into the bus.

Today, during a long day filled with work, I have calmed down a little, and what I have written doesn't seem as senseless as it did in the night. My healthy common sense, that faithful servant who looks after me so well, although I despise him, has convinced me that you can't possibly know what no one knows except Uri. I have no idea what you were thinking of when you spoke those words as the bus rattled on. Probably you had simply grasped the fact that it couldn't have been pleasant to be expecting the child of a dead man during a time of starvation.

But back to the past, the pre-past! We have arrived at the interrogation by the Gestapo, the secret police. It was the most feared institution in the Third Reich. At the time I thought naturally that only those who had something to hide were afraid. It didn't seem as important to me as it did to my father whether the measures taken by the authorities always corresponded exactly to the law. We had been taught: whatever serves the nation is right, and the people, especially in wartime, had to render the traitors harmless *before* they could act. A confirmed suspicion justified taking them into custody, just as those threatened by an infectious disease, and not only the sick, have to be quarantined. It was probably true that the suspects weren't exactly treated with kid gloves, but in what other way could they be forced to confess their sinister designs? And he who had a clear conscience ...

Oh Gottfried! He who is accused and stands face to face with power never has a clear conscience! I soon found that out ...

We had been back in Vienna for some weeks. We were in school again and Walter had had his friends at the house on one or two evenings. Although I was free now, he didn't invite me to join them, and I was quite happy about it because I saw Christianity as something of historic interest only, a grandiose effort that in the end had failed. I respected Clemens Schindler because he was fighting for a lost cause, perhaps quite consciously, but it was regrettable that a mind as good as his should be satisfied with shadow-boxing. Well, there was no way I could convert him to the present; I had enough perception to know that. And for Walter it was probably a good thing to come to grips with intellectual problems, I thought arrogantly. Or perhaps there was something quite different about this group of young men, a homoerotic interest of which not all of them were necessarily aware? I couldn't see through it and didn't really care. Let everyone mind his own business. I had a very high opinion of my own tolerance.

Until, at the end of September 1940, when they rang our doorbell loud and long at six in the morning. I was startled out of my sleep. In a dream I had just been talking to my grandmother. "You don't understand!" I had cried, and her reply, "But there they are!" still rang in my ears. I was afraid. Could she be right in the end?

Right about what? I jumped out of bed and ran barefoot to the telephone. I was sure that Grandmother was calling us from the country. It wasn't until I was holding the receiver in my hand that I realized it was the doorbell ringing. Walter stuck his head out of his door and said softly, "Put on your coat first."

My coat was hanging beside me, still damp from last evening's rain. I slipped it on and went to open the door. I didn't look through the peephole first. Only someone in terrible trouble would ring like that. Perhaps something had happened to our neighbor! The old man had been ailing for a long time.

"Well, at last!" said the SA man who was standing between two others in the doorway. With a quick motion of his arm he pushed me aside and walked in. My fear subsided like a breathless dog. "We were still asleep," I said calmly. "Do you want to see us?"

Four doors opened out from the foyer. The men walked through three of them. The only one they didn't open was the door that led to the kitchen. Indistinctly I could hear my father protesting. "Shut up!" he was told. "Stay where you are!" "But the keys ..." I heard Mother say in a strange, lackluster voice. Not a sound from Walter's room. Was the third man starting his search in the dining room or in my small room which lay behind it?

I was trembling and had to pull myself together and try to think straight, or I would simply have run away. But that would have been a clear proof of guilt. What guilt? I had no idea. Since that moment of panic I know how hopeless it must seem to someone under suspicion to prove his innocence. That is when people seek refuge in the stupidest lies because the truth is rarely plausible.

Nothing can happen to me, I thought, trying to compose myself, which was just as futile as the auto-suggestion at the dentist when the drill touches a nerve: *it doesn't hurt.* The youngest of the three stuck his head out of the dining room door and waved to me to come in. He didn't look unfriendly. "You'll catch cold, Fräulein," he said as he walked on ahead of me. He spoke a Viennese dialect. "Put on your slippers. Since when have you been with the BdM?"

"Since April 1938," I said, and noticed that my voice was just as cold and lackluster as my mother's. My brown jacket with the leader insignia hung over a chair.

"Well then," he mumbled, evidently satisfied, turned his back on me and began to rummage through the drawer of my table. "Is that Greek?" he asked, sarcastically. "Yes." "And what are you learning it for?" "I'm going to study medicine," I answered promptly. "Is that so?" he said with respect, but not so friendly any more.

He took a fat notebook with him: my diary (but I had written only a few pages in it.) Then he went through my bureau. Grinning, he held a pair of my thin summer panties up to the light from the window and gave me a look. I was furious. Then his comrade next door called out to him, "You through, Freddy? We're taking the men along. Get dressed! Keep moving!"

"So now you can sleep off your fright," the young man said to me.

"I'm not frightened," I lied.

"No?" He grinned again. "That'll come. You'll see." And he left, closing the door behind him.

For a moment or two everybody outside seemed to be speaking at once, then the front door closed and it was deathly still. I crawled into bed and curled up to get warm. Now surely Mother would come ... But she didn't come. Had they taken her with them too?

I got up and went to her bedroom to see. I opened the door softly, "Mammi ..."

She didn't hear me. She was kneeling beside her bed, her head on her folded arms. Was she crying? Her shoulders weren't moving. Could she possibly be praying? I wanted to tiptoe away, but she heard me. She got up, looked at me with dry, inflamed eyes and said "We've been ordered to go too. At eleven."

"Where to?"

"To Morzinplatz. For interrogation."

"I have a physics exam," I said.

She didn't hear me. "Tell the truth, Helga. Whatever they ask you, tell the truth. Do you hear me? Otherwise they'll find out."

"Find out what?" I stammered. "I don't know anything."

"That's just it," Mother said drily.

She sat down at her dressing table and began to comb her hair.

"It's a dirty trick to come at six in the morning when one isn't even up yet."

"Come, Helga. Get dressed. I'd like to tidy things before we leave." She looked around. Pieces of underwear lay on the floor, all the drawers were open. "Vandals!" she said scornfully.

I didn't understand my mother, I never did understand her, but some of her coolness rubbed off on me.

Before we left we drank a glass of milk, sitting at the kitchen table. "Today I don't have to cook," said Mother, "Everything has its good side." She could joke again. Or was she trying to calm me? "One is only frightened like this the first time," she went on. "How could people stand it otherwise? I'm sure Dr. Niehensky has grown used to it. They've been to see him five times."

"Why?"

"Nobody knows. He went to school with the chancellor. They were friends when they were young. That's all they need."

The chancellor. For my parents Dr. Schuschnigg was still chancellor. "Well, if his conscience is clear," I said dully.

"My dear child," said my mother, rinsing our mugs carefully under the faucet, "whoever has a clear conscience today must have a devilishly bad conscience, if he had one at all."

That was Mother. I laughed, and thought secretly, isn't she worrying at all about her husband and son? I didn't ask how she meant it. Did I know anyway, or didn't I want to know? I told her what I had dreamt about my grandmother. "Perhaps, in an emergency, we could go to her," she said, And again I didn't ask when such an emergency might arise.

I don't remember how we got to Morzinplatz, only my feeling of finality when the wrought-iron gate closed behind us: we'll never get out of here. And when they separated us: I'll never see her again. But then I had to wait for a long time and at last I began to wonder what they were going to ask me.

I knew my father. He couldn't possibly be involved in any kind of conspiracy, he was "subordinate to the authorities," any authority, as a matter of principle, if only because he considered it his Christian duty, perhaps the most dignified Christian duty. That he was disappointed, sometimes even indignant over some things that took place, that he occasionally spoke about the "hubris" of the new masters ... should I deny this if they asked me directly? Mother had warned me; stick to the truth. Her answer: "That's just it" to my: "But I don't know anything" had quite clearly betrayed the fact that there was something going on about which I knew nothing. Was hubris a bad word? Defamation of the Führer was punished as treason. How could I make it sound less harsh? Megalomania? Bravado? They all sounded worse.

Gottfried, please, imagine my situation! For hours a young girl sits in front of a closed door. Civilians and men in uniform come and go, everybody is in a hurry, hardly anybody looks at her, nobody smiles. The girl knows that the fate of her parents depends on her statement. She therefore has to find answers that are correct yet have several meanings, leaving a way out.

I looked at my watch. Physics class. My professor wanted to give me a chance to save my "excellent." He had urged me: "Today every educated person should know how a radio functions." I was therefore to familiarize myself with the subject before the next lesson. And that's what I'd done.

Involuntarily I began to memorize, and suddenly it dawned on me what they were going to ask me. Sometimes a stopped up ear will open with a click and you can hear again, just as I realized suddenly what they could accuse Father of. He must have listened to the London station that broadcasts the enemy news in German! Then he may have betrayed himself by a careless remark, and somebody had denounced him. How like him! But thank God I knew nothing about it and could swear to that. Never had a broadcast been interrupted when I had entered the room unexpectedly. Never, when I had wanted to listen, had the radio been tuned to a foreign station. How lucky that my father was such a pedantic man!

At this point I imagine you would like to ask me — and I ask myself — would I have admitted it if I had caught my parents listening to a foreign station? I think: yes. I say I *think*, because a hellishly wide abyss lies between intention and action. I wanted to save my parents but not at the price of my own loyalty to the movement to which I belonged, to the idea that I was convinced was right. A conviction for which one isn't willing to sacrifice everything doesn't deserve the name. What does testimony consist of but sacrifice? One can never choose what to admit and what to deny. But to inform the Gestapo of things I could only surmise ... nobody, not even I, could demand that of me. Was I so happy that I knew nothing because it permitted me to protect my parents, or was it primarily a case of my own position, my reputation — and my "honor"?

As we were leaving the apartment Mother cast a glance at my coat and hesitated before locking the door. "Don't you think you should wear your uniform?" she asked. "I should say not!" I cried angrily. She locked the door without another word. She understood me. I was afraid one of my girls or colleagues might see me ... doing what? It might suffice that I was simply entering the notorious building. But I could think of more horrible things. Hadn't they forced people to wash the streets in broad daylight? Would I have it in me to run away, would I want to, if they humiliated my father in public in this or any other similar way? But they had done things like that only to Jews ...

At last it was my turn. I was allowed to enter, sit down, give my name and address (as if they didn't know them already). Then I was handed a piece of paper across the desk with the words, "Do you know this hand-writing?"

I stared at the paper incredulously and stammered, "But of course! Horst wrote that!" The feeling of being saved warmed me like a taste of wine.

"What Horst?"

"Horst Ulbig, my fiancé." Eagerly I gave his name, rank, *Waffen SS*.

"But this message isn't addressed to you but to ..." The man interviewing me pretended that he was only now trying to make it out.

"To Walter." I helped him. "That's my brother." And suddenly I knew word for word what was written on the paper.

"Did your fiancé correspond with your brother?"

"Of course not. That's just a greeting he enclosed in a letter to me."

"Weren't they friends?"

"No. Albert, my older brother, was a friend of Horst's"

"Do you happen to remember what he wrote on this piece of paper?"

"Yes, Exactly. Horst apologized for not coming to a ... a Bible group meeting to which Walter had invited him. He had suddenly been transferred."

"And you ... did you take part in these Bible group meetings?"

The indifference of his tone alerted me. "No," I said curtly.

"Why not?"

"I always had a first-aid class on Wednesday."

"But they asked you to join them?"

"Yes, of course."

"Once or more often?"

"I can't remember exactly."

"Couldn't they have moved these meetings to another evening, or did it suit your brother that you didn't join them?"

I considered the question for a moment, then answered calmly, "Could be. I wouldn't have been interested anyway."

"But your brother is interested in ... religious matters?"

"Evidently." I began to find the questioning foolish. My fear was gone.

"Did he go to mass regularly?"

"I don't know. I was always on the go." Then I remembered something. "But in the summer we went to the village church because the schoolteacher played the organ so beautifully."

"So you declare that on those Wednesday evenings religious questions were actually discussed?"

"How should I know? Probably. Certainly when Clemens Schindler was there. He is ..."

"I know," he interrupted me. But in the meantime I had thought of something else and I was smiling as I said, "Anyway, two weeks ago they listened to the big football match. Clemens was ..."

"I know exactly everything he was." My interviewer looked stern "Thank you, Fräulein. You may go. Your Frau Mama will be waiting longingly for you." Now he was trying to tell me that I was still a child. That was probably his revenge. I felt I had passed my test well, my "Heil Hitler" sounded vigorous, but in the dark corridor I was overcome by fear again. Why hadn't they even mentioned my father?

Mother was standing besides the entrance. Her face was red. "Come," was all she said. "Father's gone on ahead."

"Really?" I cried, relieved.

"Yes, But Walter ... they kept him." Her voice was high-pitched and brittle.

"He'll join us soon," I said, to calm her. "What could they possibly want from *him*?"

While we were waiting for the streetcar I was overwhelmed with the joy of freedom. I looked at my surroundings — no, I took them in as if I had just escaped weeks of incarceration. The sun was shining, a warm, golden, autumnal sun. I would have liked to lie down flat on the pavement and let it warm me through and through. That I felt so cold was probably the result of my coat, which was still damp.

Never before had it occurred to me to find this view of the city beautiful. Now the irregular plaza with its coffee house tables, most of them empty, the broad quay busy with traffic, the bridge, the shallow gray-green water of the Danube canal, and above all the Leopoldsberg, its nose standing out against the clear sky, delighted me. But the best thing of all were the many, many people going about their harmless business in an evident hurry, brushing against me without noticing it because I was standing awkwardly in their way ... I had often heard my parents talk about the joy of being alone, about the beauty of untouched nature. I too liked to go for walks alone in the Tirol. I had adopted their preferences without testing them. Then, suddenly I had discovered the charm of being part of a community, the security of the group. But then I had become a leader all too soon and again was separate.

In those moments on the quay it came clear to me that I liked to live in the big city, unnoticed, one of many, none of them alike but different from many different ones. I thought that in a big city one was most easily oneself. Nobody could pin you down, you didn't have to exert yourself to break loose, you didn't attract attention ... "Helga! The streetcar!" Even the shabby streetcar, its windows smeared blue, looked beautiful to me.

My parents didn't ask me about the interrogation until we got home. They too seemed relieved. Walter had probably aroused suspicion only because of his contact with Schindler, one of the "black ones," a cleric. All the misunderstandings would soon be cleared up. But the way my parents looked belied their optimistic words. I began to wonder if Schindler had actually been trying to influence the boys against the regime. That was perhaps why Walter, who was vacillating, wanted Horst to join them.

Walter came home that same week. He looked thinner, was pale and taciturn. Brusquely he informed us that he had volunteered and asked Father for the necessary signature. Father gave it to him at once. There was no talk anymore of his taking his exams first. All of a sudden my parents didn't seem to think them important, and when Walter turned up for the first time in uniform, I could see that he wasn't a boy any longer but a victorious radiant young warrior, the like of which one didn't often see anymore.

Whenever he visited us during his training period, he devoured all the good things Mother prepared for him, praised bath and bed, but assured us that he certainly liked being in the service a thousand times more than in school. Albert, on the other hand, wrote melancholy letters: how bleak it was to be exposed to the boredom of the northern winter, crowded together with hordes of men. We were to send him books, but again only stuff that could be thrown away, preferably detective stories. Mother shook her head sadly. She had two copies of Stifter's *Nachsommer* ... "Don't bother, Mammi," Said Walter. "He'll never get around to reading it. I've just finished this whodunit. Pack it in with the rest."

"Since when do you underline things in detective stories?" I asked, surprised, as I leafed through the book.

"Anything wrong with that?" he said, his tone sharp, and explained that it helped him to get on the track of the murderer.

After finishing his training, Walter was sent to the western front right away. That Christmas I was alone with my parents. A package came from Walter with all sorts of precious things: perfume, silk stockings. "You can see that war is the father of all things, as Heraclitus already told us," he wrote sarcastically. "How can you doubt it anymore?"

"He'll be the death of us!" Father cried angrily.

"No he won't!" Mother tried to calm him. "The soldiers at the front can risk a thing or two." I thought scornfully: at the front? In France?

Albert's letters were despondent. Perhaps he would find it easier to grasp the true meaning of Christmas up there, far from all the traditional sentimentality and homeyness that was often so successfully buried under the hubbub of gift-giving and the smell of roast goose.

What would he say today, Gottfried, if he had lived to see people in the stores making a down payment on refrigerators and washing machines to the strains of "Silent Night," and children being tempted not only with the latest model electric train, but also with tin soldiers, toy tanks and rockets, to the sound of "O Christmas Tree" ...?

My life went on in its humdrum way. In the morning I was a
schoolgirl like all the others. When on duty I made a special effort to
make up for what I saw more and more clearly as an invisible flaw: that I
did not come from a family of old party fighters, although some fathers
seemed to have come by this honor in strange ways. Like the father of
one of my school mates, who during the "infamous" days of the old regime, 1934–38, was a history professor and a civil servant, yet at the same
time a member of the forbidden National Socialist party; or, in another
case, the owner of a grocery shop in a major business street, who had
kept a precise account of the life style of his rich Jewish customers and
had handed their names over to the Party, together with a request to become a member, immediately after the seizure of power, when they
didn't interest him anymore commercially. His daughter told me about it
after swearing me to secrecy, because she was so thrilled that as a reward
he had been given a very low membership number. When I confessed to
her, also confidentially, that my father wasn't a party member, wasn't
even on a waiting list, she consoled me with the fact that my fiancé was a
member of the SS and I was a BdM leader, and after all, I hadn't chosen
my parents. Since she knew I was engaged, she respected me. But she
wasn't very smart, not Marietta with her brown curly hair, who probably
had the pre-German era of her progenitor to thank for her pretty un-
German name. Didn't she realize what a mortal sin against our racial
creed she had committed with her remark? I didn't draw her attention to
it. I had learned to keep silent when it came to things one wasn't allowed
to say: the morning on Morzinplatz had taught me that.

Given such scruples, how did I come to terms with myself? Well,
Gottfried, we had a convenient master key to the small cell that housed
our clear conscience, the password used by us idealists, young and old,
when infamy simply couldn't be overlooked: the Führer doesn't know
about it. But a thought became increasingly persistent, gnawing at my
conscience — wouldn't it have been the duty of every one of us to inform
him of it?

Nothing remains undone as easily as that which is every man's duty.
Why does it have to be me? you ask yourself. Now I know that the answer is: Because it's up to you, perhaps to you and to everyone. Perhaps
just to you alone. You can't really be sure, and anyway it doesn't matter.
There isn't a system on earth that functions flawlessly. Human vileness
can seize upon every means, including those invented to eliminate it.
Church history gives us classic examples of that. If, as we believe today,
democracy comes closest to the old human ideal of a just state, couldn't it
have been possible to destroy the earlier democracies from the outside
only?

Today, with Christmas over once more — what a relief! — what am I
doing wrong?

It was my intention to go on with the plot — is there such a thing in an account of one's life? From my viewpoint, very little was plotted, nearly everything was endured — when I received a disconcerting letter from my brother Walter. For three long years, ever since he married an American girl, I had heard nothing from him except New Year's wishes on hideous colored cards. I suppose the letter I wrote at the time, congratulating them, was pretty conventional, and why not? I hadn't seen Walter for ten years when he informed me that he had married a girl "from an old family." I wondered what was meant over there by that. A girl from a family with several generations in the States behind her? Or perhaps only a family who had been wealthy a long time? Her name was Marjorie, she couldn't speak a word of German, and was "of course very pretty." And then, yesterday, out of the blue, a handwritten letter, pages of it. Was Walter suddenly confiding in me, I wondered, curbing my emotions with irony: why?

Because he was sad, very sad. He evidently felt this was the right moment to get in touch with us again. Perhaps all these years he had had the feeling that he should be comforting me, but those who are happy don't know quite how to go about it. He couldn't know that I was already consoled.

I have known for a long time now that it is impossible to recapitulate one's life briefly, unless in a curriculum vitae for a job application. When I began writing this I thought it would take me two or three weeks. Now months have gone by in spite of the fact that I have written almost daily. The thing is that one doesn't have only one past but several, all of them interwoven. The most confusing thing, however, is the discovery that one simply can't differentiate between past and present! I feel like a traveler who has crossed the equator without having noticed anything special, and is disappointed. As I write, the past that is to be included grows to the same extent as it diminishes at the other end through having been included. And I may find myself in the position of an awkward seamstress who keeps threading a ribbon through a hem until she has drawn it out again at the other end.

At first I wanted to insert Walter's letter, but that won't do. It is addressed only to me, and you — although a part of me — are a stranger as far as Walter is concerned. He mentions that too, regrets it, and would like to know what sort of a boy you've turned out to be. "Perhaps you are having difficulties with him," he writes.

At sixteen everybody is insufferable! Anyway, I thought I was terribly smart when I was sixteen and was even proud of my ignorance! To some extent Marjorie broke me of that. But whatever he's like, Helga, I envy you Gottfried, and Marjorie, who knows all about you, says to tell you that she envies you too. We are his only close relatives, and our old grandmother can't have much longer to live, if she is still alive.

I skimmed through the letter with an uneasy feeling, What was he after?

During the last months, while Marjorie was expecting our child, I kept having to talk about home and all of you. And suddenly everything came to life again. For oneself one may be able to burn the bridges to one's past — the arrival of a child brings it all back. I am sure you sense that these are not my words but reflect Marjorie's sentiments. She wanted to name the child Helga, if it was a girl. But it was a boy, and he only lived for five terrible days.

If he had been a frail baby, Helga, or premature, but he was a beautiful child! According to the doctors, he couldn't live because our blood types weren't compatible. Did you ever hear of anything so dreadful? It sounds like an invention of dear departed Adolf! (Of course this is nothing new, we just didn't know about it. How can it be possible for two people to be as close as we are, and their child can't live? But children by Negroes and whites, or by old men and teenagers, children of alcoholics and whores live and grow old?)

At first I didn't have time to think of the child, there was nothing on my mind but Marjorie. A thing like this shouldn't happen to a woman, least of all an American! She never smoked since she knew she was pregnant, she didn't drink a drop of alcohol, nothing but vitamins, the right exercises, and books on the care and upbringing of children. I laughed at her. She laughed too, but it didn't stop her. She simply couldn't put her mind on anything else. Did I write and tell you that she is a little older than I? She imagined right from the start that it was too late for her to have a child.

I was so astonished, I stopped reading. "From an old family ... and of course very pretty ... " Well, today a woman in her late thirties can still be very attractive, but I had visualized someone young. There were more surprises to come ...

Walter wrote that his wife had infantile paralysis when she was young and it left her with a stiff leg. So she was alone a lot, with a tendency to be moody. But then, "oddly enough," she had fallen in love with him in spite of it and had had the idée fixe that she would have to pay for a happiness she didn't really have coming to her.

I guess she meant that I wouldn't be faithful to her, and I often teased her about it, but now, after this hideous thing, I can't laugh any more. I even gave in to my mother-in-law's urging and dragged Marjorie to a psychotherapist, in spite of my European antipathy toward the fellows. He knew his business — Marjorie is all right again. She goes to her club meetings and can talk about it. In other words, she can mix socially with people again. All this happened six months ago.

She will never really get over it because we can't have any more children, although it would be possible if the doctors were prepared for it and replaced the blood of the newborn baby from a reserve blood bank. You can do things like that today. Did you know? But that's not for me!

That I can understand! I sighed. I felt sorry for the poor woman. But at the end Walter wrote something very strange:

Sometimes it seems to me as if I were forced to think Albert's thoughts through to the end, perhaps as a punishment, because he so often made me angry with the way he would weigh things back and forth, which finally cost him his life, and poor Clemens with him. Think of the two of us sometimes. We keep trying to imagine how you manage with an unsuspecting child and a probably senile old woman. You must be very lonely. Now we are too.

Although I was deeply moved, perhaps just because of it, I couldn't write more than ten lines of condolence. I sent them a picture of you and wrote, "This is Gottfried. He is all I have. Soon he will be a grown man and leave me, which is his good right." Then I wrote that Uri was by no means senile as they seemed to believe, but I admitted that what she had to say was sometimes cryptic and in its significance somehow distressing, like an odor that reminds one of something past which one can't put one's finger on. But then I crossed the words out again. Walter never really knew Uri, nobody knew her but me, and you, Gottfried. I hope you know her too, and that years from now it will suddenly come clear to you, what she is ...

"You never have time for me!" That hurt me deeply. You wanted me to play chess with you, but I had my accounts to do, and then I wanted to spend the evening writing. That was when you grumbled, "You never have time for me, and you don't let me go into town either!"

"Of course not! Do you expect me to let you ride your bicycle home on glare ice, on a country road with not a soul around? And the train doesn't leave until around midnight."

"I could stay with my friend until then."

"Where does your friend live?"

"Right near the station."

Subconsciously I had expected you to say, "At the pharmacy," and was relieved, and asked, "What's his name, anyway?"

"Biermeier. You don't know him."

"What does his father do?"

"No idea. Why?"

"Bring him to the house first."

That was when you walked out and slammed the door.

Just a short time ago your principal warned us at a parents' meeting, "Don't be too easy on your children! See to it that they're home by nine and keep an eye on whom they're associating with. You not only have the right to discipline them, it is your duty. And we here at school can only partly relieve you of it."

Sharp words, golden words. All of us looked a little ashamed. Nobody dared to say, "That's all well and good, but how do you go about it nowadays"

I walked after you into your room, ignored your sulky expression and told you briefly about Uncle Walter's letter. You have questioned me so often about your uncle in America, and you actually did forget your resentment and asked me a hundred questions, none of which I could answer: What did he really do as an advertising man? Did he travel a lot? Did he draw? Did he make up slogans? What sort of a car did I think he had, and did he have a big house with a swimming pool?

"I'm sure he doesn't!" I cried. "They don't live in a Hollywood villa."

"How do you know?"

"But isn't it sad that their child died and they can't have any more children?"

"They could adopt one," you said thoughtfully.

"Yes. But it wouldn't be the same."

You shrugged and said knowingly. "According to the laws of heredity, children mostly take after their grandparents. That's why they often don't get along so well with their parents."

"Don't we get along?" I asked, laughing to hide how hurt I was.

"Sometimes ... sure," you granted. "But why do you still want to keep me locked up like a baby?"

The fruitless debate went on and on, and in the end you recited your Latin vocabulary and I threw the notebook at your head. And now I am sitting through half the night again, trying to tell the same boy, to whom I usually can't address a sensible word, *everything*, everything I know and what nobody else knows, which I have to experience and endure all over again for his sake alone ...

Horst wrote regularly, entirely meaningless letters. Once he mentioned that "by chance" he had gone to an organ concert. Now at last he knew how right he had been, as a soldier, to steer clear of music. He wouldn't indulge in a setback like that again. I replied that I could understand him, but it was an exaggeration. I felt sorry for him, but he did seem to be a little too sorry for himself, and it made me impatient. Didn't he have anything positive to say?

Walter was quite different. In a cheerful letter he informed us that he had received the Iron Cross First Class. "We broke up a partisans' hideout. I'm telling you ... quite a nice little arsenal of weapons they'd collected for themselves! My hat off to them! Unfortunately the fellows slipped through our fingers ..." A short while later he mentioned casually that he hoped he would soon get leave as the result of a possible "change of address."

My parents sighed. "At last!" Neither son had been home for a long time. But then, suddenly, there was no more news at all, and Mother paled every time the doorbell rang. She thought surely she would find Walter standing outside. But she never did.

Finally, weeks later, a postcard arrived. After several incidents Walter had ended up in the most beautiful country in the world and with a pleasant job. In a postcard he wrote, "This sky is always blue!" Mother said, "Oh God!" and Father looked her straight in the eye and took her hand in his. What's the matter with them? I wondered. This was definitely good news. A few days later we were informed that Walter had not returned from a "requisition" raid. It was hoped that he had found his way to another unit while fleeing from the partisans.

Had my mother felt it coming? Now they clung to a different ray of hope. Even after the official notification that Walter was missing, they answered, when asked, "We hope he has been taken prisoner."

Oh, growing up wouldn't be nearly so difficult if besides the exciting surprises one experiences with oneself, one didn't also have to cope with insight into the nature of one's parents. It so rarely tallies with one's childish, idealized image. Admiration is just as necessary for the growth of the spirit as ultraviolet rays are for the development of one's bones. Where there is no possibility for admiration, the soul becomes deformed and perverted. In this respect my brothers and I were lucky. We could admire Mother's gentleness and wit and Father's integrity without reservation. But at the time I missed in both my parents that which the hungry spirit demands most: the essential element of veracity.

I don't think I have recovered yet from this lack, just as it doesn't help the grown up hunchback any more to feed him oranges and lemons: the time for healing is irrevocably past.

Life at home was exceptionally quiet. My parents had never led a very social life. Now only one room was heated and our sparse rations didn't suffice for entertaining guests. I didn't even know that you could buy things on the black market. For my father it didn't come into question. Uri sent us food packages which we usually passed on, unless there was room in the small army packages.

Once — I want to confess this now so that I don't seem so incomprehensibly serious to you, Gottfried — I was alone at home when an unexpected package came from Uri. Just before it arrived, I had found it difficult to concentrate on my homework. I had been watching the raindrops running down the cloudy pane of the room that faced the courtyard; I was feeling unfulfilled and miserable. If only something decisive would happen at last! If only Horst could get leave! If only I could win first prize in the next debating contest! But I knew I didn't have a chance. Only the unattainable seemed truly desirable ... And then the bell rang, shrill and long. Horst! I thought, completely unreasonably. it had to be Horst! I ran to the door. It was the mailman. With a package. I took it, signed for it, then I began to unpack it and found, besides the usual things — bacon, poppy seed and flour — an earthenware pot of honey, lovingly packed in wood shavings. I opened it, and uncontrollable greed made me taste it. I tasted it until the little pot was half-empty. Then I carried it to my room and hid it in my closet between my sweaters and caps. After that I went into the kitchen, threw the wood shavings into the stove and burnt them. I packed the carton again and tied the string around it carefully. I was ashamed of my uncontrollable desire for something sweet which now I couldn't understand at all. I simply couldn't confess what I had done; my parents would never take me seriously again.

Every child has probably done something similar; the only thing I can't understand is why I should have done something as childish as that at my age. And I wasn't spared having to make the theft worse by a lie, because on the following day there was a letter from Uri in which she wrote, "The honey is for Helga."

"What honey?" I cried, a shade too fast.

Mother smiled. "She forgot to put it in."

"She's getting old," said Father. "That wouldn't have happened to her years ago."

"Oh ... but that can happen to anybody!" I said.

"To you, yes," teased Father, "but not to a woman who runs a farm and counts every apple."

"Poor Helga! But I guess we can't tell her about it; she'd be mortified."

"Of course not," I said hastily. "It doesn't matter anyway."

Why am I telling this silly story? Because I can see it so clearly, much more clearly than almost any of the important events, because since then I know that every person is capable of doing something, sometimes, that is a complete surprise to him. Even if it is trifling. If it upsets the conception one has of oneself at the time, one keeps it secret, fearfully, and would rather confess a crime and take all the consequences than admit laughingly: yes, don't be angry. I don't know how it happened, but I did it. Did it? Wrong. It *happened* to me, and that's the shameful part of it.

No. I couldn't confess it, but I reflected on this new aspect of my character, and in the evening, when I had locked my door to get undressed. I dipped into the little pot again. Three or four times this secret gratification delighted me. Its triviality was what made the sin so sweet.

I just tore up twenty pages. I had dutifully written down everything I could think of from that time on, arranged it as chronologically as possible, "according to the best of my knowledge," as the phrase goes. It was horrible work, like washing turnips in the months after the war, with hands frozen blue and feet you could get warm only in hot water, after which they hurt for hours. My artificially thawed-out heart had hurt too, yet when I read my work, it tasted like strudel dough that had lain around too long — cardboardy — and I asked myself: why on earth am I doing this? Why do I torture myself with establishing in what month we invaded Russia and when America declared war, or try to remember if

Horst was transferred to Africa before or after Albert was wounded? None of it really matters. Yes. But I want everything to be correct. Otherwise you might think nothing is correct. I'm afraid it's the wrong thing to want. Our memory is not a film that can recapture the past. Just this, however, had been my intention — to achieve an "authentic account," a completely factual one. After which you were supposed to pass judgment and, if you felt you had to, judge me. I didn't want to anticipate anything.

As if every account were not an effort to influence! Poor Gottfried! And yet our words are the only bridge from I to you, except ...

Today's courtroom column in the paper helped to open my eyes. A former concentration-camp guard, who for years had been living under a false name, generally respected, and with a modest business of his own, was recognized by one of his prisoners, identified by the police, and put on trial for murder, many murders. Yesterday he was declared not guilty. A witness had given false testimony: he remembered having seen the accused trample his son to death in the year 1940. The defendant denied it, and his lawyer was able to prove that his client had not been on duty in that particular camp until the following year. With proof of the error of one witness, the jury seemed to find the testimony of the others worthless. How, I asked myself, is such an error possible? Doesn't the old man know in what year his son died? Quite possibly the years were all hideously alike. Or was the defendant really not the murderer? Did all torturers look alike in some horrible fashion?

*Les jours passent, les instants restent!* is written on the cover of the calendar that hangs in Uri's room. The days pass, the moments remain. I have to give up the idea of a precise chronicle. There was the hour of the roses in which my youth began. I thought it was the overture but it was also the finale.

I wonder if it is only my peculiarity to accept things as they are as permanent? Don't I have sufficient foresight, or does this happen to most of us? I was unable to imagine anything under the heading of "after the war," not even as our defeat began to take shape. What could possibly follow? According to our propaganda, Bolshevik dictatorship, a faceless phantom, absolute horror, no more specific than New Jerusalem.

I have already mentioned that I couldn't imagine my marriage with Horst and longed for it therefore only vaguely, interpolating my presentiment that it would never be realized. Am I right? When you were little, Gottfried, a chubby-chested, blond, trumpeting angel, affectionate and devoted, I simply couldn't imagine what you would be like as a rowdy teenager. Thank God you grew up to be one anyway! How the future develops out of the bud of the past is as conclusive as if it couldn't have been different, yet all analytical conclusions of future events or developments fail. I have heard so many wise people forecast — my father, for instance. All of them were wrong. The true prophets probably really see what lies ahead of us, not the reflected past. I have never met one.

Albert sometimes asked if we knew anything about Clemens
Schindler. He hadn't heard from him in such a long time. What could we
know? None of the young people came to the house any more since
Walter had gone. But some time later — was it weeks? Months? — the
young priest was standing in our living room when I came home for
lunch. It startled me because I thought: He's bringing news of Walter, bad
news. But that wasn't the case. He only asked us to give Albert his new
address. (Why didn't he write to Albert himself? I wondered, but didn't
feel like asking.)

Clemens had always looked like an ascetic — tall, lean, hollow-eyed
— but now his bright assurance was gone. He seemed very depressed.
He's not having an easy time either, I thought, but my sympathy cooled
when he asked me, on leaving, if I was still with the BdM. "Why
shouldn't I be?" I replied, my tone sharp.

"I just thought perhaps you weren't enjoying it anymore," he said,
with a sad smile.

"My daughter is enjoying it very much!" said my father. He sounded
irritated.

Schindler didn't accept our invitation to stay for lunch. When he was
gone we were silent. My parents didn't seem to have welcomed his visit; I
didn't understand why. But I didn't ask. I never asked.

Horst had put in for a transfer to the African theater of operations.
Now he wrote that the transfer was imminent, and I shouldn't write for a
while. I could appreciate his satisfaction. What was there for him to do in
France, which had been conquered long ago?He had written once that
there were very important duties to perform there too. But he wasn't
suited to being an agent, nor did he have a gift for organization. I understood only vaguely what he meant, but in any case felt that nothing worse
could happen to a young man who had decided against his nature to be a
hero — "because the times need fighters more than musicians " — than to
be moved into a world of unreal peace, while others, even if their instru-
ments were not in tune, were still fiddling away in a cultural orchestra.
The mere fact that such entertainment was held solely for the purpose of
lifting the soldiers' morale would seem to Horst like suggesting to a
young nurse, during a lack of wounded, that for patriotic reasons she
should volunteer for service in a brothel. So I was happy that Horst was
finally being sent to where decisive events were in the offing. "I only
hope he can stand the climate," said Mother.

I must understand, he wrote at the end, that he hadn't asked for home
leave, which he would probably have had coming to him before being
moved to the front, but he didn't know what he would be recuperating
from! Unfortunately he would have to while away a week or two in
Naples anyway, for acclimatization and to make the necessary
adjustment.

This last sentence was a blow, its power palpable only after the numbness of shock was over. So Horst didn't want to see me! If he felt he didn't need to recuperate, all the better — the detour of a few days' leave in Vienna would have been more exerting than a rest. Was he afraid of our meeting? Certainly! So was I! All the more reason to talk to each other at last.

"If he can't come here," I declared, "I shall go to Naples."

"Impossible!"

It was my protesting parents who made me fully conscious of my resolve, "Why not?" I asked calmly. Travel to Italy was no problem. Plenty of people were still vacationing on the Adriatic ... That was something quite different, and anyway, a schoolgirl didn't travel alone in Italy, and on top of everything without speaking the language. Besides, I couldn't miss school, and I had no idea when Horst would be in Naples. Naples was a big city. I would never find him. That was what they had to say, no longer in unison but assisting each other with fresh arguments. It was their scruples that first made the trip seem a possibility. Were these the only difficulties I had to overcome? I could certainly afford to miss a week of school. And would one need Italian to find out from our military authorities there where Horst was? And didn't my BdM uniform protect me from any untoward advances?

"I will not permit it!" cried my father, and left the room. That was a command; I had hardly ever received one from him. Relieved, I fell into the role of the hurt child who has been treated unfairly. I wept. Then the door flew open, he came back and said to my mother, "Then you go with her."

He stroked my hair gently. I cried harder. So I wasn't permitted to be a child anymore. What I wanted would take place. I had to do it. I was afraid.

I remember only dimly our going to various bureaus, the overcrowded trains, smiling and friendly officers who gave me unofficial information, a repulsive, teeming, dirty and loud city, and my first experience with bedbugs. I felt sorry for my mother. She was so miserable and so tired. Rain showers gave way to oppressive heat. The clothes we had with us were too warm. The men were impertinent, more to her than to me. She seemed so defenseless. I begged her to wait for me in a cool cafeteria while I ran from one office to another, but she didn't dare. What would Father say? As if that were all that mattered and her own judgment didn't count at all! And I was disconcerted to realize that she had none. Never had! Her light, slightly ironic tone had feigned superiority. She loved us children in a wholly primitive, helpless fashion. Many mothers tend to think, if not to say: Don't do this to me! Don't get ill or I will have to watch over you! Don't be bad! Since I brought you up, the blame will fall on me! Our tenderness doesn't want to accept the fact that the child has been born: we would like to protect and spare it all its life, as if it were still a part of us. Just as you are too, Gottfried. And I accepted this at the time: my mother had to bring me back to my father in good shape; that anything should happen to me was something I couldn't "do to her."

So I dragged her along wherever I had to go and had her with me the only time I went somewhere just to please her. Because I felt I had nothing to lose on the magnificent embankment that led from the harbor to the old fortress. I was tired and hopeless. It was the hour when the street lights were turned on. Venus was already shining in the translucent emerald-light sky above a motionless gray sea with amethyst reflections. The cone of Vesuvius lay behind us with its slanting pennant of smoke, around us a chattering, gesticulating crowd; a lot of fancily dressed, noisy children; nurses with perambulators; army trucks whizzing by on the wide road to our left; far out to sea, the turtle back of the island of Capri. All this my mother had wanted to see, "Since we're here anyway." She quoted, "*Veder Napoli e poi muori!*" and treated me to some things Goethe had written about the city. Shouldn't we take a look at the collection of Greek vases in the museum? Tomorrow morning, perhaps? Before we went home? I agreed vaguely. Her energy amazed me. I preferred to rest on some bench or other. I was finished, in every sense of the word. It was as if I had always known that my childish willfulness would lead nowhere. And what had I been expecting anyway from meeting Horst, who had no desire to see me? It was better that nothing had come of it.

Mother sat down on the corner of a bench and asked me to buy a few postcards at a nearby kiosk. I looked at her, flabbergasted. Not to write, she reassured me, only as a souvenir. So I walked over to the kiosk. Two men ahead of me bought cigarettes I glanced at the headlines of the German papers. Goebbels on the iron resistance of the German *Geist* against barbarism and nihilism ...

"Thank you very much," one of the men said in German, and turned to leave. I remember thinking: he might have learned to say *thank you* in Italian, and looked a little absentmindedly at his pale face, to which incredulous astonishment now lent a mark almost of horror. "Helga?"

"Horst!" I said. "Why aren't you in uniform?"

"What are you doing here?" he stammered.

"I've been looking for you," I said. "I was just going home again ..."

At that moment I no longer knew why I had been looking for him. I felt neither joy nor wonder over my success.

"*Permesso!*" We were standing in the way of a fat Italian who now pushed me aside. For a moment he hid Horst, that utterly strange man. What did I want from him? I stepped back farther than was necessary. When I saw Horst again his arm was around my mother's shoulder. He was looking down at her black hair and saying, "But this can't be true!"

My mother was smiling, there were tears in her eyes. "Helga wanted to find you. That's why she found you."

*Now* she had to say that! I thought rebelliously. If she had told me that on the train ... this morning ... five minutes ago! But now? Several

Italians were already crowding around us, exuberantly sympathetic. "Where can we go?" I said peremptorily.

Mother took Horst's arm, I walked on his other side. I didn't look at him. I hadn't touched him yet. "How long can you stay?" Now he was talking in the same casual way I was.

I answered quickly, "Until tomorrow morning," and paid no attention to my mother's look of surprise.

"Shall we go somewhere to eat?"

We said yes. Anything to get away from the shrill noise around us, to sit down. We entered a small dark trattoria with a few tables. The light came from a hearth. Illuminated from below like that Horst looked even more hollow-eyed, even stranger. And more beautiful. Mother said he looked as if he could do very well with a rest before leaving for "the murderous climate" down there. "I'm perfectly well," he said brusquely. After a pause he added, "If one's climbing a mountain with a sack on one's back, there's not much point in putting it down a few meters from one's goal to catch one's breath."

"So you think the war will be over soon?" Mother asked casually, the way one asks for a weather forecast. She seemed to have forgotten already that she had embraced Horst like a son on seeing him.

"But of course!" Horst cried, and turning to me "I'm glad I'm getting to Africa in time. I don't like to loaf around in a country others have conquered. While I was in France I thought sometimes that I might just as well have gone on fiddling!"

The innkeeper brought our hot spicy pizzas. I was surprised at how good they tasted. When we were finished, Horst looked at his watch and said he had to be in barracks by ten. So we had barely two more hours. "Now I'm going to leave you to yourselves," said Mother. "Just find me a taxi that will take me back to the hotel, and Helga, you'll take one too, to get back ... Won't she, Horst?"

We waited for a while at the curb, silently; at last a taxi stopped. "Don't be too late," Mother said, and to Horst, "So you'll keep up the good work, won't you?" How salutary are our small lies!

Horst turned to me and said uncertainly, "Where shall we go now?"

"Away from all this noise. I've got to be alone with you."

Horst said softly, "Aren't we alone anyway, among all these strangers? They don't even understand our language."

Now! I thought. Now I have to put it absolutely clearly. I felt as if I were on a vibrating trampoline, ten meters above water. If I didn't want to fall, I had to jump. "Horst," I said. "I don't want to talk to you. I want to feel you."

He stopped abruptly and grasped my hands. "Helga! You are so sweet!" There were tears in his voice. "Thank you. Thank you for coming."

I avoided his eyes. Didn't he understand me? "I suppose you can't take me with you to your barracks."

"Of course not."

"Then take a room in a hotel."

It was out. And I hadn't bitten my tongue saying it. But Horst didn't understand what he didn't think was possible. "Just around the corner," he said cheerfully, "there's a good restaurant and I'm sure it'll be empty. The Italians eat so late," and he took me by the hand to lead me.

"Horst! Don't you want to be alone with me? We don't have much time. Ask the waiter over there where there's a hotel nearby and take a room for us."

"You're crazy," he whispered.

"Maybe I am," I said. "But if we use this hour and a half for nothing but pretense, then I know I'll be even crazier." And I began to cry. It was the tension that I couldn't stand any longer, and my despair that he let me spell it all out so blatantly.

Horst stood perfectly still for a moment, his face expressionless, then he went over to the waiter and spoke softly to him. The man grinned appreciatively and described the way with many words and gestures. Horst gave him a tip, came back, put one arm around my shoulders (as he had done to Mother, I thought scornfully) and led me a few steps. Then he let go of me suddenly, his right hand shot up: a German officer, paying no attention to us, had just passed by. Horst had to ask his way once more; then at last we were there. I can recall exactly the doorman's sharp, critical look, but that bothered me less than the imperious way Horst asked for a "decent" room.

At last we were alone. Horst locked the door. I walked straight over to the window and looked out at the narrow alley with its fluttering rags. "There, Helga," Horst said, apparently unabashed. "Here we can talk without being disturbed. Come. Close the window, lock out all the noise."

I obeyed. There was only one chair in the room. I sat down quickly on the bed. I didn't dare to walk up to the small mirror or wash my face or at last fix my hair after all the running around. What did I look like? But my courage was gone.

Horst moved up the chair. "It was sweet of you to come. I shall never forget it." How carefully he chose his words! "And if I don't come back, then I shall think of it ... I mean if ..."

"I understand."

"Please don't cry, Helga. I have the sure feeling ... I will come back."

Can a piece of wood cry? I sat there stiff as a board. "That's good," I said. They seemed the right cue words in the script.

"And now I know that you are really waiting for me! I will come back. But if I don't ..."

He hesitated. Didn't he know his part? I knew only too well how it went on: I wasn't to grieve too long for him. Life demanded its rights. The German Fatherland. The Führer. But he said something quite different. "Then at least something in my life will have been worth while."

Now *I* didn't know how to go on. I sat perfectly still. Suddenly he knelt down in front of me, clung to my legs, and managed to say painfully, "You are going to have to have a great deal of patience with me. I am not worthy of you."

"What nonsense!" I cried, and tried to free myself. It was all so distressing. I stroked his hair a few times, but I was observing myself as I did it, despising myself because I couldn't take him seriously, not even when he mumbled that this alone would give him strength, to know that a girl like me was waiting for him ... the strength to endure everything.

A girl like me? He didn't even know me! What he meant probably was: any girl. Mechanically I asked, "What must you endure?"

"That one can no longer tell the truth from a lie! That one is so ... so vile, and is praised and rewarded for the vilest things!" He lifted his head. He wanted to look me in the eye. "It is hideous to belong to the victors! Can you understand that, Helga?"

"Not yet," I said. "Explain it to me."

"I didn't want to come back," he whispered, "and you sensed it. That's what brought you here. That's why you were there suddenly, standing in my way. And brought me here ... all just to prove to me that in spite of everything, I should come back. Isn't that it, Helga?"

"Yes," I said, my tongue leaden. "You must come back to me, Horst."

"That there are women like you! Who don't think of themselves!"

And it went on and on like this for a long time. I was burning with shame ... because he was still kneeling and because I wasn't contradicting him. I hadn't been thinking of him when I had come here. Only of myself. But I could not tell him that now.

At last he got up, kissed my hand. "I shall be eternally grateful to you."

"What for?" I cried in despair.

He walked over to the window and said, his back turned, "Because you are so true and chaste and fearless. Because you will stick to me, whatever happens. I need that. My mother abandoned me when I was young, I scarcely remember her."

At that I went over to him and promised him, "I shall never abandon you."

At last a feeling of compassion, almost skin to love, warmed my heart. But I thought: if I was a real woman I wouldn't have to say anything more. I would only have to look at him, my eyes veiled. I would only have to hold him close, make him feel what I wanted. But I can't do that because he doesn't want it! He wants to take the picture of a saint to Africa with him! Come on, Helga! Pose for the picture of a saint! Didn't you just feel a spark of compassion? The fire of love can blaze up from it, God willing ...

So his mother had run away. Surely to follow a strange man. And it was therefore my singular duty toward this poor soul not to be like his mother. He was a disappointed son, a wounded child. And this was the man whom I had wanted to make a mother of me. I had wanted to bear his child. That, and that alone, was why I had come.

A good thing he didn't know it.

"We must go," I said. "Let's walk by the sea for a little while."

We walked hand in hand like brother and sister. The fact that he seemed to be so happy appeased me. In the end he said, "When I come back we'll get married right away, won't we? Then we'll never be parted again."

"Just come back!" I said. I didn't believe it, I didn't even really wish for it. My dream was over. But I would do whatever I could to let him keep his.

Did I really see all this so sharply at the time, at seventeen? Hardly. But I felt it in a muted way. No. My violinist had not turned into a hero, and he didn't love me as I was. He didn't know me. He didn't know anything about me. But could I reproach him for it? I had counted coldly on his death and wanted to create a substitute in his child, just as I was a substitute for him for his missing mother.

The next time he comes on leave, I thought, dozing for hours in the crowded train on our way home, I'll get my child and won't ask him if he wants it. Then I shall defraud him with himself just as he defrauded me yesterday. Is that what they call love? Perhaps there is no other kind.

I felt old and experienced. I had truly lost my innocence, but in a different, more painful way than I had wished.

One knows and forgets. One has forgotten and is reminded. That is living. Sometimes it seems as if it simply lasts too long. Over and over again we have to experience the same thing in order to see what we recognized long ago in a new light. To forget is a stipulation of living on. The ingenuousness of the soul renews itself in a naturally enigmatic fashion, just as the body gathers fresh strength as we sleep. The soul does the same thing — it sleeps, it dreams, time passes; it wakens again and is hungry and strong and willing to squander its strength: the soul loves as if for the first time. But there comes the day when one has to try to wake up completely, to remember exactly and to renounce all gentle dreams. For he who forgets has loved in vain.

What happened after our return from Italy? Hadn't everything changed for me? Wasn't I obliged to re-examine my political attitude? To ask myself if all of us were perhaps moving in the wrong direction and to turn around if I had to answer this question in the affirmative?

I did nothing of the sort. I avoided calling myself to account and I have only one excuse: since I was alone I would scarcely have been equal to it. I simply didn't know enough. Something was wrong in our new state. Even Horst, who had given himself up body and soul evidently no longer believed in it, but why? That he hadn't told me.

And then came the war with Russia.

I remember exactly how things were when we heard about it: that our armies were marching as triumphant conquerors into the land of our ally. This time I couldn't say that the Führer knew nothing about it.

Probably the only way to total victory had been this chess move of an alliance with Russia and had been a demand of prudence. Probably the Führer had found it terribly difficult, but for the glory of Germany no sacrifice was too great. So we had to be thankful to him for it. I tried to see things like that. I didn't want to talk to anyone about it; to write anything of the sort to Horst was impossible.

My parents were profoundly depressed. "This means a year-long bloody struggle," said my father. "How can we possibly hold out? Our raw materials will be exhausted, our people too ..." But Mother sighed, "I worry so about Albert." And the next news from him did come from the east. He wrote, "It's no fun, but now at least we know what they saved us for!"

In his next letter he told about the flaming gold of the birches in autumn. Sometimes he thought he could see, in one of the bearded peasants, the old Tolstoy, with his bulbous nose and bright, clever little black eyes. "Then I am reminded of Clemens (why Clemens of all people, with his lean, ascetic face?) and I wonder again why he writes so rarely. Do you know anything about him? We live here in a world without time or space (because it seems endless); our lives have no connection any more with the past, with everything we used to enjoy: friends, books, feelings. Actually one realizes that one is alive only through what one lacks. But compared with the others, I must say we live riotously!"

With what "others" was Albert comparing himself? Probably with the natives who were totally impoverished after decades of forced labor; probably also with the enemy soldiers who we heard were hurled against ours as cannon fodder, without proper equipment and training. At the outbreak of the war with Russia, optimists had declared that in six weeks we would be in the Urals.

Six months later we still weren't in the Urals, but we had a new enemy who was not only superior to us in numbers but also in technology: America. Strangely enough, this left most of us unmoved. We had grown accustomed to accepting the events of war like weather catastrophes. The sun couldn't shine all the time. Naturally there were occasional setbacks.

But in any case, we would be victorious because we had to be victorious. There wasn't a soul who would even have hinted to me of any other possibility.

Soon the advances in Russia came to a halt. Horst's letters were brief and said nothing. And we hadn't heard from Albert in weeks. Then, one winter evening, the doorbell rang loudly. It was Albert. He had had infectious hepatitis, and after a short stay in an army hospital just behind the front, had been sent home for three weeks to recuperate and be checked medically.

His presence, greeted with such jubilation, soon began to weigh upon us like a nightmare. He had lost so much weight, and a veil seemed to be drawn over his beautiful eyes that had once been so expressive. A nervous twitch on the right side of his face marred his regular, rather small features. He told us right away not to ask about his experiences at the front. "Was it so bad?" Mother couldn't help asking the first evening, when she could scarcely hide her shock.

"Oh Mother ... bad?" Albert said with a twisted smile I didn't like. "There are enough things in life that one had better not talk about. So much that one may do but not say ..."

"I'm sure that's right," said Father, and turning to us, "Even children don't like it when they come home from school and one asks them: how did it go? Let's leave Albert in peace for a while. He'll talk when he feels like it."

But Albert didn't talk. He was rarely home. "I like to sit in the coffee house," was the only excuse he gave for his absence. But before he left I had a talk with him, just the two of us, while he was packing. I was sitting on his bed, my legs drawn up, watching him. Because he asked me about it, I talked about school. "Do you still like to write compositions?"

"Oh yes, very much."

"I hated it. They always wanted to know something that was no concern of theirs."

"You don't have to write anything like that!" I said. "But there are some things that come clear to you only when you write them down."

"A reason never to take pencil in hand again," he said passionately. "I wish I could still stagger around in a colorful fog as blithely as all of you!"

He seemed like a little boy who would have liked to cry and didn't dare to because he was a man. I felt sorry for him. "Albert, are you afraid?"

He sat down besides me and put one arm around my shoulders. "No, Helga. Not the way you mean it. Not of dying. On the contrary: death would mean to be released at last from always having to make fresh decisions and always doing everything wrong."

"What did you ever do wrong?"

"If only I knew! Then next time I wouldn't do it. There are fortunate people — you and Walter — you always know what you want to do and go ahead and do it. And then it's right, or at least you think it's right, even when it ends badly. I try to do it too, but nothing ever comes of it, little sentimental gestures that don't help anybody ... I could puke!"

He got up, walked silently up and down a few times, then stopped and looked down at me. In a quite different voice — now he was my big brother again — he said urgently, "Helga. Listen to me. If ever the Russian come here —don't stay. Drop everything and run as fast as you can."

"Albert!" I cried, half-laughing, half-horrified. "Have you gone crazy? The Russians — here? In Vienna?"

"I'm not saying they'll come, all I'm saying, Helga, is — if they do, run away, as quickly and as far as you can."

Was it his fear, was it his ... cowardice that was transferred to me? I tried to hide my shudders, to answer coolly, "I'll remember, Albert. But that's never going to happen." And then, when he remained silent, I couldn't resist asking, "So they're really as ... as inhuman as we're told?"

Albert turned away abruptly, walked over to the blacked-out window, stood there as if he could see through it and said with such effort to control himself that his voice sounded strangely high-pitched, "If they were human, they wouldn't be soldiers."

I didn't dare reply to that.


Then we were alone again. The weeks that followed were busy yet meaningless. When I was home I had to help Mother and try to distract her a little. Father wasn't able to. He was out of sorts, occasionally even unable to control it, and beside him and me, she scarcely saw anyone. Sometimes I was able to get cheap theater tickets from Strength through Joy, then I had to go with her. She wouldn't go alone. Frequently I was giving up time for something that was hardly worth while. But once I was given tickets for the Burgtheater, and we saw Gerhart Hauptmann's *Iphigenia in Aulis*. Both of us were deeply moved. I found everything represented in the drama that I had tried in vain to explain after my Greek class that day when Horst had come to visit us: the presumptuousness of wanting to sacrifice a beloved life, the infamy of unconditional obedience.

When I said as much during the intermission, Mother was surprised. She thought I was interpreting the play too subjectively; she would never have seen it that way. I got excited and asked what was, in her opinion, the meaning of the play? "Must it have a meaning?" She asked, with the gay-ironic undertone of happier days. "It simply gives a magnificent presentation of life as it is. All of you always want to see a moral in the story, but for that we have Wilhelm Busch, and possibly Marlitt. A work of art isn't a tract."

"So life has no meaning either?" I asked.

"Probably not," my mother admitted.

Did she notice how hurt I was? She took my arm and led me gently back into the theater. When we were seated again she said softly and with feeling, "But we may be here to give it meaning." I nodded, but I was thinking: that I can't do. And I don't even want to do it.

I had decided to graduate with German as my major subject. To do that I had to hand in a long paper. I suggested, "The Idea of Sacrifice in Tragedy" to my professor as a theme. He smiled. "You know, Wegscheider, that would be too ambitious even for a thesis. You must learn to recognize your limitations. And I'd really rather see you write something more topical." The good man had no idea how topical my theme was.

Since I wasn't allowed to use it, I chose another subject. My main interest at this point was mathematics, which I had once found so difficult. It seemed to me more refreshing to work with numbers than with words. Numbers were unequivocal; the results could be proved. They belonged to a realm of absolute order, far removed from conflicting opinions. We learned nothing about Einstein and his theory because he was a Jew.

I dutifully kept up the evenings spent with my group of girls, told them about our new expanded Fatherland, about the "unique constellation," the fateful hour, that had given us the Führer, and didn't know that I was using the expression of an outlawed poet. I said, "Many enemies, much horror!" or, "And though this world be filled with devils, the Reich must remain ours!" And sometimes also, "If all become unfaithful ..."

The girls were enthusiastic. Every time I walked into my neat, cool room after one of our meetings, my feelings of disillusionment became more oppressive.

At about this time my grandmother came to stay with us, her first lengthy visit. One morning — we had just finished breakfast — there she was, standing at the front door between two large suitcases. One of them, we soon found out, contained nothing but food. "May I stay with you, or should I go to a hotel?" she asked gaily.

Of course we took her in. The boys' room was empty. But my parents seemed disconcerted rather than pleased. "However did you manage to get here at a time like this?" asked Father. "Why ... with the first train that leaves at four ten, of course," she said.

She unpacked the bread that smelled of fennel, and a pot of lard; we poured another round of tea, and I decided to miss the first school period in order to find out what this visit was all about.

As soon as Mother had sat down with us too — it seemed to me that she sat only on the edge of her chair so as to be able to jump right up again to get something, and that's how she behaved the whole time Grandmother was there: the more relaxed Grandmother was, the more my mother's nervousness increased ... yes, well ... Grandmother said she could feel something, "this and that," going on inside her, and her doctor had advised a thorough check up. She rejected our expressions of sympathy: it wasn't going to be anything serious. "Maybe I'll have to go on a diet, maybe the change of air in itself will do me good. At home all sorts of things haven't been agreeing with me lately."

"We're all suffering from that." said Father.

"And now at least I'll get to know my only granddaughter properly!" said Grandmother, looking at me affectionately.

I could feel her sincere interest and was glad. And in the days to come her presence did me good. I couldn't understand what was bothering my mother. Once I asked her. "Oh, you know," she mumbled, "your grandmother has quite different standards when it comes to running a house. I'm really not basically a hausfrau. Everything I do is improvised, and I don't like to be watched while I'm doing it."

"But she isn't watching you. You're only imagining it."

Both of us were right. Nothing was farther from Uri's mind than criticizing the way Mother attended to her household duties, yet there was no doubt about it — her lively, piercing eyes saw everything.

Much later it became clear to me what good reason Mother had to fear those eyes — not the way Uri looked at dull floors and hazy window panes, but the insight she had into Mother's fearful heart. Later, when Uri said to me, "I warned Theo not to marry her ..." that was when I knew. Even if Mother never found out — and I hope she never did — still it was the subconscious reason for her feeling of insecurity. Because nothing gives us as much strength as to be trusted. If, however, one is expected to fail, then one's good intentions don't suffice. One needs other aids.

Beside Grandmother, Mother looked frail, although Uri was only a little taller and not at all heavy. But she held herself so straight, her shoulders were broad, her step firm, all of which made her look stately. Her voice was loud but pleasing, yet she spoke rarely. She preferred to listen. She had the gift of making others talk — not my mother, however. At the time only a few streaks of white mingled with her thick, dark hair. She wore it braided in a knot at the back of her head. Her dark dresses, narrow at the waist, were timeless, like the dresses of a queen on stage, only not as long, in spite of which she didn't really attract attention. Nobody in the street ever turned around to look at her. But the person sitting opposite her in the streetcar, or a passer by whom she might have asked for some information, was more likely to look thoughtfully and with interest at her face. Then nearly always the trace of a friendly smile would light up his features.

My father recovered quickly from his ill humor. He simply didn't like to be surprised and faced with a *fait accompli*. Now it pleased him that his mother's questions about his work betrayed her respect and interest. He began to talk about all sorts of minor irritations and slights, and she listened with sympathy but advised him to ignore things like that. "They're beneath us." But once — I can't remember what brought it on — she said *this* time he couldn't let what had happened pass. He must defend himself in the interest of those who couldn't. One should never back away from threats; that was cowardly. Or injustice would grow bigger and bigger. That was more or less the gist of the discussion.

My father said she was seeing things too simply. He sounded annoyed, He had no desire to pick the chestnuts out of the fire and burn his fingers. "I am a civil servant. I do my duty. That suffices."

"It would suffice in a law-abiding nation," said my grandmother.

"How do you mean that?" I asked, interrupting them, but my father wouldn't let her answer. He gave her a sharp look and said to me, "Your grandmother means that now we are at war. That naturally brings irregularities which everyone has to put up with."

I realized that this explanation was intended to end the dispute, and my grandmother got the message. She began to talk about the pleasant weather and how much she would like to go to the Türkenschanzpark before leaving. She had been there only once in her life, in her youth. "Would you take me, Helga?" she asked. "But it would have to be today or tomorrow. The day after tomorrow I'm going home."

This announcement was just as sudden as the way she had turned up. Yes, tomorrow she would get her final reports from the doctors. All tests had turned out negative, which meant that nothing was wrong and she could at last attend to things at home again.

I was able to free myself for the following afternoon, and we went to the park together. Grandmother enjoyed the mild air, the wide view across the gently sloping, greening meadows to the hills of the Vienna Woods. She kept stopping to look, but without interrupting the conversation. "You're looking forward to going home?" I asked casually.

"Yes. I'll be glad to get back. Because I hope everybody will have calmed down in the meantime and we'll be left in peace."

"What was wrong?" This time I couldn't resist asking.

"I'll tell you about it, Helga," she said. "This is what happened: Our priest told me I was in danger of getting a morals demerit. I was being too good to my Poles."

"To your ...?"

"To my Polish foreign laborers, the slaves they've taken prisoner and brought here and distributed among the farms. They're good-natured, they work hard if one treats them like human beings, which they are. Or aren't they?"

I was silent.

"So my neighbors complained that I was spoiling my Poles, and theirs were starting to make demands. I of course was giving them the same things to eat as the servants and myself. Suddenly two Gold Pheasants came to inspect me in their bright gold-brown uniforms, and to their horror found out that I didn't lock my Poles up at night! They could run away! 'But they're not running away, as you can see,' I told them. They could rape the girls! 'But they could do that in the daytime too,' I countered. 'And you're giving them our rations,is that right?' they asked. I got angry and therefore rash, and said, 'In the Bible there is a communist message: He who does not work shall not eat. But that he who works must also eat is so self-evident, you can't even find it in the Bible!' You should have seen their faces, Helga! Like ripe tomatoes before they burst. I wanted to be more reasonable, justify myself, calm them, so I showed them the fields. We were almost finished with the planting, the first in the area. And that was a mistake, because they promptly took my Poles away from me. I didn't need them anymore. There was one, though, who didn't want to go. Vladimir. He said he would hide. He was *not* going to leave. With great difficulty our priest managed to make clear to him that if he didn't go they'd put his Resi in a concentration camp, and they'd take her child — his child — from her before it was born."

"Who is Resi?"

"An orphan. I've had her with me since she was twelve. A good girl. She's seventeen now, just your age, Helga. And she fell in love with Vladimir. He's so handsome. Imagine it — she had to translate everything the priest told him, had to implore him to disappear ..."

"And what happened to her?"

"Before anybody could notice her condition, the priest took her to a home for unwed mothers. Here, near Vienna. He knows the Mother Superior. But Resi must say she doesn't know who the child's father is, even to the nuns. Reverend Father is probably afraid that nuns haven't learned to lie very well. Better not put them to the test. That's why I had to promise him not to visit her. I don't know whether it was the right thing to do ..."

"Shall I visit her, Grandmother? And then write to you?"

Grandmother looked at me, her expression warm. "No, no, Helga. I don't think that would be the right thing. Because you have everything the poor little creature lacks: solicitous parents, a home, you are engaged. You have a future. You wouldn't understand each other."

"But will you take her back when ... when she's had the child?"

"That would be much too dangerous. When the war's over — perhaps."

"Will ... will the man go back to her, do you think?"

"If he survives, perhaps he'll come to see ..." She sounded tired.

I asked her if the whole medical examination had only been an excuse. "What an idea!" she cried. "I don't put on an act for you and sit around in hospitals for pleasure! It was a fortunate little coincidence. Tomorrow I'll go home with five different reports. I'll take them to the district doctor and he'll see to it that soon everybody knows why I was in Vienna. For those dear people I'll now count as doomed to die, and that will save me a lot of inconvenience. In the meantime they've assigned me three Frenchmen. I hope they come soon."

"But ... but you'll spoil *them* too."

"Maybe not. I can talk to them. I mean, I can apologize ... and now and then see that they get something secretly."

"Be careful!" I begged, and asked her why she hadn't told my parents any of this. She considered for a moment, then she said, "They're so frightened. I feel sorry for them."

Did Uri know what she was doing to me with these revelations? Into what tortuous doubts she had thrown me? I'm sure she did. It was just what she wanted.

As soon as I was alone, I tried to think according to my teachings: It served the girl right. Under no circumstances should one become that intimate with an enemy. (I don't think the word subhuman occurred to me — I hope not.) It was Grandmother's fault too ...

All in vain! I didn't believe it! I didn't believe it for a single moment! It *was* Grandmother's fault, but only because she had had to send the girl away, because she wasn't permitted to express her pity, because the only way she had been able to help the girl was by this cruel expulsion. Only *that* was why it was her fault. Why all of us were at fault.

I must tell you right away: we lost track of Resi. Uri was still able to find out that she had gone with her child to work for a farmer. In autumn 1945, when the mails gradually began to function again, Uri wrote to her that she could come back any time she felt like it. There was no answer, and when asked, the district clerk replied curtly that said person, according to hearsay, had wandered off with a Russian. It could have been Vladimir. Pole or Russian — for our peasants one was as good or as bad as the other in those days. But I prefer to believe that she simply wanted to get away to a country where she could make a fresh start.

Where was the comforting excuse when I thought of Resi: the Führer knows nothing about it? He knew! It was he who had divided people according to their origins into worthwhile, worthless and harmful. But if this was wrong, what could still be considered right in this new Reich? Everything was one gigantic web of lies which we had zealously helped to spin. And now we were stuck in it. Nothing we could do about it but hold still. Whoever struggled, strangled. A senseless end ...

To the astonishment of my parents, I clung to my grandmother when she left. My arms around her neck, weeping, I begged, "Come back soon! Promise me you'll come back!"

She freed herself gently, took my hand and pressed it silently, like a secret ally.

Was it weeks later, or months, that I came home and found Mother in tears? Somebody had told her — she didn't betray who it had been —

that in Rumania a railroad car full of children, who were allegedly being moved to Germany for safety, had been gassed.

"Gassed?" I repeated uncomprehendingly. I knew the word only in connection with insect extermination. What *was* she talking about?

"They locked them in and killed them with poison gas. They say it took a quarter of an hour until all of them were dead. Children, Helga! Innocent children!"

"That's a lie!" I screamed. "Who tells lies like that? That can't be true! Who would do anything like that?"

"The SS," my mother said very softly, her face turned away.

"A lie!" I screamed. "Who says so? Who dared to make such a statement? The English radio, right? You believe everything they say!"

She shook her head. "It wasn't the radio," she said. "We don't listen to it anymore. We never listen to foreign broadcasts, you know that, don't you?"

"Just the same ... it can only be infamous foreign propaganda! Don't you remember, Mother? In 1914 they said that German soldiers hacked off the hands of Belgian children! They stop at nothing to set the world against us!"

"Perhaps," my mother granted, and wiped her face. "But that one could even make up a thing like that ... and Helga ... think of Dr. Feldstein. Why have we never heard from her?"

"I don't know," I said, "but that ... that's something quite different."

Gottfried — not until the spring of 1945, when the war was over, did I ever hear anything of gassing again. You'll simply have to believe this. But in my heart I felt that everything was possible when I thought of Resi, who wasn't allowed to give birth to her child because the father was a Pole. Suddenly I didn't understand any of it anymore. Because I knew that the Prussians, for instance, who are distinguished by so many German attributes that to us seem exemplary, have a lot of Slavic blood. I even knew that racially pure human beings, in the strictest sense, could be found today only in very small, isolated areas. I don't want to explain anything away; perhaps I could have tried to justify the enforced abortion of a Jewish cross breed to myself. For years the Jews had been pointed out to us as the essential corrupters of the people. But was it right, even in such a case, to take a child from a mother who wanted to give birth to it?

I pushed the tormenting question away. Fortunately I didn't have to make the decision. I could never be a doctor. That was clear to me now. Albert's words, half forgotten, pursued me again. "When they come, run as far as you can!" We had reason to be afraid.

Do you know, Gottfried, with what I calmed myself? I read Shakespeare, Aeschylus. The world was always a "vale of blood and tears." One probably had to say yes to that, and try somehow to salvage one's own small happiness, had to build a house of cards in the calm between two storms. Just as all of us are doing again now ...

Because of my impending final exams, I had been released from most of my duties at the BdM, but I had been entered in a civil defense course. I studied diligently. It was so uncomplicated and I found it fun. Sometimes I wrote to my grandmother. Her answers were affectionate, but didn't tell me much. Once I dared to ask, "How is Resi?" She didn't answer the question.

I passed my finals with honors. "This is the first happy day in a long time," my father said, and to my consternation I saw tears in his eyes. Was I really important to him? I had the uneasy feeling that I was not going to give him much more joy, and pretended to be gay and satisfied. Mother, too, seemed more relaxed than usual. She busied herself preparing a small, festive meal, most of the food provided by Uri, who hadn't been able to come. They were just beginning to harvest and she had to keep an eye on her three Frenchmen. Not one of them had ever cleaned a stable or driven a tractor, but all three were good-natured — the mechanic, the hairdresser and the student, even if they didn't know very much about anything. And they were half-starved too! "Well, they won't stay that way long," said Father. "Not with your grandmother ..."

Oh, how do I go on now and finish the sentence after what has happened? I don't even know what I was going to write. Or did I want to say that Father was probably so gay and gentle because a bottle of "army" champagne was once more on the table? Did I want to write that he was sociable and took an interest in us only when he had had something to drink? He was never one — how do they put it? — to say no to a drink ... But I am sure I didn't want to bring this up yet because it was only much later, shortly before the collapse, that I found empty bottles in his wardrobe. Only from then on did single memories take on a different aspect ...

I have already mentioned that my boy looks like my father. I am glad he does. Because my father had clearly defined features, shy, clever eyes, and so much poise in the best sense of the word. So why shouldn't I be glad that my boy is like him, including a habit of drawing his mouth up sideways a little when he laughs, and supporting his temple lightly with his right forefinger when he reads?

This similarity with my father has startled me only since Tuesday. I was tidying Gottfried's room, and behind all the empty bottles of lemonade, which he always forgets to return, I found an empty bottle of cognac! Panic-stricken, I thought at once: he's drinking secretly, like my father. What can one do about it? Nothing.

Toward evening, when he had done his homework and wanted to listen to the radio, I said, "You've collected such a lot of bottles again. Do you want me to return them?"

"I'll see to that," you said, not in the least embarrassed, from which I concluded that this wasn't the first time a schnapps bottle had been among the others, or you would have thought of it now. I went and got it and held it under your nose. "And what's this?"

You blushed and said rudely. "You can see what it is. But it's empty, isn't it?"

"I can see that." I said.

You turned the radio on. I took a big step, turned it off and said, "I want an explanation."

At last you noticed that I wasn't joking, and cooked up the following story: Your class had won the football game. You had all bet on it. "Bet cognac?"

"My God, Mother, everybody had one go at it! There were thirty of us! It was a joke!"

"And who had this great idea?" You said nothing. "You?" I asked. "Tell me the truth, Gottfried, *please.*"

"Why me?" you said, angry now. "Do you think I get it cheaper?"

Then I knew where it came from: from the pharmacist's boys, the only ones I didn't want Gottfried to have anything to do with, and whom Gottfried seemed to prefer to anyone else. "If you start talking about this," he said, half-threatening, half-imploring, "I'll never live it down at school."

"And why did you take home the bottle, not Friedel?"

"But Friedel is a class above us! He wasn't even there! You mean Bert! I got the bottle because ... there was still some left and I was the quarterback. Now can I listen to my program?"

"No, for God's sake!" I cried, and lost my temper. "I have to talk to you!"

You waited in provocative silence. I picked up the sweater I was knitting. Needlework is calming. "Listen," I said, finding it difficult to speak. "I want you to promise me something. Don't have anything to do with the pharmacist's boys. I don't want it. I have my reasons."

"Then tell me for God's sake what they are. Friedel is my friend!"

"His mother was almost my friend," I said. "We went to school together and were both in the Labor Service ..."

"And you never see her now?"

"She behaved very badly toward me. I don't want to talk about it, Gottfried. I can't even prove it. It isn't anything you can prove, but I know she did, and she knows it too. It would be ..." I wanted to say "undignified," but groped for a less pompous word ... "It isn't fair to me if you go there."

"Did you have political differences?" you asked hesitantly.

"Among other things," I said curtly.

"All right," said my son, "then I won't go there anymore. But I like Bert, and Friedel is my friend. To skate and fish and ride our bikes together, that'll be all right, won't it? After all, Mother, it's not our fault."

"You're right. It not your fault."

Oh ... there hadn't been any differences; we never quarreled, Marietta and I, and there was no political enmity either, rather a human animosity, no — worse. A female one. And that sort of thing isn't easily erased. A scar remains that hurts when you touch it. Gottfried will soon understand. I was just about to pick up that stitch in my writing when the present crossed my path again.

I told Uri the story of the class bet. She listened attentively. "Do you believe it?" I asked.

"Why not?" she asked me.

"But that just our Gottfried got the bottle to take home ... I'm afraid, Uri," I admitted. "He's so like Father. And during his last years ... do you know this?"

"Yes, I know," Uri said quietly.

She was silent for a while, and not until I was getting up to leave did she say, "Today I have to think of how once, when you were a young girl, you came to me and wanted to know why my cousin, Uncle Herbert, ended up in a mental institution. 'Hardening of the arteries,' I told you 'Senility. It isn't hereditary.' How relieved you were!"

"Yes," I replied. "I remember. I thought otherwise I'd have to tell Horst before we got married."

"Very well. But now listen to me. My mother died of tuberculosis at the age of twenty-three. My father and my brother both died of cancer in middle age. Uncle Herbert and your mother ended up mentally incompetent. Your mother's grandfather shot himself. And about my Janosh they used to say: a good thing he met with a fatal accident. He would have gone crazy soon anyway."

I looked at her, horrified. There she sat peacefully in her place at the window; behind her, branches were moving in the wind, a gentle rain was beating against the window. Her wrinkled skin was light and delicate, and her black lace cap was perched tidily on her carefully groomed hair. She had spoken softly, with long pauses between sentences, as if she were trying to remember more and more bad examples, and she threaded her words, one after the other, into a whole chain of sentences, something she rarely felt was worth the effort anymore. She had closed her eyes. I was just going to ask her why she was telling me all this now and had never mentioned it before, when she went on speaking, without opening her eyes. "Yet all three of you turned out to be happy, healthy, well-bred children."

Happy, I thought. Were we happy? I wasn't, and Albert certainly not. She went on. "And now it's really lucky that you can't figure out what Gottfried's father, and his father and mother, bestowed upon him ... and can't be watching all the time for it to come out in him."

I was startled to hear myself laugh loudly. It didn't sound good. "Really lucky!" I sobbed.

"Yes," she said firmly. "Because in your imagination the cognac is vodka. You must know as well as I do that Theo was not an alcoholic."

Was she right? I still don't know. I said nothing.

"Leave the boy in peace, Helga," she said. "Or he won't be able to breathe beside you. Write the old stories out of your heart; that is good, that is healing. I always did want you to go to confession, don't you remember? Leave the wound open, let the pus run out. Otherwise it goes on festering and will poison all of you. Let the blood flow. Blood purifies ..."

She's spinning the threads of her own experiences, I thought angrily. She hasn't had an easy life. But I — what was I supposed to confess? Facts are what I have to present to Gottfried. I have to inform him and at the same time try to explain why I am doing all this so late. Leave him in peace? That's just what I've done for much too long a time. Out of cowardice.

"Bring me another glass of currant juice, please, Helga. I'm thirsty ..."

When she had put the empty glass aside she said lovingly, "It wasn't meant as a reproach, child. We mothers nearly always do the same thing. We worry too much and have too little hope. I loved my first child to death."

"What on earth do you mean, Grandmother?"

She smiled sadly. "You haven't called me that in a long time. I mean what I say. But now I'm tired. Another time, perhaps, I'll tell you all about it ..."

She looked exhausted. I reproached myself as I silently helped her to undress. But with whom else could I have talked about it? Should I write to Walter? No. Besides, he had stopped writing.

When she was in bed and I was already at the door, I heard her say, "Don't be afraid, my child. Original sin is wiped out."

What was I to make of that? She was already probably half-asleep. Because Uri usually thinks just as little as I do in outdated metaphors. She was getting all mixed up. In future I would leave her in peace with my problems.

Yesterday, new from Walter! He wasn't going to write any more, perhaps we would be seeing each other soon! He had a chance to come to Germany on business. "You'll hear from me as soon as I know."

And I am looking forward to seeing him again immensely. I can't think of anything else. I wonder if his hair is gray already, if he's grown heavier as so many men do around forty. That would be a pity. Gottfried is thrilled at the prospect of meeting his uncle from America. I ask myself suddenly: am I that fond of Walter? I didn't know I was. And I stand still — I am vacuuming — because a recollection flashes through my mind: I've thought just this once before ... and now I know when that was ...

But I've not got that far yet. How is the boy ever going to find his way through this labyrinth?

I was called up for Labor Service. All girls who wanted to study had to go through with it first. It was all right with me. I was even looking forward to living in the country and escaping parental authority for a while. My need to be independent was aroused if for no other reason than that my parents always knew when I had received a letter from Horst, and asked me if I had already answered it. I was also depressed by their increasing depression. Their mutual consideration seemed formal and empty. When we were children, Father had admired Mother and teased her. Now he treated her with the politeness of a guilty conscience. He hated to see her working in the house or kitchen. Often he urged me sternly to help her; but I hardly ever had time, and she didn't want me to anyway.

I looked forward to life with people my own age. Hannelore, who had come to us from North Germany, and Marietta, the daughter of the grocer with the low party number, both from my class, were sent to the same camp. Marietta stuck close to me. She was spoiled and needed someone to complain to.

During the day we were sent out singly to the surrounding farms. We were supposed to help the overburdened women with their work. On some harvest days we had to go into the fields with them, but for the most part we were required to stay in their musty houses, looking after a horde of dirty little children, do the washing, cook, wash dishes — in short do things that didn't take much gumption and demanded no experience.

I did my best to please my house mother. I didn't succeed right away. The house was dilapidated, the children were neglected, the work was much too hard for the woman and her help. There was nothing I could do about it. The money they received toward child support was spent on the most necessary repairs, the payment of veterinary bills, the midwife, even the doctor when no household remedies or advice from the calendar helped anymore. The infant was wrapped in old, torn bed linen which couldn't be washed properly because it would have fallen apart.

How often my mother complained about the scant rations for washing powder and soap! Here they let the coupons expire and cooked a thick broth from what was left over after slaughtering, which seemed suitable enough for loosening the worst dirt but couldn't be used on the children's skin. I redeemed the coupons, sent half the stuff home and used the rest for the general cleansing of the children and the rags they wore. The two school-age girls begged me to plait their wet hair in a lot of little braids. Next morning they were delighted with their wavy hair. Their mother smiled indulgently. And when I bandaged her sprained ankle one day so expertly that she was soon out of pain and on the following day could hobble around, she asked me how long I was going to stay, and couldn't grasp that this didn't depend on me. "If it suits you here with us ..." I was glad she didn't notice how little it suited me. And I was ashamed because I couldn't really like any of the children. I only did my duty. That was when I noticed for the first time how little that sufficed.

The only one who might have understood my feelings was Hannelore, but her judgment of the people, the dirt and the general apathy was so disparaging that I kept having to contradict her and even defend what was depressing me too. Perhaps the proximity of an industrial city, for decades now, had resulted in such a "bad element," because all the capable, intelligent and adventurous people had wandered away?

"Bad element!" Hannelore agreed enthusiastically. "You can say that again! Do you know what it's like where I am? The father drinks, one of the children is an idiot, another has a harelip! When will they start sterilizing people like this?"

"I hope never!" I protested vigorously. "There must be a reason why the man drinks! Perhaps if he'd had a better start ..."

"You're just theorizing," said Marietta in an effort to appease us. "I'm telling you one thing — if it weren't for this war we'd all be better off. Isn't it crazy that we have to go to the dance tomorrow in uniform? We'll sweat like pigs and the boys will be bored stiff when they see all of us looking alike."

Hannelore had something to say about that. I wasn't listening anymore. Our assertions and conjectures echoed in my mind. If ... if ... if ... My thoughts went farther, If we didn't win? If history proved the others right? It was unthinkable! Yet the thought was already boring its way secretly into everyone's mind. Because the summer of the great triumphs lay behind us; instead the destruction of German cities had begun. We weren't making any headway in Russia. Reports of "a straightening of the front" were persistent. One shook off one's doubts and thought: we simply *can't* lose the war. After all ...

After what? After so much hope, so many big words, after so much sacrifice. And ... didn't we sense it? Didn't we young girls know very well: after so much guilt?

History forgives the victor, the "world to come" absolves him of all guilt. Perhaps — and this is our only hope, my son — God prefers to forgive the conquered.

Two words flowed from my pen yesterday which I didn't want to use: *God* and *guilt*. Doesn't one function more clearly without them, since they are so elastic that scarcely two people visualize them the same way? But I know that they are indissolubly bound together, that whoever uses one means the other as well. If only I were not so impelled to write this report to the end! Now, after months of writing, the end seems farther away than when I began! At the time I thought: in two or three weeks I'll be done. And I've barely clarified the conditions precedent; everything essential is still to come. (At first I thought I had to recall the past: now it becomes evident that no one who still breathes should speak of "the past"; that things are completely past only from the perspective of death.)

But I suppose I should finish my sentence if I want Gottfried to understand me. So ... if these pages are not solely for the simple purpose of showing my son something he does not yet know, I would be tempted to dabble in philosophy at this point and examine why there can be no guilt without God, and without guilt, no God. The person who says, "it is my fault" or "I am guilty" admits explicitly that he believes in God, perhaps without realizing it. "I can't help it" means in other words: what do you want from me? I am the result of an endless series of coincidences and am their helpless victim because there is no God.

So. From now on I shall try not to use the two words. Recently I saw a young foreigner who wanted to buy a *pampelmuse* in a village store. "We don't have 'em," he was told. He bought oranges instead. Then he saw a box full of grapefruit. "But you have some over there."

"Yes, sir. If that's what you mean."

One must speak the language of the country one is in, but also of the times in which one lives. I'll go on trying, and if I stick closely to facts, it will probably be easier.

Nothing to be done about it. We had to go to the dance in our brown uniforms. This time the invitation had come from an SS unit, stationed for the time being in barracks in the nearby city, that was shortly going to be moved east. For the most part they were very young men, going to the front for the first time. A lot of them couldn't dance. The festivities were being held in a rural inn with a big, tree-filled garden, at the edge of a wood. We were driven there in two trucks — like cattle, we joked. All of us had nine hours of work behind us, many a long march on foot as well, and the prospect of a free Sunday ahead didn't dispel our weariness. "Be nice to the boys," our leader had begged us, and added that we should behave like respectable German girls. So we had a choice. I was ready and willing to be nice to anyone wearing the same uniform as Horst, perhaps with the same fate in store for him, maybe a sweetheart too, in some far-off German city.

Marietta, Hannelore and I sat at a table in the garden with three young men. We told each other where we came from, what movie we had seen last; we stared out into the increasing darkness of the wood. None of the three boys could or wanted to dance. When one of them suggested taking a little walk, we all agreed happily. I noticed how quickly Marietta took the arm of the blond young man who until then had been addressing me. Did she like him so much? He was the handsomest, in spite of his very short nose. "We'll lead the way!" she cried. "I can see in the dark like a cat!"

"I've already noticed that you have cat's eyes," said the boy.

They hurried on ahead. "Have fun," I thought angrily, and didn't really listen to what my partner was saying. Suddenly a screech owl hooted. It startled me. "Don't be afraid. I'll look after you," said the young man, and tried to kiss me. "I'm engaged," I said, pushing him away. "That doesn't bother me." He was laughing. "But it bothers me!" I said angrily. "Oh. I beg your pardon," and with that our conversation was over. We turned around and walked back silently. Soon after that Hannelore and her partner jumped out from behind some trees to frighten us. They didn't seem to have had much fun either, but Marietta and the blond boy were gone for a long time.

Later we saw them again on the dance floor. She was teaching him, both of them laughing, and their cheeks were very red. As we were rattling back in the truck she leaned against me and whispered, "He's sweet." I said drily, "You're tipsy. Tomorrow you won't know what he looks like."

But she knew very well. She even remembered his whole name, and the following Sunday she wrote him a long letter. "Don't you think he looks like your fiancé? I always did like him," she said innocently.

"His nose is quite different." I said. Still there was perhaps something to it. Was that why it had irritated me for a moment that she had attached herself to him? "What's his name," I asked.

"Karl. But I'm going to call him Siegfried because that's what he looks like."

I laughed and couldn't be angry with her anymore. "You have my blessing." She was as happy as a child who had found the doll she admired in a shop window under the Christmas tree. I felt old beside her, and thought: I hope you get the chance to call him anything, then I sat down and wrote to Horst, a detailed letter. His news, which reached me at intervals, was so meager.

When we were warned to behave like respectable German girls, it meant that we weren't supposed to drink more than we could tolerate, smoking was forbidden, and whatever else might happen should be kept from the narrow-minded populace. This we didn't succeed in doing. During the following days there was malicious gossip; even the priest had something unfriendly to say in church. I personally hadn't seen anything you could really call offensive, but some of the girls kept revealing more and more details the farther into the past the dance receded. Like me, Marietta listened silently. One day I found her sitting on her bed, weeping. "Have you had bad news?" I asked.

She handed me an army letter that had been returned to her as undeliverable. "Your Karl has probably been transferred," I tried to console her. "Because if he had been killed ..."

"That's all the same to me," she interrupted me harshly. "I'll never find him again!"

"If he wants to, he'll find you."

She turned away. "He doesn't even know my name," she said, and blew her nose noisily to stop crying.

I felt sorry for her, but I found it stupid of her to have harbored any hopes after this one encounter. Again I felt old and weary beside her, since I had every reason to be seriously worried about the man to whom I had been engaged for three years. And yet, even well-founded fears lose their sting when they become chronic. It seemed to me that my true self had crept into a snail house long ago, and the girl who worked, spoke, listened to the radio and wrote letters was a stranger, my only concern being to hide behind her back ...

How I had looked forward to the free and easy life among those my own age! Now I realized that I had little in common with them, perhaps just because we shared everything externally: we were dressed the same, our washing habits were alike, we ate the same food, got up at the same time, wrote our letters on Sunday and used the same three dozen expressions when we spoke. Although we had been thrown together from every province in the Reich, every one of us anxiously repressed anything that might have betrayed she was different.

After a few weeks of this I noticed that I was living an absolutely mute life. I longed for a talk with my grandmother. She was the only one who had spoken her real thoughts to me, with no consideration for my youth and preconceived opinions. I decided to write to her. But then I was just as afraid to ask about her foreign workers as to question her about poor Resi. I can remember sitting in front of a sheet of paper with nothing written on it but *Dear Grandmother*, with the feeling of being locked up such as I had never had before, nor since: a prisoner robbed of the desire to communicate by the censors of the prison administration.

Slowly I tore up the paper. "Wasteful," said Marietta, the grocer's daughter. "It's none of your business!" I cried, furious that this too had registered. "I know," she said, and began to cry. Now I had to apologize. It was hateful.

Marietta cried a lot during this time. I guess the work was too hard for her. I wanted to suggest to our leader that she be moved to a farm nearer to the camp. but it turned out that Marietta preferred to stay where she had painstakingly succeeded in getting used to things. She would feel better in the autumn, she said: she had never felt well in the heat. All right ... she should know.

The closer we live with people, the stronger the tough skin of our soul becomes and protects us from the pain of contact.

At last! A letter from Horst! It began: Don't be alarmed! This aroused hope and fear in me, emotions that had been sleeping. He had come down with malaria and had been sent to an army hospital in the Alps to recover. He would not be allowed to return to Africa. Then, after a few casual personal words, he wrote, "I am sure you are behaving splendidly, as usual." He, however, didn't feel at all right in the beautiful surroundings. It was like being in a comfortable waiting room which is heated: one can stretch one's legs, one is even fed well. Just the same, one is constantly watching the clock and counting the minutes until the train arrives. Nothing is really lacking; one isn't present but in the baggage room! Hopefully one would soon be redeemed. "You understand, I am sure," he wrote at the end, "that this is hardly the place for a meeting."

I skimmed through the letter, still standing. I had just come back from work, dead tired, sweating and dirty; my hands were trembling. But this letter had to be answered at once. It couldn't wait until Sunday. I sat down on my bed and wrote impetuous, passionate words on the paper.

So this meant that he was again nearby and there was a possibility of seeing him, but he didn't want to see me. He needn't have worried — I wasn't going to get in his way a second time without being asked. For me, of course, any place would have been a place for a meeting, if I could see the person again with whom I wanted to be united for the rest of my life, and whom I scarcely knew.

Do you think you're the only one sitting in that waiting room? Right now everybody is living provisionally. We're putting everything off: until the war is over ... or the Labor Service ... or until we've finished studying. But it may just be the purpose of this uncertainty and lack of a future that we should learn to fulfill the present. The one thing that is definitely past and will never return are the dreams of the romantics that require a rose arbor to be realized, a "place for a meeting." I would have needed nothing but your cry: come! But that unconditionally! However, I shall never pursue you again. At best I shall forget you.

*At best I shall forget you.* That's what I wrote in my fury, and not a word of concern about his health. I didn't think of it until the letter was in the mailbox and I was trotting back to the camp. But malaria could be fatal! He was having terrible fever attacks, and I wrote, *I shall forget you.* But what was the use? I thought. It's true. I've already begun to forget him and he'd better know it. What use is it to either of us if he loves someone that isn't me? Faithful. He thinks I'm faithful. Some people perhaps call it being faithful when one doesn't love anyone else. I can live without that sort of faithfulness.

I couldn't cry or they would have asked me right away what had happened. Sometimes the worst thing that can happen, I thought, is when nothing happens. And perhaps I was right, in spite of everything that happened later.

I was afraid of what Horst might answer. He could reproach me for not having thought of his condition, only of myself, and he would have been right. For not having tried to imagine the hell from which he had escaped, and that, burning up with fever, one needed a glass of water a lot more than the sight of one's sweetheart. And I would have to admit that I was an unrealistic romantic. More often than not one has only to turn a reproach against someone else in order to see an unvarnished portrait of oneself.

A mother would have written quite differently. I knew that Horst was still longing for the mother who had left him. Instead of rebelling jealously I should have tried to take her place, at least as long as he was ill and weak. Oh, if only he would write and hold it against me! But why should he write to me when I had decided to forget him? He was much too proud to impose himself on me. He would grit his teeth, or ... perhaps he wouldn't find that necessary because the dark flood of forgetfulness had already reached his heart too?

For three weeks I heard nothing, as I expected, and tried to persuade myself that it was for the best. I worked like mad so as to be so tired that I fell into bed at night like a stone. I neglected my appearance, I did everything contrarily, my hair darkened and became brittle, my hands were rough, I looked haggard. I became aware of the impression one makes on others when one hates oneself. The girls avoided me. They said I had become a "striver."

They spoke of nothing but the approaching harvest festival. The year before, according to some, it had been wild, and as had been the case then, it was again to be celebrated together with the boys who were constructing the autobahn. I was afraid of the festival. I would probably have to drink a lot so as not to attract attention with my dejection. I hoped it would help. Wasn't there something called abject misery? Perhaps I could stay home. But loneliness and silence frightened me almost more than confusion.

I wanted to make my decision at the last minute, so I got ready just like the others, only let them know casually that I had a splitting headache. One of the girls said, "I hope you're not getting a fever." And Hannelore threw in sarcastically, "That would just suit our chaste Helga. She despises our vulgar amusements and prefers to pine for her soul mate." From the way the others laughed I knew that they felt the same way about me. So my engagement wasn't an alibi any more, as it had been in my school days.

"Soul mate! I like that!" I said smartly. "Anyway, he's already been gone too long. You only live once!"

That was the way they thought, wasn't it? So why were they looking so shocked? "Well now, look here ..." Marietta started to speak, then stopped, at a loss. but Hannelore, who had just ridiculed me, said seriously, "Only once, and certainly too briefly. Have you heard about the saturation bombing of Hannover?"

She came from Hannover. None of us had thought of it. "Is your family there?" we asked, embarrassed. She shook her head. "But our house is. I always thought I'd go back to it some day. Oh well, skip it! You're going to get it too, in spite of St. Stephen's Cathedral and Schubert ..."

"And you're glad about that!" cried Marietta.

"It makes one feel better," said Hannelore.

Now the girls began to protest indignantly: What did she get out of it? Why did she hate our homeland? Did she want to see everything destroyed? Didn't she know that a lot of the arms industry had been moved here, so victory might quite possibly depend on our being spared?

"Look here!" said Hannelore. "What do you want from me? I'm not a magician who can wish or curse on cue! Let me think as I please! Whoever's having a bad time wants everybody else to have a bad time, and if our house burned to the ground I don't want to see others go on living in theirs!"

"*Pfui Teufel!*" cried Marietta. "That's mean! That's ... that's subhuman!" But I was staring in fascination at Hannelore's beautiful face, its merciless expression, and realized how much strength it took to be that honest.

"You're wrong," I told Marietta. "All of us feel just as Hannelore says when disaster strikes. Only we don't admit it. The opposite would be ..."

"Heroic!" one of the girls cried.

"No. Christian," I said softly.

I noticed a quick exchange of glances and heard a murmuring, "Oh ... so that's why ..." Later Hannelore came over to me.

"I certainly made an ass of myself," she admitted. "But sometimes I can't take it anymore — all these pious lies! I didn't mean to hurt your feelings. I didn't know you were religious."

"I'm not," I said hastily. "I only meant it ... theoretically."

"Religious people do that too," said Hannelore with a bitter smile. "I should know! My father was a pastor. But come now, we've got to get dressed."

If I hadn't gone with them they probably would have stared at each other again and said, "So that's why ... " Hannelore took a bottle out of her locker, had a quick drink herself, and handed it to me. "Drink." she said. "But don't betray me."

"What is it?"

"Homemade rye. For services rendered ..."

I tasted it. "It burns like fire."

"It's supposed to. That's what they expect of us today: fire. But now rinse your mouth." As I obeyed, she said, her back turned, "I guess that was bad news today."

"What are you talking about?"

"Your letter. Forgive me, but one can tell."

A letter? I tore to the front door. Just this one time I had forgotten to look in our mailbox, and the letter — army mail — was lying in it!

His retaliation, I thought. I guess I had wanted to put it off ...

"Girls! Fall in!"

I couldn't read the letter right then, and it wouldn't be possible in the bus or at the festival either. So ... quick! Just a look at the last sentence ... I still do that to this day when an important letter arrives. I start with the last sentence because it prepares one for everything else. I expected to read: Farewell ... or: think well of me ...

"Come on!" said Hannelore. "They're tooting like crazy. Is it very bad?"

"No ... not very."

I was staring at three words that were underlined: *"more than ever!"* My eyes took in the line before them, then I stuck the letter in my pocket. I walked down stairs that felt like cotton. Thank you, dear Lord, I thought. I shall never despair again. I shall never hate anyone as I hated myself before this letter came. I shall be patient, as you have been patient with me. Was I speaking to the dear Lord or to Horst? Oh, I believe in the *You* who recognizes and forgives and loves us even more because of our errors. That is God, the only God I know.

*"I want to forget you."* That was what I had written to Horst in the loneliness of his feverish nights, and he wrote back: *"I love you more than ever!"* And from the jubilation in my heart I realized how much I too loved him.

And then — the festival. It flows together in my memory with a very different event that Mother had often told us children about: her first ball. She could still describe her sea-green, low-necked dress, her white satin shoes, the flowers, the heat, the floating through a slightly smoky brilliance, and again and again she had told us about the rather stiff, dogged dancer who had made her laugh with his banal compliments, and whom she had liked so much, who with all his conventionality had had to turn up in this dreamlike atmosphere, never to leave her side again, our father. Only years later, after quite a few inner conflicts, had she become engaged to him. The First World War lay in between, the abrupt awakening to a brutal reality for which no one was prepared, least of all the young girl who saw the threshold to life in a ballroom. And still my mother had felt on that first night that everything had been decided that had to be revitalized later, happily or painstakingly.

Our youth was clearer and more sober; our relationships with young men more direct and practical. We were familiar with rough sport, honest comradeship, meaningless flirtations, and the grave, wordless seriousness of desire, but not with that charming interplay between a smiling and a merry denial, the indecisive balance between Always and Never.

But why, if this is so, do I always have to think simultaneously of the white washed, garishly lit hall of our inn, with its oiled brown-black floor, a picture of the Führer wreathed in oak leaves, a waiting huddle of boys, their hair cropped short; sunburnt, freshly washed girls with quick evaluating looks and ungroomed hands, whose white blouses broke away from their skirts when they danced ... and at the same time see the white-and-gold vaulted ballroom, wide, undulating voile skirts, snow-white arms, elaborate curls piled high, between the black-and-white penguins with monocles and mustaches, and hear myself ask, "Where do you come from?"

"From the Ötztal. Saw right off, didn't you, that I'm a yokel!"

"I was in the Pitztal often when I was a child. Do you ski?"

"Sure do! Wouldn't ha' got to school in the winter without skis."

"I'm sorry about my skis. We had to give them up."

"But when the war's over, there'll be new ones, an' you'll be comin' to us for winter sport, an' I'll take you up ... some place ... whadda you say?"

"We'll do just that, Sepp!"

"*Prost!*"

"Cheers!"

After the war ... Meanwhile you'll be sent to the front, I thought, and the bombs will fall on us too. And when it's over you'll stand watch somewhere in the Ukraine or on the island of Korcula or in Norway, or on a herring cutter, and have to see to it that they work properly, all the people we have "freed"...

Had I heard something to this effect? And from whom? From someone who "by mistake" had turned on a foreign radio station? From someone who confessed the thoughts of his sleepless nights: And what faces us if we do win? From the stepson of my peasant woman who had to work in a munitions factory. When he was free, he drank, and when he drank he talked and didn't always care with whom ...

And now, when my dance hall was like the one Mother had told us about so often with a nostalgic smile, "Because those times will never come again," it was probably because the same jubilation that had filled her then filled me now and took away all bitter presentiments of the future; the jubilation that there still was love, the age-old, highly praised love that had just penetrated the ground soil of my soul with a first green shoot. It will grow, it will blossom, for me too, and in me!

There was a pause in the music. There was sausage, beer, and sour wine. The windows were open. A warm, steady rain was falling outside. Marietta was sitting at the same table as we were, with a short, brunet boy. Both were wet. "The rain surprised us," she said casually. The boy seemed embarrassed. Didn't she have a jacket? She'd catch cold. "You'll just have to dance with me till I'm dry again," said Marietta, "Whether you like it or not!" She was laughing at him. "But I want to," he said, blushing slowly. With the first note she took him by the hand, "Come!"

"She's pretty sharp, isn't she?" Hannelore said sarcastically.

"Leave her alone. If it makes her happy ..."

"I'm afraid not for long."

"That doesn't matter!" I cried.

My Ötztal boy nodded, his chin resting on his hands. "It doesn't make any difference," he agreed, and began hesitantly to tell me about his girl at home and that his mother wanted no part of her because she was poor, and did I think she'd wait for him? And I said, "Yes. She'll wait. But you must write to her every week and tell her that you love her."

"Every week?" he cried, astounded. "I can't do that!"

We laughed and settled for once a month, then we danced again in a Ländler rhythm, sedately, in our clumsy shoes: nothing can happen to me anymore ... nothing can happen to me anymore ...

Suddenly there was a crowd: Marietta had collapsed. They stretched her out on a couple of chairs pushed together and put a wet handkerchief on her forehead. "It's only the dancing," she whispered. "Are you still there?" "Yes," said her partner, "I'm here. Just lie still." "My name is Marietta. Will you tell me your name?" "But you know my name." He leaned closer. "My name is Herbert ..."

That's all I heard. Then I remembered how desperate she had been when her letter had come back, and I had comforted her: "But surely he'll write to you!" and she had replied, "But he doesn't know my name!"

Uneasily I thought: this time she's going to do better. And now I could hear the sound of the rain louder, and the wind. I left my partner. "I'm sorry, but I'm tired ..."

For whom ... for whom have I written all this in so much detail! Did I just let myself be swept along, and in a sort of trance placed note beside note, picture beside picture, as they sounded, as they flickered by, while the hum of the cars outside subsided and the reflection of their headlights passed less and less often across the old prints? Was I the involuntary medium for the ghost of my departed self? The ghosts one summons have a way of confusing sense and nonsense, and weaving trivialities into the glamorous veil of the irrational.

But, my son, I have never lost sight of the one question that is of importance to you: how it all came to pass. And poor Marietta, like the fly that makes a lot of noise as soon as it notices it is stuck in the glue that smelled so good and so harmless, and gradually grows silent ... and one doesn't know: is it still enjoying the taste or is it dead? ... she is a part of it too. And so that you don't think I carelessly forget half the people I have taken such trouble to introduce you to: my partner from the Ötztal was killed in action a few weeks later. All this was in a letter Marietta received from her partner, and the sad news gave her the idea to get married *in absentia*. "Because," she said, "Why should the poor little thing have no legitimate name if my boy gets killed too?"

"Are you sure?" I asked, perplexed by so much practicality. She nodded, looking me boldly in the eye. "That's why I feel sick so often."

"Well then ... I hope your friend will want to."

"Oh, he will!"

She sounded very sure of herself, and she was right. They even gave him leave, I found out later, for the baptism. Soon after that he was disabled by a wound, allowed to resume his studies, worked hard, passed his exams quickly and became a pharmacist. His mother died, and his father took the couple. with their child, into his home, and gave them the apartment over the pharmacy. The child is your school friend, Friedel, the brother of Bert, who is in your class. Siegfried! A proper name, like every name given to a new human soul in a Christian baptism. Marietta remained quietly stuck on her fly paper and enjoyed it. I don't envy her. And you? Do you envy Friedel?

Of course you are not telling your son any of this. That was only a pretense to help you to begin, an expedient to start you talking. Because in your stupid arrogance you thought you knew all about yourself and didn't need anything like this, namely my couch, on which you could tell all. I know — you're too stingy for that. If necessary, then preferably the confessional. At least that costs nothing!

But I believe just as little in science as I do in the dear Lord. So I tell my story to the night, to the prints on the wall, to the great silence, and to you, lying in bed, probably dreaming of the last football game; and to Walter in America and to his wife, who envies me because of you. I want them too to know someday what really happened. But to recognize that, I have to summon everything I can find in my memory and express it, not only put it on paper, but really make it talk. Now, before continuing, I always read aloud to myself the pages I wrote the preceding night. Sometimes I go straight on writing, but frequently, like today ... how could I go on talking in such a wrong tone? Has Christianity, the semi-Christianity of our forefathers, impregnated us with cowardice to such an extent (Judge not that ye may not be judged!) that we only feign compassion? Poor Marietta! Instead of stamping my foot, which is what I felt like doing, and shouting, "Now at last you know why I don't want you to go there and let her feed you cookies, this person who was too much of a coward to acknowledge her child; who betrayed an hour of passionate love in a thousand embraces for the face value of an honorable name for the fruit of her sin; who after that one night in the bushes crept into the comfortable bourgeois bed of a secure existence, still with a sentimental eye on the past; placing in front of her husband's honorable name the dream name of her first lover, thus every time she speaks to the child, again betraying the man who isn't his father?"

Not to mention what she did to me. That comes later. Let's keep things chronological — one step at a time.

No, I can't take the next step. I must go back to the last one, which led onto a totally wrong track. Not only because it is out of the question to tell Gottfried all this about his friend. That would be the least of my worries because he'll never see these pages — not as they are, anyway; at best he'll read a digest. I realized that long ago. This whole story of Marietta, though, is nothing but a version, my version, and now that I see it in front of me, black and white, I realize that it need not necessarily be correct.

Have I the right to call calculation what was perhaps only utter despair? The clinging to a last straw that miraculously held? The burnt child remembered the name of her second lover, but could she have any idea where he came from, or that his parents were well-to-do? And why did I impute such knowledge to her? Because I begrudged her the fact that her frivolity, her lies, should go unpunished? Or did it rankle — which I would never have admitted — that she took the man who looked like my Horst, and in her way — yes, yes — gave birth to the son for whom I had wished in vain? Do I hate her for that? Oh dear heaven, then I'd do better to start off by venting my scorn on myself.

I am beginning to doubt if it is really possible to report *facts*. Perhaps it is always only *version*.

Today it sounds as if I had nothing on my mind but Marietta. However, in spite of the fact that all these incidents have remained clearly stored in my memory, they only became a continuous story when the connection between them was illuminated abruptly by something vile that happened, for which I could never find an explanation. At the same time I found Hannelore more interesting, but she soon disappeared from my life. And basically, like all very young people, I was concerned solely with myself.

I was glad to get home before Christmas. My own room, the prospect of at last facing life without a strict schedule for every day, the possibility of reading for hours, going to the theater, meeting people whom one wanted to see — it was almost too much freedom at once. And my parents too had reconciled themselves to the idea that I was now grownup. I no longer had to account for every hour spent outside the house.

My father was pleased with my decision to study history the following autumn, after I had put my stint in the armament industry behind me. One morning I woke up with the thought that one should study what one lacked most. I didn't want to learn what came easiest to me, but rather the subjects I found difficult: historical, economic and political relationships. I might just as well have decided to study music because I have no ear for music, but nobody brought that up. My father only wanted to know what had deflected me from my plan to be a doctor. I kept silent about the decisive reason — that the idea of bearing the responsibility for life and death frightened me; to judge which existence was "valuable" and therefore worth preserving. I mentioned the second reason: I didn't want a profession in which my mind would be constantly tied to the wretchedness of physical deterioration. During the last six months I had proved that I was capable of overcoming revulsion. But weren't there already more good doctors than competent interpreters of history, and the national economy, to say nothing of politicians? My father agreed happily; nothing would be more important after the war than worldwide economic and social planning. Never again should wheat be burnt or coffee dumped into the sea while elsewhere people were starving. How my father's gray, wrinkled face began to glow when there was talk of what would happen the day after tomorrow! We didn't touch upon what would have to take place tomorrow, or in between.

Horst was in Russia, had been for a long time. Weakened by malaria, he was not at the front yet, he wrote, to reassure me; he had administrative duties to discharge.

There may be no "impossible" when it comes to carrying out orders. Often the only truly impossible thing seems to be to get home! I try not to think of it, but I dream of it. Last night my neighbor woke me. "For God's sake, Ulbig, be quiet!" How can I be what I don't have in me to be? Forgive this feverish nonsense. I love you when I am myself. Keep me in your heart so that I may be somewhere.

I have the letter in front of me now, Gottfried. Today I can't read it without tears. At the time all I did was shake my head: I don't understand it. I was slightly annoyed that Horst seemed suddenly to be regressing into the plaintive sensibility of an artist, that he was mourning his precious "I" because the hardships and homelessness of a soldier's life no longer gave him the chance to read, to think of music, or — of me. I thought I understood him, I excused him, but I despised him a little too.

At the time I read the letter hastily; that may explain my lack of response. We were just leaving; Mother was waiting for me. "It's raining," she said. "Wear your old coat." She had taken it out of the closet and was holding it out to me. I slipped into it and put the letter in my pocket. On the street she was the one who said, "No, you really can't wear that coat anymore!" So the first chance we had, we sent it to Grandmother. She was always asking for discarded clothes for the Ukrainians in her village. She found the letter and kept it. One evening, five years later, she laid it down in front of me. "Didn't you ever read it?" she asked sternly.

I must have said something sharp about Horst, that he had "let me down," something to that effect. But as I read the letter again just now, I was horrified to feel my numbness, which had lasted for years, beginning to dissolve, to feel something akin to compassion ... But I didn't want to feel anything! Feeling meant suffering torture! I didn't want to waken from the anesthesia! I said brusquely, "I didn't understand any of it then."

"Put the letter away carefully," Uri told me. And I obeyed. I put it away so carefully that I have never laid eyes on it again until today. Because when I wanted to write that Horst had reported nothing from Russia during those last two winters, I remembered this letter and went to look for it. He wrote everything in it, and at last I am ready to understand him.

When we three children were still small, we spent a few weeks in the summer at the seaside with our parents. All I can remember are the sand castles and mounds my brothers built, and that sometimes I was allowed to help them. For the most part, though, I had to watch. "Let her play with you," Mother would say. But the boys would tell her, "We can't. She's too little! She'd ruin everything!"

Once they had made a big cone-shaped mound with wet sand, patted it smooth carefully, and hoisted my blue hair ribbon on a little stick as a flag. Now they wanted to dig a tunnel through it. Cautiously Albert's hand drew closer to Walter's. I watched, fascinated, and was the first to see the crack in the surface, and cried out triumphantly, "You're ruining it yourselves!"

"So come on," said Albert, drew out his hand and patted the mound firm again. "You try it. Slowly ... slowly! You'll be in the middle right away and touch Walter's hand ..."

I lay flat on my stomach, trembling with excitement. Warily I loosened the sand with my nails, holding my hand straight at the wrist, and then — really! The tips of my fingers touched Walter's! Careful! Now back ... slowly ... very slowly ... There! Walter pushed the little toy car into the opening. "And that's the Gotthard Tunnel," he said. I ran to Mother. "I just made the Gotthard Tunnel! I did! I did! We net in the middle! The mountain didn't crack!"

Today, when I woke up, it seemed to me that I was again crouched in front of the mound of sand, boring into it with my right hand, but with no brother to help me. I tried to dig my way in from the other side with my left, and thought ... how strange! This way I'll meet myself in the middle, and then Uri said, "You see, when you meet yourself — *that* is the present!"

And since we always feel that an intensive dream wants to teach us something, I am wondering now — perhaps it would really be better to dig toward the center of my life from both sides. But ... haven't I been doing that all along? I must dare to view the past with today's vision, which already knows the future of those days, and perhaps grasp it from today's viewpoint.

From today? I wrote the words so harmlessly ten days ago. But my "today" didn't begin until the following morning. Perhaps I felt it coming, but didn't know it yet. To be alone. What that means. Gottfried is gone. He has left me. He ran away.

From what?

I could bring him back but I don't dare. Am I too proud or too cowardly? Or is it that I can't ever do anything in life and must always let everything happen?

One thing I must admit: he spared me the greatest fear, that of uncertainty. Before I had a chance to be alarmed, Walter's telegram from Hamburg reached me: "Gottfried with me. Don't worry. Writing."

Walter had announced his business trip shortly before. His stay would be brief, but if the examination he was taking should be successful, he would be travelling through Europe for several weeks next winter, would bring his wife along and visit us. Gottfried seemed upset that his uncle was so lightheartedly postponing his visit for almost a year. At his age a year is a small eternity.

Gottfried's class was to spend a so-called country school week in the Burgenland. He protested vehemently when I offered to accompany him to the station. Did I want to carry his suitcase? I wasn't to disgrace him! "So I am not allowed to meet you when you come back either?" I joked dejectedly. "That's different," he replied, and I wondered why he blushed so deeply when he said it.

When I helped her to bed, Uri said, "Gottfried gave me a kiss. Is anything wrong with him?"

"He's gone away, Uri. He was saying good bye."

"Oh I see," she said, and was lost in thought. As I was going to leave her, she clung to my hand for a moment. "Don't take it too much to heart, Helga. He needs something like this."

I sighed. It was so tiresome to have to explain everything to her all over again. "Yes, yes," I said impatiently. "He'll be back in a week."

Later I found out that Gottfried had asked a colleague to tell his professor he couldn't go, he had a sprained foot. He must have taken the next train to Vienna and gone straight from there. He had a little money in his savings account; moreover, as it turned out, he had sold his bicycle a few days before. I thought it was in the repair shop. And instead of the postcard I had expected from the Burgenland, I received Walter's telegram. At first I was more astounded than angry. I ran to Uri with it. Whether she understood or not, I had to speak to somebody.

"The boy always did want to go to America," she said. That's when I was really startled and began to suspect what Walter would have to say in his letter.

"What can I do?" he wrote.

I like your son. He's too old for a whipping. If I buy him a ticket home he's quite likely to get out on the way and try the Foreign Legion, or something like it. He's not the kind to give in silently once his mind is set on a thing. "I must get away," he says. "I can't stand it any longer." "Is Mother so strict?" "No. Not at all." "Is she after you all the time?" "I wouldn't say that." In the end he explained: "Everything gets on my nerves — school, the small town, everybody knows your name and who are you ... and all they talk about is the past. I'm not at all interested in the past ..."

He wants me to take him with me for a year, Helga. "Your wife won't mind, will she?" he asked, and from the way he looked at me, I knew that you'd told him about us. "But your mother will mind a lot!" I said sternly. "She'll see that it's good for me, I know she will," he declared. And you said yourself not so long ago: a year is very short.

Yes, a year is short when it means waiting for Walter, whom I haven't
seen for thirteen years; then the fourteenth doesn't matter. But a whole
year without Gottfried? How is that going to pass?

"Dear Mu," he writes.

Please don't be angry with me. You have always said, if one really wants to
do something, one must do it. And I really want to go to America. I always
did. I am sure I will learn a lot there and will enjoy everything. Uncle Walter
is happy to take me with him, if only you will give your permission. Forgive
me for deceiving you. I didn't know what else to do! Please don't be angry
with me! Then I'm sure I'll be very happy (even if one day things go badly
for me.) Just think how well I will speak English afterwards.

So ... be happy, Gottfried, if you can't be happy here. I don't count.

Uri: "You mustn't talk like that, Helga! Much better if you'd cry your
heart out. Cry. Do cry. It hurts. Everything hurts the first time. When my
little boy died, I did nothing but cry for four weeks. Then it was over."

"Then you forgot him? But I don't want to forget Gottfried! And after
all, he's coming back!"

"Not forgotten. No. To this day not forgotten. I can still see what he
looks like. I had four children after him and don't know how any of them
looked when they were three months old. I can still see little Johann, see
him smiling. I haven't forgotten him. I have gotten over it. I have washed
away all the pain with my tears; my love I kept. Your teeth are clenched
and you feel sorry for yourself. That's not good!"

"I don't feel at all sorry for myself," I said, and left the room quickly.

But why must I give up everything? Everything! Always I! And what
will Marjorie think of me when my child runs away from me? And what
will the people here say? They'll bring up everything all over again ...
And that's what I'm crying about now ... or is it I who is crying about it?

Let oneself go. All right. I remained lying on my bed with my clothes
on, as I was. Then I heard how it began to splash against the overhang
and the wind whipped the branches of the nut tree against the window
and the rain for which the peasants had been waiting longingly began to
fall. And I thought: Gottfried won't be able to take his bicycle tomorrow
... Yes, I did. Although I was crying because he was gone. For just that
moment I forgot it. I wanted to forget, altogether forget it all! Just as one
crosses out a sum one has set up incorrectly and that can therefore never
come out right. Best of all — not to go on living. Not kill oneself. What a
strong will is needed for that! It would be easier to carry on or even to
start all over again. Only not to have to go along with everyday things
any more: undressing, washing, going to bed, getting dressed, cooking,
sweeping, deciding with Hilde what to eat, scolding, praising, smiling —
what for? For whom? Write to Walter. What? Why? Or visit them as he
suggests. I'm not seventeen any more, I don't run after anyone who
doesn't want to see me! Forgive Gottfried?

For months I had wished him out of my womb, out of my life. Now he *is* gone. God's mills grind slowly, the old people say. It was our mistake if in the meantime we believed we could experience a little happiness ...

Then I fell asleep. Crying makes one tired and one sleeps well when one has nothing planned. And when it's pouring outside.

Hilde looked in on me in the morning. "Don't you feel well? Aren't you going to get up?"

"No."

"Shall I go to your grandmother?"

"Of course," I said, and turned my face to the wall. "I don't need anything. Let me sleep."

But toward evening the old woman came, leaning on Hilde's arm, let her push the armchair up to my bed, sent the girl away, and sat besides me silently until I couldn't stand it any longer. "What do you want. Uri? Leave me alone. I'm finished."

"You have to start all over again," she replied calmly. The same words as at that time seventeen years ago. Doesn't she realize it?

"How often?" I asked scornfully. "The last time you persuaded me: I owe it to the child. I didn't count at all. Oh, you were smart! You said, 'Give birth to it and feed it for a few weeks. Then it can go on living without you, and I promise you I'll take it away and you won't see it again.' But with what are you going to persuade me now? Why should I go on this time?"

"You must consent. Give him courage, Helga. Let him go!"

I laughed aloud. Uri sat there, snuffed out, and begged, "Take me back to bed. I'm tired."

I called for Hilde.

"I told her to go to the movies," said Uri. "It's her afternoon off."

If I didn't want the old woman to go on sitting there or go upstairs alone and perhaps fall, I had to get up. "You're horrid!" I said. "Are things going to go on and on like this? What for? Why? I've done everything wrong."

"So have I," said Uri. "But I'm over eighty, and that's worse."

I took her to bed. I went to the pantry and got her juice for the night, and I already knew that when she was asleep I would go up to the attic, look for a carton, gather Gottfried's things together and get the package ready for mailing. I would also write a note for Hilde, telling her what to do next morning. I was filled with a terrible resentment, and before I put out the light in Uri's room, I turned around and asked, "Why can't you leave me in peace?"

Then something frightful happened. Her aged features became jumbled, like those of a whimpering child, and with her toothless mouth the ancient woman stammered, "I can't stand your going the way your mother went ... not as long as I'm alive, I beg of you, Helga ..."

I knelt down beside her and stroked her hand and promised her, "I won't. Be calm, Uri. I certainly won't."

Then I pulled myself together and spoke about ordinary things, and after a while I asked her, "Will you be able to sleep now?" But she replied, "If you don't mind, read something to me. Only a few lines ..."

"Goethe," I said, with a sigh, because I knew she liked nothing better. She nodded.

I took the volume, *Conversations with Eckermann*, and opened it where there was a bookmark, One paragraph was underlined. I glanced at it briefly and hesitated, because Uri rarely spoke of death. "Go on, read it," she said. "I feel exactly as he does about it."

So I read:

"When one is seventy-five years old," he continued with great serenity, "it is impossible not to think of death on occasion. This thought leaves me completely unperturbed, for I have the firm conviction that our spirit is of a totally indestructible nature. It is something that continues to operate from aeon to aeon, similar to the sun which seems to set only to our earthly eyes, whereas in reality it never sets but dispenses light without cease ..."

"Amen!" said Uri. "Thank you. And now you sleep well too, my child."

I have the feeling that none of this is right. Because our conversation yesterday wasn't like this at all. And the only reason I wrote it down the same night, after making the package and addressing it, was not to let the night, not to let sleep falsify anything. To put everything down on paper right away. If I have to submit to my other duties again, then certainly to this one too — to go on writing. To go on hollowing out the tunnel with my other hand and from the other side ... But it isn't possible for Uri to speak at such length! She only intimated it all with a few words and often lost the thread, just as she didn't differentiate between her promise to take the child from me as soon as it didn't need me any more, and Gottfried's running away. Yes ... I tossed my accusations at her without any consideration for her frailty. But *did* she discuss it with me as consistently as this "record" seems to attest? Did she at least say, "The way your mother went," that being what really matters? Not even that! She mumbled ... "Not like Hedwig ... I can't stand it anymore," and in the middle of a sentence called my father by his first name and wanted to make it clear to him: "That was why I wanted to prevent you from marrying her! Because she wants to be blind ... she would rather tear her eyes out ..." And I, in my zeal to render everything so that a third person could understand it, again make it sound like a school composition. Should I have tried to capture every word as on a tape recording? Even then the decisive thing wouldn't have been preserved. That penetrated suddenly when her features became distorted so that I finally grasped: My God, she loves me! There is a living creature at my side who loves me!

What next? It sounds self-evident: now I take care of her. She saw me through when my parents left me in the lurch. Since then I have been her child. I know that, don't I? But I never understood it. Moreover, I did not return her love.

Was it yesterday or a long time ago that I replied in distressed embarrassment to a confession that sounded absolutely unbelievable to me: "But Grandmother ... aren't there many kinds of love?" I hoped that now she would begin to retreat, but no. She said quite frankly, "I know of only *one* feeling that deserves the name. Because lukewarm love is no love at all, Helga." I was irritated. Did she know something about which I knew nothing? And why did she speak about it? It was unseemly, almost repulsive. A good thing that my parents had no inkling of it!

I am supposed to let him go whom I want to keep, but the one whom I could easily let go (because wouldn't it be only natural if she went?) clings to me now, needs me like the air to breathe, loves me.

When I think how unconcerned I was when I began to write, with the intention not to leave out anything important! It seemed only to be a question of honesty. Now sometimes it seems that the only way toward this goal is not to leave out anything *un*important. Because what is really "important" will only become evident at the end. And that can take quite some time, and gives me a new purpose in life: to write my memoirs. I obey, invisible Master Soul-Saver! I am lying on the couch, letting myself go.

"Your laughter didn't sound right." A director would have said, "Try it again, Frau Wegscheider. More restrained. More dignified. That was 'cheesy.' " Well, yes. What did you expect? Compulsive behavior, Mister Diabolus, shatterer of souls! Longing, exhibitionism, a passion for meaning, a search for meaning ... Pretty thin, the whole thing. Perhaps a little watering down, if you don't mind, with some 'spirits'? It helped once, didn't it?

That was a good idea. After the third glass I managed to write a letter to Walter, three lines to Gottfried. I ask Walter what he needs for the boy. He should take him along, by all means. He must have a reason for running away. Probably connected with the past which doesn't "interest" him and which I force upon him inescapably by my presence. "Until now he knows only what is in his papers, Walter, but if you think it's right, tell him the truth. I meant to do so long ago" (With which all that I have written here would be superfluous!) To Gottfried I send only greetings and kisses and he should remain a good boy. Is he still a good boy? How should I know?

Why am I writing all this?

Because I fear that one can't live without an opposite. One must be able to grasp a hand in the center of darkness, even if it is only one's own.

On February first I began my stint in a munitions factory. That suited me because the depressive atmosphere at home, after my first sighs of relief, soon made any unconstrained enjoyment of my new freedom impossible. We knew Albert was near Stalingrad. Since Christmas there had been no mail from him. Even from the official news reports one could gather that a whole army was being encircled there and in the end would be rubbed out. Reports of hideous details came over enemy broadcasts. And some wounded had been flown back from the front and described what was going on there. A catastrophe of such proportion cannot be kept secret even in a reign of terror.

My new work wasn't difficult; all it demanded was good eyesight, a little dexterity and attentiveness. After the rigors of labor service, it seemed child's play to me, so that I didn't grasp why the other women — mainly older housewives — complained about it. The most disagreeable part was the long daily ride in a cold, crowded streetcar. Long pants and woolen socks couldn't prevent you from freezing. The windows were painted blue. I am surprised to this day that I didn't ruin my eyes forever, because whenever possible, I tried to read. In those days I read in every spare moment — besides the books on history which Father suggested, many of my parents' books which hadn't interested me before because I'd considered them dated. Now I discovered how much period color, even critique of the times, was contained in so-called beautiful literature (which at that time usually was really beautiful) often, perhaps, without the author's intention. That this could especially be applied to Albert's favorite poet, timeless Adalbert Stifter, I found out later. I couldn't get through *Nachsommer*. Only years later did I become exceptionally fond of this dream picture of an unscathed world, which probably never existed.

In the spring, Uri came to stay with us a second time, for a few weeks. Medical checkups had become necessary, she explained. I had the feeling that either she was seriously ill or had good reason for once more keeping out of sight of the party functionaries. I didn't ask her. Whenever possible I tried to avoid all concrete information. Hadn't I even managed to keep from inquiring about Resi and her child? In any case, I can't remember doing so. My whole spirit was filled with the exertion of gaining what I called a "historical perspective." So I tried to convince my father that this Austria, for which he was still grieving, had only been a short intermezzo. My father, on the other hand, spoke of cultural groups, of the proven strength of conquered nations to make their own imprint ...

Formerly Father had conversed like this with Albert. I did my best to take his place. Our statements always remained theoretical; we did not speak about the ruling system. In the middle of the war nothing could be changed anyway.

Only once I asked him if it wasn't really the duty of his church to protest against evident injustices. He referred excitedly to the opposition of the Bishop of Münster against the killing of the mentally disturbed and incurably ill. But it was just this protest that had failed to convince me.

Although I didn't want to be responsible for such decisions as a doctor, this was only because the criteria for what deserved to live still seemed so vague. I considered eugenics necessary, and felt that the Church had no right to force its teaching of the meaning of suffering on a nation that for the most part was no longer Christian. I was surprised, and still am, that the Church had the courage to demand that incurably crippled children be raised, and to brand abortion as a crime, when at the same time it tolerated the war. My father, however, seemed to find this perfectly all right. Religion, I told myself, was evidently his last illusion.

Grandmother didn't take part in such conversations. I knew that she might be thinking differently but certainly felt as I did. I looked often at her serene face, so thin, and was afraid that she might die soon. Then I would be all alone ...

Nor did she come to my aid in an hour I shall never forget. I had realized at once that something inconceivable had taken place: that behind this seeming senselessness a hindsight was hidden, perhaps the solution to the riddle. But I let them talk me out of it.

I was walking on the right side of Währingerstrasse. The sun was shining, the spires of the Votivkirche stabbed into the deep blue sky. A few days before I had been at the Burgtheater with Father, to see Goethe's *Iphigenia*. We had walked home and now, in the same place on the street, I began to reflect that whereas Hauptmann's Iphigenia was a girl like myself, Goethe's priestess lived in another world, in the world of the gods. And even today we expect a priest to be rooted in a certainty that is denied us. Wasn't something like this perceptible even in young Clemens? The priestess is beyond time. Yet some of her words have an immediacy that may still touch us when the words of the other Iphigenia have long since faded away.

"It is he! Shall I refer to the resemblance to our father, to the inner exultation of my heart as witness to the assurance ..."

I could feel that someone was looking at me. I had probably murmured the verse half-aloud, as I often did in my school days, and with which I made a slightly disturbing impression. But the man coming toward me wasn't looking at me at all. I stopped dead, as one says; thunderstruck. No. Because thunder couldn't have paralyzed me so completely — this was lightning itself. The lightning of recognition. My heart had skipped a beat; now it was fluttering wildly. Because coming toward me, only two steps away now, was my brother Walter. It couldn't be he, but it was.

He was in civilian clothes, dressed very well, almost elegantly. He was wearing a hat. I had never seen Walter wearing a hat.

"Walter!" I cried. He didn't react. Now he had already passed me. I turned around. It seemed to me that he was walking faster. I caught up with him, grasped his arm. "Walter!"

He turned to face me, gave me a piercing look, a strange, icy look, and said in a hoarse voice. "I beg your pardon. You are mistaken," doffed his hat briefly and walked on.

"Pardon me," I echoed, and pretended to be looking at a photographer's showcase. I saw mirrored in the glass how the man moved off calmly, walking more slowly again. I made sure that no one had witnessed the incident. So it was true — there was such a thing as a double. I couldn't believe it.

I walk into the dining room. Mother is sitting on the window seat, sewing. I suppose I should spare her, but I can't, and cry breathlessly, "I saw Walter!"

She lets her work sink onto her hap. Her lips are trembling. "Where is he?" she stammers.

"He walked away! He didn't recognize me!" And I am immediately aware of the absurdity of the statement. "Or didn't want to know me!"

My mother tries to get up but has to sit down again right away. "So tell me ... how does he look?" And then, sadly, "But that can't be ... that he didn't know you ... and that he's wearing civilian clothes ... Then he must have ..."

"Deserted!" I finish for her, and not until the word is out do I realize clearly what it means.

"That isn't possible," Mother says firmly. "Don't tell Father anything about it. It would only excite him."

But then, at dinner, she brought it up herself. She couldn't keep silent about it any more than I could. "Helga met a man who looked exactly like Walter."

My father said, without looking up from his plate. "Yes. There are resemblances like that."

"But it *was* he!" I cried angrily.

He flew at me. "Have you gone crazy? If Walter ... was here, don't you think he would have come to us? Or would at least have called? Just think what you're saying and have a little consideration for your poor mother ..."

I looked at my grandmother helplessly. She had put down her knife and fork and was looking sharply from one to the other. Now she asked quietly, "What was he wearing?"

"A gray coat and a hat. Civilian clothes."

"And did you speak to him?"

"Yes ... no, not really. I grabbed his arm ..."

"And he?" Father asked quickly.

I repeated what Walter had said, Father emitted a profound sigh. "Forget the incident, Helga," he said, not angry any more. "There are such resemblances. Our Walter is dead."

"You mean missing," Grandmother corrected him.

"No. Dead," said Father. "I just wanted ... I didn't want to rob Mother of her last hope."

Mother sat perfectly still, looking down at her plate as if none of this concerned her, as if she were far away from all of us.

I burst into tears and ran into my room. I lay down on my bed. They left me alone for a long time. Much later Grandmother came with a cup of tea. She made me drink some of it. I was very thirsty from crying. "Why was I so overjoyed?" I murmured, because this astonished me more than anything else — my overwhelming joy at the moment of recognition. "The inner exultation of the heart" ... There wasn't a more precise way of expressing it.

Grandmother sat down on the edge of the bed and stroked me. "Joy is never for nothing, Helga," she said, to console me.

Dark words. Did she mean that one had to pay for every joy? Or that we didn't need any special reason for our joy and should therefore not complain that we had rejoiced without reason? I went on brooding: had the verse about recognition come to me when I had already set eyes on Walter, and had I recognized him only in this roundabout way — *thought* I had recognized him? Had I tried to conjure him up in order to have a reason for my exultation? But then why Walter, while I was imagining Orestes? In that case I should rather have been thinking of Albert. The stranger, though, had looked like Walter, no doubt about it. Only his voice had been unfamiliar.

Now all I could do was rack my brains: how could I possibly have been so mistaken? Any dog would have been smarter. An animal will perhaps let itself be forced to do what it doesn't want to do, but it can still tell a real bone from a sham. No man can talk a dog our of his master when he meets him.

Oh Gottfried, believe yourself more than the others!

Perhaps that's why you ran away, because you're sick and tired of evasive explanations. Still, I didn't lie to you as my parents lied to me ...

No? Didn't I? What have I been doing all this time?

That's something else again.

Yes, indeed — it's always something else yet always the same. I can understand you so well. You would like to live as if the world were just beginning with you; you want to find out everything for yourself. Is that why you ran away? Instead of stopping, standing still and facing things? What I am doing here ... trying to do? Standing still in the middle of the flight into tomorrow and letting yesterday approach me. Perhaps then it will turn out to be harmless, like Uri's lion. All of us feel the hot breath of the pursuer on our necks, the reality emanating from everything realized in the world. The evil that must ceaselessly procreate evil is after us, and the faster we flee, the more likely it is to catch up with us. But the good thing always stands there, arms open wide, and demands silently: Stop. Stand still. Look around you. The lion pursues you only so long as you flee from him. Turn around! Let him eat you! That's the worst thing that can happen to you!

Am I saying this to my child? I am saying it to myself. If I hadn't run, he wouldn't have run away ...

Where are you now, my son? Yesterday you smiled at me as if I had never cursed you, never hated you; as if I had conceived you with love, borne you in hope and swaddled you with concern, and hadn't counted the days I still had to have you with me until Uri kept her promise and took you away to a children's home or to a strange woman. She had promised not to tell me where. She was never going to remind me of you. Only one more week left of the six I had to feed you. My breast was slightly inflamed and you hurt me every time I nursed you. I didn't take care of you, Uri didn't ask me to. She attended to that herself. I didn't watch her do it. I was to nurse you only for six weeks; we had agreed upon that. Then I was to be free again. I intended to find work in the city, among strangers who knew nothing about me. In this way I could perhaps forget. Because what remains without consequences seems never to have happened.

After I fed you for twenty minutes, Uri always came to take you from me. Then she would hold you up straight as she carried you out of the room so that you could burp and wouldn't become colicky. Today she didn't come on time; something must have delayed her. You let go of me and were almost asleep. I sat up and patted your back a little, the way she always did. You opened your eyes again slowly, and then, suddenly, your face lit up. You beamed at me. "No!" I cried. "No!"

I put you down on the bed hastily and buried my face in the covers. I didn't hear Uri come in. She grasped me firmly by the shoulders. "Helga! Stop! Tell me what happened!" I burst out with, "He smiled at me!"

Uri said drily, "I don't believe it. He's too young for that. Sometimes he makes faces when he's asleep, probably if something's pinching him."

"Hasn't he ever smiled at you?"

"No, Helga. I just told you — he's too little."

I bent over the child. He was pale and sleeping peacefully. He wasn't pretty. He looked like a little monkey — low forehead, broad nose. His little face twitched. "You see?" said Uri, who was watching us. "Something's bothering him. Have you burped him?"

Hadn't I gone through all this before? "There are resemblances like that" ... "Walter is dead" ... Now they want to fool me again. But I know: my boy looked at me, he smiled at me: Do what you like with me — I know that you love me.

Is that loving? This fear, this torture, and the promise: I will protect you. I don't want to love you but now it has happened. I won't give you away.

Colic ... he makes faces ... he's still too young. Am I going to believe the others again? "You're lying!" I cried. "You're lying. But I'm not going to give him away!" And I carried you to the table and changed your diapers, and Uri stood beside me and helped me without saying a word. Since then you were my child.

Did Uri achieve what she wanted? Did she get it with old wives' wisdom and artifice? Probably. But in the evening she said very seriously, "Now think it over once more, clearly and soberly. I could find a good place for the child; he would be treated well there."

"Where?"

"I won't tell you where. If you give him away, it must be forever. The other woman wants to adopt him."

"But he's my child, and I'm not giving him away!" I said.

Uri spared me nothing. "Why not?" she asked gravely. "All of a sudden? Because he smiled? Every child does that when it's six or seven weeks old."

"Because I love him!" I said.

She kissed me hastily, blew her nose hard and said, "Then everything's all right, Helga. Because I love him too."

All that happened yesterday, it seems to me. And now you are gone and don't want to know anything about the past! But since that day I have lived for you. What am I to do now? Why am I still here? To finish knitting my stocking? For all I care ... one's got to do something.

I didn't get around to writing for a few days. Uri worries me. She doesn't want to get up anymore. She says she's too tired. There is no reason why she couldn't stay in bed except that in older people this is dangerous because of their lungs. Besides, she seems somewhat confused, she can't keep time and names apart. "Has Theo written to you?" she asks, and of course means Gottfried, not my father. And I don't know: should I correct her or let it pass? And she doesn't want to be alone anymore. "Do you have to cook now?" she asked once when I got up. She sounded fearful.

"No, no. Hilde attends to that. I'm only going to get the bills." And then I cleaned all the silver, sitting beside her, the things we brought from Vienna when we gave up the apartment. They carried away everything Uri had, the time she came to the city to get me. "The Russians!" people said. But there were others who knew it wasn't the Russians. "Go and have a look over there ... and there ..." We didn't go and look.

"Are you still writing down everything?" she asked suddenly, as I sat working silently beside her, and when I said yes, she asked, "How far have you got?" I conceded that the time elements had become a little confused. "That doesn't matter," she said. "If you can only hold onto everything. I forget such a lot of things now. It's a pity. How happy one was often, and how discouraged! And then the snow comes and covers everything. Have you written about Janosh and Vicky and little Johann? It all hangs together, one just doesn't know how. Janosh planted the apple tree on Johann's birthday. Are there any apples left?"

"Yes, Uri. Do you want me to get you one?"

"Not now. Now you must write. The girls were really pretty, pretty but stupid. And you must write about Alphonse. make a note of it: Alphonse Pêret. I loved him, and he loved me too."

"I could never understand that," I said obstinately.

"I couldn't either," she said smiling. "But what does one understand anyway? After all, you did know him ..."

She stopped speaking, she smiled, she was asleep. Can I write down what the old woman is dreaming? I'll try. It is not a story for Gottfried, but I've known for some time now — the whole thing isn't a story for Gottfried. And anyway, he's not here anymore ...

I lived a part of Uri's story with her without being aware of it. In the summer of 1943 it was easy; the following summer it took some effort on my part to look away.

Now, after leafing back and reading everything again, I understand why I have placed these three events, between which so much time elapsed, side by side: all of them belong in the same area of experience. As in a fairy tale, I seem to have had to pass three tests, and the last, finally, my Gottfried, I passed! I recognized your trusting smile and succumbed to it. I let them talk me out of my living brother when all of them banded against me and "personal observation," I was even too cowardly to stand my ground against my brother himself who had said, "No!" And I didn't want to believe Uri's story: that can't be! I must be mistaken! So ... look away with a clear conscience, for of what concern was all this to me? I almost became angry when she asked harmlessly, "But you must know! After all, weren't you there?"

The whole business though didn't suit me at all. It didn't fit in with my view of the world which was still romantic-idealistic. We never welcome a disappointment because the truth always seems to be an inferior exchange for an illusion. To rejoice over the disillusion — that would be wise. But one grows wise against one's will, especially if one is a woman

Uri left us after this second visit with various doctors' reports, all of them good, but she seemed tired and enervated. We urged her to avoid heavy physical work when she got home, but she said, "On the contrary. The vegetable garden is waiting for me."

"And your Frenchmen?" Father asked. "I suppose they just get fed."

"No, they don't," she replied. "They behave very well. After all, they have to do the men's work."

As she got into the train she invited me for the summer and I accepted the invitation gladly. I waved to her, my grandmother, this forthright old woman who, I believed, could understand me. But I hadn't sought any opportunity to find out and didn't know if she had been waiting for it.

Shortly after her departure we heard from Albert at last. He had escaped from the inferno at the last moment and was in an army hospital with severe frostbite. "Don't worry, they'll patch me up again," he wrote. That wasn't Albert's way of expressing himself; it sounded bitter. But he had survived and still had all four limbs.

My parents' spirits rose. They completely overlooked what Albert had scribbled at the end of the letter: "What's Clemens up to? Be sure to let me know." And when I asked once, "Haven't you heard anything from Clemens Schindler? Albert seems worried about him," they avoided a direct answer: they didn't know anything definite. He was supposed to have left Vienna long ago. But to Albert Mother wrote, "Clemens is all right." So apparently I was the one from whom something was to be kept. That was all right with me.

I still find it difficult to ask questions, and it isn't always cowardice; sometimes it is discretion. Confidences that don't concern one are embarrassing for both parties. Children pressed too hard with questions involuntarily become liars. Their talents need the obscurity of semiconsciousness to mature. As a child one already senses and feels everything but one isn't capable of evaluating and deciding. Since I knew this so well from my own experience, I wanted to preserve this protection of an unconscious dawning for Gottfried as long as possible. Now, with his flight, he has placed my whole life in doubt, perhaps because this need only to be there for him was nothing but a highly questionable alibi.

What should I have done?

Accused! You are not here to ask questions; you are here to justify yourself. Take advantage of the respite. It is still your turn. But the present is cutting you short. I can feel the hand approaching from the other side of the tunnel. The future impinges upon the past. *Death has entered.*

That these words should present such a trite picture ... Can't one express it more precisely, more briefly, in a soberer fashion? Evidently not. The myth becomes a scientific statement. The circle of experience is closed. (Yesterday I read a newspaper report on a native African language that distinguishes the present from the past and future. For these people past and future are the same thing, the Not-now. Perhaps they know better than we that he who has no past, who doesn't incorporate his past into the present, doesn't drag it along with him — isn't that the way to put it? — that he has also thrown away his future? Do you hear me, Gottfried?)

This morning, when I entered her room with her breakfast tray, Uri asked in a hoarse voice, "Tell me, Helga, are the dandelions out yet?"

I was glad. She was feeling better. I opened the window, let in the fresh morning air, the bird sounds. Only the day before yesterday she had said, "Winter is snowing everything under!" Today she senses it again, that it is summer. "Yes, Uri, the dandelions should be blooming."

Do you remember, Gottfried, how you got ten groschen from her when you were a little boy for every fifty dandelion heads you picked? Because she didn't want the weeds to multiply and ruin the hay. That was when you earned your first money. Was Uri thinking of it when she asked me now, "Go pick a few for me. I like the color so much."

I was surprised. She loved only roses. I had had to fight for room for my irises, phlox, asters, hollyhocks, carnations and zinnias because she thought: roses are perfect. Why bother with anything inferior? And now I was to place these weeds beside her bed? Dandelions?

Perhaps it was only a pretext to send me outdoors. She might have noticed that since you went away I have scarcely left the house. She is quite right: no reporters are crowding against our fence to find out why my son ran away from me.

I have written a short, polite note to the school principal, asking him for a money order for the rest of the tuition payment. His German teacher, his gym teacher ... when they meet me on the street they'll stop and ask, all sympathy, how you are; and I shall reply, "Wonderful! My brother is taking him to America. We had planned it anyway, but he was supposed to finish his term first ..." So why this fear of every encounter, every question? Probably because I don't want my sore spot to be touched.

Are the dandelions in bloom? What ideas old people have!

I closed the gate of the vegetable garden and walked out onto the big meadow with the apple trees, on which the last tired pink-white blossoms hung between the light green leaves. But the grass was spattered with yellow dandelions. The bees love them. I walked carefully along the edge so as not to step on the grass. To our Herr Stadler the quality of the hay doesn't seem as important as it used to be to Uri. The transparent, dust-colored seed balls are already standing between the short, deep yellow blossoms. The sun burns on my neck. Cabbage and brimstone butterflies weave through the shimmering air. From far off the call of the cuckoo, and I almost count them as I used to do with you: fourteen, eighteen, twenty years more ... Well, of course, I have to live until Gottfried is grownup, has a profession, perhaps a wife ... innumerable years the cuckoo calls for me. Again today. Why? Uri needs me. A new, threadbare alibi.

"Here are the flowers. It's lovely outside. Perhaps I'll take you out to the summer house this afternoon with Hilde." She looked at me, looked at the flowers, astonished. "You wanted some dandelions, Uri, didn't you?"

"Oh yes," she said. "But don't forget Clemens."

"Clemens? What do you mean?"

"The poor fellow ... and my little Johann. Write everything down, Helga. I've forgotten so much. Sometimes I'm afraid I won't recognize them anymore ... It all happened so long ago."

One look at her sunken, yellow face told me that I mustn't contradict or question. "Yes, yes," I said soothingly, as if talking to a child. "Don't worry about it. I'll write down everything." But inwardly I rebelled. The manuscript is already much too thick, and I know about Uri's life only from hearsay, and what I know about it doesn't coincide with what I saw. I never did see through it. What does it all have to do with me, Gottfried? But Uri repeated, her eyes closed, "Tell the whole story. With all the names. Don't forget the names ...

"Every night he runs after me ... You see, Helga, he has come back ... he runs after me ... then I call out a name to him and he sniffs at it ... In the meantime I am behind the next door ... if only I don't run out of names before I am safe ... I don't know anymore ... Helga, quick! Read them aloud to me ..."

She was panting. I hurried to her and held her fast. She looked through me, horrified, and clung to my arm. "Nobody is pursuing you, Uri. There's nobody here."

Her gaze reverted to me. It fell on the dandelions. "Alphonse!" she said, and looked relieved. Her hands let go of me, her eyelids drooped, covered her eyes. Gently I laid her back on her pillow.

She slept to her death. It didn't last long. She slept for an hour, maybe two. Her breathing became more and more labored, then her heart stopped, like a clock, at the same time her eyes opened wide as if in great astonishment. "Grandmama," I whispered. "It's me. I am with you." But she was already gone. And I could hear the cuckoo still calling outside.

I don't understand her last dream. It seems to me that she wanted to tell me something quite different, but in her fear she broke through language as through a mirror. There was nothing left but splinters ... no picture ...

Oh, if I could have prayed then! Perhaps then the splinters would gradually have fitted themselves together again, so that I could see what she wanted to show me. But if I could pray, I wouldn't write.

In the summer of 1943 my parents found I wasn't looking well and welcomed Grandmother's invitation. She made my visit possible by requesting my assistance for harvest duty. She invited my parents as well, but my father wanted to spend his vacation on the Alpine farm as usual. As a child I had spent a few summers on Grandmother's farm, but my father had never joined us. He found it too painful to see all the changes that had taken place since his youth. He admired the fact that his mother had managed to adjust to the changing times, but didn't want to be witness to it. The boys had grown up there like princes, each had had his own horse, they had hunted with their father since childhood; reading, writing and arithmetic had been nothing but a sideline. At the age of fourteen they had gone to boarding school — Hans, the oldest, first; my father a year later. In the winter my grandfather shot himself while cleaning his rifle. Naturally it was an accident; I don't think anyone doubted it, in spite of the enormous debts he left behind and although it gradually leaked out that he had tried in vain to make up for them by gambling.

Grandmother was left with four children. Cautiously and discreetly she began to sell one piece of property after the other. What should they have lived on otherwise? Poor little Johann, over whom she had wept so passionately, was followed by the two boys — first Hans (my grandfather had insisted that his name be passed on), then Theo, my father, and three years later, Aunt Vicky, who committed suicide when she was twenty because of an unhappy love affair, in a very romantic fashion. Still, she was dead, poor thing. This did not prevent her fiancé, who had turned his attention to the daughter of a rich industrialist after a thorough check of her dowry, from marrying the girl. "My poor Vicky!" Whenever Uri said it she seemed to be mourning her daughter's limited intellect rather than her sad fate. Uncle Hans became an officer. He was killed in 1916 at the battle of Isonzo. So of her five children, Uri kept only two — my father and the youngest, my Aunt Mimi, who when she was in her twenties married a wealthy Canadian owner of a sawmill, and since then lived with him, childless, in the northern wilds. After the war she sent packages regularly, but for a long time now had been writing only at Christmas: they were well, she hoped we were too, and if we needed anything, we were to write. We sent pictures of Gottfried and also wished her a Merry Christmas and a Happy New Year. God preserve the peace!

"Wouldn't you like to see Aunt Mimi again? Why don't you invite them? Maybe they'll come over," I suggested once, but Uri rejected the idea, almost startled. "We never understood each other."

"Don't look so shocked, Helga! It happens often that old parents have nothing more to say to their children who grew up long ago. Of course, if I lived in a little old palais in the inner city, surrounded by Biedermeier furniture and Waldmüller pictures, and elegant people came to see me, then I would have to invite them because then she could impress her Ted." Suddenly her voice was soft. "She was an adorable little girl. Everybody liked her. And she wanted to listen to fairy tales all the time. Did I tell the children too many fairy tales? She was like Janosh's mother, who was a beautiful woman, really someone to admire and cherish, as women in those days were supposed to be. But we, Helga child, unfortunately seem to be the women of tomorrow, and there's nothing we can do about it. But sometimes we have to disguise ourselves a little because, you know, men like a dream ..."

"I know," I said.

I have written all this by the light of the seven tall white candles I have placed at the head of the dead woman. She is lying on her bed. I have covered her because of the flies. I don't want to leave her alone tonight. The peasants, the poor — they never leave their dead alone, not the dead, not the newborn. Both are too close to the edge of the great sea. I can never do anything for Uri any more, so I want to watch over her body tonight. Perhaps, if she is lying beside me, I won't write anything completely false about her.

But it just occurred to me that I must compose the text for her obituary. So I went and got her papers, which have been in my desk for a long time. It is odd that we have no first name for Mother and Father, even less for Grandmother and Grandfather. It sounds very strange: Anna Katharina Wegscheider, née Kirchner ... died suddenly and unexpectedly at the age of eighty-five. Unexpectedly? At that age? people will say. But that's the way it is — the thing that has been expected for a long time surprises us most. I really should add Aunt Mimi's name to the bottom, but she doesn't know anything about it. I haven't even sent her a cable! That occurs to me only now. I should have sent Walter one too, but I intentionally didn't do so because if everything goes according to the plan, he'll be leaving with Gottfried tomorrow. I don't want to see Gottfried standing beside Uri's grave and then leaving with Walter. That would be more than I could bear. Now that they have left me alone, we can manage without them, right?

Strange that I can't wholly realize that a dead woman is lying beside me. I don't feel any different than if I were alone. In some countries people believe that during the first hours and days the souls of the dead remain close to the body they left behind; that is why one should change nothing in the room, nor give away their clothes. I am in no hurry to do either. I am glad to push all thoughts away as to what must happen next, because once I have settled everything, there will be no reason for me to go on living here, nor will I be able to afford it. But this is something I want to think of in the daytime. Candlelight is much more suited to illuminate the past than the future.

So what do I still know about my stay during that hot summer? I remember the first night, the pleasant awakening in the morning — nothing planned, no factory to go to, no air-raid drill, no standing in line for food. The sun stood high in the heavens when I woke up, and it smelled of hay because the grass in front of the house had been mowed the day before. Grandmother had insisted that I sleep a lot. The big kitchen downstairs was clean and empty. Old Frieda was clomping across the courtyard. She took off her wooden shoes and put down two heavy cans. My breakfast was ready on the terrace for me, she said. How long was it since I had been given milk to drink? And there was even some butter with the bread, and a little pot of honey. "Land of milk and honey!" I said, because Frieda was watching me, looking pleased. "And you can sure do with it," she said.

I found you, Uri, in the vegetable garden. You had turned two beds and were already raking them. "We want to plant young strawberry shoots," you explained. I could go right ahead and cut the furrows. The shoots were lying in the shade in a covered basket. "You're doing all right, Helga. Better than I do. I never get my furrows straight."

Did I really ask you that morning how old you were, full of admiration for your vitality, because my back was soon aching? I can see the sly look in your gray eyes in the shadow of your big straw hat that hid the fine wrinkles. "Must I tell you just because you are my granddaughter? Remember this, Helga — that's a question one asks only of a woman under thirty or over seventy!" The thought that you could be close to seventy didn't occur to me. To me you seemed neither old nor young.

After lunch you said I should lie down in the shade. I took it for granted that you were going to rest in your room. At five o'clock we had high tea — some kind of herb tea — and ate bread and cheese and greengages; even in those days you had your evening meal early. You drew up a hassock and put your feet on it. "Shall we go for a little walk?" I asked, as it grew cooler. "You go, Helga. Have a look around, but when twilight falls, come home. I'm too tired. I was out in the fields for three hours. We harvested the last of the rye. I think there's going to be a change in the weather ..."

"Now see here!" I cried. "I'm to rest on a chaise longue while you go out in the fields at noon?" She said, "It was an exception. Because of the threatening weather. Otherwise my Frenchmen always work alone. We're running things according to a strict regime now." Did they know anything about farming? I asked. Hias, the old man with only one leg, was supervising the work. In that way he could see he was still good for something. And when he bawled them out, they didn't understand him anyway.

"Where do they live?"

"In the former stables. Tomorrow I'll show you everything. Now, if you'll be so good, water the newly planted beds once more. Did you see where I left the watering cans?"

You picked up the paper and put on your glasses. I crossed the yard. The watering cans weren't where they should have been. I didn't want to go back, but sauntered off and soon heard voices in a strange rhythm. The Frenchmen. What were they doing here? What did the enemy look like? I was ashamed of my prickly curiosity, and walked on. I didn't choose the broad center path, though, but walked around the square bed where the raspberries were planted, until I came to the gooseberries, which hadn't been picked yet. I began to eat some as if that were why I had come there, and listened. Now the boys were speaking softly. They turned their backs on me. Two laughed and chatted, the third never stopped working. Carefully, at short intervals, he was watering what had ben freshly planted.

I knew that the young men had noticed me long ago, but not one of them looked my way. What to do? Were they allowed to greet me, and should I reply? I decided to reply, only now they walked off without looking at me, jauntily, as if they weren't at all tired, like young men walk when a girl is watching them. One of them picked a carnation and stuck it behind his ear. "*Mais Alphonse, qu'en dirait Mère Cathèrine?*" one of the others teased him. That much French I could understand, but I only grasped a moment later whom they meant, and realized that they had come here to please you, Grandmama, to do something no one had ordered them to do. They — the "slaves"— were free enough to be generous. Thoughtfully and strangely amused I walked through the little back gate, across to the edge of the wood. So the enemy loved you. I was proud to be your granddaughter.

And I am to this day, Uri. But during the time in between I sometimes found it difficult. Because you never had any consideration for my need to admire without reservation. You were always yourself, whether we liked it or not.

No, I won't hold a memorial service now! The good parson will do that at your open grave. I'm worried about it already, although I know he'll do his best. He will talk about your good deeds and surely praise as well the fearlessness with which you always took the part of the weaker one. You were not a faithful churchgoer; you went to church only on Holy Days. But the years of the Russian occupation were evidently Holy Days for you too, because then you never missed Sunday mass. One had to prove to people, you said, that it doesn't have to cost you your life if you remain true to your convictions. Then, when you gradually stopped going again, the parson angrily labelled it "defiant religion." You smiled as you agreed with him. But he never withdrew his friendship and respect. I should really have gone to fetch him today, but that occurs to me too late. He'll know that this has to be held against me, not you.

But let me feel my way back to that first summer. I can recall the most important events as if they had happened yesterday. One morning a man came with a bill, and you sent me to your room to get your purse. "It must be on my desk," you said. "And then there's a twenty-mark bill in the middle drawer. Bring that along too."

I ran upstairs, found the purse, opened the drawer and stopped short because I had caught sight of a piece of lined paper with regular, slanting, very fluent writing on it that didn't go at all with the soiled copybook page it was written on. I glanced at the signature: " ... embrace you. Your forever grateful Clemens." With bated breath I saw the stamp of a prison censor. Without giving a thought as to whether I was doing right or wrong, I read the address and the first sentence: "Dear Mother, when you come to see me again, please bring me ..." Then I took the money, ran down the stairs, gave it to you and went back into the kitchen where we had just been stringing beans.

I didn't know what to think. You didn't have a child or any in-laws called Clemens. It was ... and I didn't doubt it for a moment ... my brother's friend who was in jail. But how did you happen to know him? Visit him? And how did he happen to call you Mother? I felt as if I were in a dream in which familiar surroundings are suddenly transformed into strange and threatening ones.

Then you came in, sat down with me, and silently went on stringing the beans. But after a while you swept the beans together, emptied your apron in the pail and said, "No. This won't do. Come upstairs with me for a minute." When we got upstairs, you looked around. I had closed the drawer again. "There's a letter in it you were not supposed to see. I only thought of it later. I guess you read it, my child. Or ... didn't you read it? It's up to you."

It sounded grave and solemn, Uri, the way you said "It's up to you." Without a trace of irony. That was why, for once, I couldn't remain harmlessly ignorant; this one time I had to take the harm upon myself and had to answer. "Yes, Grandmama. I read Clemens Schindler's letter. But how do you happen to know him? And why did they lock him up?"

"I don't know," you said, sounding a little impatient as you took out the letter. "Anyway, somebody's got to look after him and only close relatives may do that. But his mother is ill, so I went there with her papers ..."

"Oh," I said, feeling relieved. "So the letter is for her?" Whereupon she became very thoughtful and answered slowly, "I never asked myself that, Helga: is the letter for her or for me? I wonder if even Clemens knows. In any case, the message is for me because only I can go there. You read it?" I shook my head. So she read it aloud to me. He needed zinc salve and absorbent cotton, and if possible, a lemon ... "I left a few black currents on the bushes. I'll take them with me next time. They have just as much vitamin C ..."

"*La Mère Cathèrine*," I murmured. "You are Mother to a lot of people."

You put the letter back in its envelope and in the drawer, and locked it. When you turned your face to me again it was red, and I felt that you were finding it difficult to control your voice so that it would sound kind and gentle. "Helga, I think I told you already — I lost my first child whom I loved above everything else. After that ... then I had only the choice of hating everything and burying myself in defiant grief as in a tomb, to be dead myself, or ..."

I whispered, "Forgive me," and the tears welled up in my eyes.

She walked up to me quickly, kissed me and said, "Or I had to love all the more, not only my husband and my own children who were born after that, but ... all of you. Because for me you remain children." she said with finality, as if I had protested. "As long as you need me. But now let's finish the beans or we'll have to keep the stove heated until evening."

Uri ... do you know what surprised me more than anything else in this exciting discovery of your relationship to Clemens Schindler ... and I can only say comforted me? That you didn't find it necessary to impress upon me to keep silent about it. That it never occurred to you for a moment that I could wittingly or unwittingly betray you.

Why did I never ask you — yesterday there would still have been time for it — whether you left the letter lying in the drawer on purpose? Because I only thought of this possibility just now.

I made myself a cup of tea because I had begun to feel cold. I smoked a cigarette with it and my thoughts wandered ... whether Gottfried had already packed his bags, whether he enjoyed the idea of traveling or didn't sometimes think: if only I were in my bed at home and was only going to travel across the big map on the wall with my eyes!

One has to be able to let go. You have told me that so often, Uri. Some learn how to do so under good circumstances; you had to learn under bad ones. I shall never learn it. I am too poor for that. But I am obeying you, Uri. I didn't whistle for Gottfried to come back; I let him go. But my feelings may be hurt, no? And then your voice said, suddenly sharp, as it had sounded so often during those months of dreadful waiting, when I sat there, apathetic, staring straight ahead, "Come on, Helga! Do something! Work! I can't do it all myself! Do something sensible!" Well, now perhaps it would be sensible at last to get to the end of these confessions. Very well then, to continue with the text ...

So ... I glanced over the last pages and asked myself suddenly: perhaps she had laid the letter beside the twenty-mark bill on purpose, to open my eyes at last. Had she expected further questions? Had she come to Vienna only to find out where Clemens was, and to help him? Perhaps to restore the connection between him and Albert? All I would have had to do was ask and she would have let me in on her secret, and I wouldn't have been standing alone anymore on the other side! Why couldn't I ask her? Perhaps because I wanted to stay on the same side as Horst. I don't know.I suppose it suffices to tell what I did and what happened. Where would I end up if I wanted to cast light on what didn't happen and what I failed to do? Then I would still be sitting in front of these pages with white hair, and my memoirs would finally have become my purpose in life, as in the case of a retired army general. Except for the fact that he has an audience, or thinks he has, whereas my Gottfried chose to run away from all these disclosures ...

That he has inherited from me. He would like to remain innocent at any price. But perhaps a young person has the right to make such demands. One should keep the chick in its egg until it breaks the shell of its own accord. And if I want so much to tell my son where he really came from, then it is perhaps only in order to get rid of this secret at last, because for seventeen years it has stunted every other knowledge in my soul and hasn't let any new, budding experience develop.

I had always felt that with Gottfried's origin (I don't want to say "procreation" because there must be a will behind every procreation) my life ended. You, beloved dead one, taught me that I had to endure it in order to protect his. You said to me, "With every soul the world begins anew, and if you let it die, you not only destroy a life to be but you say no to life itself."

Oh, Uri, how often I reproached you in bitter silence for bringing me around to a feeble "All right then ... in God's name ..."

I keep these pages in a folder. Sometimes I make notes on the cover of things I mustn't forget to insert but that only fit in later. I see: "I have my future behind me," and under it, "Beware of the pseudonymous words, child: *peace, freedom, honor, God* ... and so on. Every person hides his own experiences behind them. One thinks one has come to an agreement only to find oneself all alone in the midst of an intimate conversation, or one has started to quarrel and meant the same thing."

So how can I tell your story, Uri? That would be like throwing a lasso over a colt and expecting it to go on prancing. Doesn't it come clear anyway out of such sentences? But if I tried now to recall the little scene that revealed your strange secret to me ...

We were standing in the vegetable garden early in the morning, when Alphonse came and brought two pails full of wood soil for a flower bed. He had brought it from far away, at dawn, before his daily work began. He accepted your thanks gaily with the words, *"Moi aussi, j'aime bien les choses inutiles,"* then off he went again with the easygoing walk of a young man women like to watch. I looked at you and looked away, startled, because tears were glistening in your eyes. Alphonse was just closing the gate and he turned around and waved in a comradely fashion, almost a little condescendingly. And you said, as if I had expressed my thoughts, "Yes. That's the way it is. The prisoners are our superiors. They may be the masters of tomorrow."

I didn't want to believe that you were acknowledging a quite different superiority, so I said, "They're very grateful to you."

"Paul and Louis," you said, "are perhaps grateful. Alphonse only puts up with the fact that I love him."

"Grandmama!" I cried heatedly. "What are you talking about? I don't know what I'm supposed to think!"

"Neither do I," you said quietly. "But it makes me happy. Happiness is a fire and fire shines. That can't be kept secret. What could happen anyway? I've just come to life again. That's all."

And then I asked — I did, young creature that I was, I asked the old woman — "But what's going to become of it?" She laughed and answered, "Nothing. Nothing more is going to 'become' of anything. My future lies behind me, so time has lost its power over me ..."

On the right side of your desk, Uri, the calendar of the year 1947 is still hanging. You have never torn off the cover. Straight across it, in big, firm letters, is written: *Les jours passent, les instants restent. Noel 1946. Alphonse.*

I believe that was the only sign of life from Alphonse after his return home. Paul wrote you that he had passed his master-craftsman examination; Louis sent the announcement of his engagement, and a few years later a snapshot of his two little girls, all dressed up.

*Les jours passent, les instants restent!* Perhaps that would be a motto for my book. How many days, weeks, months have gone forever; only moments have remained. The encounter with Walter didn't last more than two minutes. That last conversation with Albert, his "run as far away as you can." Frau Feldstein's sorrowful glance from the truck ... and your first smile, Gottfried, that entrusted you to me forever.

I can hardly make a story out of all these moments, just as I can't distill a philosophy out of your sayings, Uri, which are noted on the cover of my folder. 'The moment one wants to hold fast onto something, come what may, one has already lost it.' That's the third one ...

How was it with your first baby? You conceived him right after the wedding and were so happy, the way every very young wife is happy: with a little resignation. Because you didn't feel well and now couldn't ride anymore, couldn't go along on the hunt, and soon wouldn't be able to dance any longer and make merry with your charming Janosh. And just as the worst was over, you got appendicitis and had to have an operation. Only then, when they told you they hadn't had to take your child, when between the pains of the wound you could suddenly again feel its gentle stirring, then all of a sudden the child meant everything to you. You had stayed alive only to give it life. You almost felt indifference for your husband. He had played his part. You didn't go back to your shared bedroom when you came home, nor did you after the birth: you didn't want to disturb your husband, you said. Actually you thought he might disturb the child. You barely parted from him for the time it took to eat your meals. Everybody said the boy looked like you. You would have liked to be a boy; that's why you saw in him all the possibilities you might have had. "I expected him to live my life. He didn't want to do that. That is why he died."

"But what did he die of, Grandmama?" I protested against any such interpretation. A child dies of an illness, not of an imputation.

"He refused all nourishment. He was extinguished like a little light in the wind."

And then? Grandfather must have tried everything, good and bad. Your resistance was a total lack of will. Nothing meant anything to you. And soon, when you felt you were pregnant again, you only wept. When Grandfather saw all his efforts to heal you fail, he became cross, sad, worried. Finally he asked the parson: would he help to put you together again. The parson spoke of humility and the resignation to one's fate, of your duty as a wife and the mistress of a farm. "I do everything," you replied. "I just can't feel happy about anything anymore."

"And that is the greatest sin of all!" he cried, and got up, groaning — he was old and fat. He looked at you sorrowfully and, deep in thought, tried to think of an appropriate quote from the Bible. Whatever came to his mind, though, didn't seem to fit. He only mumbled it softly between his lips. But you looked up suddenly and begged, "Say that again, Reverend Father."

"To have as if one had not," he repeated, "That is what Saint Paul demands of us Christians All our worldly goods are only a loan from God. Do you understand?"

"Yes, that I understand," you said. "Thank you, Reverend Father. That way it may be possible ..."

"And from then on I could live again, Helga. I enjoyed the children, the flowers, the animals, and my poor merry Janosh, God rest his soul. Also things that should have been cause for weeping rather than for joy. Everything is easily bearable once one has grasped the fact that there is nothing definitive. *Nothing*, Helga."

You stressed the word. I was silent. What had happened to me was definitive. I wasn't going to let anyone talk me out of that.

How short the nights are already! I can blow out the candles now, Uri, can't I? And surely I can let you rest alone now with your past ... and with mine. Because if I were to cheat now ... you as the only witness could not testify against me anymore. But who has accused me? Why am I constantly defending myself?

If it is possible to "have as if one had not," it should also be possible to speak about a third person. I mean in the third person. A pity that didn't occur to me before. But perhaps I shall still come back to it ...

Out of these summer weeks with you, Uri, three moments have remained present: the discovery of Clemens Schindler's letter to you; the discovery that love is not bound to the seasons of life; and ... the astonishment when I found myself face to face with Marietta in the pharmacy. I hadn't heard from her since she had left the Labor Service ahead of time because of her marriage.

I had ridden Grandmother's bicycle into town to buy a few things at the pharmacy. An old man was waiting on me, slowly, fussily, but still, when totaling the amount he made a mistake. A young woman had come up to him from the back door and was watching him with obvious impatience. In the meantime I was counting my cash. When the old pharmacist gave me the bill, she said hastily, "Father, there's a letter from Herbert. I'll leave it here for you," and walked over to the door. Meanwhile I had looked up, had just looked into Marietta's startled, defensive eyes, and with that had perhaps made a move of surprise or pleasure. She walked out quickly.

I couldn't understand it. "But that was ..."

"What did you say?" asked the old man. "The absorbent cotton costs seventy pfennigs."

"All right," I said, and paid. And he took the letter in his trembling hand.

It was all really quite simple to reconstruct. This had to be the father of the harvest-festival Herbert whom Marietta had married *in absentia*. But didn't she know me anymore? Or didn't she want to know me? And why not? I don't understand it to this day. Since she greeted me with great joy when we met again a year later, I have concluded that in the first moment of shock she simply didn't want to believe in my reappearance in her life. Her defensive look was equivalent to the no that lies on the tip of one's tongue as a response to all unpleasant news. I, however, began gradually to doubt my senses. Just as surely as Walter three months ago, Marietta had now looked me in the eye, and both of them had slammed the door on me as it I had been a suspicious-looking beggar. I walked around the shop, to the back entrance, and saw a baby carriage there, and diapers fluttering in the open window. For a moment I wondered if I shouldn't walk in, go up the stairs and say, "But Marietta! Don't you know me anymore? It is I, Helga!" Certainly that would have been the right thing to do, but I couldn't make myself do it.

I asked grandmother what she knew about the pharmacist's family. Did he have a son? Yes. "Unfortunately he is in Russia, his only son. And the pharmacist's wife died miserably six months ago of cancer. I hope the boy comes back. He has a wife now too, and a child."

"Is she from here?"

"No. They say she's from Vienna. A very young girl. Why are you asking?"

"Oh ... just because ..."

I wanted to finish this account of my first holiday with you before they buried you, Grandmama, but now it is all over. Nothing left to do but engrave your name on the black marble. The place beside Janosh, above the two Johanns, was left free for it more than sixty years ago. And now I am being given a courtesy delay before they come and ask: what are you going to do now? Because you had the right to live here until your death; I have no rights whatsoever. So it will come to pass that Gottfried won't find his maternal home when he gets back. This may be good for both of us. It forces us to begin all over again.

Meanwhile Herr Stadler, the owner, has already called on me, and I was a little surprised that he was in such a hurry. But he assured me at once: I had nothing to worry about, for heaven's sake! Nobody had any thought of rushing me. (Who was there to rush me besides him?) It was too late in the season now anyway to undertake anything. "What are you planning to do?" I must have asked, and gradually got out of him that he wanted to turn our old home into a guest house for tourists. Because farming hadn't been profitable for years now, nor was he able to make up the deficit with his fish hatchery. Naturally a great deal would have to be invested — running water in all the rooms, eventually central heating, but there was time for all that "Until, let's say, Christmas ..."

"Until New Year," I said firmly. In the meantime I would look for an apartment in Vienna.

"You want to move to Vienna?" He seemed surprised. Then he said, "Well, of course ... an efficient young woman like you. I'm sure you will ..." and his lips told me what he wanted to say — "be lucky" — but he corrected himself hastily and said, "make a go of it."

"I hope so," I said, with a confidence I didn't feel. "I have earned money before." But he didn't mean that. He didn't doubt for a moment ... but would I like it in the big city after so many years in the country? "Your garden ... how it all blooms and flourishes down there ... and you know how to get along with people too," he said, with an admiring grin. "Nobody's going to get the best of you. First it was Gretl, and now Hilde ..."

I had no idea what he was after, but I hastily suggested that he hire Hilde because now I didn't need her anymore. She was very efficient, although a little lacking in independence.

"Fine," he said. "We can do that." But he looked at me through his glasses, from under his dark, deeply furrowed brow, strangely distressed. "I am grateful that you are going to leave me Hilde because I am sure you have trained her well. But actually ... first and foremost I would need something quite different, namely someone for the management, to take charge ..." He got up quickly. It was too soon to talk about it, but perhaps I would think it over. Before I took something else in Vienna.

I must have looked dubious. Quickly, to prevent a rejection, he added, "I know you'll get a job there any day, an efficient person like you ... and with your appearance. They'll come running. And with me ... I know ... it's dull. I'm not very sociable and you don't care about cards. Although I want to buy a television set anyway. In the winter, when there are no guests, one would have time for it, right? That would be nice ..."

My heart was beating so wildly, I was afraid he might notice it. I pulled myself together and said calmly, "Thank you very much, Herr Stadler. It's very friendly of you. Unfortunately it doesn't come into question. I have already decided on Vienna."

He bowed a little too low and walked over to the door, but there he stopped once more. "If you would only consider the fact that then the boy wouldn't lose his home." His ruddy face became even redder, and he added, "Because I'm really very fond of Gottfried."

"Thank you, Herr Stadler," I said, touched and embarrassed. "I'm truly very sorry. But it doesn't come into question."

"I thought that's the way it would be," he murmured. "*Küss die Hand*," and he left.

I must tell Uri, I thought, before it occurred to me that I can never run to her and tell her anything anymore. Then, involuntarily, I walked over to the mirror. A pale face, a wry, ironically bitter mouth, startled eyes ... Calm down. What can happen to you anyway? You said no right away ...

But isn't it funny, Uri? *"It doesn't surprise me at all. And actually you should have thought it over"* "But there's nothing to think over!" *"No? What did you write the day before yesterday about not wanting to recognize Marietta, about the no that lies always on one's lips with every surprise attack?"* "It's a no of defense, Uri!" *"All right ... all right. So stick with it."*

During this "conversation" I had picked up a comb and fixed my hair. I had looked at my profile, then stepped back so that I could see my whole figure, and had decided: black really does make one look thinner. When I finally sat down with my accounts again, I was in good spirits, probably because I had explained my position to Herr Stadler so briskly and unmistakably.

I must try to express myself more briefly because even if there is no-body any more to disturb me during the day, I simply have to be finished by Christmas. That gives me six months, but the last weeks before I move can scarcely be counted; and in the autumn I shall have to see about find-ing a place to live and getting a job, and before that refresh my knowl-edge of stenography and typing. When I think that I have been working on this since All Souls, and by now have covered three years, I should be able to finish off the other two by December. If only I didn't have the feel-ing that everything essential is yet to come!

Well, I can at least treat the following winter, 1943–44 summarily be-cause I can recall hardly any details. I heard lectures on history, political economy and sociology besides attending civil defense courses in order to be able to teach that myself.News from Russia was rare and sporadic, so that we soon had to worry about Albert, then about Horst. There were steady heavy bombing raids on German cities. We too had night alerts, but the squadrons still passed over us. Together with our air-raid warden I was responsible for everyone going down into the cellar as soon as there was an alert. The young woman on the fourth floor refused to tear her lit-tle children out of their beds — nothing was going to happen here any-way! I urged her to comply. I always hurried straight up to her, helped her to dress the children, carried her things to the cellar. My mother went down only because of me.

Silently we listened to the news every evening. Frequently a fresh re-treat was referred to as "a straightening of the front." The German troops had already been forced to leave Africa in the summer; Italy had toppled Mussolini and done away with fascism; yet there were a lot of people who still believed in "final victory," all those who couldn't imagine sur-vival after defeat. It happened as it does often with seriously ill people: as long as the diagnosis is doubtful, they can look death in the face, even make preparations for the burial. But as soon as the fatal symptoms ap-pear, they begin to plan the future, and no one knows if this is self-decep-tion or to spare the others.

All the people I heard talking were of the opinion that there could be no question of capitulation, not under any circumstances, after there had been so much sacrifice for a better future. One began to whisper about German miracle weapons that were being readied, as if this were something as certain as the coming of spring, and would turn the situation around. Until then we had to endure. What did we have left? No one had pointed out a different possibility to me, and the only one who might have been able to do so at the time wanted to pass me by with a silent greeting: Clemens Schindler. I met him one day at the streetcar stop on my way home from the university. He got out, I wanted to get in. He nodded, surprised, as I stared at him. To the annoyance of those behind me I stepped down again and hurried after him. Obviously hesitant, he grasped my outstretched hand. I was so pleased to see him. How was he? "Thank you. Well," he said. "And you?"

But I didn't feel like a mere exchange of formalities. I told him that I had spent the summer with my grandmother, making it sound significant. Without paying attention to this bit of information, he asked, "Have you had news from Albert?"

"Yes," I said. "Two weeks ago. But we can't make out where he actually is."

"If only he is alive." he said.

"My fiancé is in Russia too," I told him, and suddenly it slipped out. "It's terrible! All one can do is wait!"

"And pray," the young priest said softly, smiled sadly, as if to apologize for this advice, drew his hand out of mine — I hadn't noticed that I was still holding it — and walked away. I thought: But surely they didn't lock you up because of waiting and praying! And I was angry that he had brushed me off like that. Later I understood his behavior ...

At home nobody seemed surprised about my encounter. Just the same, Father begged me, "Write to Albert about it." I did so, but I didn't dare mention it to Grandmother because on leaving she had begged me to keep in mind that letters were now sometimes read by outsiders.

During the lectures of my professors I felt as insecure as I did sometimes with my own family. They too gave the impression that they didn't know how much the next man knew, how much capacity for independent thinking one could assume. The various disciplines were therefore alike in that the ruling official viewpoint was pronounced as wisdom's latest conclusion. With some teachers I suspected that they couldn't possibly mean it seriously, but I had no confirmation of my suspicions. To my astonishment I noticed that now, as the same theories which I had accepted and defended since my schooldays were being served up to me again and again, but with a somewhat more complicated terminology, I began to have severe doubts. Things couldn't be that simple. And I had pictured university as something quite different.

I fled into practical work and instructed people enthusiastically: how, in cases of emergency, they should hold wet cloths against their mouths if trapped by collapsing walls; conserve oxygen by not talking and not moving, at the same time making their presence known to the outside world by regular signals ... In those days I sometimes went to the movies with Mother, to give her a little break. But soon neither of us wanted to see the war scenes in the weekly newsreels any more. The apathetic faces of Russian prisoners, stamped with deprivation and suffering, made us conscious of the fact that perhaps now Albert or Horst were standing in line for hours in the bitter cold, a bowl in their hands, for a ladleful of soup. A helmet sticking up out of the snow or the toe of a boot in a village that had been retaken, betrayed that a human being was lying there, frozen stiff, one of thousands, and there was no difference between friend and foe. And everywhere ... the waiting mothers and sweethearts of those who would never come back. The face of the Führer, who was shown with partiality pinning medals on the chests of brave boys, was bloated, pasty, his gaze fixed, his movements jerky. I felt sorry for him. Mother whispered, "I can't stand the sight of him anymore." Two girls in front of us turned around and giggled. I broke out in a sweat. After that we didn't go to the movies together.

At this point there is something I would like to tell you, Gottfried. This man Hitler is often represented today as a sort of demonic buffoon, an inflated zero who was only able to fool people stupefied by slogans or blinded by resentment. But I think that his power rested on the fact that he was filled with a gigantic sense of mission. He really did see himself as the savior of the German people and knew how to transfer this belief to others, to simple people as well as intellectuals. When some call him the Antichrist, I agree. There will be not only one but many Antichrists before the end of time. And all of them have one thing in common: they scorn the simple joys of life. The real and the false prophet — both are permeated by their calling, right up to the sacrificial death.

Now I hear the wild protests of all those who believe that millions fell for the simple tricks of a power-hungry clown. How can anybody speak of a sacrificial death? He died like a rat when its last hole is surrounded. Right! And yet ... whoever tried during those days to oppose the devil isn't here today to ridicule him. And there must be some people who feel sorry for him whom all of us encouraged in his power, who was first our idol, then our scapegoat. Besides, I would rather pity him and with that at last forget to feel sorry for myself.

Evidently one easily becomes rhetorical when faced with nothing but one's four walls. As long as you were asleep in the room next door, my Gottfried, I expressed myself in a simpler fashion, especially when I still believed you would one day read all this. Now you are in America. Today a letter came from Marjorie.

She writes that she likes to see how friendly and modest you are, better behaved than the boys there. She is astonished that in spite of your height, you are still "such a child." You have little difficulty in making yourself understood, and when you have found young friends — she hopes soon — the two years in America will be advantageous to your future. Then she consoled me: so many parents in far-off areas have to bear the sacrifice of much longer separations!

What pleases me especially about the letter is the postscript: "Please let me know as soon as possible if Gottfried has been vaccinated for tetanus. He isn't quite sure. Otherwise we'll attend to it at once ..." She is fond of you, she worries about you, she is considering all sorts of possibilities ...

I fell asleep last night with pleasant thoughts like these, but soon woke up and was conscious of the absolute emptiness of my life. Because I could have had this sixteen years ago — given my child to people who would have been good to him! A few days later he would have had the same smile for them as the one that had seduced me. And I could have built a life of my own, could have gone on studying, developed my talents, accomplished something ... Phrases, all phrases! At the first convenient moment I would have killed myself. And at least I won't do that now.

Perhaps it is always an illusion that one "lives for somebody," waterwings of a sort that are useful only so that one can someday do without them. I confess that I am a little curious about what is to become of me ...

On my twentieth birthday I received a letter from Horst. He hadn't sounded so hopeful in a long time. "I can't bring you twenty roses, beloved, but a thousand wishes that are redder and more beautiful and heartfelt, that will come to full bloom when the storm that would like to defoliate them is over ..."

My mother had received a letter too. She had opened it at once in the foyer. She murmured, "It must be a mistake ..."

I looked up impatiently from Horst's letter and asked, "What's the matter?" and my smile over Horst's unaccustomed enthusiasm died.

Albert's captain was writing, Captain Knolle. Albert had sometimes mentioned him. "... for the Führer and Fatherland. You can be proud of your son. He was a courageous soldier and a good comrade ... Unfortunately I did not see him myself. There can be no doubt though that he died right away. But the enemy was on our heels. Please accept my sincerest condolences. We shall never forget your son ..."

"It must be a mistake!" This conviction frequently averts the first deadly blow. Mother repeated the words, her lips trembling, then she sank to the floor.

I got her to bed and called Father. He was to come right away, she was ill. "News from Albert?" he asked.

"Yes."

"I'm coming."

Then he was sitting beside her, holding her hand. "Look ... it's all over for him," and the tears were running down his face. She didn't cry. "I can't believe it," she kept saying.

I thought: and now they have only me, and wondered why neither of them said it. Quietly I put away all the things on my birthday table. The cake I took up to the little girls on the fourth floor.

Toward evening Father called the doctor. He gave Mother an injection after which she slept for twelve hours. But I too slept as if drugged. Why wake up? Only to wait until I received such a letter too?

Father woke me before he left the apartment. "You must look after your mother, Helga. Try to distract her. Give her something to do."

"Yes. I'll try."

He leaned over and kissed me on the forehead. "My poor child," he said. "Your youth is anything but beautiful."

I began to cry for joy that he felt sorry for me. But he freed himself and said, "We must control ourselves. I hope God preserves your Horst." I would have liked to ask: Do you still believe in God? But he had to go to his office. He left as punctually as he did every other day.

Mother tormented herself with reproaches. Why had she tried to protect the susceptible boy from every cold and forbidden him so many things? Why had she constantly urged him, who had been ambitious anyway, to study, and stopped him from daydreaming, from idling away his time? Why hadn't she let him attend the mountain-climbing classes with his comrades, why had she forbidden him to swim across the Danube? All so that he might perish miserably in this accursed war!

I tried to reason with her. I didn't feel right about it, but I said, "Isn't it better to die *for* something than *of* something? Cancer, polio, leukemia ..."

"Die for what?" Mother asked, looking at me wide-eyed.

Did I dare to say: for the Fatherland? Our Fatherland perished in 1938. "For our homeland, Mother," I said.

"Who can take that from us? Oh yes, they could drive us out! We already have them among us, all the refugees! Albert wasn't defending his homeland — he was driving others out of theirs. But at least he didn't like doing it, the poor boy. He had to do it and I have to bear it 'in proud grief!' We go on lying all the time, all the time. And with a lie everything dreadful begins ..."

"Mother, would you peel the potatoes for me? Otherwise I won't get through in time. I have a class at two."

She took the knife in her hand willingly, but soon her hands sank on her lap, her eyes stared unseeingly at the wall. She murmured again, "It must be a mistake ..." and began her senseless talk again. "He liked to play with dolls ... Albert should have married young and had children ... That would have made him happy and I would so have liked to live to see my grandchildren ... Perhaps it is better for them never to be born ..."

"Mother," I said, as gently as I could. "We may have children, Horst and I." And when she didn't answer: "I want to have children."

"Oh, the things one wants!" she said contemptuously.

I was often afraid of the moment, Gottfried, when you would realize that you were born unwanted. I wished above all to spare you this insight as long as possible. I hoped to fortify your soul with a hundred proofs of my love before it was exposed to this burden. Now it has dawned on me that I too lived through this moment. Perhaps almost everyone experiences it once. My mother had wanted children, but now she told me to my face, "Oh, the things one wants!" And could say it with such bitter indifference because my presence meant nothing to her. I virtually didn't exist for her.

I had no time to lick this wound; like the man buried in a cellar dragging someone who has fainted to the light can't stop to take care of his minor scratches. Mother willingly did all the things I asked her to do. Once I dared to give her the older of the children on the fourth floor to look after while their mother took the younger one to the doctor. I stayed in the next room with the door ajar. The child played happily with the glossy threads Mother had used formerly for her flower embroidery. "The gold is the queen!" I heard the child's peepsy voice say, and the friendly monotone answer, "Yes. And look ... the blue and the red are the court ladies." "And what is this one?" asked the child. "That's the little dwarf who makes everyone laugh." "How does he do that?" I heard Mother's thimble jingle. "And the poisonous toadstool, the traitor — now he chases him away!" The child laughed aloud.

Afterwards I asked, "May I bring her down to you often?" But she said, "Can't somebody else look after her sometimes?" During those weeks she didn't once mention Walter.

Grandmother wrote to me: "You simply must come again during your vacation. You need fresh air, milk and unbroken sleep, and I need you." When I replied that I couldn't leave Mother, she wrote, "So bring her with you." Father agreed; Mother just shrugged her shoulders. "Whatever you say. It's all the same to me."

"Will you take us there?" I asked Father.

Startled, he refused. "What for? I'll put you on the train."

"That isn't necessary," I replied.

Father tried to explain his refusal. "Now a tractor is rattling around where I used to accompany my father in the dawn to hear the mountain cock's mating call. In those days I used to sit on the box with deaf Joseph when we drove into the city to shop. Try to understand, Helga! I don't want to see my old mother in pants, getting onto a bicycle with a basket of apples for the market on the back!"

"But she doesn't do anything of the sort! You've got it all wrong, Father!"

"But I have the right memories," he said, "and I want to keep them."

After our arrival I took heart again because Mother looked at everything with interest and sometimes was almost as she had been before. Grandmother watched over her unobtrusively. "How good it smells here!" said my mother. "In the city it's as if you were living in catacombs. Funny that we put up with it. If I were young, I'd travel around the world with a tent."

"In a car?" Grandmother asked drily.

"Oh no!" Mother wasn't thinking in such concrete terms; nor was she considering the fact that the world was divided by iron curtains, and that practically only prisoners lived in it.

We scarcely noticed the three Frenchmen who were working here, but one evening we met them, looking for snails, which they intended to eat. Mother stopped, watched them for a while, then asked casually, "Do they really taste good?" Grandmother walked on, smiling to herself.

"*Pardon, Madame?*" asked Alphonse.

"Oh. Can't they speak German yet." Mother groped for words, then she asked, "*Ta mère, sait'elle que tu vis?*"

"*Elle est déja morte, elle-même,*" he replied.

"*Tant mieux.*" Mother sighed. I murmured, "*Excusez.*" Alphonse, bent over again, said politely, "*Pas de quoi!*"

"It is forbidden to fraternize with the foreign workers," Grandmother said when we caught up with her. "Please be careful."

"Why?" asked mother. "Nothing makes any difference anymore, does it?"

"Oh yes, it does!" Grandmother contradicted her. "They plant our grain and harvest it; they help us to survive and we help them."

"What for?" asked mother.

"Because life goes on! ... Whom are you looking for?"

I can still hear it — Grandmother's harsh "Because life goes on!" Her sharp "Whom are you looking for?" with which she angrily addressed a man who had walked toward us slowly on the narrow field path and was looking us over, one after the other. He seemed especially interested in my bare feet. Now he stepped aside to let us pass. I can still see my mother's startled movement of negation, caused either by the statement that life went on or by the obvious curiosity of the stranger. I took her arm and led her past him while he said, "I'm looking for a Mrs. Wegscheider."

"I am Mrs. Wegscheider," said Grandmother. "What do you want?" I had never seen her so churlish. He had been entrusted with a message, said the man. "Go ahead! I have no secrets from my family." But it was a confidential message, he said, and he didn't feel right about ... A little more politely Grandmother now asked him to come to her office next morning. Was she thinking, as I was, that it could have something to do with Clemens Schindler?

The stranger said, "Yes, ma'am. I'll do that." He shifted his cap and walked off. The Frenchmen had passed out of sight long ago. "Who was that?" asked my mother.

"I'm afraid someone who has no business being here,"Grandmother said brusquely. She took Mother's other arm gently and said, "Look up, Hedwig! How the stars are coming out one by one!" "And how the crickets chirp and the grass smells!" said Mother. I suppose all of us were thinking: and how beautiful the world could be!

Next morning, after breakfast, I was sitting on the terrace with Mother. We were stripping red currents off their stems when Grandmother came up to us quickly and said, "Hedwig, please come with me! You have to sign a receipt." Mother got up obediently, shook her apron and said, "Are you coming with me, Helga?"

"No," said Grandmother. "Let Helga go on with her work." The old woman was trying to detach my mother gently from my guardianship. As long as I gave her things to do she sometimes seemed almost gay, but left to herself she would begin to cry silently.

How long were things to go on like this? Is it true that time heals all wounds? And how would Horst behave toward my mother when he came back at last? Would he be good to her? The only son she had left?

I hardly ever thought of how things would be between Horst and me in that inconceivable future called "after the war." But I still know today that I was trying to make clear to myself — while the shiny red beads popped into the pail and I shooed away the wasps whirring around me with a light shake of my head — how these intricately curved pieces, Horst and my mother, could be fitted together in the puzzle of the future.

I remember how as a child I had for some time preferred jigsaw puzzles to any other games. To form colorful fairy-tale pictures out of a scrambled heap of small pieces. The pattern had been taken from us, otherwise the thing would be too easy. Actually the real fun was to anticipate, simply by looking at them, how the different parts could be assembled, before placing the notched pieces where they fitted with a quick move of the hand. The color transitions were a help. Who would ever have thought that the little light gold spot was the tip of Cinderella's shoe? Now you could already see her slender ankle under the coarse gray skirt, and the delicate rosy hand, and looked for the same gray for the sleeve and found the knee ... and what was this? A blue semicircle. Look, there's the rest of it, and it fits without any gaps! And that must be the bowl she's still holding on her lap. The prince enters suddenly, demanding that everyone try on the slipper, yes, the one over there in the dark corner by the fireplace too, because it doesn't fit the proud sisters in spite of tears and blood ...

We didn't have the pattern, but the title was printed inside the cover, and we knew the fairy tale well, or we would never have succeeded in creating a wholeness out of the hundred little pieces. Now I could perhaps find the wing of a dove shimmering somewhere in the pile, because the first pigeon had to be beside the bowl of lentils. So we knew the content of the picture, but not the form, the *what*, not the *how*. And now, as I sit and write and the light flickers because of the storm raging outside, it seems to me that I see a picture reflected in mirrors so that it is duplicated and appears finally in a misty vacuum: the twenty-year-old girl in the shade of the greenery, busily stripping the little red balls from their stems with a fork, scarcely noticing the annoying wasps because she is looking at where the five-year-old sits, fitting colored pieces together, moving her lips silently so as not to disturb her brothers who are doing their homework at the same table. Her mother sits on the window seat and sometimes looks across at them and admonishes: "Albert, don't hold your work so close to your eyes ... Walter, you're finished? Let me see ... Oh no! You've got to write that again! That isn't an *o*, that's a dumpling! You can't hand it in like that!" And I hear and see it all — the scratching of Walter's slate pencil, Albert's tongue between his teeth, but the only living thing is the incomplete puzzle in front of me, and if I don't find the beginning of Cinderella's hand then the shoe won't fit, the prince won't recognize her, and the little magic tree will have bestowed the wedding dress upon her for nothing ...

A heap of colored pieces lie scrambled on top of each other, the past results in no picture. I know what happened, dear God, but not why and how! Nothing fits together! They should give me a pattern at last! Other children get the pattern! I don't want things to be more difficult for me than for the others! I don't want to learn patience! Now I'll break the whole thing apart again so that they can't say: see! It's coming! Nothing's coming! Iwon'tIwon'tIwon't ...

Mother! My picture is ruined. Walter punches me in the ribs. I barely feel it but now it is I who have been treated unjustly. I sob and scream: "Ow! Ow!" and throw everything on the floor and stamp on it so that it shall be ruined.

What happened? Why is it so quiet? I know: Mother slapped me. Slapped my face. My nose started to bleed right away. Now I'm lying on my bed in the dark room, cotton in my nostrils, a sweet taste in my mouth, listening to my own breathing. And to Mother's last words that sounded like a threat but were actually a wonderful promise: "Never ... this child is never to play with a jig saw puzzle again!"

Did the pieces break under my feet? Or had my mother in her perplexity discovered the wisdom of capitulation: not to "allow" the child to do what it doesn't want to do?

But even if I wished to imitate her now, Gottfried, I couldn't spare you anything. Nobody can do that. Mother promised too much that time, because week after week I have been sitting here until late in the night, trying to put my picture together, and again I know what it is to depict but not what it will look like. The pieces are indestructible, so there's no use stamping on them. And the ones I have pushed farthest away I am going to have to look for on my hands and knees.

I was finished with stripping the berries and carried them into the kitchen. Mother was standing beside Grandmother, who was stoking the fire, and was looking with a lost little smile at the flames. "Now I can go on," she said, as I walked in, and both of them turned to me. "Helga, the man who came yesterday was here and brought us news of Albert," said my grandmother. "He was with him to the end," said Mother, and the smile never left her face. She was holding a watch in her hand. Her smile indicated hope. I couldn't understand. "To ... the end?"

"Your mother is glad to have certainty at last," Grandmother murmured.

I couldn't understand anything. The pieces didn't fit, so I let them lie. A connecting piece was missing. Mother held the watch to her ear and smiled as if she could hear her son's living heart beating.

I saw Herr Schneider — that was the name of the man who had introduced himself as Albert's comrade at the front — once more when he came to say goodbye and receive a food package. "When were you discharged?" I asked. He didn't look like a soldier to me.

"Three months now," he said, "'cause me arm stayed stiff after a wound. Nuthin' so bad it don't have its good side!" he joked. But since we women remained serious, he quickly frowned again and said, "Well, no tellin' what your brother was spared!"

What was his profession now, I wanted to know. Same as before, he said: grocer. "Uster be fruit from the south ... well, we 'ad to switch from that!" He guffawed again. He did business in Vienna too, and he'd like to try right now to find out how he could contact Reverend Schindler ... my brother's friend. Did I happen to have his address? I glanced at Grandmother, but she didn't look up. "We haven't heard anything from him in a long time," said my mother. "But why don't you ask at St. Stephen's? They should know."

"We'll find out all right," Herr Schneider assured us, and rose.

"Have you something for him from Albert?" I asked.

"Jest a little souvenir, nuthin' valuable," answered Herr Schneider, and took a small diary bound in green out of his pocket. "See? 'Sgot his name inside. 'Clemens Schindler, my friend, should he survive me,' and some poetry. Cain't read it proper; an' understand it? No way!"

"Give it to me!" I cried.

Puzzled, he let me take the little book from him. "Read it aloud!" said Mother, and looked at me greedily with her dark eyes. Yes, it was Albert's handwriting. I read:

> Once the lonely ones created lovingly
> Their secret world, known only to the gods ...

I read it softly. "It is beautiful that you are bringing a friend the words of his friend," my mother said seriously. She took the diary out of my hand and gave it back to Herr Schneider. "Jest gotta find him!" he said. "Cause cain't stay more than a coupla days in Vienna."

Now Grandmother went to get his food for the journey, a generous package. He thanked her. He'd take most of it to his children. As soon as I was alone with her I asked, "Don't you really know the address? Aren't you in touch with Clemens any more?"

"He was let out long ago," she said quietly. "So he doesn't need me. And if he ever does ... he knows where to find me."

"But will Herr Schneider find him?"

"I'm afraid so." In explanation she added, "I don't like him. He doesn't look you in the eye."

That evening she told us that my father was coming the day after tomorrow. "Things like that have to be discussed in person," she told Mother. Would he really come? I wondered.

We anticipated everything in our games, Walter! Albert! Everything! Again and again I would like to ask you: do you remember ...? For instance, when we had our big children's party once a year and hid the thimble, and the child waiting outside came in and had to look for it. Somewhere it was shining where everyone could see it, but the child, not knowing where it was, didn't see it, and still couldn't see it when everybody laughed and cried, "Hot! Hot!" and walked away again, groping helplessly. At the time I knew very well that I was close to the others' shared secret and could hear "Hot! Hot!" whispered in my ear, still I walked past it.

Father really did come and we didn't notice any signs of pain from destroyed memories. Mother showed him around quite proudly, brought him a blanket for his chaise longue, remembered his favorite dishes, and finally declared that on Sunday she would go back with him. It was high time for her to lead an orderly life again. Father was affectionate and grateful. "But Helga must stay here!" said Grandmother. "I need her." And I said quickly, "I'll gladly stay."

I looked for the little faded purple volume of Hölderlin's poems and took it with me to my room. I didn't know the verse Albert had inscribed for Clemens but it was probably Hölderlin. Or Schiller?

I soon found the poem, and then I knew that when Albert had written those two first lines, he must have meant especially the last two that end the poem:

> They who true to the most heartfelt love and godlike
> > spirit,
> Hoping and suffering patiently, victorious over fate ...

Certainly both friends knew the poem by heart, and when one of them began it, the other would go on in spirit. That I could feel this with them made me very happy. At last I could cry over Albert's death! And I was almost able to feel with my mother why certainty had clarified things for her in the most literal sense: it had torn away the veil that had clouded her consciousness! How close all three had been drawn to each other now: Mother, Albert and Clemens!

To be sure Herr Schneider was a strange middleman for such a union, but he was only the instrument, I consoled myself. Whenever Mother mentioned him later she always referred to him as "the cheese merchant." And when we corrected her: "Fruit, Mother!" she said every time, "Cheese suits him better."

When I didn't succeed in finding the next piece of Cinderella's hand in the heap of pieces, there, suddenly — the pigeon's wing was shining, and I was able to close the gap next to her shoulder. So now I'll leave Herr Schneider unfinished and tell rather about my second meeting with Marietta.

But why? Why don't I go straight ahead with Herr Schneider and the circumstances of Albert's "heroic death" in action, and reveal all the facts I gradually found out later? I imagine because of the comprehensibility. What I didn't know then I shouldn't tell yet or everything will become unreal. I want to tell how it came to pass ... ah ... how it came to pass, not what happened. My God, with that I would have been finished long ago! But whom would that help? Not Gottfried, because Walter could tell it to him in a few sentences, probably has done so already. And it wouldn't help me at all. So ... not what happened but how it came to me, step by step. By reporting, revealing, and bringing it all together, I may at last understand my story. And if not? Then it was all for nothing, like the horror I thought would save Horst's life, which was in vain because it resulted in his death. But something else that could not have been foreseen resulted from it: the life of my child. Have I perhaps resigned myself to it in the meantime? What happened had to happen to animate the son in me. Certainly in the beginning I wanted to give my whole story this comforting interpretation: when the end is good, all is good. What meaning could it have? You, Gottfried, were the meaning. You, my son. Indissolubly united, nothing can separate us, no one stand between us ... So much Albert lives in me, so much poesy! And the same short sightedness that could see a winged messenger in the cheese merchant. Nothing could separate us? Oh yes: a ticket to Hamburg sufficed! Perhaps you sensed this manuscript in my drawer, the lasso with which I wanted to capture you forever, and saved yourself the imprisonment. Or my disgrace in not knowing how to throw the rope far enough ...

So why do I go on writing, trying so carefully to highlight every point correctly? Whom do I want to convince with it, and of *what*?

Perhaps it will yet come clear.

And so I thought: If I go back to that day in spring in the year 1940, and begin with how Horst visited us for the first time as an SS man, then I'd have the beginning of the "plot." As if one could leave out one's childhood! Now I suppose I have to make up for it from case to case: the sandcastle with the Gotthard Tunnel; the puzzle pieces under my feet; dear Jesus who died for me whether I wanted Him to or not. After so many years, I am still the same, still full of longing, still recalcitrant, and have still not learned patience. Is it the latter that I lack more than anything else? Would I marry Herr Stadler otherwise and stuff all this paper into the oven and give up all claim to knowing how it came to pass?

I can't do that.

So come, silver-blue pigeon, settle down on Cinderella's shoulder. Stop calling, "Guru, guru, blood is in the shoe." Everybody's known that forever.

"Alphonse has cut his foot!" Grandmother said as she came to lunch, breathless. "He's lost quite a lot of blood. They were cutting the corn when some partridges flew up and something moved directly in front of him. He had already started to swing the scythe and wanted to change direction, that's how he cut his shin."

"Did you bandage it?" I asked.

"Yes. But you must go and get more bandage. And ask the pharmacist what we can do to prevent fever from the wound. Take my bicycle. No, first finish eating. They don't open until two."

"Is that the only pharmacy?"

"The other one's much too far away and nobody knows me there. At the Pelican just tell them my name if they should ask for a prescription."

All right then, I thought. Perhaps only the old man would be there again. And if Marietta should cross my path ... then I won't acknowledge her either! If one wants to live with people, one must conform to their rules, even if they remain incomprehensible.

This time a young man who limped badly waited on me. Was this the dancer from the harvest festival? He had been short and brunet; this man was too. He gave me something to prevent fever. I read the directions, found a bill and laid it on the counter. The pharmacist looked across it and smiled as the doorbell rang shrilly. "Close the door!" he cried. "Come on, close the door!"

I looked around. A little flaxen-haired boy trotted spraddle-legged up to the counter, laughing proudly. "Pa-pa-pa-pa!" Involuntarily I stretched out my hand to him; he still seemed so unsteady on his legs! Meanwhile his mother had come in, hot, sunburnt, in a light red dirndl, her curly brown hair like a halo around her forehead. "Thank you," she said, "but don't bother. He can manage alone."

The little boy had already passed me and toddled around the counter. The man picked him up, the boy shouted with joy. Marietta asked, "Did the lady get everything she wanted?" and only then raised her head to face me.

The shock didn't have time to reach her eyes, but a sudden reddening, as if with pleasure, darkened her cheeks, and she said, "Helga! Helga Wegscheider! Is it possible?" She took my hand. I stood stiff as a board.

"Herbert," she cried, "this is my school friend, my friend. Don't you remember? What are you doing here?"

I could hear Grandmother's voice: "Just tell them my name ..." and I had the same name. Why did Marietta pretend to be astonished?

An old woman came in, dug a creased prescription out of the pocket of her coat; Marietta took her child from her husband and said, "Come, Helga! Come with me!"

We walked around the house, into the courtyard. I explained that I couldn't stay because they were waiting at home for the medicine. "What a pity!" said Marietta. "Then you'll have to come another time, perhaps in the evening when Herbert is free. We have so much to tell each other! Look, Friedel, this is Aunt Helga!"

We looked at each other, the child and I. The boy had light eyes and, under his little snubnose, a long upper lip. "He's adorable." I said. "His name is Friedel?"

"Yes. Siegfried," said Mariette, and brushed a silver-blond curl off his forehead. "He's our treasure. You see, we'd like a lot of children."

"How nice," I said, but explained that I had to go back to Vienna in a few days.

"But you'll soon be coming to see your grandmother again, won't you?" asked Marietta, as if she had never wondered about my being here. "Then do let us know."

"I certainly will," I assured her, and now I was blushing.

She watched me go on my bicycle. Before I turned the corner, I looked back. She was standing there smiling and waving to me with the child's hand. I waved back.

Why hadn't she wanted to recognize me the other day and today greeted me right away, I wondered. Perhaps because she had found out in the meantime that my father hails from here and a meeting was unavoidable? But her behavior made me angry. After one has just learned the multiplication table in school, somebody comes along and says boldly: "But sometimes two and two make five! Didn't you see what a happy family we are? Could you find a sweeter child anywhere? A more contented wife? Surely God loves me very much that He arranged all this so splendidly! Yes, yes — they are right who say: God helps those who help themselves!"

I hadn't wished Marietta any bad luck. Certainly not. I had felt sorry for her. I would have liked to help her and comfort her in her misery. But that she didn't need anything of the sort and had found happiness so simply — was that right? Gottfried, I don't think there is a darker impulse in us than this outcry for the justice that punishes those who do wrong. Nothing is so difficult to comprehend as God's evident forbearance.

Is it only forbearance? Or indifference? Is it indifference and not already ... injustice? Why did only Abel's sacrificial smoke rise to heaven? Cain saw it, became jealous, and hated his brother. Why did the laborer in the vineyard, who only started to work in the evening, get the same pay as the man who had been toiling since dawn? Why did the Savior love all his disciples, but one of them most? Why should the shepherd leave his obedient flock and seek the one sheep that has strayed? If there is more rejoicing in heaven over the sinner who has repented than over the ninety-nine who have been righteous, then it really doesn't pay to be righteous. We shall have to recognize the fact that God Almighty doesn't ask what we consider just. I haven't reached that point yet. Anyway, I don't find it right.

I looked for Grandmother in the house and didn't find her, so I went over to the stables where the Frenchmen lived. Alphonse was lying on a cot, his foot raised, and was eating the raspberries Grandmother had just brought in. She was watching him eat. "Now we're getting fresh bandages," she said, smiling. Alphonse said, "*Merci, Mademoiselle.*" I asked if he was in pain. He said: not worth mentioning. Grandmother gave him a pill. I left quietly.

I helped old Frieda clear the kitchen. When I went outdoors again, only the sky above the courtyard was light. The hens crowded around me, clucking excitedly. Grandmother had missed their feeding time. She was still sitting beside the Frenchman. Just then the other two came in from the fields, chatting. They greeted me politely; I barely responded. I thought of Horst. Why couldn't he be as well off as these boys? Work in the sun and wind, enough to eat, at night a roof over their heads, waiting peacefully until it was all over ... whoever wins the war makes no difference ... There is no justice anywhere, right from the start. Some are born with a harelip, others with a damaged brain. Or as Jews. Some die with their first-born after a Caesarean, others have eight children and are run over by a car. Albert was twenty-four and is rotting under a birch tree. But Mother is perfectly satisfied since she is wearing his watch on her wrist ... They have only me ... They're not going to get much joy out of me ...

Frieda brought me the pan with the chicken feed. I scattered it and watched the birds fall on the seed, their feathers puffed up. Then grandmother came from the stable and walked up to me. "Thank you, Helga," she said pleasantly. "Nice of you to take over."

"*Pas de quoi!*" I said pertly.

Grandmother glanced quickly at my face. "Be patient, child," she said. "There comes a time when we understand everything." She must have been thinking of Herr Schneider's message as she said it, of all the unspoken lies that had separated me from my family for years, but I thought she meant: to understand means to forgive, and answered quickly, "That's isn't necessary. I am not ... curious."

The pan was empty. I turned around and went into the house. She followed me and said softly, "But child, you have your Horst. Why are you so ... so sad?"

The tears shot to my eyes, and to my astonishment I heard myself reply, "One can't love from a distance forever."

"What do you mean, child?"

"I'm sure he's changed in the meantime, just as I have, probably more because he's going through a lot more. But both of us think of the other as he used to be!"

Grandmother laid one arm lightly on my shoulder and walked ahead of me to her office. She sat down beside me on the old black oilcloth sofa that stands opposite her desk. "Helga!" she said. "One always loves from a distance, especially at the beginning of life, and then again at the end."

Grandfather, whose life-size picture hung over the desk, looked across at us, amused. "But you married when you were sixteen, Grandmama!"

"My first love, though, was when I was twelve," she explained. "Our tutor. With all the passion of which a woman is capable"

"Yes. But you saw him daily."

"That's right. Yet he was so far away that he didn't even notice me. I could do whatever I liked. Aside from the progress I made in learning, I didn't exist for him. I was only a child. And I knew nothing about him except for a little kitchen gossip, not what he was thinking, feeling, hoping. He was on another planet, absolutely!"

"And he really didn't notice anything? You were so ... reserved?"

"My youth made me invisible for him, like a magic cap. I couldn't tear it off. Now I have a magic cap again." She got up, stepped in front of the little mirror beside the door and shifted her kerchief into position over her white-sprinkled hair. "But now I am grateful for it," she said, smiling at herself in the mirror.

"I don't understand any of it!" I declared stubbornly.

"How does Christian Morgenstern put it?" she said serenely. "What must not be, can't be! But actually, Helga," very seriously now, her eyes darkened, "We love him who is the same person yesterday and tomorrow. The only thing that changes is the surface. Don't be afraid of the many kilometers. Of course the two of you will have to start all over again from the beginning, but what's so bad about that?"

"No, Grandmama," I said, partially consoled. "That wouldn't be so bad." And when she said, "Well, then, let's go and have supper at last. Frieda is going to scold ..." I took her hand and kissed it. I had never done this before and never did again.

What a relief it was when I returned to the city! Mother now attended to her household duties as a matter of course and didn't need to be watched or reminded of anything. I was rid of an enormous responsibility and paid for it willingly with increased compliance. Still, the normal, regular life of a diligent student was clouded by the knowledge that it wouldn't last much longer. Because now the war became total. Our city became the target of bombing attacks more and more frequently. One didn't have to force anyone to go down into the cellar any longer. Many people felt that the cellars of their houses weren't safe enough. Every day they put up with walking long distances, setting out early in the morning with their children, baby carriages, knapsacks and suitcases in order to be in the catacombs of St. Stephen's Cathedral in the Inner City before eleven. The bombers usually came around noon.

Soon every free room was claimed for those who were homeless, and an old woman moved with two boys into my brothers' room. Her son had been killed in action, her daughter-in-law had died. The children were pale and quiet. Mostly they stayed in their room. My mother washed their dishes together with ours. "Why do you do that?" I protested. "The old woman doesn't have anything to do anyway."

"So that she retires earlier. She stinks!"

Mother's way of calling a spade a spade shocked me. In former days, when referring to pretty and jolly things, we had found it original. To be honest, I didn't like our lodgers either. The four-year-old boy was cross-eyed and sucked his thumb all the time, the ten-year-old looked around him with sharp, darting eyes. I discovered that he took some of our bread. I didn't say anything, but I locked up the bread. Once the woman talked to Mother about her son. He had been such a smart salesman! By now he certainly would have been head of a department ... if the war hadn't come ... and if he hadn't married that slut! The old woman hesitated, crossed herself, and mumbled, "God rest her soul!"

Mother was laughing as she told Father about it, but he remained serious. "That at least ..." he said hesitantly. "At least what?" I asked sharply, but he only shrugged wearily. Then, sounding depressed, he said, "There are no more walls, there is no more private life. Everything is jumbled ..."

I could sense that Mother's laughter hadn't offended but had hurt him, and he asked suddenly whether we wouldn't rather go back to Grandmother. He would be glad to take us there. After all, it couldn't go on forever ... I realized that he hoped a small residue of yesterday's world might be preserved there, where the life of the individual was safe between his own four walls.

Before I could answer, Mother cried, "What are you talking about? Then they'll take the whole apartment from us and leave you nothing but a small room, and then we can never come back!"

"You're right," he said quietly, and after a while, "There's no escape anyway from what lies ahead of us now ..."

For the first time that Christmas we didn't have a tree. We waited so long before buying it that there were none left. Perhaps otherwise we would have felt we had to ask the old woman and the boys into our festive room. Now it sufficed that Mother sent me to our lodgers with a plate of oatmeal cookies and gingerbread (made with artificial honey).

It was cold in their room. I asked them if they didn't have any more coal. They did, but had to conserve it. So I went down to the cellar and got a pail of our scant reserve, knelt in front of the stove and made a fire. "Noble of me!" I scoffed to myself. "How many days indulgence can you hope to get for it?" My heart had less warmth to dispense than the stinking, smoldering brown coal on the grate of the old tiled stove.

"You didn't have to do that," said the old woman, who was lying on the bed and had spread a greenish-black coat over her. She was probably thinking: before the room gets warm we'll be sleeping anyway, and she was right. Two prettily decorated candles stood on the table and between a few fir twigs lay the wretched presents which I now had to admire. I said, "And what beautiful peace candles you have!"

She chuckled. "Peace candles? Them's the boys' baptismal candles. Come on," she told the older one, whom we called Little Rat, "light 'em again so's Miss Wegscheider can see how good they burn. Pure beeswax! You can't get nothin' like 'em any more. And then recite your poem as a 'God bless' for the cookies."

I protested in vain. The candles were lit, the woman sat up, the little boy took his thumb out of his mouth. Now he looked quite cute. The big one took his hand, they stood side by side and rattled off breathlessly:

> Jesus Christ be praised,
> That you became a man.
> Born of a Virgin, as is true!
> The angel host rejoiceth!
> Kyrie eleison!

"Kyrie eleison!" croaked the old woman.

"Very pretty," I said, embarrassed. "You did that nicely. Thank you very much!"

"Good night, Merry Christmas!" the old woman cried as I left, and went on in the same breath, "Slobs! Have you gotta eat the whole thing in one go?"

With the blue-dimmed flashlight, which was indispensable for going out at night, my parents went to midnight mass at the cathedral. I wrote to Horst: "Perhaps next Christmas we will be together." But I didn't believe it. I didn't believe in the peace. I couldn't imagine what it would be like any more; it seemed much more probable that people would kill each other off until there was nobody left. And in this thought there was a certain consolation. The old woman in the next room began to pray, and I turned on the radio. And I heard, as if sung by angels, so pure and clear, the last verse of the song of which the boys had been compelled to recite the first:

Christendom rejoiceth
On earth both far and wide,
Sings praises to the Lord
From where sun rises to sunset!
Kyrie eleis ...

I trembled in powerless fury. I thought: the dear Lord ... if there was a
dear Lord ... would have finished all of us off long ago!

During the day thoughts like this didn't plague me because there was
always something that had to be done. One had to stand in line for hours
now for food, and the time spent in the cellar was lost time too.

It was February, I think, when I had an errand to do on the Wieden,
and was taken by surprise by an air-raid alarm that came earlier than
usual. I walked into the next house, which was the thing to do. I helped
an old woman on crutches down into an already crowded cellar; then I
told the strange children a fairy tale. I drowned out the woman's grum-
bling and everybody listened to me. But when the first powerful shock
caused the walls to tremble, she started her litany all over again, and
since the light had already gone out, some found the courage to join in
the supplication: Pray for us! Then, when the light of an electric bulb
gleamed dimly through clouds of dust, everybody, with the instinct of
scared animals, pressed forward to the door and up the stairs. My warning echoed ineffectually. So I joined them, and we reached the hallway.
The heavy door hung aslant on its hinges; dense, caustic smoke was
pouring in. Where were the wet cloths now that we were supposed to
hold against our mouths? The children gasped for air, screaming. Then
the sound of the all-clear signal. Unhesitatingly everybody turned around
and went up to their apartments in this house, which was still standing.

I ran out into the street with the air-raid warden, a little old man. He
was dutifully holding his "fire beater," a broom with a cloth wound
around it, and there we stood in front of a gigantic heap of rubble, bricks
and glowing beams. A house diagonally opposite had been cut in half.
Fire engines roared up; later soldiers came with spades and started to dig.
The heat almost scorched us, the hoses wet us to the skin. Only a part of
the staircase had collapsed, so we were able to work our way to the cellar
steps. Now we heard knocking signals and muffled cries. "They're all still
alive!" somebody said. Then I saw the child.

All of us saw her at the same time. There seemed to be nothing wrong
with her. She sat hunched in front of the cellar door, staring at us. "She's
in shock," somebody said. "Carry her upstairs."

I went over to the little girl and picked her up and held her in my
arms. She was thin, perhaps six years old, but limp and very heavy.
"Come," I whispered. "It's all over. Now everything is going to be all
right." "Yes, Grandma," said the child, and with a last sigh closed her
eyes as if now at last she dared to sleep.

No. I can't describe it. How they came up one by one, what they looked like, how they protested yet submitted humbly when the women with the NS Welfare insignia came and began to assign emergency quarters. I stood there with the lifeless child in my arms. It was as if I no longer belonged, nor the child. An energetic woman asked me if it was my child. I said no. "Then put it down!" she cried. "Help us! We've got to see to the living!"

I obeyed. I put the child down on the curb and helped to carry a stretcher with wounded five or six times from the cellar entrance to the open truck that was waiting. It began to snow hard. When all the wounded had been taken away and I could go home, the little girl was lying under a thin, white cover. If her grandmother came now, she wouldn't recognize her.

I had lost my bag with my purse in it, so I had to walk home, almost an hour's walk. Mechanically I put one foot in front of the other, still with the feeling of not being wholly there. Some people turned to stare at me — at home, in front of the mirror, I realized why — and I twisted around to find out what there was about me to stare at. At the same time I was thinking: I must write to Horst right away. Everything is completely changed. I have to tell him.

But when I had washed and changed my clothes, I was able to put only one sentence on the paper, with benumbed fingers: Today there were dead ... Then I didn't know how to go on. There was no way to express it. In the end I tore up the paper, went into the kitchen and made myself a cup of tea.

Later I saw worse things than this pale, ostensibly unhurt child. I helped to dig out a twelve-year-old boy whose legs were smashed, while his mother stood beside us, screaming, "At least he won't have to go to the front! Hitler won't get him!" and something akin to demonic triumph trembled in her voice. But beside her stood an old lady in an expensive fur coat, wailing because her Meissen porcelain was destroyed; she had inherited it from her grandmother, and all her life had washed it herself ... I was witness to what man is when faced with the destruction of his world, and I tried to stand firm and think: that's the way it is. And whether we deserve it or not, we've got to bear it somehow, we've got to see it through.

"Aren't you the least bit afraid?" a strange woman asked me when I wanted to go out into the street during an attack because we could hear the screams of the wounded. Afraid? I thought. That will come in due course. But not now. Now we're in the thick of it.

At home I told my parents nothing, nor did they ask me.

My mother accepted the daily hardships as fate, but my father accused those in power more and more openly: the Allies, who had negotiated with Hitler until he had finished arming and been able to choose the best moment for his war. Who were now holding the entire German nation, including us, responsible for the crimes of this clique, which they themselves had nurtured! If only they had conceded to Reichskanzler Brüning half of what they would later grant this blackmailer! If only they had promised Schuschnigg the support of their weapons instead of mere "moral support"! But now they were bombing civilians; the whole German nation deserved to be destroyed!

What was I supposed to reply? If you had thoughts like this, you shouldn't have sworn allegiance to Hitler as a civil servant. But don't you really remember how you wept for joy when your old dream was fulfilled: One People, One Reich! And were glad to put up with Hitler.

I had gradually learned to be silent. Walter was dead, Albert was dead, so could I say to my father: you and your kind ... it's more your fault than anyone else's, if one can speak of fault and not only of disastrous fate? I didn't have the heart to do it. but he took my silence for agreement, and next time he was already saying, "These criminals! They won't capitulate until nothing's left standing. That's the revenge of the peddler who couldn't sell his postcards."

When a North German woman walked into a store and started to speak, expressions became stony and the merchandise she wanted was rarely there. As soon as she was outside, it started: They had let us in for all this! They had always been the smart ones and had ordered us around, had eaten our butter and guzzled our wine, stolen our gold and even decamped with the Kaiser's crown! "But the Führer is Austrian!" I burst out once in childish anger, and was told, "That's right! But he didn't get anywhere with us! *They* made a Führer of him!"

I didn't dare to insist: "Didn't we shout with joy when he came in all his glory with soup kitchens and air squadrons?" Because I knew they would reply with coquettish naiveté: "Sure! We always shout for joy when we're well off! Live and let live!" "We didn't let the Jews live!" "We didn't chase them away. Matter of fact, I always used to buy from Jews. Of course we moved into their apartments when they were gone! Should they have remained empty? Of course we Aryanized a few stores! They diddled us often enough! It was our turn! ... I always said maybe we shouldn't have burnt down their synagogues. But only a few devils did that! ... Perhaps we should have stopped them ... But I ask you — what do we need synagogues for in a Christian country? We're religious people. The Jews remind us of the Savior's death, that's why we couldn't stand them. But we did them no harm. We didn't ... Didn't we watch them wash the streets? ... So what? Our soldiers in Russia had to put up with worse! They say ... come closer ... in the concentration camps they are murdered, with their wives and children ... And you believe that? That's propaganda from the London station. And anyway, it's not *our* fault!"

What would you like, miss? Thread? Don't have none. Paper thread, if you like ... There you are! Heil Hitler! Home to the Reich with the Heinies!

And I was one of them, one of these shabby cowards who only shout with joy for the rich and mighty and despise the loser.


In February, after a long pause, there was at last news from Horst. He had suffered a shoulder wound, was in an army hospital, and hoped for sick leave. "But my arm, if it can be saved, will remain stiff, Helga. So I'm coming back a cripple. Is that bad?"

"Thank God!" Mother cried. "For him the war is over!" She embraced me with tears in her eyes. "Child, be glad!"

"He's a violinist, Mother. What will he do now?"

"Something will turn up," said Mother, sounding a little unsure. "The main thing is, he's alive!"

"I'll believe it when I see him standing in front of me," I said. "Then I'll be happy too."

"I hope so," Mother said reproachfully.

She couldn't understand me. Nobody understood anybody anymore. I can remember though what I felt at the time; but that it is the same person who is writing all this and will soon be packing her things for Vienna in a small suitcase and be looking for a room and work there the day after tomorrow — that is almost impossible to grasp. Am I saying this in order to be able to go on writing? It's not happening to me, but to that other girl? All, right, perhaps that's a useful device. And when I no longer write *I* but *she*, then I am not lying any more than I have been lying until now: because we look back at our past *I* and its experiences as something outside us. But we experience our true *I* as beyond the passage of time, as independent of our age. When I look at your picture, Gottfried, at age two — I've placed it beside my bed now — then you look at me so shyly and inquiringly, as you did yesterday, not desiring but requesting an answer.

I call myself to order! The facts, please! The whole thing is supposed to be a factual report or even a settling of accounts. So on with the text.

Our lodgers, the old woman with her grandchildren, were evacuated. Children and old people were a hindrance. Away with them! Oddly enough, the room wasn't requisitioned any more. Perhaps a file card got misplaced. At the time many things got mixed up because a lot of people disappeared overnight from Vienna whom one would have liked to keep. They fled west from the approaching Red Army, leaving their homes and possessions behind.

Not only the lady with the little girls left our house, but the capable (and therefore throughout the entire war "deferred") manager of a big food distribution firm disappeared without leaving a trace, as did the secretary of the central radio station who spoke so many languages. Often I thought of Albert's warning: "Run as far away as you can!" But how far would I get? And I think I tend only to flee forwards. I want to put fear behind me. And that one can do only if one stands firm.

In the night, after writing these lines, I tried to find my way back to the state of mind I was in at that time. What did I actually fear, wish or hope for? Certainly that both of us would somehow be spared, Horst and I. I didn't ask myself how this was going to happen. I had no goal anymore. I was afraid of meeting him again. We had lost the ground under our feet because we could no longer believe in what had formed the basis of our union: in the Führer, in the German people, chosen to save and lead Europe, in all the ghastly sacrifices for which we were to blame. How could we look each other in the eye? One would hold the other responsible because both of us had succumbed to the illusion longer than necessary for the other's sake, so as not to leave the other alone with his illusions, so as not to disappoint him. How could we respect each other, and how love without respect? "I'll find out when he stands before me" ... that's what I told myself and probably meant that it would be possible somehow to conceal everything.

Now that I have written this, I think for the first time: a good thing it happened differently.


It means so much to me to prove to Gottfried now, before Christmas, that I am not the least bit angry with him anymore. So I sent him a long account of my visit to Vienna and am fitting a copy in here.

You know that I want to move to the city and earn money, and to be in a position to live with you when you come back to study. You will be a grown man then, my Gottfried. I shall feel it more strongly than other mothers because we will have been separated for such a long time, and I think it will be good for both of us. Just imagine the main problem — namely, where to stay — resolved itself in almost fairy-tale fashion in the first few hours!

I checked my suitcase at the station and took the streetcar into the city. I stood next to a fat lady who looked me over in a friendly way and finally asked, "Aren't you the daughter of Frau Hofrat Wegscheider?" With this question I recognized her as the daughter of the lame old lady with whom grandmother shared a room. We had often met on visiting days at the old people's home. When she heard that I was going to be in Vienna only for a few days and had just arrived, she invited me to stay with her. She happened to have a room free and wouldn't be renting it anyway until the New Year. I accepted gladly, and as soon as we had arrived at her old two-story house in Nussdorferstrasse and I had walked into "my" room, I was determined, if at all possible, to stay there. Because from the loud, ugly street you walk through a broad entry way into a wide courtyard with wintry grass and one huge tree, and look up at a real Old Vienna balcony that runs around the whole first floor. Many doors open out onto it, as does the door to my room too.

The landlady lives in two rooms that face the street — I can't imagine why. The walls shake with every passing truck. Evidently this doesn't bother her.

She quickly made tea for us and I let her tell me her story as I sat amidst her beautiful, lovingly cared for Biedermeier furniture. She never married, and is able to defray her everyday expenses by renting three rooms, but her only joy, she explained, is the yearly trip she takes to foreign countries; for that she is using up the interest of what had once been a considerable fortune. Until now she had only been able to travel in the summer, when her lodgers were away. Wasn't it a problem to find new ones on her return? She said no; the young people paid a fair share of their rent even in the summer, because it wasn't easy to find quarters like this. Each room had a hot plate, and the rooms were electrically heated. "I had to install stronger circuits. Everybody can get water in the courtyard, as much as they want." Of course there had to be some supervision. "That they don't bring in girls, that sort of thing. After all, nobody's got to stay who doesn't like it. Oh, sometimes we have trouble. But I tell myself, for twenty-five hundred schillings I'd have to sit eight hours a day in an office, wouldn't I?"

She gets eight hundred schillings for a gloomy, sparsely furnished room with a wobbly washstand! She explained: "I only rent to colored people. They don't have much choice, so they pay better. The one over there in number two is an Indonesian; has his doctor's degree. He's been here five years. In one there's an Arab. He's studying economics — that's what he says! I think he's just having a good time at his father's expense! Well, that's none of my business." I asked who had been living in my room. She said, "A real African! Coal black! Do you mind?"

Now she confessed that it was her intention to find a person she could trust for this room because she'd like to see Egypt and Palestine, where it was too hot in the summer. "But then you'll get less rent," I told her. Fräulein Wermuth had already thought of that: she felt sure she could make up for any such loss in the summer months if she rented to tourists by the day or week ... obviously the rooms of the students who were away but who were still paying for them.

I rose. Then she asked me point blank, "What would you pay for this room?" "Four hundred, perhaps," I replied. "But you must take the central location and the ideal quiet into consideration," she pointed out. "I know,"said your businesslike mother. "But the stairs too, in summer and winter, to get water, and to the toilet." "Well, think it over," she said. "This time you're my guest, of course." "How do you know, by the way, that I'm a trustworthy person?" I asked. She laughed and patted her towering blond hairdo in front of the mirror. "My knowledge of human nature," she said, but then she added, "After all, I know who your family were."

I could only wonder how quickly all this had happened because I am determined to move in there on January first and see what Fräulein Wermuth expects from her "trustworthy person."

My second effort was not quite so successful. After answering a few job offers in a coffee house, I decided to look up Herr Lukesch, the owner of a literary agency for which I once worked briefly. In the telephone book I saw that he was now a publisher. I found him in; he hardly seemed older, only fatter and a trace more reserved than formerly. Why, for heaven's sake, had I stopped working for ten years? he wanted to know. Surely I must be out of practice! "I've been reading a lot of French," I told him. "I mean out of practice in German!" he said. I laughed as I replied, "You don't know that I have a son whom I always helped with his German homework. Besides ..." He raised his eyebrows. "Besides?" "I write a lot of letters ... and so on ..." I was already feeling quite foolish. He shrugged in disbelief. "Whoever writes letters today?" he said. "I do," I said, suddenly annoyed. Now he explained calmly that there wasn't the same demand for translations as there had been then. The main difficulty was to find suitable material, and for that one had to follow the French papers constantly, visit the libraries, et cetera, and above all have a "nose" for what people wanted to read. "Shocking stuff, you know. Shocking," he repeated, and looked at me meaningfully. "You can't sell anything else."

I felt like a convent girl presenting herself to a film director as a sex bomb! He warned me in a fatherly fashion that I couldn't count on making a living that way. That wasn't what I was after, I lied, but now I had more free time and would like to work again. I was moving to Vienna soon. "Well, then come and see me again when you get here," he said. "Maybe something will turn up." I couldn't help but think that he only vaguely remembered me, and the work I had done for him, so I decided to write to the dentist who was looking for a receptionist for January first. And I can ask Fräulein Wermuth's advice eventually too. She is shrewd.

All the best, my dear Gottfried. You'll hear from me before Christmas. What are you planning to do for the holidays? Besides writing a letter to your old Mother?

Now I am home again and not even downcast at the thought that this house, Uri's dear, sprawling old house, will be home for me only for a few days. I am interested in getting to know people like Fräulein Wermuth, so carefree, so assured. I could almost say so harmless, since they don't seem aware of any harm. At best it vexes them. Oh, if only I had money, I would study philosophy. Because I think he who traces words to their origin might also come upon the origin of things ...

I am hungry for new people, as if I had used up the old ones with whom or among whom I have been living for such a long time. Like a coat that can't be reversed any more because the material is equally worn on both sides. Dear God, if only Herr Stadler restrains himself and doesn't feel that two lonely hearts like us should at least get together on Christmas Eve! Perhaps, as a precaution, I will go away.

But my only duty now, really, is at last to get to the end of this writing. The preparations for moving must not serve as an excuse. Because since I want to start all over again in Vienna, mind and energies must be free for present and future ...

And with this I have finally reached the exact point where I should have started my memoirs. It was a long detour. Did I have to make it? Perhaps simply as training for the last steep part? Now I shall leave my heavy knapsack at the edge of the road, all the imaginary necessities one always drags along and so rarely needs. The "provender" remains behind too, the refreshing little by-products of the plot. No more resting now for an enjoyable look around. Only an obdurate one-step-after-the-other on the path that has narrowed. Not a drop from the bottle, not a look in the mirror. Just to be safe, I throw the mirror away. My *I* shatters into a thousand pieces, nothing left of it. My report will be fragmentary because I am going to adhere even more strictly to writing only that which I really still know. Most of it sank long ago into the mire of the times.

The girl was celebrating her twenty-first birthday. Her mother had baked the bean cake which was so popular at the time, and as usual had laid violets and primula around it. She had parted from her old seal coat, cut away the worn parts, and had a jacket made for her daughter. Helga looked at herself in the mirror, pleased with her reflection. The shiny black enhanced her complexion and her light hair. But now spring was coming. "I did so want to give you something valuable," her mother said apologetically. "It will be autumn again so soon."

"And what will you wear then?"

"I ... we'll figure out something. It's still such a long way off."

Her father, evidently wishing not to be outdone, also wanted to give his child something special. He gave her his beloved rosary which his father had given to him. Helga had to laugh when she thought of Uri's merry Janosh, how he ... but aside from that, the present embarrassed her. How distressing it is when someone denies himself something he treasures and for which we have no use whatsoever! Helga thought that the season for fur jackets might perhaps come again, but that the season for rosaries was gone forever. She didn't know what to say when her father spoke a few regretful words about her bitter youth. He said, "We may have tried to keep you out of the worst conflicts whenever we could, but after all, you weren't blind ..." Was he trying to say something special? she wondered. It didn't seem very important any more.

Now I am of age and can do as I please ... but what is there still to do as one pleases in this world of destruction? I know exactly what I don't want: to be buried in an air attack. To suffocate or to survive as a cripple, to be disfigured. But a direct hit — why not? I am sure one doesn't miss much if one dies young. What an unredeemed promise the sixteen red roses have remained which Horst gave me five years ago! And today I didn't even get a sign of life from him. I am sure he is thinking of me as I am thinking of him: without a wish and without hope.

At noon, as the girl let herself in, her mother met her, looking upset. "What's the matter?"

"Father wants to speak to you."

He was waiting in the dining room where he was pacing the floor, his hands folded behind his back. The table was set. Bewildered Helga had to look again: she wasn't wrong — the table was set for four.

My spring flowers in the middle. For a moment I was shocked: Horst! Did I said it aloud? "Yes," said Father. "So you know already. But child, this is insanity! He can't stay here. They saw him coming, in uniform ..."

"Where is he?"

I wanted to pass Father and rush to my room, but he held onto me with surprising strength. "Wait a minute, Helga! Listen to me! You've got to send him away right after we've eaten! Go with him, so that you're seen together, and say goodbye to him at the streetcar stop ... yes, that's a good place: in front of the window of the grocery store ..."

I didn't try to free myself. Astonished, I stood still. Mother had taken her place at the table and was sitting, her hands hiding her face. Now she took her hands away, and I could see the tears in her eyes, but her voice was perfectly steady. "But Theo," she said, "At midday the shutters are down and there's not a soul around."

"Oh. That's right." My father sounded as disappointed as a general whose whole strategy has collapsed. "Well then, you must go down there at three sharp, when they open up again."

And all the time I was listening for a sound in my room! If Horst were here, he wouldn't stay in there without making a noise. There was only one explanation: my father had gone crazy. He had been drinking again too. I could smell the wine on his breath. That was why my mother was crying, and she was playing along with him, I supposed, so that he wouldn't start raving. She winked at me reassuringly. *Of age!* I thought bitterly. How was I going to cope with these two minors?

"Where is Horst?" I asked quietly.

"In your room," said Father. "He must have fallen asleep. He was dead tired," said Mother, and began to cry again.

"Promise you'll send him away," Father urged, "otherwise all of us are lost!"

"*You* send him away," I said. And now, as I saw the expression on his face: the torture, the mixture of guilt and rebellion, the hope in my heart began to tick again like a clock ... perhaps ... perhaps ...

"I can't do that!" Father groaned as he picked up the chair he was standing in front of and banged it hard on the floor three times. Mother said anxiously, "What will the neighbors think?" That stopped him.

And then the door to my room opened, and Horst was standing there, his left hand on the knob. "I'll go of my own accord," he said, looking first at Father, then at me, not reproachfully, just infinitely tired.

"You do understand, don't you?" Father murmured. "It's only in your best interest. But first let's eat."

"I'm not quite ready yet," said Mother, got up and walked into the kitchen.

"Come," I said to Horst.

We walked into my room and I closed the door. "You know, I didn't believe him. I thought he'd gone crazy."

"He's being very sensible," said Horst. "I was the crazy one. please let me go now. It's only going to be torture!"

"Oh no!" I said. "I won't let my birthday present be taken from me again." I could see he hadn't even realized that it was my birthday. That shamed me. How important I still felt I was!

I touched his right arm, which hung down stiffly. "Does it still hurt?" As if continuing my thought, he said brusquely, "That's not important."

"What is important, Horst?"

"Nothing," he said, gritting his teeth. "It isn't worth it anymore."

"Then why did you come?"

"I wanted to see you once more."

"Oh no! You wanted to stay with me and I'm not letting you go! Never again, Horst! Do you hear?"

"But I must!"

"No! We mustn't anything. Now at last we're going to do what we want."

Horst lay down on the bed. Evidently he couldn't stand on his feet another moment. "But your father," he murmured, his eyes closed. "We'll fool him," I said. "That's what he's aiming at anyway. Then he can keep his clear conscience, his white shirt, his clean hands!"

"Have you become cruel too, Helga?"

I laughed nervously. "Today I am of age. Let me do as I please. The only thing you may do now is rest." I stroked his thin, faded hair.

"And your mother?"

"I know she'll help us."

Do other people sometimes experience the same thing: that just in a decisive hour of their lives, when word and glance decide the future, they feel pressured into a role they don't want to play at all? Thus, filled with motherly compassion, I had to gaze at his haggard face and into his dull, sunken eyes, and speak to him as if he were still the same man who had said goodbye to me five years ago with a long, passionate kiss and in the complete harmony of faith and love. The faith was gone — I had to try to save the love even if I no longer felt it. As if at some time or other, perhaps in deepest sleep, the scene had been rehearsed, every word was right and my hands knew what they had to do ...

"How strong you are!" he said.

"Only as long as you are there," I replied, and this was not a lie.

At table Horst confirmed what my father had hoped: that until now he had just barely overstepped his leave and would be able to excuse his tardiness with the irregular running of the trains. The wounded, all those who could still walk, were to leave Vienna today, late in the evening. The rest had to stay behind because trains were being run now only for important war business.

Horst asked my father why he wasn't in the last reserve. Father replied, embarrassed, that that still lay ahead, but Mother explained eagerly that he was the only one left in his department and would carry out the evacuation of his office as soon as he got the order.

Horst burst out laughing. "Then are you going to govern from the Rax Alp?"

After the meal he lay down on my bed again and I sat beside him. We decided that we would leave together and say goodbye at the streetcar stop, but that he would come back in the night. At two o'clock I would be waiting at the house entrance. "But what will you do until then?" I asked.

"I'll sit in some café or other."

"But what if a military patrol comes by?"

"Then I'll say I don't have a train until six. They don't know so exactly now."

"And if they come later?"

We racked our brains as to where it would be safest for him to spend the long evening. I thought of Clemens, but didn't know where he was staying, and he probably wouldn't have been able to help us either. The best thing would be if a girl would take him with her, but that was something he would have to think of himself. "You *must* save yourself!" I implored him. "I don't care how. That isn't important. Promise me that you won't let me wait behind the entrance for nothing tonight! I couldn't bear that! Not now!"

The tears were pouring down my cheeks. "If I'm not there on time, Helga," he said, "then I am dead. Then you don't have to wait anymore. Then you'll know how things stand."

"But you will come, Horst? And soon we'll have forgotten everything. And we'll start all over again from the beginning."

He smiled like a child falling asleep while his mother tells him a fairy tale. I remained seated on the edge of the bed, although my back was beginning to ache. Punctually at three I woke him. Father came out into the hall and said cordially, "Do your bit, boy! It won't be much longer now."

Horst thanked him for the meal. He overlooked Father's hand, whereupon my heart sided with the old man. For what was Horst blaming him? Hadn't he played along himself to the end?

"I'll be right back," I told Father gently, but he called after us on the stairs: "God bless and *auf Wiedersehen!*"

"Thank you!" Horst called back, "*Sieg Heil!*" To me he whispered mischievously, "You never can tell ..."

"You're not being fair to him," I said softly. "Don't forget, you're his only son now!"

Horst's face was serious at once, and he mumbled, "A cripple and a failure, but the only son of two fathers."

"And my only husband."

He pressed my hand. "That's why I haven't given up yet."

When we got to the streetcar stop there was a long line in front of the shop. That was the right moment for tears. I threw my arms around Horst and whispered, "Tonight!" He, suddenly grasping the situation, freed himself and said, "Let's make it brief, Helga."

I covered my eyes with my arm and ran off. When I looked back, before turning the corner, I could see him getting into the streetcar. I must tell Mother to get in line, I thought. Perhaps they have oil ... and I began to think how I would feed Horst without my parents noticing.

In the evening I lay down on my bed, dressed. I didn't dare fall asleep for fear of missing the hour we had agreed on. I would have liked to go down earlier, but I wanted to stand behind the door for as short a time as possible. Somebody might come. And what if there was an air raid alarm? The whole house would be up.

We hadn't thought about that. Dear God, please ... I was ashamed of myself and stopped praying. As I finally crept downstairs, I groped frantically in my mind for an excuse in case I met anybody. I couldn't think of one. I simply had to chance it.

I unlocked the door softly. I wanted to see if the coast was clear ... and recoiled. A man in uniform was standing in front of me. All was lost!

"But Helga, what's the matter?"

I sobbed. "I didn't recognize you!"

We hurried up the stairs, then it seemed to me that the rattling of my keys, which fell out of my hand, would waken the whole house ... but all was still. I drew Horst by the hand through the dark hall, he bumped into a chest, the compote glasses tinkled. Then, at last, we were in my room. With my blue flashlight I gave us light until Horst was sitting on my bed. "I'll help you undress," I said, but he objected. "I can do that myself." We bickered about who should sleep in the bed and who on the floor. Finally he agreed that for this first night he would sleep in the bed. I wrapped myself up in a blanket, turned and waited until he was finished and lying quietly. But he couldn't fall asleep any more than I could. "Move over to the wall," I said. "There's room for both of us." I crept into the bed and began to cry.

"What's the matter?"

"Nothing. I'm just tired."

"Do you really still love me?"

"Why do you ask? Would you be here if I didn't, and would I be lying beside you? Don't you care for me anymore? Why don't you kiss me?"

He said after a pause, "I want you forever. If we do it now ... then we spoil everything."

I didn't understand him. He couldn't possibly believe in the blessing of a priest! Did he need wedding ring and bridal wreath? "Now is 'forever,' Horst," I whispered. "We may have only this one night."

"Just the same," he said. "Don't be angry with me, Helga. Something at least must remain whole. Can't you understand that?"

"Yes," I lied.

He stroked my arm gently. At some time or other I must have fallen asleep, then suddenly the morning light was filtering through the black paper on the window. I sat up, startled; he groaned but didn't wake up.

I locked the door from the outside while I fixed breakfast quickly in the kitchen. Mother came in, her hair in curlers, smiling, animated. "You can take the skimmed milk," she whispered. "Do you think one of Walter's suits would fit him? Do you want me to find the knickerbockers? Because the long pants will be too short for him."

"Yes, please, Mother. But what will we do with the uniform?"

"We've got to get rid of it," she said.

Everything seemed quite natural. "Did you hear us in the night?"

"I waited. I didn't go to sleep until you were back."

"And ... he?"

She smiled. She had urged him to take a sleeping pill. "A good thing you've reminded me of it. Now I have to wake him up."

Everything seemed so simple. One only had to make up one's mind to play one's part, then the drama ran all by itself to a happy ending. With wedding ring and bridal wreath? Perhaps Horst was right. Perhaps one just had to have enough confidence.

But when I came back with the malt coffee and bread and jam, and looked at him asleep, his mouth half-open, the stubble on his hollow cheeks, his forehead furrowed, his hair sparse and faded, I suddenly thought, "Perhaps he can't ... I'm a damned fool! I harassed him. he doesn't need a woman, all he needs is a bed, food, and a suit of clothes ..."

In spite of my shame I felt immensely relieved and had to ask myself: "Did I want to get it behind me only because I ... was afraid of it?" And in my gratitude, as I sat there waiting for him to wake up ... I had to be careful that it happened soundlessly ... in my shame and disenchantment I began to hope that in an undetermined future we might really be able to begin all over again to love each other.

At breakfast Father said, "If we're lucky, the Red Army will be in Vienna a week from now. Unless these criminals intend to defend the city!"

"So ... one is a criminal when things go wrong, a hero when things turn out right," I said rebelliously.

"No." My father sounded irritated. "But a man who sacrifices other lives in a hopeless situation in order to save his own a few weeks longer is a cowardly criminal. Whatever he may have been before!"

"I must go to the butcher's," Mother said, to distract him. "We're supposed to be getting extra rations for Easter."

I had forgotten that the holidays lay ahead. That would make our position more difficult because Father would be home all day and Horst wouldn't be able to leave the room. As if she had guessed what was on my mind, Mother said later, "Don't worry. Father has a lot planned for Sunday and Monday."

"On the holidays?"

"Well ... yes. There are people he wants to meet. Now everything has to be properly prepared ..."

"The evacuation?"

"No, no. The liberation," Mother said naively, and I didn't ask any more but reminded her, "What do we do with Horst's uniform?"

It had grown so warm that no one was heating so to burn it would have been conspicuous. Mother said I should make a package and she would "forget" it somewhere ... on her way through the little park or in a public toilet. "Leave it to me," she said. "Good," I told her.

How often I have reproached myself later when she started up out of her semiconscious state and began to look for the package, or when she cried fearfully, "No, no, no! It doesn't belong to me! I didn't have a package! You must be mistaken."

She was not away longer than usual. I ran into the hall when I heard her unlocking the front door. "Did you get rid of it?" "Of course," she said proudly. "I hid it behind the toilet bowl!"

She was young, gay and filled with confidence. I hadn't seen her like this for a long time. Was she so fond of Horst? I wondered, touched. Actually I imagined she had simply triumphed over danger, like a happy trapeze artist after a moment of extreme tension. In one hour, lassitude, age and anxiety were wiped away and hope shone in her every word and movement.

After Horst's return the day before, while we were still eating, the telephone rang and Mother, on her way to the kitchen, had picked up the receiver. "Yes?" she had asked brusquely, as she always did. Then there was a pause and she gave her name. "No, no, it doesn't matter," and she hung up. When she came back she explained to Father, "Wrong number." And now I was convinced that this call must have been a signal agreed upon for the beginning of those "talks," and that this was why she and Father had looked at each other so meaningfully.

I asked Horst if he would like to read something, since all he was doing was lying on the bed, staring up at the ceiling. He said he couldn't read, but wondered if the St. Matthew's Passion would be broadcast on the radio this year. Could we turn it on for a while?

I did so, and stayed in the dining room, waves of sound all around me, drawing me gradually away from the shores of the present into the very heart of the times. Finally I was imbued with a feeling of dejected calm. Nothing was over and nothing was on its way to us. Everything was being decided now, in the innermost heart of the world.

When I went in to Horst, I thought he had fallen asleep, he lay there so motionlessly. But as I came closer he grasped my hand, kissed it and murmured, "Can you forgive me?"

I asked, "What am I supposed to forgive?"

"Everything," he said.

"Very well then — everything." I said, and smiled at him

To this day I haven't kept my promise.

To forgive is a result of giving up. I know that only now. That is why it is so difficult: because who forgives renounces a claim.

It used to disturb me that in the Lord's prayer we say: *as we forgive our debtors*. I consider this a poor translation. Surely "to those who are indebted to us" was meant. But now I recognize how specific it is: when we annul a debt or give up a claim, we forgive. Only by renouncing do we pardon. That is why we so rarely succeed in doing so. Because the claim was just, we often feel we should cling to it for the sake of justice. I have no idea that I had charged the debt to Horst with double interest to this very day.

Perhaps it is just as the old priest said when he told me, "You feel like a sacrificial lamb, and that is *your* guilt."

How furious I was at the time! I had been defrauded of all my natural rights, debased and destroyed. Was I supposed to say thank you? I never went to him again, and Uri didn't urge me to go anymore. But I haven't forgotten his words, as this proves.

I can barely recall any detailed events between Holy Saturday and the arrival of the Russian army. I only know that I felt dreadfully uneasy during the alarms because I knew Horst was in the unlocked apartment. We weren't allowed to lock up because of the danger of fire.

Our situation became increasingly critical when Little Rat, the older grandchild of our former lodger, suddenly turned up at our apartment and begged to be let in. The NS Welfare had taken the whole transport only an hour's distance away, then simply requisitioned quarters from the peasants somewhere along the Westbahn line. The three of them had been given one bed only, so their grandmother had sent the boy back a few days later: he was to get through to us and hang on to the room so that they'd know where to go after the war. This obscure cloud, "after the war," which we had seen in the sky, motionless, for such a long time ... now the storm was blowing it toward us. It might be here the day after tomorrow, or next week. We could already hear the muffled thunder of artillery.

Now we had to feed Little Rat too. That was bad. To hide Horst from him was also difficult. Fortunately the boy was seldom home. He roamed around a lot in the streets and made himself useful in his way. For instance, once he asked if we had any old bottles. He brought them back a few hours later, filled with wine. With the end near, the innkeepers had decided to unload their secret reserves. "We'd rather have bread and lard," Mother said, looking worried. The boy took one of the bottles under his arm and came back in the evening with half a loaf of bread and a roll of toilet paper. I can still remember how all of us laughed, and how offended he was that we didn't take his businesslike efficiency seriously enough ...

Since all our window panes had been replaced long ago by paper and cardboard, we enjoyed the warm spring days more than ever because now we didn't have to live in semi darkness anymore, except in my room, where Horst was. Although a wide tree-lined street separated the next house from ours, we were still afraid someone might wonder about the presence of a young man.

Mother had given me Albert's mattress. During the day we pushed it under the bed. At night Horst slept on it, close beside me, so that I could lean over him and press my hand over his mouth when he groaned aloud in his dreams and gave short, sharp commands. Once he didn't come to at once and tried to push me away, shouting, "Fire!"

"Be quiet, Horst! You're with me. The war is over."

As his panting changed to heavy, sobbing breathing, I heard a strange noise outside. Then he heard it too and held his breath. Both of us sat up, motionless, in the dark. Steps. The shuffling, weary, uninterrupted tread of many feet. Countless! I crept to the window and opened it softly. Now the sound was clear, more hurried.

"They are here!" I whispered.

Horst was surrounded by danger, like a trapped animal, whichever army was marching outside. He fell back on his bed. "You had a bad dream?" I asked.

"We were walking past huts ... all sleeping," he murmured. "Suddenly two shadows ran along the wooden fence. I shot. One of them fell. But the other jumped at me and tried to stuff a gag in my mouth ..."

"That was my hand, Horst. You shouted 'Fire!' and I can't let you shout."

"Yes. And I recognized your face. You cried out, 'You killed the child!' and pointed to the body lying there, and I saw it really was a little boy. I had killed him with my own hands."

"Your right arm is lame, Horst," I whispered, and stroked his shoulder. "You were only dreaming. You won't kill anybody any more."

"Nobody any more," he mumbled contentedly, and soon fell asleep again. But I listened to the steps, the steps that passed by all through the night.

In the morning the street was empty again. Nothing to be heard but the early morning twittering of the birds and the muffled sound of Russian rockets in the south, the "Stalin Organ." At breakfast we confirmed to each other that the war was over. Father looked confident, but warned me not to leave the house. "And what about you?" I asked.

He was going to stay home, of course. He had to talk to the Russians when they came. I stared at him. "Do you speak Russian?" No, he didn't. But he had asked someone to write down a few sentences for him and hoped they would have the right effect. "What makes you think that?" I insisted on knowing, and he explained, somewhat embarrassed, that it was a statement saying that he belonged to the resistance movement that had prepared for the arrival of the Russians and would support them. Insofar as they proceeded legally, of course, he added.

I had never heard the expression: *resistance movement*. Suddenly I understood everything. So they were traitors, I thought. Objectively and with no exceptional excitement I realized that my family were traitors. "Why didn't you tell me this before?" I asked.

Mother answered quickly before Father could, "Look, child ... we didn't want you involved too." Father changed the subject. "I'm sure Helga still has her uniform in her room. That's got to go, fast!"

"I threw it away long ago," Mother said proudly. "Last week. And the child never even noticed it."

That was true. I wasn't tidy. I didn't notice when any of my things were missing as long as I didn't need them.

"That's good," said Father, sounding satisfied. "But I'd like to take a look ..." and he pressed down the door handle of my room. "Why did you lock it?"

"Oh," Mother said, "you know ... Little Rat is so curious ... into everything ..."

"Unlock it." said Father.

I looked him straight in the eye and said, "I can't do that because Horst is in there and he's going to stay there."

It seemed to me that my father swayed. So he really hadn't noticed anything. One never notices what one doesn't want to know.

He walked over to the window and leaned his forehead against the frame. "Then we are lost," he said.

"But why?" Mother tried to console him. "I got his uniform out of the house long ago, and he's wounded. They won't do anything to a cripple." And when Father didn't reply, she said firmly, "After all, he's a member of the family."

"That's right," said Father, his expression inscrutable. "But unlock the door now and don't lock it anymore. And when they come, don't show any fear. Understand?"

I opened the door. Horst got up slowly from the bed. I couldn't tell by looking at him how much he had overheard. "It's all right with Father that you're here," I said.

The two men looked at each other. The fact that each saw shame and embarrassment in the other's face gave them a fleeting sense of security. "Forgive me," Horst murmured, "But Helga ..."

"Don't worry about it," said my father, "but call me ... address me with *Du*." "At last!" cried Mother, and kissed Horst quickly on the cheek. But I though: And that's supposed to prove he's a member of the family.

A picture of the Führer still hung over my desk. My father took it down from the wall. "Put it away!" he said. But the place where it had hung was lighter. He took the photograph out of its frame and handed the latter to Mother. "Find something else that will fit into it." She went back into the living room and Father followed her.

I didn't dare to look at Horst. "Nice of your father," he said with effort.

"There was nothing else he could do," I replied. I didn't want either of us to feel grateful to the traitor.

Little Rat came out of his room, sleepy. "This is my husband," I told him, pointing to Horst. "He has been dismissed from an army hospital and will be staying with us now." "In our room?" the boy asked, startled. "No. In mine," I said. "Oh, I see," and he went to look if there was any coffee left in the pot.

Was our calm real or were we just showing off because neither of us wanted to admit his fear to the other? Because if sorrow shared is sorrow halved, and joy shared is doubled, then fear shared is fear ten times over. That is probably why we behaved as if nothing could happen to us. Because if we had really been confident, why hadn't our soldiers deserted to the other side months ago? Why hadn't our workers torn the armbands with the *Hakenkreuz* off their leaders' arms long ago and stuck on the Soviet star? But perhaps they had done so, here and there — we just didn't know about it. So who were they, these men of the Resistance? I asked myself suddenly if perhaps Clemens Schindler wasn't one of them, and if Grandmother had known it? And me, only me they had left on the other side! Horst and me! Now they were bringing us across at the last moment. For years we had been their alibi: the black and the brown uniform! For thanks we were now being protected. Our foolishness and delusion had been very useful to them ...

Mother gave me the new picture in its frame. It had been in the frame before it had had to make way for the Führer, a reproduction of the Sistine Madonna, whom I had looked up to as a little girl during my evening prayers.

"A pious exchange!" Horst said derisively.

He shouldn't scoff, I thought, because he wasn't objecting to the role my parents were forcing him to play. Hadn't he wanted to be a hero once, something so much better than an artist? But now he dreamed that he was shooting fleeing children. It would have been heroic if he had kept his uniform on and said: "I won't go along with all this. I believed in the Führer and his Reich, and if it all goes under now, I don't want to live anymore!" Heroic? A pretty opera aria, I thought soberly. In reality everything looks different. There was nothing left for us to do but keep our mouths shut. We had been marionettes and we hadn't known it. Now we knew. That was the only difference.

A new act could begin.

Theoretically I know that next morning some Russians came and walked quietly through all the rooms after Father had shown them his scrap of paper, but I no longer remember it clearly. Later it was often mentioned that they had given Little Rat a bar of chocolate and he had shared it with us. All the tenants except us were living in the cellar. The rockets were whining and one could hear the roar of planes. But what was feared most was a revenge attack by the Germans in those districts that had surrendered to the Red Army with little resistance. At the Danube Canal they said there was still bitter fighting. We didn't go into the cellar because we didn't think it advisable to display Horst's presence so openly. If Little Rat spoke about it, there was nothing much we could do, but the boy found the cellar dull and preferred to run around in the street.

So he wasn't there when the Russians came a second time. We were having our midday soup. "Don't get up. Go on eating." Father ordered, and quickly slipped a red-and-white armband, which Mother had meanwhile sewn for him, over his sleeve. "So go!" she begged him, "or they'll break down the door!"

This time however nobody seemed interested in deciphering Father's papers, or paid any attention to his laboriously learned words. We heard rough cries, trampling feet, laughter, then they were already pouring into the room. Five, six, seven ... don't pretend you didn't count them.

The girl counted them. Later. Perhaps by that time all of them were gone. Now they seemed to fill the whole room with noise, warmth, with the smell of wine and sweat and leather. The girl thought: "Don't look! Don't be startled! Don't pay any attention!" She raised the spoon to her mouth. With the next spoonful the soup splashed on her dress. One of them grabbed her arm and said, "Come." She thought: a good thing there's no fat in it, the spots will come out easily. That's the sort of thing one thinks of ... At the same time she thought: what do I do now? If I resist, Horst will come to my defense and they'll kill him.

She ducked quickly under the fellow's arm and ran into her little room, but she was no longer able to close the door behind her. She squeezed herself into the narrow space between bed and bureau. Protect your back, she thought. The men followed her. Now they were silent, and the girl could understand clearly what her father was saying to Horst outside. "No! Stay here or they'll kill you! You can't help her!"

"But we can't just let her ..." Mother cried, and began to sob aloud. It was dreadful.

A chair was knocked over, and then, beside the shoulder of the last Red soldier, the totally distorted face of her mother bobbed up ... "Go away!" the girl screamed.

At that moment she grasped the fact that she was totally abandoned. Her mother could only wail, not help. Her face disappeared. "Father!" the girl screamed, but outside all was silent. Then she let her hands fall that until now had pushed back the attacker, clutched his throat, beaten his nose bloody; her right knee, raised for a well-aimed blow, sank down powerlessly. They hadn't been prudes at the BdM; they had shown the girls how to defend themselves from a man. A shot in the next room. "Father!" the girl screamed once more in senseless hope. She heard a curse, a gruff, incomprehensible order from the next room, heard chairs being overturned, china breaking, and her mother screaming like an animal. But then, in the doorway, clear and soft, the voice of her father. "You have to endure it child. Everything passes."

So she gave herself up for lost and therefore was lost.

But that wasn't all. Because in the interval of one or two minutes, as she still stood with her back to the wall, defending herself, many thoughts passed through her mind: I won't put up with it, I can't bear it, I'd rather die. But then they'll take Horst with them. Then they'll find the mark on his arm and torture him to death ... no ... I must endure it. It's the only thing I can do for him ...

Was she filled with the certainty that Horst couldn't go on living without her, that he needed her? Was that why she gave in? Or was it only the cowardly wish to get everything behind her as quickly as possible? suddenly it came to her, like a flash: that's what we thought the Russians were like, it's good that they are like that! We were right ... And this too: Horst shot on fleeing people in his dream ... surely he killed defenseless people, that's why he can't protect me now and I can't defend myself anymore ... High up on the truck, Frau Dr. Feldstein is standing, looking down at the girl with pain and compassion ... so that's why, she thinks, confused ... that's why she felt sorry for me ...

But there wasn't time to think so many things. And yet ... if people plunging to their death can recall their entire life, why shouldn't all these reflections have risen up simultaneously, independent of the passing of time, amid the tumult of shame, pain, fury, revulsion and hatred, beside the sharpest, that is most objective perception (and we perceive with eyes and ears, with nose and skin, yet actually only in the innermost core of our being, where we think and feel the most objective perception of all details).

Which has nothing to do with the case. Which I shan't enumerate even to myself. Enough that through so many years I was never able to get rid of them. Now at last the veil that we call the past hangs over them. What happened that *was*, isn't anymore. It happened to me but it doesn't concern me any longer. Involuntarily I wrote in the third person and it seems to me now that is *was* somebody else who was destroyed. And who consented. But I am alive and intact.

My God, is that true? Can that be true?

Perhaps it will come clear when I go on, because it can't be clarified in one sentence. But the puzzle must be completed. Not until nothing is missing can one recognize the whole picture.

After the tumult — the void. The last one had closed the door behind him. From outside, muffled voices, a scraping of boots, and sobbing still penetrated, but as if from another world. The girl lay in a black silence, as in a tomb. Bleed to death, she thought. That happened. If only nobody comes first ... and then she heard the door open softly. *I should cover myself. I don't want to. I don't want to do anything anymore. Never.* But the thin, shrill scream tore open her eyes and she stared into the eyes of a little boy, glittering with the delight of horror. "What do you want? Go away!" she heard herself stammer, because her bitten lips were stiff. She pulled down her skirt.

"My grandmother," he said, but couldn't finish the sentence. His teeth were chattering. "She is tired. The dead man is lying on her bed ... but she wants to sleep ..."

"What dead man?" the girl asked indifferently. She had forgotten the shot.

"Your husband. He killed himself."

"That's like him," the girl said, and sank back again.

And I'd wanted to save him.There was no saving him. How often had he said during the last days, "I'm not good enough for you." And now she hadn't been good enough for him. Loud and clearly she said, "Go to hell!"

Little Rat ran out.

No, no. I can't have said that. Because if there is a hell, then all of us have been right in the middle of it for a long time. One should be able to wipe the sentence off the blackboard of silence, like a false equation. With what? With tears, of course. If only I could cry! Or pray! Why can't I? I could pray when I was five.

One says the words ... the words ... all gone. I can remember only those for which Mother folded my hands ... here she sat, beside me, and then she didn't look at me but at the picture. Now it's hanging over the desk. *Today if any wrong I did* ... Wrong? The banal word caused the girl to tremble with rage ... *I beg the Lord don't look at it ...*

That would just suit you! Look at it, dear Lord, please! Look at what has become of me! And now they discard me like a dirty rag! Even Horst hadn't wanted to look at me again, and Father doesn't come to see if am still alive. Self-pity released the tears that led to a lessening of tension and passed over into a light sleep. But while sleeping, and how often after that ... how often ... everything began all over again from the beginning ...

Father sat beside my bed. He had covered me with a blanket. The window was open, the birds were singing. I closed my eyes again and listened reluctantly to the birds and my father's halting words. A Russian doctor had been called in and examined Horst's body but had not discovered the SS blood-type mark, thank God! So for my father there was again something he could thank God for. Horst had evidently aimed well with his left hand. Good boy. Otherwise they would certainly have noticed the

SS mark of infamy in the hospital, and then what would have become of us? To play it safe, he was to be buried right away. The air-raid warden was already digging a grave beside the garden fence. Staunch fellow! They hadn't occasionally shared Grandmother's food packages with him for nothing.

"Perhaps, Helga child, it was better for Horst ... the way things happened. He couldn't have played the violin again. You must be brave now. Mother is in a state of total collapse. It worries me very much. Look after her. I have to go now. We must form a government as quickly as possible so that the Russians have no excuse ... Renner will be at the head. What good fortune it is that spared us this great man!"

Renner? Wasn't he a Red? a Socialist? A Red was suddenly a great man for Father? I could hear him saying, "Adolf Hitler, whatever people may think of him, is a great man because he has united the Reich." But then he had let Father down, and the bottles in the closet had to console him while he waited for the next great man. "Bring me a glass of wine." I said, interrupting him rudely.

"Wine, Helga? On an empty stomach?"

"That's why."

Father left the room and came back with a piece of bread and lard. "Eat this first." But I put it aside and waited until he came with a full glass of wine. "Perhaps it will really do you good," he mumbled anxiously. I looked at him scornfully. "As much good as it did you." When I saw the red rising from his neck to his cheeks, I looked away. Honor your father and mother so that you may live a long time ...

Live a long time? I raised the glass to my lips. The smell of the wine was nauseating. I vomited.

My father went away and came back with a pail and a rag and tried awkwardly to clean up. I lay there and didn't move. Finally he laid a wet handkerchief on my burning eyes and brought me a cup of tea before he left. As soon as he was gone, I drank the tea greedily. After that I felt hungry and ate the bread.

I must have fallen asleep again. "There you have her. So take her," my mother said, and put Mimi in my arms. Once Mimi had been my favorite doll.

Why was Mimi suddenly there? Racking my brains woke me up. I had only dreamt the doll, but Mother was sitting beside me, reading aloud to me as she used to do, quickly and without any intonation, but correctly, word for word. She hadn't combed her black hair. Half loose, it hung to her shoulders, and she was barefoot in her nightgown. I had to see that she got back to bed. So I interrupted her. "Mother, what's the name of the story you're reading?"

She looked at me, her eyes blank. "I don't know."

"Let me see." I sat up. The witch's knife shot through my body. No, that doesn't belong here. That's from Andersen's fairy tale about the little mermaid who wants to sacrifice her tail so that the prince can love her. The name of the fairy tale is The Singing, Soaring Lark.

"I want to sleep some more, Mother. Go back to bed."

"But you wanted to hear it."

"Yes, I did ... then. Now it's too late."

"Too bad," said Mother. "Well, then let's go back to sleep."

She never read again, not to me nor silently to herself. After any short attempt she would lay the book aside. "It's too late," she would murmur. Toward the end, during the last year, it used to give her pleasure to tear newspaper into shreds. The first relationship of many children to the printed word was also her last. But if I had wanted to listen to her longer at the time ...? *If*. There is no *if* in life.

I don't know any more — in the days that followed, did she look after me or I after her? Or did Father do everything when he came home toward evening, dead tired from walking long distances, from hunger and the exertion of making difficult decisions? Exhausted, thin, dark shadows around the bags under his eyes, yet cheerful, full of hope and a confidence he couldn't hide. He dragged water hundreds of meters, he lit a fire in the little cooking stove in front of the tiled oven while we peeled potatoes and sorted through dried peas for worms ... Russian rations. He said, "Things are going to change in Austria! We're sticking together! We've learned ..."

"What?" I asked.

"Respect for the convictions of our adversaries! Tolerance as a precondition for freedom ..."

How old I felt beside him! He was starting all over again, while I was finished. I didn't want to listen anymore. Of what concern was all this to me? Then I caught a few words. "And when the boys are here again ..." I raised my head. "*Who*?"

"Yes, Helga. You have to know now. They're alive. Walter in the Tirol, working with the Americans; and Albert was able to save his life too, with the papers of a dead comrade. Then he joined the underground."

What was that again?

"He went underground in Berlin, with a false name, and from there he sent a messenger ..."

"The cheese merchant!" I said, and could hear Grandmother, "I don't like him ..." Had she really known everything and not told me? Now I asked straight out, "And what happened to Clemens Schindler?"

Father's shoulders sagged. "Alas," he said. "They got him again. He was executed two weeks ago. Here, at the County Court. With nine others. At the last minute ... these murderers!"

Two weeks ago. Had Father known it at the time? Executed. We had eaten and slept as usual.

My mother said dreamily, "He had such pretty hands. He wanted to be a pianist. He was always going to play something for me. Everybody promises things but they don't keep their promises. Traitors all of them ..."

The word on the tip of my tongue, that I had been trying to choke down all the time — she said it so easily! As if she weren't herself anymore, only a membrane for promises that had faded away, or for angry thoughts ...

"Come eat," Father said tenderly, and filled her plate. "The soup's ready. We may be able to get oil tomorrow. Isn't there any bread?"

"No," I said.

"Didn't you queue up?"

"No,"I said. "I don't go out."

"Then I'll ask Little Rat,"

"No!" I screamed. "I'll go!" And I started to cry. Because we didn't have any more bread or because I shuddered at the very thought of seeing Little Rat again? (Until now I had managed to avoid him.) Because Clemens Schindler was dead. Because my father was a traitor and my mother beginning to lose her mind. And because we were all still alive, even the boys. I can't go on, I decided. I can't go on.

But you turn on the gas, no gas comes out. The clothesline is made of paper. Shall I slash my wrists? What a mess! And they'd surely find me too soon. And I don't want the air-raid warden to bury me with Horst beside the garden fence. I don't want anything, absolutely nothing at all. To die isn't enough! Never to have been ...

"Helga, please wash the dishes as long as there's still warm water. I have to finish work on a file." We have files again. Hallelujah!

I washed the dishes and got Mother back to bed. But I was determined not to get up next morning; they could do what they liked. Even if Mother ran naked through the hall.

"You're coming with me. I need you!" Grandmother said sternly. She was sitting beside my bed, watching me as I slowly drank hot milk and honey, sip by sip. At the same time I was watching her. She had changed. Her lean face was sharper and her eyes were filled with an energy I was much too weak to resist. Her hair was almost white now.

"I can't," I said. "Mother ..." She waved the objection aside. "We'll take her along. Get up. Get dressed. Where's your knapsack?"

"In the hall," I said. "In the chest."

I crawled out of bed and heard her say outside, "Hurry up, Hedwig. Take your warmest coat. We've got to leave in twenty minutes."

"But I'm hungry," Mother whined. "Let me eat this sandwich first."

"No. Give it to me," Grandmother said sternly. "You can eat it in the truck. Put on stout shoes and pack only what you need most." She's speaking to her as if she were a child, I thought ... to me too. What is she planning to do with us?

I had given up all opposition and was dressing slowly. I still felt pain with every careless move. Meanwhile Grandmother had come into the room again, and as she stuffed underwear and clothes into the knapsack, the explained, "Alphonse took me with him. He made friends with an officer who had to drive to Vienna today. He took us along. Otherwise I'd have come on foot to get you, but this way is better, of course."

"What am I supposed to do at your place?" I asked.

Suddenly there were tears in her eyes and she embraced me hastily. "*Live*, child!" she whispered.

"I don't want to anymore, Grandmama."

"I know. But you must. It's like being born — there's no way back so you've got to get out."

The knapsack was full; only the side pockets were still empty. Grandmother stuffed my gloves into one, then she went over to the desk and took Horst's picture, which was standing on it, out of its frame. It was a picture of him in civilian clothes, with his violin. I guess I made a gesture of objection. "But we're going to take it with us," she said emphatically. "Hedwig, are you ready? We've got to go now."

Mother seemed to have put very little into her old shopping bag. She was already waiting in her shabby winter coat that smelled penetratingly of naphthalene. She had put on mittens too, and a woolen scarf. "Shouldn't I rather stay with Theo?" She sounded troubled.

"You've got to decide that for yourself," Grandmother replied, and walked out into the hall. Mother let the door close behind her and followed us hesitantly.

The spring morning washed over us, blue and gold, when we unlocked the heavy house door and pushed it open. A truck, spattered with mud, stood outside; a few Russians in it, smoking, laughing, playing cards. Alphonse, leaning nonchalantly beside the driver's seat, spat out his cigarette and said, smiling, "*Enfin.*" My mother, however, when she saw the Russians and realized that we were going to ride on the truck, cried, "Oh no! Oh no!" and fled back into the house. Grandmother took me by the hand. "Get in. They won't harm you."

I got in and sat down on the seat beside the steering wheel. Alphonse put the knapsack in the back, and grandmother held the bag my mother had left on the sidewalk up to him. A young Russian got in, whistling, and started the motor. My heart, which I had believed dead, began to race, because the truck was starting and Grandmother hadn't gotten in yet! "Hey!" I heard her cry, and she ran a few steps after us, panting. The young soldier stopped the truck, laughed loudly, and Grandmother got in. "There!" she said, with finality, and pressed close to me. It sounded odd. "Where is Alphonse?" I asked involuntarily.

"He stays here. They'll be allowed to go home soon," she replied calmly. "And we two, we'll start all over again together, from the beginning." She let her cool, rough hand rest on mine and looked straight ahead.

Through the windshield I could see the almost empty streets, the windowless houses, heaps of rubble in between, a woman pulling a big child in a handcart ... perhaps it was dead. Apple trees in pink blossom glory. The sky covered with rapidly moving cirrus clouds. Two boys playing ball. We rattled across the Danube on a wooden emergency bridge. The little church on Leopoldsberg gleamed white above the sharp curve of the nose. Mass had been held there once, before the big defensive battle against the Turks. "Maria help!" Not us! Not me! But had anyone had the courage to ask her? Clemens ... perhaps. If he had been given time for it. If he had believed at all. Perhaps he had only become a priest for appearance's sake, in order to be a better traitor. To what had he wanted to convert me that time when I ran away from him on the stairs: to Christ or against Hitler? Had he really felt it was the same thing?

My father, like most people, had said "Heil Hitler" on the street, and in church "Praised be Jesus Christ!" To each his own and everything at the right time. First we praised God for the Anschluss, now for the liberation. Dear God, in any case we praise Thee ... for Thine is the kingdom and the power ... and we always praise him who just happens to have the power.

But Clemens must have meant something different. A pity that I'd never known what. Because Walter ... he was just a naughty boy playing Indians. The way he had looked through me. With that icy look he had killed all my joy that he was still alive. "Excuse me, you must be mistaken." And there would be no reviving it if he came back now. A good thing that I didn't have to see him. I wasn't curious about him anymore ...

As if she were following my thread of thought, Grandmother asked "You know that Walter is alive, don't you?" I nodded. "I hope he comes home soon and helps your father."

How? With governing? Or with taking care of Mother? I didn't want to know. Grandmother went on, "But they got poor Albert. At the last moment."

"That's like him," I said.

Grandmother's hand pressed mine down as if it had been my mouth. She said nothing more. Later she handed me the sandwich she had taken from my mother. I ate obediently. To obey without thinking ... that was almost as good as not being alive anymore.

"Babushka," the Russians called her, and they seemed to obey her too. I wasn't afraid of them when she was with me, and she stayed with me all the time. At night, too ...

But before I go on, I must admit that I startled myself when I said, "That's like him" for a second time; for the second time I used such contemptuous words for someone lost. But it's true, I justified myself.

When I thought of Albert: his indecisiveness, his constant deliberation of all motives, his dissatisfaction with everything, most of all with himself, then I knew that he couldn't have been able to hold out in such a dangerous game of hide-and-seek. I thought how even as a child, when I was supposed to look for the boys in the vicinity of the Berghof, he always stepped forward. laughing, when I came near him. "Here I am! You won!" Whereas Walter, the younger one, would rather have gone without a meal than step forward of his own accord. And later he often complained that Albert didn't stick to the rules of a game, and Albert just laughed: That's why it was a game, he said, so that one could think it over whenever one liked: be the robber now, and a few minutes later, when one was tired of it, begin all over again as a policeman.Walter was furious. Finally he walked out on Albert and found other playmates. For him every game was serious, and it was the only thing he could be serious about. It was like him to saunter through Vienna in the middle of a war in civilian clothes, with false papers. It was like him too, to be collaborating with the Americans now. I wondered if he'd come back as an occupation soldier. That would be like him too.

When he came, he would ask, "But where is Helga?" and they would tell him: your grandmother took her away. She was finished, poor child. A lot of Russians ... you know ... right on the first day ... Would he answer: That's like her. No, no. No one would say or think anything like that. Forgive me, Albert. Forgive me, Horst. Because "That's like him" doesn't mean anything but "Serves him right."

But I had thought that of the others! Only I had suffered injustice, no, much more than injustice: disgrace. From the very beginning they spared me, wouldn't permit me to participate in their thoughts, plans, actions, because my innocence was their security. That in the course of this I became guilty didn't worry them; that in the end I had to pay they probably found reasonable, because at some time or other I had to learn.

The priest in the confessional didn't like this interpretation. "You feel like a sacrificial lamb," he said, "But no one is without guilt except the Lord. I cannot give you absolution until you recognize your guilt and repent. Weren't you lacking in love toward your fiancé?"

"Yes," I said. "Always!"

"In respect and obedience to your parents?"

"I despised them."

"Do you repent now?"

"There was nothing else I could do."

"Do you still despise your parents?"

I evaded the question. "I feel sorry for them now," I whispered.

Hastily, as if he feared I might recant, he gave me absolution and told me to say an act of contrition. In the evening Uri asked gently, "How was it?"

"Dreadful. If I still believed, I would have committed my greatest sin today."

"But how could you go to him if you don't believe?" she cried, more astonished than horrified.

"It wasn't altogether clear to me yet," I replied. "But how could you send me to him since you don't believe yourself?"

She looked at me sadly. "That doesn't count," she said. "You should accept any help you can get."

"Why?" I asked stubbornly.

Grandmother leaned forward and said softly, "Helga, I think you are going to have a child."

I hadn't felt well for days. I couldn't keep food down and thought it was fish poisoning. In the co-op they had handed out sardines. Surplus. But nobody else had been sick.

I jumped up. "No! No!" I cried. "Never! Never!" I already had my hand on the door handle.

"Stay here," Grandmother said harshly. "You can't run away. It runs with you."

"If it's true, I'll kill myself."

"No you won't."

"Help me! I don't want it! It's got to go!"

"Yes. I'll help you. We'll give it away just as soon as it doesn't need you any more to live."

"It is not to live! I don't want it!"

"But it is already alive, Helga. And it is a child of God like all other children. You will not kill it. Not with my help."

I sat down, laid my head on the table and wept. I sensed that her will was stronger than mine, and her confidence, which I couldn't understand, was passing over into me gently. A child of the greatest humiliation — a child of God like all children? Perhaps if I took this upon myself too ... perhaps as a penance? Because what sort of a penance was it to say the rosary three times? Perhaps if I said yes to it, I would then be free again. I felt that was possible, even if I couldn't grasp why.

The alternative caused me to shudder. An abortion. No. I was not prepared to expose my body to anything like that: a fresh outrage. It wouldn't cancel the first one. On the contrary: I would be confirming voluntarily a consent once extorted from me on the rack! That sounds complicated, but I can't express it in a simpler fashion. My impulse: "Oh no! Not again!" was entirely spontaneous — and what else could I possibly have meant by it?

I wiped away my tears and said, "But then ... I can't stand it. That everyone knows ... Tell them the child is Horst's" Grandmother agreed at once; she sounded almost relieved. "Good. If that's what you want. It's nobody's business anyway. But now I'm going to get your soup. Eat slowly. You'll see, soon you'll have the worst behind you."

Haven't I already written once that every account of life is only a "version"? I think that was when I wrote about Marietta's fate. But then I hadn't yet recognized as clearly as I do now that our own life again and again offers various versions, and nothing is more difficult than to decide on a specific one. This consideration arises before I write how I explained things to myself at the time: Actually it wasn't a lie but a superior truth of a kind to call this child Horst's. Because I had given in to save him; thus my love for him had made this new life possible ... I truly tried to see it like that; it also explains my grandmother's quick consent. Or was she thinking: with a child that one's going to give away anyway, it doesn't make much difference who the father is?

But unfortunately, on that same morning, I had admitted in the confessional that as far as love for my fiancé was concerned, I would always be found wanting. He was the only person in the world to whom I had really felt I belonged, and yet ... What fills this chasm? Perhaps hatred, disguised at first as reproach. He had worshiped me as a dream bride, an idol. And as the counterpart of his mother. "I am not worthy of you." And when the idol fell off its pedestal, life wasn't worth living anymore. He threw it away. He decamped without asking if I wanted to join him. If now, after the fact, I declared him the father of my child, of *this* child — what could you call it but an act of revenge?

So what! If as an adult person one wants finally to cast out self-pity, a shot of cynicism helps more than anything else. It works like the pills that spoil the wine for the alcoholic because he feels sick after the first glass.

The child would be born, if at all, as Horst's child. I faced the paternity case in eternity with equanimity.

In the meantime it has occurred to me: if I am counting on a reader of this manuscript, I would have to include an obvious third "version" of the reason for my false testimony, although I know for certain that it did not occur to me at the time; namely that it would be more acceptable for the child to be the product of a loving relationship, a premarital union brought about by the war. Perhaps I had this consideration to thank for Grandmother's agreement.

Haven't I given the impression that I was living with my Grandmother as in the good old days of the war summers? Not so. The house was full of strangers, of refugees and bombed-out persons; some circus people were quartered where the Frenchmen had lived; some ...

I got this far yesterday when the telegram came: "Arriving tomorrow. Looking forward. Walter."

At first I was only startled. Was he bringing Gottfried back? But if he was doing that, he would have led up to it differently. Or had something happened? But his cable read "looking forward." I cannot look forward to it. I am afraid. Not only because something may be wrong with Gottfried ...

So I am to have Walter here, sitting opposite me for hours ... An accounting will be due, and that right away. I can't put him off with this writing. And we have seen hardly anything of each other as adults. I knew him first as the rascal who managed with cunning and charm to get everything that was forbidden Albert and me; in the end I knew him as a smart soldier. But now, in his letters, I had heard things that didn't go with these memories at all. So I would scarcely recognize him, nor he me. Two total strangers were supposed to speak to each other as brother and sister, and I had to talk to him about my innermost anxieties, about my boy. I am afraid of hearing Walter's opinion of Gottfried, be it ever so friendly! I am also afraid of the question: how do you visualize the future? Why? After all, I give a lot of thought to it myself, sensible thought. I shall undoubtedly find work. If nothing comes of the translating, I can do secretarial work or something else. That's no problem today. I shall certainly not demand any help from my successful brother. Or shall I?

Yes. Hence my uneasiness, my desire to avoid him. I need his help, not for the future (I hope) but for the enlightenment of what lies behind me. Suddenly a second person turns up to help me in this cave exploration, someone who will let the ray of light from his lamp fall in a different direction and perhaps make it easier for me to orient myself. Thus I may be able to recognize how it was.

Just then Herr Stadler interrupted me. He knocked, came in, all apologies, and said, very embarrassed: "Frau Wegscheider, please don't misunderstand ... I don't want to force myself on you, but I keep having to think of Christmas 1949 ... after the death of my wife ... when your grandmother was so good to me. And because you're all alone this year ... you don't have to be afraid that I'll refer to what I spoke about last time ..."

What a relief it was to be able to show him the telegram and say, "It's really very good of you, Herr Stadler, but look ... my brother is arriving tomorrow."

"Oh well, that's different. I'm so happy for you." If he was disappointed he didn't show it, the good man.

Walter was here for three days. Three days and three nights. On the twenty-third, twenty-fourth and twenty-fifth of December. Today, on St. Stephen's Day, I still have time to write everything down. Then I must definitely bring this to a conclusion.

I may put the furniture in one room for the time being; the dishes go up in the attic, the books in the cellar. On the twenty-eighth I get the crates, on the second I want to leave for Vienna. By then I must be finished with the past, with the spatial past, because I don't want to have to come back to this house for a long time once I have left it. And with the temporal past, with these pages. But there is nothing left to do with them but give a general report of our three-day conversation. It was one long conversation, interrupted only by meals, some housework and a little sleep. As Walter was leaving, he said, "I've never talked so much in my life! Marjorie would be jealous. She calls me a reticent man and declares that to get an opinion out of me is like pulling teeth! But you know, Helga, that comes because on most things I don't have any opinion, as most people don't. Things aren't all that simple, so why talk about them since ..."

"Walter!" I cried, laughing. "You'll miss your train! Shall I go with you to the station so that we don't have to stop in the middle of a sentence?"

"No. Stay here," he said. "We'd be in the middle of a sentence anyway! Do your best, *Mädi* ..." He walked away fast, and I melted a peephole on the window pane with my breath and pressed my nose against it. I am five years old again, watching my brother, who already goes to school, his satchel on his back, as he slides on the sidewalk, leaving long glare-ice tracks, to the annoyance of the janitor. As soon as I began to go to school, *Mädi*, the little sister of two big boys, became Helga, and she was never called *Mädi* again until now. She had almost forgotten the nickname.

Almost forgotten! All the almost but not irrevocably forgotten was the basis of our endless talks ... after the benumbing embarrassment of our first fumbling efforts had been overcome.

"Oh Walter! You're just the same."

My surprise was genuine. I had prepared myself to welcome a stranger, a complacent, middle-aged gentleman, and here was Walter, slim as ever, erratic in his movements, running his fingers through his hair as he had always done when he was considering an answer, cracking his knuckles, my telling him not to ... we looked at each other and laughed. "Now I know you again," he said. "You haven't grown more conciliatory, you just look as if you had!"

"What do I look like?" I asked curiously.

"Old, wise, mature ... My God, do you still take everything at face value? You look wonderful, *Mädi*! Like a school teacher, not a day over thirty, who is determined to subdue a graduating class. No wonder Gottfried ran way from you!"

That was Walter! If one can't let the hot soup stand until it is cool, then better jump into it! Nothing I could do about it. "How is he?" I asked.

"Do you mean: does he look well, does he eat enough, does he get out often enough and takes an occasional bath?"

"No. I mean: is he content now?"

"Since I gave him your message," said Walter, stretching his legs and pushing himself into the armchair so that his head rested on the back and he could look up at the ceiling, "since then he seems enormously relieved."

"What do you mean?" I asked reluctantly. My brother hadn't been in the house an hour; why didn't he wait until we had drawn closer? Why did he have to start talking about this thing as if it were a football game? My opposition to his approach was so strong that I didn't grasp his answer at first.

"... the boy was convinced," I heard Walter saying, "that he was the son of a war criminal. For years he had tried to be loyal to his father, to believe he had been a dazzled idealist who had tried to do his best. I guess that's just about the way you put it."

"Yes," I said, perplexed. "But that's the way it really was. You know that."

"Certainly," Walter said drily. "Only it didn't really follow that this hero, as soon as things began to go downhill, withdrew from all responsibility. And *that* only when things were going badly for him, when the Russians were going to nab him."

"But Walter!" I cried.

"Yes, I know," said my brother. "And you can be assured I gave Gottfried a different version."

*Version*, he said.

"But," he went on, "it turned out that the boy couldn't understand why the man didn't prefer to go to Siberia rather than leave his pregnant wife in the lurch. Uncanny, the things children think of, isn't it? But actually a quite logical thought."

"What did you tell him?"

"What you told me to tell him: he shouldn't rack his brains any more about the gentleman's character because he wasn't related to him. There was absolutely no knowing who his real father was. He therefore couldn't use him as an excuse for any good or bad traits."

"And ... what did he say?"

"At first he looked at me, flabbergasted. It really was a bit sudden. Then he looked down and mumbled, 'So it was the Russians,' and when I confirmed this, he was very quiet for a while. He looked stunned. I was a little worried, although I think your son is a robust fellow who can take a thing or two. Suddenly he grabbed me by the arm and looked me straight in the eye. 'Uncle Walter ... are they quite sure that ... that Horst Ulbig isn't my father?' I said, 'Yes. Your mother knows it for a fact.' 'But then why didn't she ever tell me?' he cried. After that he thought things over for a while and asked finally, 'Or was that what she was always wanting to tell me?' 'Yes,' I said. 'Just that.' "

"And I thought he wouldn't be able to bear the truth."

I looked at Walter. How soft his mouth was, and his chin! But those gray eyes had been capable of looking through me with icy alienation when I had stopped him on Währingerstrasse. We call upon all our sternness, all our will power, to lie to those closest to us, and always we tell ourselves it is to protect them. It had been my intention to ask Walter,

"How could you do that to me?" Now it was Gottfried asking me through Walter, "How could you, Mother? How could you lie to me for such a long time ...?"

"The strange thing is," I went on thinking aloud, "that it never occurred to me that Gottfried might be ashamed of his father. If he had really been Horst's son, I'm sure I would have worried about it. He had to cope with everything all by himself. Why didn't he simply ask me?"

"We usually prefer uncertainty," Walter said thoughtfully.

"And now? I mean, are you sure it isn't tormenting him? You should know that one doesn't remember the Russians kindly here. That's why I didn't want them to call out to him on his way to school: 'Here comes Ivan!' " (I was looking for excuses. Gradually I scraped a few together.)

"But that's just what they did, Helga. Some big pharmacist's son wouldn't shut up until Gottfried gave him a good thrashing. The ten-year-old against the twelve-year-old. Since then they've been best friends; at any rate, he's the only one who writes to him."

This was a blow. So I was right, I thought. My hatred of Marietta flared up, my suspicions seemed confirmed. But I wanted to hide my agitation from Walter, and interrupted our conversation by pretending that I had to attend to supper.

"And Marjorie?" I asked, when we were sitting together again. "Isn't it difficult for her to have this finished product of a teenager delivered into the house from a totally different world?" I was already adjusting my way of expressing myself to Water. As in the old days ...

"Not really. Marjorie gets along with everybody, perhaps because she's so tolerant. And why is she tolerant? Not as a matter of principle, because she has very strict, one might say narrow principles. She can't deny her Puritan heritage and doesn't want to. She simply has an innate respect for all people. She speaks to everybody as if they were superior to her in cleverness, kindness and, above all, sophistication. She really wants to learn, and who doesn't like to teach? That's how she wins people."

"You too," I said, smiling, "and that must have really taken something."

"Yes," Walter answered, very seriously. "I thought to myself: Let's see now ... there must be something in me when she looks at me so steadily with those big blue eyes. Could this woman possibly find me interesting? An unmarried woman who never goes in for the usual flirtations, and converses in just as friendly and interested a way with me as with an eighty-year-old businessman or a famous boxer. I didn't know whether I should consider this a distinction or a slight! I wanted to find out. I asked her for a date. She accepted, not at all surprised. Later she admitted she had thought I wanted a recommendation from her father because I had just started a new job, and the more connections I had, the better."

"You still have so much to tell about your work." I interrupted him.

"Oh ..." He waved the idea away. "One earns money ... That was when I got my first inkling that it can be good for a man to be lucky, strange as that may sound. But isn't it really only the so-called unfortunates who try to look across their garden fence? Marjorie had a deeply rooted inferiority complex ever since polio left her with a thin, stiff leg."

"How old was she?"

"Thirteen. And wanted to be a physical education teacher! Rode, fenced, won prizes in handball for her class. And suddenly all that was over! That she was able to learn to walk at all was thanks to years of painful medical procedures, which at first were unsuccessful. She says that at the time she realized it was smarter to take the sorrows and joys and aims of other people seriously instead of thinking constantly of her own disappointments. 'I'll never ride, fence or dance again. I'll never marry and have children. Let's see if there isn't something else on earth.' A whole lot, she found out to her astonishment. You know, Helga, one really only gets to be a human being when things go wrong and one stops worshiping oneself and the idea of one's success."

"*You* say that!" I cried. "You who risked your life when you were only eighteen?"

"But more for the sport of it," he said. "To be for Hitler was out! Albert, and above all Clemens, saw to it that I realized that. So ... *against* him. The main thing being that something should happen. Out of school, into adventure. Prove that one was a *man*. If one went under, so much the worse. Civilian life didn't offer very attractive alternatives at the time ..."

Hadn't I visualized it exactly like that? What moved me to contradict my brother? "But it took great deal of courage, Walter, and courage is positive."

"That may be, like good eyesight and sharp hearing. All hunter's virtues. Our grandfather was a great hunter, but today hunting areas are scarce. Talents like that lie fallow. Perhaps that's why some people are crying: *Vive la guerre!*"

He raised his glass to me. "Do stop, Walter." I said, feeling shaky.

He smiled. "Okay ... You see, Marjorie broke me of all that long ago. Now I guess you think: because she knew better. Because actually she does. She's religious, but she keeps it to herself. People like her take 'the little chamber to pray in' absolutely literally. Just imagine — she really admired me, absolutely seriously, so much so that she thought I was joking when I asked her to be my wife. 'But why?' she asked, baffled, turning quite pale when I replied without thinking. 'Because you're the only one who never tried to catch me.' That confused her, and she said, 'But perhaps I did. Not on purpose though. Certainly not. At best subconsciously.' You know, Helga, a Viennese finds this mixture of psychoanalysis and puritanism irresistible. Just when one's thinking: that person is naive, one has to wonder if perhaps one isn't even more naive. Well, and so on ..."

"So on what, Walter?"

He shrugged. Lightly he said, "Pure bliss! Just imagine — to deny oneself something, to have consideration for someone ... all completely new sensations. And not trying to gain anything by it, no ulterior motive."

"Just like that ... for love." I said.

He got up. "I suppose so. One can never be sure. The onion always has one more skin."

"You're so complicated over there."

He laughed. "We're catching up." But all of the sudden — his mood changed all the time — he was serious again. "Especially I," he said. "I have an enormous need to catch up. Because you mustn't think that at the time, in the Thousand Year Reich, I was already thinking so to say relativistically about my share in the thing, as I do now, at a distance of twenty years! Oh no! There were two sides. One had to be on the right one. Without the influence of Albert and Clemens I would probably have become just as strapping an SS man as your Horst, if only to protest against our father's behavior. But then, that was impossible. I simply knew too much. Albert was an ardent patriot, an Austrian patriot, of course; besides, he was a Catholic. Clemens was an ardent Catholic besides being a patriot. Between the two of them I often felt like a mercenary who had let himself be hired for strange, rather nebulous goals."

"But you hoped that your side would win, and you thought it was possible."

"At the beginning probably not, no, not even then," he said thoughtfully. "But when the thing began to function, when we weren't ten or twelve any more but a hundred, five hundred — nobody knew exactly how many, and wasn't supposed to know — that's when I became passionate about it, especially after they hanged a few of us. Yes, I think it was only from then on that I felt irrevocably bound. One might have left the living in the lurch, they could look after themselves, but never the dead. And the irrevocability of this decision gave me a feeling of security. I can't tell you, for instance, how much Clemens's scruples unnerved me. After all, he was the one who started the whole thing, our group, anyway. He was the one who demonstrated to us the possibility of resistance, and he delivered the moral justification too, from the Bible!"

"So they really were Bible evenings!"

Walter smiled. "That was the least of it. The rest of us weren't overly interested in this kind of argumentation, especially not boys like Pepi Kummer, our little Red. But he got along well with Clemens. What was the fear of God for one was human rights for the other, and since one was fighting in the same cadre, one agreed, for the time being, on the same rules."

Was Walter treating everything he had believed in and they had fought for with such high stakes at the time, ironically for my sake? In order to shame me, who with my fiancé had stood in another camp? Or to justify the fact that he had never tried to bring me over to his side? I brooded about it and thus lost the thread. When I started to listen again, Walter was saying, "... that made me impatient, and even seemed despicable to me. I thought: the priests ruined him!"

"Why do you say that?" I asked.

"Clemens was temporarily free when I came to Vienna. Personally he was just as brave as he always had been. The Gestapo had injured him only physically. But he beat so strangely about the bush!"

"How, for instance?"

"For instance, he had to be doubly cautious now because he really longed for nothing so much as to die soon. But that would be getting off too easily, so for our sake he mustn't let himself be caught again. 'And that's how the mountain of guilt grows,' he said. I can still hear him say it. He sounded depressed. I replied angrily, 'If you think we're wrong, withdraw! Nobody'll hold it against you!' But he said, 'That would be even worse! For me there's just no way out any more to the right thing.' When I left him, I shook myself like a wet dog. But I was soon dry again. When I heard that they'd nabbed him a second time, I thought, without any pity: that's what he wanted. Perhaps it's better for all concerned. In a fight you can't use people with scruples. And they'd never get anything out of him. We could be sure of that."

"Walter," I said. "I have his farewell letter. Do you want to see it?"

"How do you happen to have it?" Walter looked almost shocked.

"It was written to Uri, to Grandmother. She had visited him in prison."

"How did that come about? Show me the letter." Walter seemed moved. But I said, "Tomorrow, Walter. Tomorrow I'll heat her room upstairs. I've left everything unchanged. It's the first Christmas Eve without her. We always had the tree in her room."

"I can't remember her clearly any more," said Walter.

The day before yesterday, on Christmas Eve, he couldn't resist saying, "How German!" as I lit the candles on the little tree. He meant: how sentimental! And of course he was right. I started to excuse myself. I had had no intention of having a tree, but Herr Stadler had got one out of the woods just for us. "Look how fresh it is! How it smells!" And I had hung only a little lametta between the branches.

"But of course we've got to celebrate!" Walter said. "After all, that's why I came!"

Was that why he had come? I hadn't realized it. He gave me an expensive present, a record player. "We couldn't believe it when Gottfried told us you didn't have one! When one lives isolated as you do."

"But I'm so unmusical." I said. They evidently couldn't imagine over there how little money we'd had all these years.

"And here Marjorie sends you one of her favorite records. No. Don't play it right away, please."

"Oh. Spirituals," I said politely. "I think I'll like them. I don't have anything special for you, Walter, but I'd like to give you Clemens's letter, if you want it."

"But first tell me everything," he said.

And while I told the little I knew about Uri's relationship to the young priest, Walter walked up and down the room, looking at the pictures on the wall — the yellowed daguerreotypes of Uri's parents and her Janosh, the rigid pictures of her children, the pretty, stupid little girls, and our father in the uniform of the Maria Theresa Academy, precocious and very stiff, and our parents' wedding picture. Mother with her hair very short, in a low-waist chemise dress. 1920! "How young she was!" Walter said, obviously touched. "And she just couldn't grow old!"

I wondered, "Why? She wasn't vain."

"Oh," said Walter, "I didn't mean it that way. Our women over there are old at forty, in spite of their smooth skin, rosy mouths and false eyelashes, because they've resigned themselves to the fact that no dream can be fulfilled. I don't mean Marjorie!" he added quickly, embarrassed as a schoolboy.

"I know," I said.

"Our mother refused to give up her illusions, and then she simply couldn't bear reality. But now go on and tell me about grandmother. Or don't you want to show me the letter?"

How impatient he was! As if the letter might have an explanation for him, the riddle's solution. In that case he was going to be disappointed.

I knelt down in front of Uri's old, slightly damaged desk, got the letter out of the bottom drawer and gave it to Walter, and while he looked it over, I thought back to the hour when Uri had shown it to me for the first time. I don't exactly remember the conversation that preceded it; I only know that she had assured me excitedly: No! It hadn't been like that at all! "I wouldn't have let them sacrifice you so to say as a hostage in the enemy's hands, the way you seem to think now, so that the ones on the other side could operate better. None of us were quite sure that we were standing 'on the right side,' as you put it, Helga. Because one couldn't know how things were going to turn out. Whatever succeeded was 'right', whatever went wrong was 'wrong.' And before the end one couldn't really know."

"But what is right *can't* depend on success," I replied, astounded.

"Broadly speaking, in many cases it does," Uri said drily. "Because the conqueror always tries the conquered, never the other way around."

"But there must be a final judgment!" I cried, and tried not to betray how excited I was.

It was shortly before my confinement, and I was ordinarily in a totally passive state. I was waiting for this child, which had been conceived unwillingly and which I considered a burden and a disgrace, to finally come out of me and leave me alone again. The more difficult the birth, the better. Perhaps unbearable pain could purify me. Perhaps after that I could be myself again. Until then it meant passing time in a semi-somnolent state; it passed of its own accord. Hurry! I thought, when the child moved. I was incapable of hating it. It was innocent, as innocent as the worm one steps on, the fly one kills. But if in our world success alone decided what was right, then it would have been better to kill the child right away. I felt a tortuous pity for the little creature condemned to birth in my womb.

Uri took this same thin packet of letters out of her desk. The drawer had stuck even then. "I'll show you Clemens Schindler's last letter," she said. "The answer is there."

"Read it aloud, please," said Walter, after looking at the stamp of the jail censor on the inside of the envelope, and I stepped closer to the Christmas tree. I had to think that this was how we had recited Christmas poems on Christmas Eve when we were little.

Dear Mother,

I wanted to thank you once more for everything, and tell you that you mustn't be sad because now I must die. I am glad that it has come to this at last. I thought it was necessary to commit a small wrong in order to fight a bigger one, but now I know, have known for a long time, that in the long run injustice can never be conquered by another act of injustice: power through cunning, tyranny by betrayal. After apparent success, everything always goes along in the same old way. I at least, of all my comrades, should have known this from the start. But it's always the same thing: light comes to darkness and the darkness doesn't accept it. Pray for me.

Your grateful Clemens.

Walter was silent for a long time. He put out a candle that had started a branch hanging above it to glow. Finally he asked, "Why does he call her mother?" I explained and also told him that I had asked if the letter wasn't actually addressed to his real mother, and Uri had told me that she had wanted to bring the letter to the sick woman right away, but meanwhile she had died. "And I thought you were going to explain all the connections to me at last," I said. "It would never have occurred to me that you were going to find out something from me, the outsider!"

"Everybody had his orders," Walter replied, "and knew only as much as was absolutely necessary. Anything more would only have been a burden. Thus anyone caught couldn't tell too much, even under torture. Quite a few have our father to thank for the fact that they are still alive. He was a courageous man."

"I never understood him," I admitted.

"It was a great loss for this country that he died so soon after the liberation," said Walter. "I suppose he was nothing really but a conscientious civil servant, but how many were there then who weren't hopelessly compromised in 1934 or 1938?"

"But he went along with everything, didn't he?" I asked hesitantly, not because I wanted to denigrate my father but because I would have liked to hear another word of praise for him.

"Went along with everything? What else could he have done as a civil servant? Emigrate perhaps, with us three children and a profession he could practice only in his native land?"

"You know very well that he went happily along with everything," I said sharply.

"Yes. But with what?" countered Walter.

"With the Anschluss, of course!"

"Yes. But 'Home to the Reich' was the dream of his generation! After 1938 everybody dreamt it, the Reds too! To be sure, everybody saw something different in this Reich. For the socialists it was the home of Karl Marx and destined therefore to be an experimental effort. But you've got to admit that such experiments, if they succeed at all, so only in big nations, hardly in a small mountainous country like Austria. On the other hand, our father's friends looked longingly for the old symbol: the Holy Roman Empire. Secretly these old gentlemen saw Vienna as the capital of the united German tribes. We already have the Kaiser's crown — we'll find the Kaiser too."

"So simple," I said.

Walter shook his head. "Of course not. Their misfortune lay above all in the fact that although they saw National Socialism correctly as a fly that lives for a day, their fantasy didn't suffice to imagine what could be destroyed in one day. Well, our father and several others at least learned from their mistakes. Sometimes it looks to me now as if, as soon as they're gone, it will start all over again from the beginning. Tell me, Helga, have you never thought of coming over to us?"

"No," I said honestly.

"I could understand it as long as Grandmother was still alive, but now things are different, aren't they? I think your boy likes it over there. It's an easier life in the States."

"Is that decisive?" I asked, but added hastily, "I'll think about it. Now I'm going to the city to look for work." I guess that sounded final, and Walter didn't bring up the subject again. He began walking up and down once more, straightening pictures, reading book titles. Now he stopped in front of the calendar that Alphonse had given Uri for Christmas in 1946. Inside, on the pages of the months, there were pretty views of France, but Uri had never torn off the cover with the dedication written straight across it: *Les jours passent, les instants restent. Alphonse.* "What's this?" Walter murmured, took the calendar off the wall and looked more closely. "Actually it's true. Our memory does consist of a lot of snapshots. Who was this Alphonse?"

"A French laborer. Uri liked him very much," I said, probably sounding a little embarrassed. Walter said calmly, "And he probably liked her too," and hung the calendar carefully back in its place. Then, surprisingly abrupt, he asked, "Say ... Grandmother was a practical woman, wasn't she? Didn't she ever suggest to you ... I mean, I've heard that at the time all the clinics for women in Vienna attended to that sort of thing without any difficulty."

"I didn't want it," I said quickly. "She didn't either."

Walter pressed my hand. "You had courage and you were rewarded, because your boy is a splendid fellow. Truly! We envy you, as you can imagine. But ... didn't it damn near kill you?"

For the first time a person asked me the question and I was grateful. "Almost," I said. "But you know, I didn't want to keep the child. Uri outwitted me," and I told Walter the story of Gottfried's first smile, and then he told me in great detail how it was when his poor little baby died. Finally he said, after a pause, "You see, sometimes one just has to accept the fact that one has drawn Black Peter!" I didn't understand the allusion, and he reminded me of what a poor loser I'd always been. As soon as I drew Black Peter I'd always run weeping to Mother and declare that the boys had cheated!

"I don't remember that at all," I protested, laughing.

"Oh yes," he said eagerly. "Just try to remember! And *Mädi*, when I finally came back to Vienna in '45 and heard what had happened to you, and then about Horst, I dreamt that night ... you were coming toward me on the street ..."

"Like that time on Währingerstrasse?" I asked tensely.

"Yes. But it wasn't Währingerstrasse, it was a little narrow suburban street with a lot of ruined houses. You were holding up a playing card and were weeping as you said, 'But I didn't play with you!' I looked at the card, dumbfounded. It was Black Peter! And I thought: she's right. We deceived her."

"And then?"

"Then ... then I woke up. I couldn't do anything for you. I saw to it that Mother got into a home ..."

"I know," I said. "But I must have been a horrible child. Do you remember how I trampled on the puzzle?" No. That was something he had forgotten. "And how we played together in the sand, and our hands met in the Gotthard Tunnel?"

"No idea!"

Now it became truly Christmas. I got our dinner, which was all ready, brought up the wine, and every sentence began with: Do you remember? "Do you still know the name of the game, Walter, that Albert didn't like because he was always the one left out? You need a lot of children for it, at least seven. The chairs were placed in a row, always one less than the number of children ..."

"The Chair Game. I know ..."

"No. It had a prettier name. Going to Paris? No ... I've got it! Going to Jerusalem!"

"Yes. That's right."

"The chairs were in the middle of the room, side by side, facing the door or the windows. The children marched around them, single file, and when the leader cried 'Now!' everybody had to sit down fast."

"He cried, 'Attention! The enemy!' Something like that," said Walter.

"Possibly. Makes no difference. Anyway, the thing was to find a free seat. Whoever hesitated was left out, and Albert was nearly always left out."

"Naturally," Walter said quietly. "On the voyage of life too."

He drank to me. I protested. "Do you really believe, Walter, that the dear Lord puts up too few chairs?"

"Sometimes it looks like that. But the nice thing about Albert was that he never resented anyone who was quicker. Only you, *Mädi* ... you were really a poor loser. Do you remember: we had a dice game ... Horse Race ..."

"I can see it!" I cried. "A beautiful landscape with hurdles and little forests and light blue brooks. The ground was dark green. Railway crossings ... a sports arena ..."

"And the horses were black, brown and white," said Walter. "I always wanted the black one!"

"And I the white one!"

"It started with one, a hundred was the goal. Once you were way ahead of us, but just before the goal you had to go back because you came to a raging brook, and the square said, 'Bridge destroyed by high tide. Back to square one!' "

"Then I lost, of course!"

"Lost?" cried Walter. "You never lost because you ran off crying as usual and went to bed without your supper. We were furious and had to put up with the reproach: we should let our poor little sister win once in a while."

"And what did you say to that?" I murmured.

"Nothing," said Walter. "But later we played alone."

We looked at each other; the same thought came to both of us. "So that's why," I said. My laughter sounded forced. I had just finished my third glass of wine.

"Perhaps also because of that," Walter said slowly. "Because somehow we seem to go on playing them, only with different names — all our games."

"And gradually," I said, "one also has to learn to lose."

"Yes," said Walter, suddenly serious, "Because this," and he tapped the pocket of his jacket into which he had dropped Clemens Schindler's letter, "this is certainly true, what Clemens writes. But with this truth all one can do is die. It's useless for living."

"Do you think so?"

"He who wants to act absolutely correctly, can't act at all." Walter said firmly. "You know, I have acquired enormous respect for the sober idealism of the Americans. Just look at our young president! Many of his enemies consider him a visionary, but I'm telling you — he knows how to balance the books. The sons of millionaires are usually good at figures. The Peace Corps is fine, but the atom bomb is indispensable if one wants to use the Peace Corps. To end the cold war is certainly desirable, but the use of warships against Fidel Castro was more important at the time. One always has to keep the grand concept in mind: what is useful to others is in the end useful to us, and vice versa. When our consumers are poor, we can sit on our merchandise. Alleviate poverty and sickness ... sounds great, and at the same time it's the best protection for our prosperity. I feel a lot of sympathy for this expansive egoism. Believe me — in the course of history fanatics have done more harm than all the corrupt businessmen put together."

I didn't contradict him. It sounded convincing. But perhaps he had expected agreement, because he went on, irritably, "Anyway, I infinitely prefer the Protestant work ethic over there to the decaying Catholicism here."

"What are you talking about?" I cried bewildered. "Are you drunk?"

"I do feel the wine," he admitted. "But I know what I'm talking about. Not in detail — for that I would have to live here longer, and I have no desire to do that. I'm speaking generally, about the people who carry the dear Lord in their mouths and send welcome telegrams to the devil."

"Oh. I see." Suddenly I felt tired. "That still upsets you?"

"Doesn't it upset you?" Walter retorted. "One could have forgiven anyone else at the time, but the Cardinal of Vienna?"

"Just the same — they almost threw him out of the window a few months later when he realized whom he had welcomed! You can't expect me to condemn him. We needed more time ..."

"That's true," Walter granted. "I don't have anything against Innitzer personally either. Perhaps he would even have liked to be a martyr. But the Church only grants that to little people. The influential ones have to see to it that as soon as the wind changes, they reef their sails so that the ship can't capsize. That the institutions are safe and the apparatus functioning — that's the main thing every time. So first it was the church of the feudal lords, then of the big industrialists, and now, once more, an *aggiornamento* is due: since democracy has been victorious all along the line, let's be democrats for a while."

I listened, flabbergasted. To whom was Walter making his speech? And why did I know next to nothing about these things? After all, I listened to the radio occasionally, read the newspapers frequently, and even watched the newsreel every now and then. Thus I was able to give him the cue for which he seemed to be waiting. "Do you really consider Pope John an exponent of decaying Catholicism?"

Walter shrugged. "Perhaps he's really honest. If so, he doesn't see through the game that's being played. They're letting him get the chestnuts out of the fire. But before he goes too far, before anything changes seriously, just in the nick of time — they'll drop him."

"But you can't just drop a Pope!"

"Maybe he'll die in good time," said Walter. "If not, that can be helped along. Wouldn't be anything new."

The last little flames were flickering on the tree. At first Walter's cynicism had impressed me, but now I resented the vehemence with which he accused the world of his origin in order to place his new homeland in a better light. And the respect with which he had spoken of our father didn't seem sincere anymore. I sensed scars in him that might break open any time and bleed. I bear the scars myself; no wonder I could sense them in him. Perhaps both of us were suspicious of each other: had the other perhaps remained whole?

These thoughts had made me lose the thread while Walter had gone on talking, but I heard, "... Sometimes I envied you because you were safe." I felt my way back along the guiding line of these words and was just able to catch the last fading sentence: "You and Horst ... you seemed to obey these slogans blindly, without any presentiment whatsoever of what they were hiding."

"At first we really didn't see it," I explained, "and then it was too late."

Walter turned on the light. It was so bright, I closed my eyes. He said, "If you don't mind, let's play the record now. It's just ten. I arranged with Marjorie that she'd be listening to it now too, along with Gottfried ..."

In involuntary protest against so much thoughtful agreement, I said, "But then you didn't figure out the time difference! It's morning there now."

Walter put the record on the player as if he hadn't heard me, then he turned the light out again and leaned over my chair. He propped his hands on the arms so that his face was very close to mine. The wine on his breath was slightly unpleasant, and anyway, I don't like people so close to me, I'm not used to it, because it's a long time since Gottfried appreciated anything like that. And Walter said, while the muted drums and rhythmic clapping were already issuing from the record player, "You know, *Mädi*, don't take it all too seriously. Christ is supposed to have been born in November but we celebrate his birthday today. What does it matter? I think we often hold the pictures up too close to our eyes, and then we wonder when they get all hazy."

He stepped back and sat down quietly and listened, and now the voices of the Negroes also drew me into their magic spell. And subsequently it seems to me that this sentence was the wisest thing Walter ever said.

When I was finally in bed, exhausted from so much talking and listening and replying — my mind is totally untrained for such things — the misty tatters of his opinions wove through the dark, dispelling sleep. I could think of better answers, inadequate too. I simply knew too little! I knew too little about Walter's new homeland, its history, its present, hardly more than a few catchwords: free enterprise, integration, tolerance ... I could see before me the pictures in illustrated magazines: Hollywood and Harlem, exploration in outer space ... and do I know more about my own country? I share the general opinion that things are better now than they were before, even better than ever (if one doesn't take the mythical good old days into account.) Still, things are by no means good. But then, how can the many things that are not good add up to something better? For instance, does the balance of corruption add up to a fragile justice? I had never racked my brains over things like this. Like most people I accept the public climate as I do the weather: unwilling but resigned.

And is it really correct, what Walter declares: that with Clemens Schindler's insight one could only die, not live, because no action can be free of guilt? And if that's right, what possibilities are left to us? Truly only death, or anticipated death — the cell of the recluse? For our earthly life there is nothing but resignation, and redemption is valid only for above, for the Upper Room.

The hoarse, ecstatic voice of the black woman rises passionately above the clapping, shouting and wailing, and reaches an apogee of longing — the Upper Room. Again and again she repeats this symbol of invocation. The designation is simultaneously ascent and arrival, seeing and seeing again, and recognizing without seeing. Now there is no more separation from the living. Those over there, Marjorie and Gottfried, are borne upward by the voice, as I am, as we are, and the others are already waiting there: Uri and Horst and Albert. There are hundreds of doors through which they can enter because that too is what makes this room Upper, that all those who have been parted find each other and become one in joy in the Upper Room ... the Upper Room ...

I woke up in the middle of the night and asked myself: why am I so happy? Oh yes, Walter is still here and we have another whole day together. That suits me fine, but it can't be the reason I'm so happy. Because I am also a little afraid of him. He is always so positive about everything. I'm sure that's good for Gottfried because that's just what he was lacking with us. A young person must have a solid wall against which he can ram his horns, not a lot of perhaps ... could be ... on the one hand, on the other hand. When babies teethe, one gives them the hardest rind to bite on ... But why am I so happy?

Perhaps because of my decision, as I fell asleep, to interest myself more in the world. I was really a backworld person. (Shouldn't it be *backwater*? Makes no difference.) "I won't play anymore!" I had cried as a child when I had been on the verge of losing. Now, for seventeen years I have been sitting in a dark room and have heard unwillingly what the others are doing next door, and have clung stubbornly to my decision: I won't play anymore! It takes courage to come out so late and say: Here I am again! But fortunately they are so engrossed in their game, they'll hardly notice me. Then I'll step into the circle just as soon as they count again: eeny, meeny, miney, mo ... or: Kaiser, king, nobleman ... why haven't they modernized that yet? Film star, director, statesman, doctor, teacher, mailman ...

Why am I so happy, so filled with courage, suddenly in such high spirits?

In the Upper Room.

There's nothing new about it. But for me it is new. I had forgotten that one could get in, that everybody could, even I! At any time, even now! Beside this revelation everything that has happened becomes unreal. Because what happens is petrified, remains preserved in layers, a mere reproduction of a form of life. But life doesn't pass — it escapes from time to time to the Upper Room ...

I am full of strength, as if I had never expended any. Joy is nothing but the readiness to begin anew, knowing very well that just before the goal one may again read: back to square one.

My little white horse has recovered; now it wants to run again.

When I awoke for the second time the sun was already shining into the room. Startled, I looked at the clock: 8:30.

"Why so horrified?" Walter asked genially. "We're not missing anything."

He was sitting on a chair beside my bed. He had thrown my clothes over the hump of the sewing machine. He apologized for having looked in on me. It had been almost eerily quiet in the house. "And I'm sure you're hungry," I said.

"That too. So get dressed, but see to it that you keep your sleeping face. When you're asleep you still look like a schoolgirl."

"Why are you wearing black anyway?" he asked, when I brought the breakfast tray into the living room. "Because of Grandmother?" Is that still customary here?

"I like to think it suits me," I said. "Black makes you look slim."

"That's something you don't need," said Walter, and trickled the dark honey onto his bread and butter. "Is it homemade? It's wonderful."

"Yes," I said. "Herr Stadler is very proud of his honey. He manages to keep bees in spite of our rugged climate. It's his hobby. I think it costs him something. Imported honey is cheaper and people don't notice the difference."

"People are stupid everywhere," Walter mumbled. "Tell me, does he have a family?"

"No," I said, and was angry when I felt the blood rising to my cheeks. "His wife was killed in an accident. She ran her bicycle into a jeep."

"And when was that?"

"Gottfried was still very small ... soon after the war."

"And since then he's been alone?"

"Yes."

"And you?"

"What about me?" Now I was really furious. "If it reassures you — he did ask me to marry him a while ago. I turned him down, of course."

"Why?"

"Why? Because I don't ... because he doesn't ... tell me, Walter, do I have to explain why? If I'd said yes I'd also have to give my reasons. I feel perfectly capable of supporting myself and the boy!"

"Of course. Don't get excited. But you shouldn't stay alone forever. You're still too young for that."

"That will come all in good time," I said, irritated, and Walter didn't bring up the subject again.

I am "still young." But I was much younger during all those years. When he met Marjorie, did he ask her: Why don't you play tennis? Surely not, because he could see she had a game leg. There are things that don't come into question for me. When Gottfried was three, he had a case of fish poisoning. Since then he doesn't touch fish, and if I had forced him to, it would certainly have made him sick. That's the way it goes, my dear. A purely physical business. Walter didn't ask any more questions, but I could read his thoughts: Didn't anyone "please" her in all these years?

More than one man "pleased" me. Hasn't any woman "pleased" you since you got married? Probably, the way I know you, one pleases you everyday. But what comes of it? Nothing. Because you are not free. Literally speaking you are unfree, can't make a move, because your wife "fetters" you. How clever language is! You are fettered by her and therefore can't run after another, even if you wanted to! In the same way, or in nearly the same way, I am unfree. They say that people still fell pain in a limb that has been amputated. They ignore it and don't talk about it; still it hurts.

Walter said the weather was glorious, that we should get out in the fresh air. He wanted to invite me to dinner in town. "Fine!" I said. "Let's go to the Golden Lamb. Do you have enough dollars? I'll heat the stove so that it'll be warm when we come home."

We walked fast. At first the trees were still covered with thick, lacy veils of hoar frost, then the sun came out. I told him how all this land had once belonged to our grandfather, but now we owned nothing anymore. And I also showed him the artificial pond that Janosh had laid out for hatching fish, which had failed as all of his other enterprises had. You could see loops and curves on the ice. "Sometimes skaters come from town, not many, because after all, it means walking four kilometers."

Walter was surprised how long it took before we met the first person. "Nobody goes for walks any more." Then Walter told me that my son already had a friend, and the two had joined a chess club. "No girlfriend?" I asked casually.

"But of course," said Walter. "A nice girl. Her name is Ruth."

"Does he play chess with her?" I asked foolishly, and Walter gave me an amused look. "No. He goes to the movies and dancing with her."

"Often?"

"Only on Saturday. That's the way they all do."

"How old is she?"

"I think she's fifteen. I'm sure he'll take a picture of her with his new camera. Shall I tell him to send you one?"

"Yes, do," I said, as naturally as possible, and changed the subject.

Could I possibly be jealous? Oh heavenly day! A good thing the poor fellow was far away!

We were pretty frozen when we walked into the restaurant. The warmth enveloped us so pleasantly that even the smoke didn't bother me. It was late, and quite a few people were eating. Walter was delighted: there was venison with cranberries on the menu. We drank red wine and enjoyed the meal. When the gentlemen at the next table got up, I recognized someone who had had his back turned to me until now. I pointed him out to Walter as one of Gottfried's former teachers, a classics scholar, a truly erudite, witty man, and I was itching to say, " See, that's one who pleased me once, pleased me very much, and how glad I am that he never noticed it!" But I was careful not to slide out on the ice voluntarily.

And then a stocky man came in who limped badly. He spoke to the headwaiter and pointed in our direction. He evidently wanted to reserve our table for the evening. I turned my eyes too late. He recognized me and greeted me woodenly; I barely nodded. "You don't like him!" Walter said as the man went out again.

"No," I said. "That's the pharmacist, and unfortunately I found out from you yesterday that his son is Gottfried's best friend."

"Tell me the whole story," said Walter, and I promised, "Yes. On the way home." Why not?

"So," he asked, as we left the houses behind us. "What's wrong with the pharmacist's family?"

"Well … his wife was a schoolmate of mine and we were together in the Labor Service. So I was present when she met her husband at a dance.

He liked her right away. And when Marietta found out that she was going to have a baby, she got married *in absentia*. Then she moved here, to his parents', and I met her again quite by chance ..."

"And?"

Strange. It had really been my intention to tell him everything, and it simply hadn't crossed my lips. In that moment, as I considered what to say, I was conscious of how shabby it would be to expose another woman like that. I expected a sign of astonishment in Walter's bland expression: why is she telling me this kitchen gossip? Things like that happen, but how do they concern us? No. If I told everything I would not only have exposed Marietta but myself as well. But now I had started and had somehow to get to the end.

"She never liked me," I lied. "And then, in '45, she sent her husband to us, with the Russians ... to me," I corrected myself.

"No, Helga," said Walter, taking my arm. "You've got to tell this properly, one thing after the other, just how it happened. So far I haven't understood a word."

Oh, all right. I could do that. Tell him the story, no interpretations, only the facts.

"I had been staying with Uri for a few weeks ... with Grandmother."

"When?"

"In the spring of '45. She came and got me."

"I know."

"The house was filled to the rafters ..."

"With Russians?"

"No. Not Russians."

Grandmother had had bombed-out people billeted in her house for quite some time: two women — between them they had seven children — and at the last moment she had taken in what was left of a disbanded circus troupe: a group of artists and the clown, and his wife, the bareback rider. Her name was Maya, and she was already well over forty, a thin woman with black hair. I think the juggler was her son, but nobody was supposed to know that. Or her lover.

"But that doesn't make any difference," said Walter.

"Yes it does, since he was also interested in hiding her from the Russians, and that happened every few days, when they were warned, God knows by whom. There's a big wall closet for the brooms, et cetera, on the landing. I'll show it to you later. The clown had put a clothes rack in front of it that you could move easily. When the woman was hidden in the closet, they quickly hung a few old jackets and aprons on the rack. It was a perfect hiding place, big enough to crouch down in or stand bent over. She probably could even stand upright in it. She was much smaller than I. But of course you didn't get much air. And after Maya had spent an hour in there two or three times, she declared she wouldn't get in it any more because anything was preferable to suffocating, and besides, she found it dull! The mothers who couldn't leave their children weren't sparing with ironic insinuations regarding the virtue of the circus rider who needed so much protection! You can take my word for it — without Uri's authority there'd have been murder, or at least quarreling and yelling from morning to evening. But she saw to it that the little children got milk from our only cow, and that potatoes were cooked every day for everybody, and that everyone did his share of work in the house, in the stables and in the fields."

"Did you have cattle?"

"We had a permit for the cow, we fed two pigs, a dozen hens, and of course a lot of rabbits. The children had to gather the food for them every day. And so there was meat on Sundays. The circus people were allowed to keep their two horses."

"Did they have other animals?"

"Only a little trained Pomeranian. The monkeys hadn't survived the cold winter, and they'd had to give away the elephant because they hadn't been able to feed him. Before the war they'd even had a lion who jumped through a flaming hoop. The clown liked to talk about it. These circus people were so confident. All they wanted was to wait for the end of the war and then go right back to work because they thought people were hungry for a little amusement, and the peasants didn't know what to do anyway with all the money the city people handed out to them for a few kilos of flour or a little pot of lard. But then it still took a long time until they had all the permits they needed, and could leave. I think in July."

It began to snow. Prickly crystals blew against our faces. "You'll get a sore throat," said Walter. "Wait until we get home!" But he had taken out a stopper and was talking now to the gurgling water: Hold it! Don't flow away! "I won't get a sore throat," I said, annoyed. "I'm used to weather like this."

"You were going to tell about the pharmacist," Walter reminded me. "How was it anyway? Did the Russian come often? And ... where were you then?"

"I'm coming to that, Walter," I said, and involuntarily walked faster. "They were often on the farm, but they came up to the house only once, two stern young officers with taciturn faces. They searched the whole house for weapons. It took several hours. I sat upstairs with the women and helped them to wash the children and put them to bed. When the Russians came in, I had one on my lap and was feeding it pap. Its mother sat next to me on the bed and was feeding the infant. I didn't look up, but my hand was trembling so that the child was getting nothing to eat and was fretting. Then one of the soldiers laid his hand on my shoulder and said, 'No afraid,' and gave the other one, who wanted to search a trunk, a sign to leave the room. Then Uri came to get me. 'God bless you,' she said to the woman who had loaned me the child. Probably because the woman smiled scornfully, Uri added, 'My granddaughter is an expectant mother, even though she doesn't show it yet.' Then the woman said, 'Ah ...' and looked at me with sympathy. So the dread moment passed in which my secret was revealed and — at least I saw it that way — became wholly irrevocable. The ridiculous designation of the authorities ... there were food cards and special rations for expectant mothers ... had come to Grandmother's lips perfectly naturally, and nobody seemed surprised that I was expecting a child or wanted to know who the father was. I noticed by the friendliness and consideration of those living with us that everybody soon knew. The clown — he was an older man with gray, stubbly hair, and daily turned a few somersaults to keep in trim — drew me into a corner and showed me a sharp knife with a horn handle ... ("A clasp knife," Walter, the expert, informed me). The clown grinned and said, 'Whoever gets too close to my Maya gets this between the ribs. House search for weapons? That's a laugh! For that the gentlemen must get up earlier.' And he stuck the knife in its leather sheath and dropped it into his practice pants. They were out of shape and full of holes.

"I should have told Uri about it. The man's intentions could have endangered all of us, but I said nothing because I was glad — and not without envy — that he was prepared to defend his lady rider.

"About a week, or at most fourteen days later, Uri was standing beside my bed in the middle of the night, shaking me awake. I slept in her room, but I slept very soundly, and the trampling of feet and the screams hadn't wakened me. She was holding a candle in front of my eye. 'Quick, Helga! Quick! You must get into the closet!' I could hear steps above us, coarse laughter, and in the hall the excited barking of the dog, the frightened weeping of the awakened children, and now the imploring voice of a woman: 'Please ... no! Please, for Jesus Christ's sake, please ... no!'

"Uri dragged me behind her, down the few steps, tore the clothes off their hooks, pushed me into the dark, said breathlessly, 'So ... stay there! And whatever happens, don't move until I come to get you!'

"I crouched down and heard her hang the clothes again. She was about to leave, but she didn't get far. A thick, unsure man's voice said, 'So where is she?' The pharmacist! He said, 'I'm sorry, but they'll kill me if I don't find her. They've been told an SS bride lives here!'

"Grandmother said, 'Here we have only mothers and children and circus people. Please translate that.' He did, and I listened, and heard how they contradicted him scornfully in their low, guttural voices. 'I can't help it! They know she's here. They want to look for her!' The pharmacist again. 'So please look for her,' said Grandmother.

"Next day Maya gave us a graphic description of what happened. the artists got together and conferred as to what could be done. The clown lost his head and was determined to hide Maya, but she refused. Then somebody brought him his baggy trousers and his dunce cap and told him, 'Quick! Change! And we'll give them a performance!' I don't know whose idea it was but everybody thought it was fine. The props were soon ready; Maya got into her tights in spite of her husband's protests. She laughed and said she wasn't afraid any more, although you could hear the children crying upstairs and chairs falling and the screams of the women begging to be spared, for Jesus Christ's sake! Maya put on her mask — black with rhinestones — and told the juggler, who was also in costume by now, 'Come! We'll get them down!' and they ran up the stairs and walked into the room, and Maya beat her drum and cried, ' Walk in, ladies and gentlemen! Walk right in!' She interrupted her account to say, 'There's a game, you know, in which, at a given signal, you can't change your position any more, and it was just like that. One Russian — he looked like a Hun — didn't let go of the woman he was dragging to the bed, but he turned his head and opened his mouth wide, and she was so surprised, she didn't take the opportunity to free herself. And the children stopped howling and the pharmacist just stammered, 'What's going on here?'

"Maya said, 'All of you come downstairs, ladies and gentlemen!' And I can imagine that she wiggled her hips a little. 'We're going to give you a performance, a big show! So come! Come!' And they followed her, all five of them, like the little children followed the Pied Piper of Hamelin. The bigger children, by the way, ran on ahead, and their mothers didn't hold them back. But the pharmacist walked straight to the front door and disappeared.

"In the dining room they had pushed the chairs and the big table against the wall and lit all the candles they could find, and when the soldiers came in, the clown somersaulted toward them in his white costume with the red dots. He bowed so low that he lost his cap and his balance. Then he pushed every one of them down on a chair, and they were already doubled up with laughter. When the juggler started playing with the balls, they had to try it too. It was wild! But they had completely forgotten the search for the SS bride and the women upstairs, and gradually they sobered up. Later Grandmother served tea, and they put the table back and sat down happily around it. Then Grandmother whispered to the clown, 'Please don't let any of them leave the room for the next few minutes,' and she took the teapot to fill it again, but she put it right down by the door and came to me and opened the closet and whispered, 'Come quick!' And we ran down the stairs to the garden. Uri had brought along a cover. She spread it out between the raspberry bushes and said again, 'Stay here until I get you.'

"I wrapped myself in the cover as best I could. Through the bushes I could see the two lighted windows and hear the laughter and noise, and up in the black sky the stars were trembling. And all I could think of was: Marietta sent them! Marietta sent them to me! And something like that, Walter, you just can't forget."

"But you're only surmising it!" he protested.

"That's true. But the pharmacist's wife was the only person in the whole neighborhood who knew anything about Horst!"

I could see that my brother didn't believe me. Now it was snowing heavily. We were almost home. I wanted to finish the story before we went in, so I took Walter's arm and walked more slowly. I said softly, "I'm sure he didn't want to do it. I never thought of that. It often happened in those days that they pounded on the door and demanded, 'Take us to some women!' And if the man said, 'Leave me alone. I don't know any women,' one of them would hold him at bay with his machine pistol while the others took care of his wife. Or when he led them into the woods and then pretended he'd lost his way — that could cost him his life. Marietta would have been trembling for his life, Walter. Perhaps that's why she said, 'Take them to the SS bride up there on the farm.' "

"Perhaps," Walter admitted hesitantly. Then he said, "Strange that the circus rider didn't interest them at all."

I noticed that he wanted to change the subject. He simply didn't believe my story. So let it be ... What happened before would really have belonged to it. So let's talk about Maya. "First of all," I said, "she was incredibly courageous. And just the fact that she wasn't afraid was protection."

"I'm sure that's right," Walter agreed. "It's the same thing in battle, only there one doesn't know: is the man afraid because the bullet is meant for him, or does he get hit because he's afraid?"

"And then," I went on, "I think the mask protected her, I've thought a lot about it. I saw her with it on when Uri brought me back. Uri said in a shy, almost servile tone, 'We thank you, Frau Maya. You really are a magician!' And Maya bowed low and said, 'Don't mention it! It's my job. You've just got to know how!' And then she took off her mask and laughed at us and cried, 'We had a ball! But you could treat us to one or two rabbits tomorrow, Frau Wegscheider. For overtime!' "

We were home. I unlocked the door. "Did you ever hear from those people again?"

"Never," I said. "Wait, Walter, stop. I'll brush you off. There's always a whisk broom behind the door so that one doesn't drag all the snow into the house."

"Now do you understand why I'm not exactly enthusiastic about Gottfried's friendship with the pharmacist's boys?" I asked. "Sure," said Walter, but it didn't sound convincing.

Perhaps I should have told him what I had felt as I lay there in the raspberry bushes. The first leaves were already sprouting from the strong stems we had let stand a short while ago, after removing all the dead stuff. Bright green in the daytime, they were black now, and the sky I was looking up at was black and sprinkled with cold, glittering stars thousands of light years away. I had thought once that a dear, a loving God lived up there, and that all of us were his children who could cry out to Him and implore His protection. That was a long time ago. Behind the stars lived Nothing, interwoven with other stars. Unfathomable.

Unthinkable. Infinity brings no comfort. The tiny thing is just as powerful and powerless as the biggest thing. The dew was cold that covered the earth and slowly also me. Cold as Marietta's hatred. I had despised her and this was her revenge. I wasn't allowed to complain. I was nothing and should be snuffed out. So it didn't matter any more. Let them find me, let them abuse me a second time. What's to stop them?

Only Uri. She wanted to save me and the child in me. Why? Why did we plant greens and fertilize the earth? Why did we give everybody eight potatoes a day and the children a quarter liter of milk? And why did we go out into the fields and weed? In order to remain alive. Why? To be there when rescue came. But what was rescue? The Allied troops with their canned food? The packages from America? The Marshall Plan?

It was worth it, that we made the effort. We were helped. The wheel was set going and is turning again. The bombs are falling somewhere else. The women are being raped somewhere else. The enemy is being killed somewhere else in order finally to build a "just world." We were helped, we were saved. What for? We haven't changed ...

That's what was going on in my mind as I made tea and Walter fanned the fire. Then he asked me what I thought my life in the city would be like; if I thought I'd get accustomed to living with the practical lady with the colored students. Gottfried must have shown him my letter.

"Why not?" I replied. "I can shut the door behind me and lock up any time. Besides, I won't be home much." But it also interested me to get out into different surroundings. Now at last I wanted to strip off the past like a snakeskin. That I tried to write it all down must certainly have accelerated the process, I admitted. "Will you show me what you've written?" he asked naively. "Yes, certainly," I said. "Fifty years from now!"

But he didn't let my feeble joke deceive him.

"I think, Helga," he said, "that we have an advantage over the young. They understand everything, we don't understand anything anymore. It's a strange thing ... but those people who get the least out of life ... the old, the sick, the poor ... cling to it most. Our marriage was truly happy, right from the start, but you know ... we're really close only now, since this dreadful disappointment. I don't think the child, if he had lived, could have united us so closely. We might have transferred everything to him that we now have to realize ourselves. Do you understand what I mean?"

"Yes," I said. "I understand. One is always tempted to use a child as an alibi. That's why it's a good thing that Gottfried ran away, not only for him but probably for me too."

"You're getting him back soon," said Walter. And then we talked about Gottfried's future, whether he would be more suited for technology or business, and while we were talking I thought for a moment: it is strange how good one can feel when actually one is without hope in one's heart and doesn't expect anything more from life. Had I finally grown up?

And then came Walter's departure during a conversation just begun, and his farewell words, "Do your best, *Mädi!*" which transformed me abruptly into the child who watches through the ice peephole in the pane her big brother slithering off to school, into life, into alien territory. To cling to Now is perhaps the most distorted lie because we are always, all at the same time, what we have ever been.

It has taken me from early morning to afternoon to describe Walter's visit and the most important things we talked about, but how fragmentary it all is now. We spoke about Albert, too, and about Mother. How terrible it was for Walter to find her in such condition when he came home full of good intentions to make up for all the fear she had had to suffer on his account. "Then I really thought ... she'd be better off dead," he confessed. "Why ... tell me, why did she have to live her life to the end so slowly, a poor neglected creature, playing with buttons ..."

"And with scraps of colored silk."

"Why did we have to see her like that? It was unfair. She would never have wanted it. If I hadn't been too much of a coward at the time, thinking more about myself than about her ..."

"Stop." I interrupted him impetuously. "One must never say anything like that."

"At least I grasped what our 'victories' looked like," Walter went on after a pause. "Our brother dangling from a lamppost, your life destroyed, Mother a senile, vegetating old woman ... only Father still reciting the old maxims with a few new rhymes. One sees it, hears it ... what can one do but salute, about face, and exit."

"Back to square one," I said, and smiled hesitantly. He understood me at once. "Exactly. One starts all over again from the beginning — makes money, enjoys life. Then one's lucky and meets a woman who thinks one is a human being. And one tries at last to be one! There are people, scholars, who say that we humans, as a species, are still walking in our baby shoes, taking our first steps, smashing whatever we touch, communicating by babbling and lashing out at everything ..."

"And smiling," I said.

"Rarely," Walter objected. "Rarely! But allegedly things are going to get better, in fifty thousand years or so, when we have matured and learned to find our way around in the world. What a pity that we two are unlucky enough to be living now!"

"Be honest! Doesn't it please you at all?" I asked.

He stopped short and laughed. "Of course. Often it pleases me a lot."

"There you are," I said. "Me too."

I have taken down the pictures and curtains in Uri's room; tomorrow I start to pack. As I held the wall calendar in my hands, I thought: to keep it would really be sentimental. I could tear off the cover with the inscription: *les jours passent, les instants restent,* and keep it with Uri's few letters, but as I leafed through it briefly, I came upon her handwriting. I read: *The steep steps of disappointment lead most quickly to the realm of truth. But most people's hearts are too weak for such a steep path.* I was perplexed. It sounded harsh. But ... wouldn't it be a good ending for my book? Because a whole book has grown out of these many sheets of paper; and now I have finished and by chance find this saying. Tear off the pages that cover it ... that's all there is to it.

My back aches, my eyes burn. I have been sitting here writing for six hours. Soon the sun will set. The frost is gone; during the night the snow melted off the branches, and it smells of spring. I'll butter some bread, put on my boots and coat, and run around a bit before I finish up. It's a good feeling to have finished something, even if one has no idea for what purpose. After all, one washes the dirty dishes, even before a trip — especially before a trip.

And now ... now I could start the whole story all over again from the beginning. Perhaps I should. Because everything has changed. Why? because *I* have changed. The whole version isn't right any more. I did my best but it was no use.

When I began to draw — I think I was three when I discovered this miracle — I ran to Mother with every picture. She was to share my delight. There! Look! Oh, unforgettable disenchantment when she looked at it with interest and with a tender little smile said, "Very pretty. But what is it supposed to be?"

And just now I felt it again: somebody looking over my shoulder lovingly, ready to admire. But how can one admire what is unrecognizable? And he says, "Very nice. But what is it supposed to be?"

When I was three, I may have drawn a house or a child or a tree. The child — me, naturally — was bigger than the house, the tree smallest of all. But every day I walked daily into a house and knew it was much bigger than I or I couldn't have got inside it. There it is — knowledge is nothing, one has to experience. That isn't the right word either. The English say realize, that is to say, perceive, but *perceive* is only passive. Perceive and realize, perhaps?

And yesterday I experienced — realized — that the house is bigger than the child. That all the proportions in this picture, which I have painted so painstakingly and with so much fervor, are wrong. The version isn't right. Still, I shall let it stand. Perhaps it is more useful as a background for that which is as difficult to hold fast and depict as lightning. If I am to give it a name, and I guess I should, then the old command over the ancient shrine of Delphi is best suited:

KNOW THYSELF

Advice that one should follow constantly, all the time, not now and again. Follow, therefore obey. *Obey*, therefore means to start off, to leave one's permanent location, to give up one's point of view. Have I given my fictitious reader the picture only now to disappear from it?

But I have no time for conjectures. The boxes are piled high in the entrance. I have to pack. I shall tell briefly what happened yesterday. And if it covers only one or two pages, although it is the most important thing of all, then I think of Alphonse's inscription: *Les jours passent, les instants restent.* I suppose there must be empty days and years in our lives so that the moments of fulfillment, of permanence, may happen. Without having remembered with such great effort all the things that happened formerly, I might not have become aware of what was happening now.

So ... I put on my boots and my loden coat and walked fast. I was hungry for exercise after writing for such a long time. The warm wind had freed the branches of ice and snow, and dark rings lay exposed around the trunks of the fruit trees. They rarely appear before February, and I was touched again by the fact that the gentle, imperceptible pulse of the trees could melt the snow,while our warm bodies could be overpowered and killed by it in a few hours.

The evening sky was a translucent green; light, streaking clouds, driven by a sultry wind, were turning sulphur yellow. So much glory in utter glassy silence! Nobody seemed to be around. I walked in the road so as not to sink in too deeply. As I came nearer to the pond and the little brook that feeds it, I heard a strange scraping noise that I took to be the crackling of a half-broken branch, until suddenly a long, high-pitched scream shrilled through the air, accompanied by the cracking sound and a splintering.

In the first moment I didn't want to believe that a human being could have screamed like that. A cat, I thought, a hoot owl! Just the same, I ran over to the sound, straight across the melting snow and through the underbrush, to the water. And as soon as the view was clear I saw and grasped everything: a boy had drawn figures on the ice with his bicycle, pretty elliptical eights, and, evidently delighted with the symmetry of his figures, had added one loop after the other and gone too near the mouth of the creek where the ice was thinner. The back wheel of a bicycle was sticking out of the water there, and beside it a groaning boy was struggling to work his way out, but the more the struggle, the larger the hole grew all around him.

At first I saw only a red stocking cap and thought it was a child. "Wait!" I shouted. "I'm coming! Don't move!" I looked around for a branch that I could push across to him, but the one I found was rotten, and I couldn't find a firm one anywhere. "Can you touch bottom?" I cried, because that would have given me more time. "No. Please ... come quickly! I can't hold out much longer!"

That was no child's voice, and the heavier the person was, the more hopeless my efforts to help him. At any rate, I had to approach him from the middle where the ice was still thick, so I ran along the shore. He screamed again. He didn't scream at me; I guess he thought I was going to get help. He cried in his despair, "Mother!"

"I'm coming! Wait! I'm coming!" I called back to him.

Now I stepped out onto the ice. It was wet on top and a little rough. I was able to make good progress. I tried to slide and listened fearfully, but I didn't hear a cracking sound or a humming in the ice, which would have meant it was breaking. Only from where the boy was came the sound of bubbling and cracking, mingled with his groans. He was still holding himself above the ice by his elbows ... there was about five meters between us. "Don't move!" I said. "I'll be there in a minute."

I went down on my knees carefully, then I stretched out. The icy water penetrated my clothes at once. I pushed myself forward cautiously. then the boy said, and it was difficult to understand him because his teeth were chattering, "The bicycle ... if you could push it over to me ..."

He was right. It was our only possibility. If I could manage to raise it without breaking through myself, then move it around him so that I could push it close to him on the side where the ice was firm ... I couldn't do it quickly, but it was our only chance.

I could not go home without this boy. I suddenly knew that. I had just recognized him. It was Siegfried, Marietta's oldest son. And when I recognized him, a wild triumph had lamed my heart and made me catch my breath, So there! I thought. But it wasn't a thought. Dare I say it was happiness? Does that golden word go with my sudden reaction? No. Don't lie! It was delight. The consuming, sensual pleasure of cruelty. The bliss of retaliation. I felt it to the depths of my soul.

From where did I take the courage, receive the strength, to say no to this deadly reaction? I recognized: that's the way I am, but with my last ounce of strength decided: *but I don't want to stay like that.*

"What shall I do?" cried the person I had just hated with all my heart.

"Pray!" I cried. "Hang on! I'm coming!"

I don't know whether he prayed, I don't know if I did. I got hold of the bicycle, but when I began to pull it, the hole where it had broken in got larger. "That's no good," Siegfried panted. "You've got to grab the hub so that the wheel doesn't turn, and then raise it!"

Impossible! I thought, but I said, "I'll try. Be patient for just one more minute!"

I thought: if he drowns, it's my fault. Because I wanted it.

Now both wheels were lying on the ice, and Siegfried cried out to tell me what I should do next. When we got to the point where he was able to grasp one of the wheels with one hand, then with his other hand, he said, "Now you must pull it back quickly, and I'll swing myself onto it ... but quickly, or the whole thing will break through!"

I said, "Yes, When?"

"Now!"

I closed my eyes and pulled and thought I had torn out my lungs, and heard a cracking and a tinkling sound and thought: it's all over ... all over ... but if it is I'll simply go on lying here ... Just then a breathless, exhausted voice beside me said, "Frau Wegscheider, we've got to crawl to the shore quickly now or we'll freeze to death!"

We began to move toward the shore, flat on our stomachs. When we tried to stand up we could hardly do so, we were so weak. We'll never get home, I thought, but the boy supported me and said, "It's only fifteen minutes from here. We can do it, can't we?"

He took my arm and I realized we had to move fast, but not fall, not even once. Or we'd never get up again. At any rate, I wouldn't be able to. And now I *wanted* to live again. "Back to square one," I murmured, and laughed foolishly to myself.

At home he was the one who collapsed and I the one who attended to everything. I called for Herr Stadler, but he wasn't there, so we had to stay in the living room. I couldn't have dragged the boy upstairs. I told him to take off his wet clothes and wrap himself in the cover on the sofa, and to lie down. I shook the grate free of ashes and opened the vent; then I put two pots of water on the stove, crept to my bedroom, undressed, let my wet clothes drop to the floor and put on the first things I could lay my hands on. I tore the blanket off my bed and went back to Siegfried, who was having severe chills. I put more covers over him. I made tea, got aspirin: perhaps it would fight the inevitable cold. Then, at last, I called the pharmacy. But Friedel's parents had gone out. I left a message for them to pick up their son at my house; he had had a little accident while skating. Then I put on my coat, placed the chaise longue near the stove and could gradually feel my limbs coming to life.

"How did it happen?" I asked. Siegfried had thought that after the long, severe frost the ice would hold a few more days. "You got too close to the mouth of the creek."

"Yes. But that wouldn't have mattered if I hadn't fallen. And if you hadn't come right away, I'd be dead by now. What will Gottfried say?" he was evidently too ashamed to cry and tried to joke. "He'd beat me up!"

"Does he tend to do that?" I asked casually.

He blushed a deep red. "Now and then," he said, smiling sheepishly.

I looked at him and found that I liked him. Very much. Suddenly I liked everything about this skinny, strange boy, even his long upper lip and his flaming jug ears, his shy glances that begged to be forgiven. I loved him as if he had been my own.

No. Wrong. A heart has its limitations. It doesn't love two people at the same time. It loved only this one. This one alone. I wanted to resist as we resist false consolations, or a medication that soothes pain momentarily but possibly makes the illness worse. Why love all of a sudden? To like, to tolerate, to grant him his place in life, that would be enough, wouldn't it? I saved his life. No, no, I realized suddenly, and in a wave of heat that dissolved the last numbing frost in my body: I saved myself when I risked my life for his. And now all's well. The false equations are erased from the blackboard.

I stand in front of the class and try to get the blackboard shiny clean; that's my duty because I am the monitor, but I can't do it. The sponge is gray with chalk; the more I wipe, the cloudier the board. I walk over to the washbowl. We have an old-fashioned one with a small brown container on top and a pretty little filigree faucet that has to be turned vertically so that a thin stream of water can run out of it and burble down through the drain into the pail underneath. But more often than not there is no water left in it. Also not today. The class giggles. I hear whispers: "Wegscheider's splashing!"

Splashing was strictly forbidden. And just today the supervisor was coming. He has a white beard and is very old. Sometimes he falls asleep while listening; he's probably heard it all so often. But when he sees the smeary blackboard he'll think we want to make fun of him. "I can be strict too," he likes to say, but nobody believes him. The tears of pity rise in my eyes, the supervisor is standing in front of the blackboard, shaking his head sorrowfully. "That doesn't look nice," he says, sounding worried. Then I quickly untie my apron strings and walk up to the board and wipe it clean with my damp apron, and now it shines, spotlessly black. "Good, good," says the supervisor. "Make a note of it: with tears everything goes away. As a reward we'll play now. What would you like to play, my child?"

"Rumor!" I answer quickly.

You see, Walter, that was one game we forgot when we thought of all our games. How we loved it when at the end of a children's party we weren't allowed to be wild any more, but were supposed to cool off before going home. All of us sat quietly around the table, and the one to start whispered a word in his neighbor's ear, as unusual a word as possible, then he had to whisper it to the one next to him. The joke came when the last one to hear it said it aloud, and his word had scarcely any similarity with the first one that had been sent on its way, neither in meaning nor in sound.

Why did we always laugh so hard over that, Walter? Isn't it rather something to cry about?

"Why are you crying? Are you in pain?"

"Because the sponge still isn't wet enough to clean the board."

The oven glows ... I close the flap ... sneeze in the rag ... I'm getting a cold ... overshoot the goal ... with the black horse ... but that's Walter's horse ... the white one's mine ... you're crazy, you know ... the ringing comes closer ...

"Frau Wegscheider, please wake up! The doorbell's ringing! Or should I open it? It may be my parents."

He is shaking my shoulder. He is standing beside me. He is alive! That's good. Then I don't have to cry any more. "Yes. Open the door."

To sleep. To sleep at last! But then Marietta's shrill voice, "For God's sake, what happened to you?"

I try to sit up. The ceiling light is circling around me. That's what it's like when I have a fever. But I have to leave. I have to pack. They mustn't notice anything ... I close my eyes again. The five china shades of the ceiling light continue to revolve around me in a circle. Strange ... this way one gets the feeling that one's circling with the earth in outer space, head down ...

"Frau Wegscheider pulled me out! She saved my life."

Now. That's better. The lights are back in place. Just the same, I don't look at them. I remain lying down and look at Marietta coming toward me, and at the funny figure swathed in a green checked plaid up to his chin, his long, hairy legs and huge, dirty feet sticking out under it. "Lie down right away," I tell him, "and cover up. Excuse me, Marietta, for not getting up, but I feel a little dizzy. I dreamt so hard ... I mean slept ..." What had I really dreamt? I was still happy about it. Oh yes, the apron. The sponge, The blackboard, "Good. Good. With tears everything goes away."

Marietta slipped out of her coat. She wanted to know exactly what had happened. She swore that she'd strictly forbidden the boys to ride their bicycles on the ice. "Your father should give you a good beating!" she said, and from Siegfried's smile I gathered that his father had never beaten him, and Marietta added hastily, "Though he doesn't have to know exactly what happened or he'd be terribly upset."

It was all right ... I could get up. I took them both to Gottfried's room and loaned Friedel clothes and shoes. Marietta looked all around her with alert brown eyes. Shyly she added, "I like your boy so much. I was always glad when he came to see us. Does he like it in America?"

"Very much," I said.

"You're still shivering, Helga. You should take a hot bath."

"Yes. I'll do that." What concern was it of hers that before taking a bath we had to heat our coal stove for hours!

"You're moving to Vienna soon, I hear."

"Yes. I'm moving to the city."

She took a look at the many boxes. "Couldn't the boys help you pack?"

I wanted to say no. I always wanted to say no first, but I thought it over and agreed. "That's a good idea. What do you say, Friedel?"

He nodded eagerly. "Of course! Gladly!"

Marietta took over. "So listen! I'll send them to you early in the morning." She was obviously relieved. This way she could do me a good turn.

But then, at the front door, came the doubt: perhaps it wasn't enough! she grasped my hand, clung to it and stammered, "Thank you, Helga ... thank you for fishing him out for me!" She tried to smile, but the tears sprang from her eyes. "With tears everything goes away!" said the rusty tired voice of the supervisor in my heart.

"I fished him out for *myself* too!" I said. "I hope he doesn't get anything worse than a cold."

I pushed her out and closed the door and locked it. I tended to the stove, then I dragged myself up the stairs for the last time, with my blanket, and crept into bed just the way I was. As I rolled up in the blanket I thought vaguely: now Gottfried has received a brother, and knew at the same time: but that is only valid when one dreams. No ... the result is right forever; it just can't be verified when one is awake.

Next morning the pharmacist came with his younger son and brought the doctor with him. They told me that Friedel had a high fever and had been given penicillin; they were surprised to find me up. But I had perspired all night and now felt quite well and fresh. The doctor examined me hastily, congratulated me on my constitution, and advised me to take a medicine he'd brought along, as a precautionary measure, and ... to take is easy.

Berthold was going to stay with me to help, the pharmacist decided, then he thanked me with tears in his eyes. I said, "Anybody would have done the same thing." Then I added, "Do you mind if I stay upstairs? You'll find your way out all right." It sounded harmless, but it was meant as an insinuation, and he understood it. He turned purple. "Once more, my most heartfelt thanks!" he murmured. At the door he turned around and said hoarsely, "You see, the boy means everything to me," and walked out fast. And there stood the younger one, who heard it all! Embarrassed, I said to him, "You know, a sick child is always the favorite."

"Yes, I know," he replied thoughtfully. How like his father he was! Broad shoulders, stocky, short neck, pale, soft brown eyes and a round forehead. "Friedel really is Father's favorite, but Mother loves me best. So that evens things up."

Again a mathematical equation and one based on false premises.

"Would you bring in one or two boxes for me? Then we can start packing the books immediately."

I am in Vienna. Sitting in my room. It is still very cold, and the little electric stove fights the frost with its feeble warmth. And to "close the door behind me," as I explained to Walter, isn't going to be so simple after all. But this doesn't really belong in here any more, or I would really have to put down "Writer" on the registration form I just filled out, so that Fräulein Wermuth can sign it before she leaves. She suggested that I do so, but then I would have to dedicate the rest of my life to writing this instead of ... living. No. Just as on every map the imaginary meridians are shown, I shall soon have to decide to ring down the curtain on the so-called past and face firmly whatever comes toward me.

I thought the curtain had to fall after the description of my farewell to the old house, with which I wanted to finish this evening. But this morning something came up, or rather some*one*, who still belongs behind the curtain. This encounter opened my eyes to a new version. You will see right away how.

You? Yes ... you. Because I am really writing this ending ... no, this beginning, for a reader. Perhaps for many readers. That too came up this morning. (Came up, as if it had already been there, hiding?) Since I wasn't writing for Gottfried anymore, I thought I was writing only for myself, to understand what I have experienced a little better. But doesn't to "understand" mean: to want to communicate? A creature alone in outer space would "think" only to the extent that it could speak, because without speech there would be no thoughts. And already, as I clarify my thoughts, I am doing something that reaches out beyond me — nothing that we do is for us alone — doing it for exactly the same reason I felt when I lay stretched out on the ice: If I can save Siegfried now, I save myself. For a brief moment I had wished him dead, in order to fly to the assistance of God is Just, so that Marietta might at last get what she deserved. That was when I recognized, as in a dazzling flash of lightning, what I was and what would happen to me if this God of our lust for revenge became Lord of the Universe ... and I gave him notice. Then, when Marietta came to fetch her boy, and her quick glance at everything, her fearful excitement, her seeming confidence, filled me with pity, I noticed that with this decision something truly fundamental had changed in me, because it wasn't so-called pity, that mixture of compassion, contempt and self-righteousness, but truly ... sorrow, the wish to help, the happiness to have been able to.

But this morning I received even clearer proof. It seems to me that this last week has consisted of many moments that will endure beyond the few days that have passed.

I'll skip the farewell to my home of so many years. Herr Stadler was friendly and worried. He helped with quite a few things because I had sent good old Berthold home after half a day. He never stopped talking. He is a boy who has to report monotonously and in great detail what he is doing, has just done and intends to do. Finally I couldn't stand it. Although Herr Stadler also had all sorts of things on his mind to tell me: how he was going to fix up everything for the comfort of his guests and for his own profit. He evidently can't imagine why I don't find his undertaking as fascinating as he does. But at heart he seems to have resigned himself to it and will soon marry again because, alarmed by my impending departure, he has fought his way through to this decision. He will be a good husband and one day I hope thank me for not having accepted him. Still he felt it necessary to suggest a little New Year's Eve farewell festivity, and to avoid this I left for Vienna on the thirty-first.

I returned to my native city full of expectation, like a young person feels traveling abroad for the first time. (But when I traveled to Italy that time, I was not at all curious. The world outside, the strange country, the lively, friendly people — none of it had existed for me because there had been no room in me for it ...) Now there is plenty of room, and the short trip to Vienna was already filled with adventure ... if that's what one wants to call the insight into other people's lives ...

Fortunately Fräulein Wermuth had been invited to a party, and after telling me a lot about her impending trip to Egypt and trying to familiarize me with the most striking characteristics of her two lodgers, she left the house at nine. I was tired enough to go to bed right away, but I did unpack the record player and tried to lift my spirits to the Upper Room with the Negro singer's hoarse song of longing. And thought at the same time of the lonely "coal black" man who had lived here before me.

Yesterday, on New Year's morning, I breakfasted quietly in a well-heated coffeehouse and read the papers. I skimmed over a report about the final meeting of the First Session of the Council in Rome. I caught myself reading with Walter's critical eyes: didn't the assembled fathers have anything more important to decide than whether they should say *Have mercy on us!* in the future instead of *Miserere nobis*? But perhaps they were right. Perhaps if we could at last understand what we heard and swore to in church, it would really help us. Because all great decisions must have been made long ago. We have only obscured them for centuries with incomprehensible words and beautiful gestures. Rather like Uri's roses, which I used to bend down and cover with earth in late autumn so that they wouldn't freeze in the severe frost. But as soon as spring comes, one has to free them and straighten them up so that they may bloom in June.

Shall I write and tell Walter that? No. Still and again we stand on opposite sides, but now we know that it is our mistakes that separate us, and we don't have to waste any words on it.

The bells were shattering the air as I walked out into the street. They were calling to where the words have been assembled that one loses elsewhere, but I withstood the sentimental impulse and did what I had intended to do: I wrote to two companies that were looking for a secretary. The dentist, by the way, never answered. A woman in her late thirties evidently didn't come into question for him.

In the afternoon I went to the Central Cemetery and at last visited the grave of my parents. And this morning, remembering his vague encouragement, I went to see Herr Lukesch, the publisher. This time he recognized me and pretended to be touchingly concerned. Where was I living? When was my son coming back? But above all — had I been to the opera yet? I simply had to go to the opera soon! "The opera is the only thing here that has world stature!" He at once gave me the address of a theater-ticket agency where I could mention his name. Translation? Oh yes ... did

I really want to start translating again? Right now the agency was only an adjunct to the publishing house, but if I wanted to bring him something, he'd be glad to take a look at it. Of course I would have to attend to getting the rights ...

I tried to say goodbye cheerfully, confidently, but somehow he must have noticed my disappointment. "How's the diary going?" he asked, keeping hold of my hand. "Couldn't you make a book of that?"

"What do you mean?" I asked, stunned. Was the man clairvoyant?

"You hinted something to that effect last time," he said.

"Really? But I never thought of publication. It wouldn't interest anybody, let alone ..."

"Why don't you leave that to me, dear Frau Wegscheider? You know, documentary material is in demand today. Nobody wants fiction."

"But you're thinking of something quite different."

"So much the better. When will you bring me the manuscript?"

"I've got to copy it first. And anyway ..."

"Copy thirty pages, no more. I'll probably say no after ten, but after thirty I'll know if it's worth reading to the end. But you mustn't be offended ..."

"Of course not. You'll soon see that the whole thing's much too private."

At last he let go of my hand, smiled and said, "When I look at you I'm only afraid that anything you're capable of putting down on paper won't be nearly 'private' enough for today's readers, dear Mrs. Wegscheider."

"You'll be surprised." I said, laughing and a trifle annoyed.

Somewhat confused, I felt my way through the gloomy anteroom and bumped into a clerk. He dropped a pile of files and I helped him to pick them up. He thanked me. As I wanted to leave, he stopped me and said, "Excuse me, miss, but didn't you live in Währing once?"

"Yes," I said, surprised. "But that was a long time ago."

"Don't you recognize me? I'm Benno!"

"What's your last name?" I asked, a little impatiently. I couldn't remember any Benno. "Benno Grätzler," he said, and when he saw that this was no help either: "But we lived with you once, with our grandmother, my brother and I."

"Then you are" ... I just caught myself before it was out: Little Rat! ... "the older one?"

"That's right," he said, so pleased.

"Is your grandmother still alive?" God knows I was totally indifferent to whether she was or not. Surely she died a long time ago, she was a hoary old woman then. It was only that I had to speak quickly about something else. At the same time I looked the young man straight in the eye. He wasn't to see I was afraid. It was a face like dozens of others, a little dull, a little pale, shy eyes behind very strong glasses. Was he short sighted? He hadn't worn glasses then.

Yes, she was still alive. Eighty-three now. Couldn't walk any more. Had been in a nursing home for the last two years. And the little one? He smiled, and that made him look sympathetic. Proudly he said, "He's an officer in the army!"

"Congratulations," I said. "So all the best. *Auf Wiedersehen.*"

"Thank you. The same to you," said Benno Grätzler, whose name I had forgotten or never known, and he held the door open for me politely as I walked out.

I stood for a few minutes in front of the house, in the icy wind. Where should I go now? Home, of course. Rest. Lie down. Come to my senses. Try to understand this strange incomprehensible person: me.

I couldn't lie down. I paced the room and asked myself: is this true or is it again only "version" — that all this long time, almost half of my life to date, has been nothing but a convulsive flight from the possibility of meeting this person?

Often, during the first years when I had to attend to something in Vienna, Uri had said, "Why not stay a few days?" I could buy cheaply in the big department stores; I should see this or that exhibition, should at last go to the Burgtheater once more or to one of the new cellar theaters. I could read the papers leisurely in the American Reading Room ... She suggested that I stay the night with some distant relatives who had always been friendly and had never "done any harm." It was wrong to burn all my bridges because I would certainly want to return to the city some day. But I didn't want to warm up relationships to people who meant nothing to me, to be obliged to them. Once she told me straight out: "You can't sit in your mousehole the rest of your life. The later you decide to come out, the harder it will be." She gave me a sharp look. "Besides, these people have their own worries, you know. They didn't sit under a glass bell either in the bad years. They were bombed out and had to start all over again. They're not dying of curiosity to see you. I think you overestimate their interest in you."

"I don't!" I said angrily. "I just don't feel like it. And I hate the city!"

"Then let it be," said Uri. "I meant well."

How could I tell her that I shuddered whenever an eight- or ten-year-old boy came toward me? Still, five or ten years after that midday hour, I was terrified only of little boys. It didn't help to explain to myself that by now he had to be much bigger. A grown boy. That insight always came too late.

Not that I expected such an encounter. I didn't think of it. I didn't conjure it up. I was in no way conscious of why I rushed through the streets in such a hurry and didn't want to stay in Vienna any longer than was necessary. Besides, in the evening, at the theater or in a museum, the likelihood of seeing this child was as good as nil. I wasn't making a fool of myself in my fear, but there I stood, waiting for a streetcar, and the boy who had just bought a cone at the ice cream parlor came out and looked at me and my heart stood still ... until he looked away, bored. Or a boy shouldered his way past me, any boy with coarse brown hair, and I prayed: don't let him look back, dear God. Not now. Not today. Tomorrow ...

Now I know that all I was afraid of was his eyes. Of the carnal horror in those eyes. If they looked at me it would all happen again, again and again. They had caught that dreadful happening. I wasn't allowed to forget because it was stored away in the eyes of this knowing child, and from them it would one day attack me again.

Not long ago I read in a newspaper article that somebody had established in an experiment that what he dreamt last remains fixed for seconds on the retina of the awakening person, until he is completely awake and the day's perceptions are superimposed on the dream. If this is true, then we have proof of the reality of our imaginings or pictorializations. But of what help are proofs? Some people don't need them at all, while others can't get enough of them.

Now I remember that Mother had laughed over the unusual name: Benno. "How do people like that get to calling a child Benno?" But when he stopped and asked, "Didn't you live in Währing once?" not a trace of recognition warned my eyes, my ears, and not a trace of uneasiness.

I felt as if a heavy burden that had bowed my head to the ground had been lifted from my shoulders. Now I can look around me freely. Because in the eyes of this strange young man there was no reflection of my torture. A little curiosity, perhaps, and grateful sympathy. How can I explain this literal relief? My common sense tells me that he hadn't forgotten that hour, that he even certainly thought of it as we talked to each other. But for him it was something like the stories he has read in the many illustrated magazines: nothing real, nothing that has any further effect, consequences, power.

It was a toothless lion, Uri, from which I ran away for such a long time.

Fräulein Wermuth came into my room just now. She simply had to speak to me again in greater detail and introduce me formally to her lodgers before she leaves tomorrow. This was the account book ... would I understand it? And the gas man came on the twenty-seventh. On that day I would have to be home in the morning. And here, these money orders should be paid on this or that day. Finally she gave me some addressed and dated aerograms, and begged me to report that everything was in order. And to mail them punctually. The rubber plant was watered only once a week, "But you'd better feel the fern. The earth should never be dry. Do you think I should pack my bathing suit? Just in case? ... That's what I think. It doesn't weigh much. There ... I can hear the little doctor coming home. Let's go right over ..."

Dear Gottfried,

A year ago neither of us would have thought that you would be celebrating your seventeenth birthday in America. Have a good time, my dear boy. Since Uncle Walter was here, I have a much better idea of your life.

We refreshed so many childhood memories, especially on Christmas Eve, as older people like to do, and we also recalled our games. I must have been a dreadful spoilsport because I was such a poor loser. Losing, though, isn't really so difficult once one has learned how! But when the house is burning we cling to the windowsill with all our strength instead of bravely jumping down onto the safety blanket. Do you understand what I mean?

I am especially happy that you have made such nice friends. Please send me a picture of them soon, especially of Aunt Marjorie! After Uncle Walter left, I had an exciting experience. Just think — I pulled your friend Friedel out of the icy fish pond! He broke through the ice on his bicycle ...

And this is followed by the version for Gottfried which somehow sounds different from the first. I wonder why? I'm trying to be honest. To whom am I lying, to him ... or to myself?

Everything we put into words is disappointingly incidental. Probably that is why I never succeed in telling the same event twice in the same words. But it is not only the hope for the more suitable expression that causes the disparity. The misunderstanding that develops in the listener during my report communicates itself to me and influences my choice of the next words which are to dispel it. And yet I must not stop! Just as one never puts one's foot down longer than is necessary when crossing unsteady ground, I hop from sentence to sentence without looking back. And if only I can come close to expressing what I want to say, I am as happy as the imperiled wanderer who, panting, again reaches firm ground.

Oh Walter, you know it too: The word that we whisper to the next person when we play Rumor becomes less and less intelligible from mouth to mouth, and what comes out in the end makes all of us laugh. Because we thought we understood but understood badly, and said the wrong thing which our neighbor in his turn distorted ... But we notice that only when we are allowed to experience what was meant.